THE PROBLEM WITH DATING

BRITTAINY CHERRY

BCHERRY BOOKS, INC

The Problem with Dating

Book One in the Problem Series

Brittainy Cherry

The Problem with Dating
By: Brittainy Cherry

The Problem with Dating
Copyright © 2023 by Brittainy Cherry
All rights reserved.

Without limiting the rights under copyright reserved above, no part of this publication may be reproduced, stored in or introduced into a retrieval system, or transmitted in any form or by any means (electronic, mechanical, photocopying, recording, or otherwise) without the prior written permission of the author of this book.

This is a work of fiction. Names, characters, places, brands, media, and incidents are either the product of the author's imagination or are used fictitiously. Any resemblance to actual events, locales, or persons, living or dead, is coincidental.

This e-book is licensed for your personal enjoyment only. This e-book may not be resold or given away to other people. If you would like to share this book with another person, please purchase an additional copy for each person you share it with. If you're reading this book and did not purchase it, or it was not purchased for your use only, then you should return it and purchase your own copy. Thank you for respecting the author's work.

Published: Brittainy Cherry 2023

Editing: Editing4Indies, Lawerence Editing, Virginia Tesi Carey, My Brother's Editor

Cover Design: Silver Grace

❦ Created with Vellum

AUTHOR'S NOTE

Throughout the novel, Spanish is used a handful of times by a few characters. I understand that there are many ways certain phrases can be translated depending on the Spanish-speaking individuals based on geography. I, along with a Spanish-speaking advisor, have decided to translate in a way we felt was most authentic for the story. Thank you, and enjoy.

To everyone trying to date again after a bad relationship, situationship, or what-the-heck-was-that-ship:

Hold on tight.
This one's for you.

"Rules for happiness: something to do, someone to love, something to hope for."
– Immanuel Kant

CHAPTER 1

Yara

A vibrant leaf floated aimlessly from the maple tree as I stood in my older sister Avery's driveway, giving me the first sign that the season of change was upon us. Summer was packing up its swimsuits and popsicles, while autumn prepared to unleash its pumpkin spice everything for the next few months. I could smell it in the crisp air—change was around the corner.

It only seemed fitting that I was also about to embark on a new season.

"You don't have to go," Avery whimpered as I moved around a box in the back of her boyfriend Wesley's blue Ford pickup truck. "We've loved having you as a roommate!"

I smiled, knowing that I wouldn't have made it through the past year if it wasn't for my two sisters. Avery pretty much bottle-fed me self-esteem slogans for the past twelve months to make sure I didn't drown in my erratic thoughts each day before she tucked me into bed with a blend of herbal tea that my younger sister, Willow, made to help me sleep.

"I have to stand on my own two feet again if I'm going to move forward," I said. It had been over a year since I'd ended my marriage with my now ex-husband, Cole. I'd been staying with my older sister and Wesley ever since.

Even though I knew they didn't seem to mind having me around, I felt it was time to shift onto my new stage of life. The small town of Honey Creek only had one apartment complex, a building that overlooked Lake Michigan. Though the view was remarkable, it was odd that I would stay in a one-bedroom apartment there after living in houses for the past ten years, but I was thrilled. Something about having my own space felt like a renewal of my energy.

"You could always come to stay with me in Big Bird," Willow offered, walking around with the final box of my things. Big Bird was the school bus Willow transformed into a mobile home. It was funny how different my sisters were from one another. When Avery was stubborn and headstrong, Willow was like a flowing stream. Where Avery planted her feet on solid ground, Willow floated away in wanderlust. While Willow wore her heart on her sleeves and allowed anyone and everyone to experience said heartbeats, Avery was as closed off as a person could get.

Sometimes, I wondered which sister I was most like, but then I realized I was probably a blend of them both. I was equal parts perfectionist and wild heart. Yet sometimes those two characteristics clashed during a crisis, and I'd be left drowning in a panic of wtf moments.

Thankfully, when that happened, my sisters would help guide me forward.

"I'll keep the Big Bird offer in mind. Thanks, Willow," I told her.

"Anytime," she said sincerely.

If it weren't for my sisters, my dad, and our family friend Tatiana, I wasn't sure I would've made it through the past year.

THE PROBLEM WITH DATING

It wasn't getting over Cole that was the problem. Oddly enough, I never had a moment of regret once I left. That was the thing about a person mentally checking out way before their feet moved. Mourning the relationship began before I even left the marriage. I'd said goodbye to him in the spirit before my lips ever spoke. Therefore, I moved through the grief of it all quickly.

However, I struggled with how much the town seemed to judge my situation. I had a few individuals remark that marriages were supposed to be fought for, not disposed of so spontaneously. Some whispered about me when they thought I was out of earshot, while others said it to my face. People in Honey Creek loved my ex-husband.

They couldn't comprehend why I'd leave such a sweet man. It made sense that they'd thought that way—Cole was an angel to the external world. He was approachable and charismatic. He was the guy who'd help baptize your baby on Sunday morning and then grab a beer with you on Monday night at a sports bar. If a cat was stuck in a tree, he was climbing it.

He was Honey Creek's leading man, the perfect gentleman and the town's new favorite chief of police. People loved that man. Cole Parker was a charmer to the outer world, and now I was the cruel woman who chose to walk away.

I supposed that was the problem with keeping your struggles to yourself—nobody understood how I was drowning behind closed doors. If only they would have stepped into our private lives and seen how Cole treated me.

They would've run, too.

Nobody even knew how bad it got sometimes, not even my family. I was too ashamed to share the worst days. They would've scolded me for not leaving sooner. My ex-husband wasn't only verbally abusive. He also had an issue with a wandering dick. That thing always ended up in places it didn't belong. I applauded any woman who had the opportunity of meeting said penis. It was probably the most mediocre three minutes of their lives—four minutes if he had caffeine.

Outside of the town's judgment, one might've asked me what the most challenging part of the divorce had been. That was an easy answer for me.

Cole. Was. Everywhere.

Legit everywhere. For a while, I thought he was stalking me. Or, perhaps, he cloned himself a few times. Then I figured he had a few other guys from the police station tracking me. Dating alone was hard. Yet dating while Cole lurked in the wings was almost impossible because everyone knew him and didn't want to step on "his property." His property? What a joke. I was as much his property as the birds in the sky belonged to the sea. It was such a 1920s concept, but the people in town seemed to follow the new chief's ridiculous rules.

It was like he was the freaking king gorilla of the town.

Me, man. She, ex-wife. You, no touch.

Insert the pounding of his chest.

Even guys who expressed interest in me told me they couldn't take me out on a date due to respect for Cole.

The idea of a date seemed so foreign to me; what I wouldn't do to have a first date again. I couldn't even recall the last date I had.

After a few years into our marriage, Cole stopped taking me out unless it was going to Chicago to watch a sporting event or have drinks with his buddies and their wives at the sports bar. Anything I considered romantic was corny to him, so we hardly participated in them. If we did, he'd complain the whole time before we left, then fake like he was having the time of his life in public before returning home and yelling at me. That just made me avoid doing activities with him.

Luckily, I spent the past year doing all the dates Cole refused to take me on. I attended candle-making classes, winery tours, and paint-and-sip nights. I even took tango lessons with my two left feet. I found a lot of happiness in my year of discovery, but that didn't remove the fact that I still yearned for companionship.

I didn't need to fall in love, but I wasn't against falling in *like*. A crush would've been satisfactory. I wanted to have a crush on somebody. I didn't even know what that felt like anymore, but the idea of butterflies thrilled me.

When it came to dating, I missed so much.

I missed handholding. The kind of handholding when someone was slightly ahead of you, not looking in your direction, but he reached backward with his hand extended, knowing you'd find your perfect fit tangled with his fingers.

And kissing!

Gosh, I missed kissing. Not just deep, passionate kisses, though those were fun. But I meant the forehead kisses. The tip of the nose kisses. The soft cheek pecks. The neck caresses that sent tingles of joy down one's spine.

I missed all of that. So year one was all about me, myself, and I. It turned out I enjoyed me, myself, and I. Now, I needed someone else to appreciate me, too. The current year would be defined as Yara out on the prowl—if only Cole would stop freaking scaring the men of Honey Creek off. Dating apps and expanding my search to Chicago was the last option on my list to try. After hearing Willow's nightmare stories from the dating apps, I was more than apprehensive to dive into that world.

Daddy walked behind us with a box as Wesley followed his steps like a puppy dog.

"Ready to get to the new place, Buttercup?" Daddy asked.

"Ready! I'm going to ride with Avery and Willow. You and Wesley can meet us there."

Daddy grimaced and leaned in. "You sure? I ain't got nothing to talk to that science nerd about," he complained.

I smiled at Daddy and patted his shoulder. "Wesley is nice,

Daddy, and he's been dating Avery for years. You might as well give him a chance."

"Last time I gave a guy a chance, he broke my baby's heart," he said, referring to Cole.

"Well, luckily, Wesley isn't Cole. He's much smarter."

"Book smart, maybe. But he's still a man, which means he's an idiot," Daddy argued. Leave it to my father to hate men more than we girls did. In his mind, no one would be good enough for us, and Wesley was *literally* a rocket scientist. He worked for a space agency in Chicago.

"Uh, you do know I can hear you, right?" Wesley asked as he raked his hand through his red hair.

"I'm not one to mince my words," Daddy replied. "Come on, Harry."

"Wesley," he corrected.

"Whatever," Daddy said. Over the past two years, Daddy had never called the guy by his actual name. I'd be scared the day he did call Wesley by his name. It would mean the end of time was near.

We headed to the apartment, and we girls gladly sat on the sofa delivered earlier that day while Daddy and Wesley moved all the boxes in for us. Daddy refused to let us help at all. Us Kingsley girls were certified princesses in our father's eyes.

Once the guys moved all the boxes in, we ordered Chinese food and ate at my new table. *My* table. It was mine. Everything in that space was mine. Sure, maybe I maxed out my credit cards to buy everything, but I didn't care because everything belonged to me. That was a freedom I couldn't express with words. The best part about life was that nothing lasted forever. Not even heartbreak.

After dinner, Avery pouted when she was getting ready to leave.

"I don't even know when I'll see you again," she dramatically whined.

THE PROBLEM WITH DATING

I laughed. "Well, we have our morning hike tomorrow at sunrise. So you'll see me in about seven hours."

She scowled. "I was hoping you forgot about that."

"Not a chance."

After our goodbyes, everyone headed off, leaving me alone in my new space with Cocoa. The hardest part of having Cocoa was that Cole requested shared custody of the sweet dog, which meant every two weeks, we had to meet up for a dog swap. I figured that was just Cole's way to keep one foot in the door of my life. Even though I wanted to slam said door against his big toe.

My phone rang as I cleaned up the food and packed the leftovers. Willow's name flashed across the screen.

"Hello?" I asked.

"Hey! There was one last box in the car. Do you want to buzz us in to bring it up or come get it?"

"I'll come get it. No worries. Be right there."

I tossed on my slippers and hurried downstairs. After grabbing the box from Willow, I thanked her and returned to my building. As someone left the building, I slipped into the door they held open. When I reached the elevator, I struggled to push the button due to the box in my hand.

"I got it!" a voice said from behind. As a muscular arm reached across the box and me, I looked up to find the most beautiful pair of hazel eyes I'd seen in a very long time, paired with a breathtaking, welcoming smile. A smile with a perfectly trimmed beard wrapped around it. A smile I had never seen in the little town of Honey Creek.

My heart skipped a few beats.

Fresh. Meat. On. Deck!

"Hi there," he said with his pearly whites fully displayed. With a British accent. *Are you kidding me?!* Um, how dare he? What was a British accent doing in Honey Creek, Illinois? I tried to wrap my thoughts around the fact while my heart was doing cartwheels of excitement within my chest. What in the Bridgerton Experience was happening right now?

"Hi?" I replied. It came out as a question because I was caught off-guard. Who was this new person standing before me who decided to steal the air within my lungs? Not only with his looks but his vocals. Who was this Prince Charming, and why hadn't I seen him in town? Why hadn't the women of Main Street mentioned him at all? Not even in passing? Gossiping was their favorite hobby, yet somehow, this man slipped through without a whisper.

Did he say something—his name, maybe? I wasn't sure because not only did I mentally check out when I found new prospects with accents in town, I forgot how to use words and how to listen. Too much time had passed to ask him to repeat his comment, so I smiled and nodded.

He gestured for me to enter the elevator first, like a gentleman.

"Which floor?" he asked.

"Six."

His smile stretched. "Same here. You must be one of my new neighbors."

"Yeah, I'm Yara. I was born and raised in Honey Creek but moved into my apartment today. The last box of the unload," I said, nodding toward the cardboard in my grip.

"Can I carry that for you?" he asked.

It was official.

I had a crush.

My first crush in decades!

The situation was worthy of a parade. Or at least a glass of cheap champagne from Jackie's Beer & Spirits store around the corner.

I had an official crush on the elevator man, Jake. Or John?

No, no. It was Jake. It had to be Jake.

And Jake was *chef's kiss* attractive. Dirty-blond buzz cut with hazel eyes, built like a contestant on *Ninja Warrior*, and a wicked smile that made my cheeks heat. And that accent!

People always say women will not meet a guy if they never leave their apartments, but the joke's on them. It just so happened that men also lived in apartment buildings.

Some of them even had accents.

CHAPTER 2

Yara

"I hate you, I hate you, I hate you," Avery complained as she collapsed dramatically against the bench in front of Peter's Café. She dripped in a pool of sweat and regret as she panted and drained every drop left in her water bottle. Her ordinarily straight black hair was frizzy and drenched as she wore a backward baseball cap. And those brown eyes of hers shot daggers my way.

I snickered at my sister's terrible morning attitude. "You're grumpy."

"We just went on a two-hour hike at six in the morning with three huskies," she said, gesturing to the three large pups sitting before us on their leashes. "I told you repeatedly, I'm not a hiker."

"You love our morning hikes," I said. "It's the highlight of your days!"

"That's just because I live bleak days," she dryly replied. "You know what my favorite part of the hike was?"

"What's that?"

THE PROBLEM WITH DATING

"The moment it was over. Remind me never to make a bet with you during a game of Scrabble."

"You do know I'm the champion of that game. You made a grave mistake thinking you could beat me."

She rolled her eyes. "Shut up, Yara."

I smirked, knowing my sister's grumpiness only made me love her more. Every Tigger needed an Eeyore. Well, I didn't even claim to be Tigger—that was Willow's role. She had an amount of energy I couldn't grasp even if I'd downed ten espressos. She was our Tigger. I was more so a Pooh Bear, if anything. I often avoided wearing pants at home, a little naive and a stickler for honey—especially when drizzled on avocado toast.

"I think hiking is growing on you," I mentioned, nudging her.

"I have enough blisters on my feet to prove that point," she replied. Just as she spoke, a car with a U-Haul hitched to the back drove past us. Avery grimaced more than before. "Have you noticed an upswing of new people moving into town? It seems odd to me."

"Our little Honey Creek is growing."

"I hate growth."

"You hate everything."

"Fair."

"Seeing people and businesses entering town is a little exciting," I said. Especially if they had penises, no wedding bands, and *zero* clue about who Cole Parker was.

She gestured across the street. "You call this exciting? It's giving 'bringing the city to small town' vibes."

Across the street from Peter's Café was the old movie theater. Well, it used to be the old theater before being transformed into a fancy-pants restaurant that would open any day now. It was called Isla Iberia, and it was the most bizarre thing that existed in our town. Don't get me wrong, it was a beautiful building. It just felt out of place.

"One of these things is not like the other," Avery sang with a deep bass tone. "It's a bit pretentious, don't you think?" she asked, staring across the street at the new restaurant. "A hair over-the-top."

"An eyesore," I playfully agreed at the multistory restaurant. Since when did restaurants have more than one level? Who did the owner think we were? Chicago?

"An atrocity," she said.

"A blot on the landscape."

"I bet they use cloth napkins instead of paper towels."

I shivered at the thought. "I bet people can't wear jeans to enter."

"Have you met the owner, Alex? Seeing as how he's your business neighbor, I figured you might've crossed paths."

"No. I haven't. I've seen him here and there, but we haven't spoken. He lives in my apartment building, too. I noticed him leaving with a gym bag on his shoulder this morning." He was quite attractive, too, with dark features. His deep, coffee eyes matched his messy brown hair and beard. He didn't smile as much as JoshJake. I wasn't certain Alex Ramírez knew how to smile at all. Yet the fact that two extremely good-looking men were in my apartment building was *very* promising.

Avery rolled her eyes. "Another morning workout freak. Wonderful." She combed her runaway hair strands out of her face. "I heard the guy is a total jerk. Mary Sue ran into him last week. She said he called her a see-you-next-Tuesday after she called him a piece of shit for ruining our town. Can you believe that? Sweet Mary Sue being called such a mean name."

I laughed, knowing my sister's words were bathed in sarcasm. The only thing sweet about Mary Sue was her pit bull named Star.

"Dad said others have been giving him a hard time in town,

too. Some kids have been vandalizing the place," I said. "I feel bad for the guy."

Imagine trying to bring your dream to life and everyone giving you an awful welcome. People like Mary Sue West gave small towns a bad rep.

"It is weird, though," Avery continued. "He could open a spot anywhere based on how fancy this restaurant is. I looked him up. He has four other exceptionally successful spots opened in the US. Two of them have Michelin stars. They don't hand those out to anyone."

That *was* strange. How did he even know about a small town like Honey Creek? Most people overlooked our home as they headed straight to Chicago. We were hardly a blip on anyone's radar.

"It's not every day a Michelin-star chef opens a restaurant in Honey Creek, Illinois," I agreed.

"Things are changing around these parts," Avery commented with a look of disappointment. "Did you hear about the stoplight that's going up next week?"

I arched an eyebrow. "You bite your tongue. They aren't adding a stoplight."

She nodded. "Right down the way on the corner of Elk Street and Honey Avenue."

I shivered at the thought. "Before you know it, Al's Hardware Shop will be a Home Depot, and our farmers' market will be a supersized grocery store."

"Watch your mouth," Avery warned, pointing a stern finger my way. "I will cause an uproar if I lose my weekly trips to the market for Ms. Ruth's fresh flowers."

"Good morning, ladies," Milly West said as she powerwalked down the street like she did every morning. She walked in place as she looked at the construction team hanging up the sign of the new restaurant. "Can you believe this? Something this sinister coming to our sweet town?"

Milly West was in her mid-sixties and known for her dramatic rants. Unsurprisingly, she and Mary Sue were *very* closely related—twins. We called them the babble belles of Honey Creek. They always yapped their gums but never really said much of anything. Just last week, Milly was going on about how a butterfly followed her home and was probably a government robot recording all her whereabouts. I didn't have the heart to tell Milly that her life wasn't intriguing enough for the government to waste their robotic butterflies.

"Sinister seems a bit much," I said with a smile.

"No. I mean it. Something about that owner is very dark. I hear he's from the south side of *Chicago*," she said, whispering the word Chicago as if it was dipped in sin.

"Oh?" Avery asked with an arched eyebrow.

"Yes. The *south side*," Milly repeated with a shiver as she kept powerwalking in place. "You know, people from that side of town do drugs! *A lot* of drugs. We don't need that kind of stuff in our sweet town."

"Yeah, you're right, Milly. We definitely *don't* have drugs in Honey Creek already. That bad boy might even be putting drugs in his dishes," Avery sarcastically remarked. There was a good chance our town had more drugs than Chicago. Our youth had a way of partying quite hard at times.

Unfortunately for us, Milly didn't pick up on sarcasm easily. She gasped and placed her hand on her chest. "Oh, you're right! I saw a video on YouTube about people putting cocaine into brownies. Or maybe it was marijuana. It's bad enough that that Nathaniel boy is back in town, and now we could have another drug lord in the place."

Avery's eyes widened. "Nathaniel who?"

"You know." She waved her hand, trying to page through her brain's yellow pages. "Lesley's boy, who was off to the Major Leagues but got wrapped up in trouble."

"Nathan Pierce?" Avery asked, alert. "He's back in town?"

"Yup. He's been seen around these parts a bit as of late. He is mostly staying on his mom's farm, though. It's a shame. He left a bad imprint on our town. I hate that he's back. Don't you?"

"I have no opinion on that man," Avery said through gritted teeth. Which meant she had a robust opinion on him. Nathan and my sister had a bit of history that only a few people in town knew about. It might've been a secret to most, but it was no secret to me that Nathan Pierce was Avery's first love. He wasn't the one who got away—but he was more so the one who ran away—*sprinted* away—and left Avery's heart in pieces.

Milly blinked a few times before looking at the restaurant and then back at us. She leaned in as if to whisper, but was just as loud as before. "What does your father think about this? It looks a little bad with his construction team helping with the build," she stated. "I can't believe Matthew was okay with such a project."

"Matthew does what he does when he does it," Daddy hollered from across the street, making Milly jump a little. She turned to see Daddy in his hard hat with his big, toothy grin. He tipped his hat toward Milly, who instantly blushed.

Daddy had that effect on many women in town. He could make even the meanest ones bashful from his charm. They acted as if he was the small-town version of Shemar Moore. The other day, I overheard a woman say she'd love my father to take his sledgehammer to pound town against the bush between her legs. Add that to my nifty list of reasons to seek out trauma therapy.

"Good morning, Matthew." Milly waved in his direction.

"Morning, Milly. That workout set looks good on you," he flirted, making Avery and me roll our eyes.

Milly smoothed her hands over her set. "Oh, this old thing? I found it at Goodwill for ten bucks."

One thing about us Midwest folks: when we found an item

for a good deal, we would spread the news to anyone who'd listen.

"Ten bucks got you looking like a ten," Daddy replied with a wink.

"Kill me now," Avery muttered, nudging me.

Milly grew even more flustered and waved Daddy off. "Oh, Matthew Kingsley, stop it right this instant and get back to work."

"Yes, ma'am," he said before he gave Avery and me a sarcastic wink. It was essential to know the difference between Daddy's winks. They all held specific meanings. The one he'd just delivered to us said, "Dang nosy Milly being rude as ever."

Milly cleared her throat. "Your father is something else, ladies."

"We hear that a lot," I said.

"Is it true he went out with Laura Wilkes last weekend for dinner?" she asked, leaning in closer, still not whispering.

"We like to stay out of our father's business," Avery said sternly. "Everyone's business, for that matter."

Milly nodded. "Yes, me too. I'm not too fond of gossips. They always have some words on their lips, yet nothing but hot air comes out. Okay, girls, I better get moving before my heart rate drops too much. Just watch out for that Alex Ramírez. Cocaine brownies are a real issue. I'll write down that YouTube address for you to watch the documentary. Bye-bye!"

"Bye, Milly," Avery and I said in unison, waving her away.

Avery made a gagging sound once Milly was out of viewpoint.

"So about the bad seed being back in town," I started. Don't get me wrong, Nathan wasn't awful. He was always kind to me and my sisters, too. But he was our town's bad boy when we were younger. I figured Avery fell for him because of his charm, wit, and filthy tongue.

"Don't bring him up," Avery warned.

"Avery…"

Her whole posture tensed up, and she shook her head as she stared at an invisible watch on her wrist. "Well, will you look at that? It's about time I head to the high school. I have to set up in the gym before practice later today." Not only was Avery the head coach of the baseball team, but during the school year, she was the head of the physical education department.

She hopped to her feet, which was a clear sign that screamed, *"I'm not talking about Nathan Pierce today, Yara."*

I received her message loud and clear, but I knew we'd have to revisit it at some point. Our town was too small to pretend Nathan wouldn't run into Avery sooner than later.

"Fine, fine. I'll see you later," I agreed.

Avery snuggled the three dogs one last time before walking off in the opposite direction of me. Avery hated most people but strongly loved dogs—my kind of girl. People had a way of letting each other down more than dogs ever had.

"Bye, Daddy!" she hollered as she waved across the street.

"Have a good day, girls," Daddy replied, waving to us both.

As I waved back, the owner, Alex, walked outside. He said something to Daddy and gestured toward the almost hung sign.

I sat straight and tilted my head toward Alex. He dressed in all black and stood with broad shoulders. He had a perfectly trimmed beard and dark brown hair that was somewhat long on top but shaved shorter on the sides. He hovered over Daddy, which was surprising, seeing as how Daddy was almost six-foot-two. The man crossed his arms over his chest and had an intensity in his stare as he listened to Daddy update him on the project. He nodded once before glancing across the street toward me.

Our eyes locked, and instantly, my whole body filled with chills. His stare was direct and cold. Brown eyes packed without a drop of gentleness. It almost felt as if he didn't see me but was looking through me. I'd never felt so invisible when being stared at. I averted my gaze straightaway, my cheeks heating from the oddity of his stare.

He had what Avery called RDF—resting dick face. A grumpy, hardened facial expression that read unapproachable.

Milly was right about one thing. That man was very dark.

Tall, dark, and handsome, that was.

Everything about him looked delicious—even his harsh gaze.

Alex might be destroying our sweet town with his restaurant, but he looked good while he did so.

CHAPTER 3

Alex

*I*n the back closet of a four-bedroom home located in Chicago sat a box of diaries that was not mine. The house echoed with silence while memories were imprinted within the walls from the past years. There were dozens and dozens of journals of all different sizes and styles.

Some were leather casings, others were wood. Some were brightly colored, others dull. Not a page was empty, and no line was spared. The words were jumbled in cursive against the pages. Some were harder to read than others. Yet all the words were hers. All the pages were filled with her heartbeat.

Within those diaries lived the life of my late great-aunt Teresa, a firecracker of a soul.

Within those diaries were her secret triumphs and pains. Her ups and downs.

I sat on the floor of the back closet of the four-bedroom home, combing through said diaries. I should've been attending to a million other tasks to get her house ready to be sold over the next few weeks, but those diaries slowed me down.

I could almost feel her in the ink droppings. I could almost see her in the letters. I could almost hear her in the words.

I wasn't sure if that was a curse or not.

As I sat, I began to organize the diaries in chronological order. They started when Teresa was sixteen years old. The idea of a young Teresa made my mind swirl. What was she like? How did her thoughts look?

There was probably a special kind of evil when it came to people who read someone else's diary entries, but seeing as how Teresa was no longer around, I figured it wouldn't hurt because I wasn't ready to let her go. I wasn't prepared to lose her completely. Reading her words, her mind, and her thoughts felt like I had a little bit more time with her.

That was all I needed—a little bit more.

Dear Diary,

I hate America. I hate Honey Creek. I want to go back to Madrid. But at least Peter is cute.

-Teresa

"You good in here?" a voice said, forcing me to shut the diary. I turned to see Noah standing behind me. We'd been best friends for years. His greasy brown hair was pulled back into a ponytail as he wiped the sweat from his forehead. He and his fiancée, Mandy, came over to help me organize the house before putting it on the market. He arched an eyebrow toward the box. "What's that?"

"Nothing. Old journals," I replied as I stood.

"Her old journals?"

"Yup."

"Dude." He sighed, brushing his hand against his forehead. "That's tough. How are you feeling?"

Busy. Tired. Overwhelmed. Sad.

Mostly sad.

"I'm good," I lied. "I'm fine."

A few hours ago, I received a call from the hospital that

THE PROBLEM WITH DATING

Teresa had passed away. My mind hadn't caught up with her being gone yet. Instead, I distracted myself.

Noah kept looking at me as if he didn't believe me, but he didn't push too hard. He knew me long enough to know I'd close up even more if pushed. I wasn't like him—expressive of my emotions. When Noah was sad, he said he was sad. He'd cry and fall apart and work through his feelings. Me, on the other hand? I'd push that shit so deep into my soul that I'd forget I had trauma to unpack until it erupted from me from someone burning something in my restaurant.

Unhealthy? Sure. True? Absolutely.

"Mandy and I got all the funeral stuff in order, so you don't have to deal with that. It's all handled," Noah said.

"Thanks," I muttered, rolling up my sleeves. I meant it, too. I didn't want to deal with that, and Noah swept in at full speed ahead, taking on the task. Mandy was there to help, too, covering any corner left undusted.

Too bad I wasn't going to attend the funeral.

It wasn't my style.

I wouldn't tell Noah that because he'd try convincing me to attend. I was too tired to argue. Too tired to feel. Too tired to exist.

I glanced down at my watch. "I've gotta get to the new restaurant to work a bit."

Noah narrowed his eyes. "Have you been sleeping, buddy?"

"I'm fine," I lied once more.

"It seems you're burning at both ends, with your new spot opening soon."

"That's life." A lot of burning.

He brushed the back of his neck. "If you need help with anything—"

"You've already done enough, Noah," I stated as Mandy entered the room. She smiled my way, and I tried my best to smile back, but it faltered. Sometimes, being around

Mandy made my mind twist because she looked so much like her sister, Catie. I thought Catie was a leading lady in my life story, but she turned out to be only a passing side character.

Maybe she was even a villain.

I blinked and looked away from them both. "I've gotta get going. Thanks again for the help, you two."

"Do you want us to move that box out of the closet?" Mandy asked, gesturing toward the diaries.

"No," I replied. "Leave it right there. I'll get to it later."

* * *

I'd been pied.

Apple, peach, and rhubarb, to be exact.

When I arrived at my new restaurant, Isla Iberia, I stood outside just in time to see some teenagers do a drive-by on their bikes with pies in their left hands.

"Get out of our town!" they shouted before throwing the pies at my display windows, not one missing the target. Five pies. Five messes. One pissed-off Alex.

Out of nowhere, another on a bike came shooting past and shot his pie in my direction, hitting me directly in the face.

The tin slid down my face and shirt before plopping against the sidewalk. Of all the days they could've harassed me, they chose the one when I was the most broken.

Livid wasn't a strong enough word for what I'd felt. My hands formed fists as I tried to keep myself from chasing down the teenagers and whooping their asses.

They all laughed as they sped off, so I did what any respectable, grown thirty-two-year-old would've done—I flipped them off.

"Is that how you always interact with kids?" someone asked behind me.

"Only when they're dicks," I replied.

"You know what they say. Boys will be boys."

As if that thought process never led to anything terrible like, oh, you know—nuclear wars.

Turning around, I found the man speaking to me, standing in uniform. I stood a bit taller and nodded once. "Officer."

"*Chief*," he corrected, tipping his hat in my direction. "But people from around here call me Cole."

"All right, Chief."

He arched an eyebrow. "I said people around here call me Cole," he repeated.

"I'm not from around here."

"Yeah, that's pretty clear."

"Shouldn't you be racing after those kids to get them for doing this to my place?" I yipped.

"This? It's just a little pie. Think of it as a welcoming gift." Great. A cop who didn't do his job. He probably would've thrown a pie, too, if he had one.

He gestured toward the building. "I grew up in that place when it was a theater. My grandfather owned it. My wife and I had our first date there. Well, *ex*-wife. But we're working on fixing that ex part."

I hated people who freely overshared their life stories with strangers. I hardly shared my story with people I'd known my whole life. I was almost certain Noah didn't even know my middle name. It took him hearing it from Catie to discover we'd broken up last year. I had ended a five-year relationship and didn't even mention it to him.

When he found out, he texted me, "Did Catie and you break up?" I replied, "Yup." That was where the conversation ended, too. Nothing more, nothing less. I liked to keep my struggles tight against my chest.

Chief Cole seemed to be the opposite of that belief. He kept telling me crap I didn't care about. "My family owns this town. Before my grandfather passed away, he signed the theater away to some old lady."

"Teresa," I said, tensing up from him calling her an old lady. She was so much more than her age. She was vibrant and lively, the kindest, gentlest person I'd ever known. I didn't find the need to tell the ass that, though. Again, I didn't overshare.

"Yeah, her. My family was pretty pissed about it, but we didn't get much say. Grandpa didn't ask for people's input. He did whatever he wanted when he wanted." He scratched at the back of his neck. "We probably would've thrown more of a fit if we knew the old broad was gonna sell it to some guy to transform it into an upscale restaurant."

My hands remained in fists as my pie remained against my skin. "Don't call her an old broad," I said through gritted teeth.

He arched an eyebrow. "You knew her personally?"

"She's my family."

"Oh." He narrowed his eyes and shook his head. Clearly, he had more to say, but he took a step back instead. "You have a good day, Mr...."

"Ramírez. Alex Ramírez."

"Alex. Welcome to Honey Creek. Don't worry if your little restaurant fails. Some small towns aren't meant for big-city visions. You can just pack up your knives and return to where you came from," he said before wandering off.

I flipped him off, too, my new favorite salute to everyone who crossed my path.

I hated this town.

If I had enough nerve, I would've hated Teresa for putting me in that town. When I promised I'd build her a restaurant wherever she wished, I didn't think she'd pick this hellhole.

Welcome to Honey Creek, Illinois, the bane of my existence.

I'd never had a whole town hate me until I made my way to Honey Creek. A bunch of people who didn't know me made it their mission to send their hatred and rude remarks my way. Apple pies included.

I didn't care how the townspeople acted toward me. I knew I

was out of place in Honey Creek and thrived on that. The last thing I wanted to do was be like the people of that forsaken place.

Still, there I was, building a part of my empire on their soil.

The things we do for love.

Getting the restaurant up and running took much longer than I'd hoped, but we'd officially be open within a few weeks. Finding staff for the restaurant was a bigger pain, seeing as most of the townspeople were anti my existence in their small town. Plus, I was almost certain the necessary paperwork and permits sat untouched simply because they didn't want me to build in their town.

That didn't matter much to me because the town didn't matter. I went as far as to hire a staff of professionals from the outskirts of Honey Creek. Finding people to work for you wasn't too hard when one had a Michelin star or two. Plus, I paid my employees well with exceptional benefits.

The only person I hired from Honey Creek was Tatiana Silva—a woman with a personality louder than a playground packed with kindergarteners.

"Do I call you chef or Alex?" she asked as she walked into the restaurant after I finished cleaning up the pie mess outside.

"I'll answer to both," I told her, guiding her to a table to start the interview process.

"I'll interchange them, then. Keep a mystery to it all." She took her seat. Tatiana wore vibrant colors of neon pinks and yellows. She was in her sixties, and her spirited outfit seemed dull compared to her animated personality.

Tatiana walked in with a confidence I'd never witnessed before. When she arrived to interview for the front-of-house manager, she already claimed she'd earned the position.

I was a bit speechless.

"I'm the best thing that can happen to your restaurant,"

Tatiana told me as she sat across from me. "I'm the best of both worlds."

"What does that mean?"

"Well, I grew up in Honey Creek. I know this town and its people. I have all the connections you might need here. Looking around the space, I can tell you need a few."

I wanted to take offense, but she didn't allow me to interrupt.

Tatiana was a hand talker. Each word that left her mouth came with a wave of her hands, making her seem bigger than her small frame did. Teresa talked the same way.

I didn't know picking up on a minor trait from Tatiana could oddly bring me comfort. It was almost as if Teresa was shining through her.

Tatiana continued. "The problem is this town is afraid of new things. Not their fault. Growing up in a small town meant you grew up with traditions. There's nothing wrong with that. Best believe I love me a good tradition, and Honey Creek is soaked in them. But I think the best things in life come from intermixing traditions and new creations. If God wanted us to remain the same, he would've never made us so different. I think that's why we're supposed to mix these things; to create something even more special. Besides, every tradition was once something new. So I can help you with the small-town people. I can help get them comfortable with you being here, and before you know it, *bam*! Dinner at Isla Iberia on Saturday nights will be their new tradition."

"How do you do that? And why do you believe you're the right person for this job?"

"I can get people in town to enter the restaurant if they see me smiling at the hostess desk. But also I spent twenty-some years working at the best five-star restaurants in Chicago. You have my résumé. You see my stats."

"I do."

"So no one else is better for this position. I'm talented, gifted, and a bridge from your big-city self to the small-town folks here. Sure, you can get others from out of town to come here, and they will. I've eaten plenty of food at your restaurant in Chicago before. You're beyond gifted at your craft, chef."

"I appreciate that compliment."

"I'm not here to flatter you, only to speak truth. So…" Tatiana held her hand out toward me. "When do I start?"

I hired her right there on the spot.

After all the tasks for the day, I headed outside and stared at the building in front of me. "There ya go, Teresa," I muttered to myself. My employees would come in for more training in a few days, and then we'd be up and running.

An overwhelming amount of guilt fell over me as I stood in front of the building. I took too long to get it together. The place should've opened months ago.

Teresa wouldn't even get to try the menu I crafted with her over a year ago. It was because of her that I combined Caribbean and Spanish cuisines. I would've never opened a fusion restaurant without her guidance.

Still, I knew she'd be proud of it. I knew it would mean a lot to her, even if it meant nothing to me.

"You got a minute to chat, Chef?" someone said behind me.

I looked over my shoulder to find someone I did not expect to see standing behind me. "You're Nathan Pierce," I blurted out, stunned to see a professional baseball player.

His dark brown hair was cut with a fade, and he hovered a few inches over me. Even though Nathan wasn't as built as he used to be when he played in the Major Leagues, it was clear he was in good shape, which was shocking after the articles I saw swirling about him over the past few years. Last I heard, he was passed out on the strip in Vegas. That was years ago, though. Not much had been said about him after that. He pretty much went ghost for years afterward.

And there he was, standing in the middle of nowhere Honey Creek, looking at me. Holding a huge box of produce in his hands.

"That's me, and you're Alex Ramírez."

"News travels fast in small towns."

He nodded. "Sure does."

"Yeah. Wow. I'm a big fan. Not that I wouldn't love to chat, but I have to get back to work," I said as I started toward the building.

"Hold up. I need a word with you," Nathan stated.

"With me?"

"Yeah. I spoke with Tatiana not long ago."

I narrowed my eyes, confused. "About?"

"I moved back to town to help with my family's farm. Rumor mills were running around about an uppity restaurant in my old stomping grounds. I had to see it for myself."

"You're from this hellscape?"

Nathan smirked with a chuckle. "Born and raised. They even named the baseball diamond Pierce Field after me. I got a feeling they have regrets about that choice. Anyway, like I said. We need to talk."

"About?"

He gestured with his head toward the box he held. "Honey Farms. My family's pride and joy. We want to partner with your restaurant and provide the produce and livestock for you and your team."

"I have all my partnerships lined up already and—"

"And you should reconsider. Nobody has better ingredients than Honey Farms. I promise you that."

"You shouldn't make promises you can't keep."

"Trust me. I keep my promises." He reached into the box and handed me an eggplant. If someone told me I'd be holding Nathan Pierce's eggplant by nightfall, I would've called their bluff.

"You can have this whole box to test out the produce. I even tossed in some eggs and meat from my brothers' butcher shop. You'll see the difference in quality. You've never had something this great."

I narrowed my eyes. "I find that very doubtful."

"I don't care if you doubt it. It's just the truth."

I shook my head. "It's not every day a professional ball player shows up requesting to be a partner with my restaurants."

"Former professional ball player. I don't do that anymore."

"Why is that?" I asked. "What happened?"

His nostrils flared slightly before he shook off his annoyance. "If you take me into your kitchen and cook some of these ingredients up, I'll tell you."

I chuckled. "No, you won't."

He shrugged. "Only one way to find out."

"Why is working with me so important to you?"

"A couple of reasons. First, my mom's health isn't doing the best, and I figured I could help her out with her farmland. My four brothers do a stand-up job, but I know it's been a lot on them. I'm the head of the family and haven't really stepped up the way I should've after my father passed. I'm back to do better. Second, you own my favorite spot in LA and my second favorite in Chicago. If I want my family's farm to become the best, I should work with the best. Having Honey Farms partner with you could change our lives. When I saw you were opening a spot in my hometown, I figured it was meant to be. It's that easy."

"No offense, Pierce, trust me, I'm a big fan. Huge, actually. If my best friend, Noah, knew I turned down the chance to partnering with you, he'd have a few choice words for me, but the truth of the matter is, I can't take on the risk."

He stepped in closer. "I'm not a risk."

Based on the articles I'd read about him, he was a bigger risk than I was willing to deal with. I already had enough going against my restaurant. I didn't need an ex-pro with past addictions floating around the gossiping mouths in town. "With your past—"

"We all have a past," he said, his deep voice dripping with regret. "But it's not what I'm defined by. Give me a shot to prove that Honey Farms is the best for you, Chef. Just give me a chance that no one else in this town will give me."

I felt a tug in my chest. I hadn't been in Honey Creek long, but I could tell that they'd probably held grudges against people and their past demons. If they treated a new person the way they'd treated me, I could only imagine the torment they'd give Nathan. The words failure and junkie came to mind.

I really, really hated that town.

I arched an eyebrow. "You swear this is good stuff?"

"Better than you can imagine."

Nathan Pierce was calling me chef. It was taking everything inside me not to ask for his autograph. Sure, he had a downfall after the Major Leagues, but no one could stop him when he was on that field. He had all-star written all over him until his injury in the final game of the World Series. After that, it appeared that he spiraled into the triple threat of darkness: partying, drugs, and depression.

I wondered what would've become of him if he hadn't gotten injured.

Noah would lose his mind after I told him this story.

"All right," I said. "Let me cook with these, and I'll get back to you."

Nathan shook my hand after he handed me the box. "I appreciate it, Chef. Thank you. My card is in the box, and you can call me. You can even visit the farm, and my brothers' butcher shop is right down the road."

As Nathan turned to leave, he paused for a second and gazed across the street at the dog daycare, The Pup Around the

Corner. A wave of sobriety washed over his face as he stared. It was as if he'd stepped into a memory that swallowed him whole.

"You good?" I asked.

He shook himself free of whatever chain had hooked onto him. When he looked my way, he forced a smile. "Yeah. I just saw a ghost. Or, well, the sister of a ghost, at least."

I didn't know if he meant an actual ghost or not. Based on the rumors, he'd done enough drugs to be able to see ghosts possibly. He'd been close enough to death from overdoses that it wasn't a bizarre idea. He muttered a goodbye and then, in haste, headed in the opposite direction than he had focused on a few seconds ago.

I looked over at the shop he'd been studying, and my chest tightened when I saw the owner walking into the shop with another person.

I'd noticed the woman a lot over the past few months of construction. There was no denying she was beautiful. Her skin was a mesmerizing dark bronze that seemed to glow whenever the sun met her. When we crossed paths at the grocery store the other day, our eyes locked for a second. Her doe eyes were walnut-colored with slight hues of honey strands throughout her irises. Annoyingly entrancing.

She had a few freckles across her cheeks and dimples that only deepened whenever she smiled. She was short, about five-foot-four, but her personality made her feel taller. If she lacked anything, it wasn't confidence, that was for certain.

She talked like Tatiana and Teresa, too, with her hands. Everything was explosive. Everything was a performance.

That afternoon, her naturally curly hair was pulled back into a ponytail. She wore a flowy red jumpsuit and a bright yellow bandanna tied around her head, pulling her whole look together.

She seemed to be the town's golden girl. Apparently, everyone liked her, which meant one thing—she was a pushover. Even Gandhi had people who hated him. No person was liked by everyone unless they allowed others to walk all over them.

That fact alone made me distrust the woman. Anyone who was a pushover was also a liar. Maybe not to others, but at least to themselves. They lied to make others comfortable, which was the stupidest thing in the world to me.

Why dull yourself in order to make others shine? It seemed ass-backward to me. I'd never met another person worth losing oneself to. Correction—I'd met one person I lost myself to, and I could vouch it wasn't worth it at all.

That woman across the street was a liar. I hated nothing more in the world than liars.

She laughed a lot, too. Nobody had that many real laughs, which only fed into her being fake. She currently laughed so loudly with the other person beside her that I swore her laughter rippled off my chest. That annoyed me. Why would anyone laugh that hard about anything? Nothing was that funny.

Just seeing her radiant personality put me in a sour mood. That wasn't shocking, though. It didn't take much to make me moody. I lived comfortably with my unpleasant attitude. Especially on that day. Everything was awful that particular afternoon. Seeing that woman only made it worse.

CHAPTER 4

Yara

I hated confrontation. My body broke out into hives whenever I was forced to have uncomfortable conversations with individuals. That made running a business a little harder than I would've liked it to be, especially when I fell behind on bills because I was, in fact, a wimp.

Some days, I wished I could get paid for daydreaming. I was fantastic at living in make-believe scenarios. I was almost certain I'd be a millionaire by now if daydreams wrote checks. My mind had a way of feeling like a delusional comfort hug when reality was kicking my behind. Which seemed to be a constant thing when I was dealing with Mrs. Levels and Shirley, her sweet golden doodle dog.

"You do understand, right, Yara? With the way prices are going up everywhere and the way my bills are set up, I cannot afford to keep Shirley in doggie day care while keeping my lights on." Mrs. Levels was a woman in her sixties, who'd been using the services at my dog spa and day care for years. She'd brought her animals to the shop long before I took over ownership from

Mr. Parker after he passed. As she told me her third sob story of the month about why she was two months behind on payments, I couldn't help but notice her sparkling diamond earrings.

"Those are beautiful earrings, Ms. Levels," I mentioned. "Are they new?"

"New? Oh gosh no. I would never spend such money on superficial items, especially when my income is so tight." She touched the palms of her hands to her ears. "These are a family heirloom. Passed down from my great-great-aunt, Anita."

I smiled and nodded. "Is that so?"

"Oh yes," she purred, waving a dismissive hand in my direction. "I could go on and on about my great-great-aunt Anita, but I don't want to bore you to death with my family history. All I came to ask is if you could keep Shirley while I go to another job interview this afternoon. I have a feeling this is the one!"

"That's very exciting news. I know you've been looking for a while. What's the position are you applying for?"

She stood and held her hand to her chest. "Well, gee, Yara. You sure are nosy today, aren't you? Mr. Parker, rest his sweet soul, never questioned me in such a manner. I simply dropped off my dogs and went on my way. Did you know he never charged me a dime, either? Sweet Mr. Parker always did so much for this town. My hope is that you honor his memory as you take over his shop," she scolded with her nose turned up.

"I hope the same thing, Mrs. Levels. Go ahead and bring Shirley in. The girls will take her into the playroom for the day."

Mrs. Levels's scolding tone shifted when she realized she was getting her way yet again. She melted into a smile and patted my hand. "You're such a saint, Yara. Truly, I hope God blesses you."

"That's very kind of you to say, Mrs. Levels."

"What can I say? I'm a very kind person," she agreed as she turned to go grab Shirley. When she came back inside, a happy-go-lucky Shirley followed her, wagging her tail. Shirley made any irritation I'd felt toward Mrs. Levels disappear quickly as she hurried over to me for cuddles. I wished people were more like dogs, minus the whole eating their own vomit and poop every now and again. Dogs were genuine. People sometimes... not so much.

As one of my favorite employees, Keri, took Shirley back for day care, Willow walked into the shop.

"Hi, Mrs. Levels," Willow greeted as she tossed her hair up into a messy bun before nodding toward Mrs. Levels. "You got something dangling from your earring."

Willow walked over and yanked off a price tag that stated that the earrings were from Royalty Yours, our town's jewelry store about a block down the way.

Mrs. Levels huffed and snatched the price tag from Willow's grip. "Well, then." She looked over at me with guilt pouring out of her eyes, but her tongue held too much pride to fold. "I thought I was wearing my other pair. These were a gift. Anyway, have a good day, ladies. I'll be back for Shirley before closing."

She hurried out of the store, brushing past Willow in a flurry, knocking my sister sideways slightly. "Whoa. What's her issue?"

"She lied about the new earrings and dodged bringing her account up to date," I explained.

Willow gave me a stern look. "Again? Yara, you can't let her get away with not paying."

I shrugged. "Mr. Parker let her go without paying, so it's fine."

"Uh, it's not. Mr. Parker was a pushover."

I laughed. "Pushover is my middle name."

"Change your middle name," Willow ordered. "Listen, not to sound like Avery, but screw Mrs. Levels's deal and arrangements with Mr. Parker. You now own this place and need to run it like you're the owner, not an employee."

I pouted. "But it's hard!"

"Hard work, big reward." She brushed her thumb against her nose. "Or you know what? I can get Avery to give Mrs. Levels a piece of our mind and get her to pay."

I shook my head. "Don't you dare? The last time I asked her to stand up for me, a girl walked away with a bloody nose in fifth grade."

"She called you brace-face," she argued.

"You both called me brace-face, too."

She waved me off. "That's different. We're your sisters. Bullying with siblings is the ultimate perk of having siblings. But anyone outside of us will get a bloody nose. I do mean it, though, Yara. You have to start standing up for yourself and your business at some point. I bet Mrs. Levels isn't the only one who got away with not paying, is she?"

I swallowed hard, not wanting to mention how much the business had been suffering lately—even with having more dogs than ever before. Perhaps I let too many people slide by missing a payment here or there. Sadly enough, it was slowly catching up to me.

"How about you head in the back to help for the day like you said you would?" I mentioned. Whenever Willow was in town—which wasn't often—she loved volunteering at my shop. If there was anything she loved as much as adventure, it was dogs.

Willow's nose scrunched up. "Is Keri working today?"

"Yeah, she is. Why do you always make that face? Keri's sweet."

"She has a bad aura, Yara."

I laughed. "Don't do that. She's just young. There's nothing wrong with her."

"If you say so, but all I'm saying is I have a sixth sense of sorts."

"You can see dead people?"

"Well, that, too, but no. Keri gives me an odd feeling."

"You're overthinking this."

"Maybe," she agreed. "Or maybe you're underthinking it—like with people paying. It would help if you spoke up," she said. "Or I'll tell Avery to do it for you."

I tossed my hands up in defeat. "Okay, okay, I'll handle it."

"If you want, you can stop by Big Bird tonight to decompress." She waved my hand. "I can feel your erratic energy."

I pouted. "I'm not erratic."

Yes, I was. The bills in my back office were enough to send me into another anxiety spiral. The number of panics I've had lately behind closed doors in my office was almost concerning. I couldn't find a way to pull myself out of the debt hole for the business I'd seemed to be digging for myself.

"I can't come tonight. I have Sip & Dish with the girls," I told Willow.

She released the most dramatic sigh. "Why are you still hanging out with those people? I thought you'd be free of them after the divorce."

"They're my friends. We've been doing Sip & Dish for years now. Plus, they're coming over to see my new place." Sip & Dish was when the wives of a few police officers and I went to one another's houses to watch either cooking reality shows or bad reality shows where we'd drink fancy cocktails and dish about our lives. We'd just finished the cooking competition show *Bite Sized* and were now onto *The Real Housewives of New York*. I started the tradition after our husbands complained about our reality show addictions. It had been going on ever since, and I looked forward to it weekly.

"Just make sure to sage your space after they leave. And stop letting people get away without paying you," Willow remarked before disappearing into the back to help out for the day.

I wished Mr. Parker would've thought about my anxiety

before he left me his pride and joy. Sure, running the shop was a dream of mine, and having him pass it down to me felt like the greatest gift he could've ever given me. But each day I allowed someone to escape without paying, I felt like I let him down.

Each day, I wished I could be bolder like Avery or less afraid like Willow. Sometimes, I wondered what it was like to have a nervous system that wasn't always in overdrive from any or all types of human interaction. I wondered what it was like not to overthink every situation and conversation during the day. But I settled into a pool of worry and anxiety that twisted my guts into such knots that I lived on the fear that, at any moment, my internal organs would erupt from the level of stress I was under. It only started when I became a business owner. What they didn't tell you about running your own business was that you'd have to run your anxiety, too. My emotions over having a business were like another full-time job—which only paid in tears and tequila shots.

I probably should've invested in therapy, but seeing how the bills were behind, I'd have to do what every other poor soul did —find TikToks where random people shared their therapists' advice and apply it to my life until I felt somewhat okay. A false Band-Aid of healing, if you will.

After work, I headed home and prepped for Sip & Dish. I made piña colada cocktails since the *Real Housewives of New York* were going on their group trip to an island that evening. It seemed very on-theme. Around seven, I was surprised when no one had arrived yet. Jenny was always on time. Rory and Rachel normally showed up early to any and every event.

I sent out a few text messages but received no replies.

Around seven thirty, Lori buzzed my door to be let inside the apartment building, easing my nerves. That was until she arrived at my door.

I smiled at my friend as she stood in the apartment hallway. "Hey, Lori! What's going on? Everyone's late and not answering my texts. The show already started, but I'm recording it so we can restart when—"

"We're having Sip & Dish at Rory's house tonight, Yara."

I arched an eyebrow. "Oh? I didn't get the update. I can grab my keys and head over—"

"You're not invited," she cut in.

"Wait, what?"

She frowned and shook her head slightly as she combed her red hair behind her ears. "Sweetie, we heard your divorce was finalized the other day."

"Yeah, I know you heard that. I was the one who told you."

"Exactly. We went along with everything over the past year because we truly thought you'd come to your senses and get back together with Cole. But when you didn't…" She sighed. "Sip & Dish was started for the wives of the police department, Yara. For the *wives*," she repeated as if she wanted to clarify that I was no longer a wife.

I stood a bit perplexed at what she was getting at. "I started the group."

"Yes," she agreed. "And you did great, trust me. But…you're not a wife anymore."

I snickered, stunned, as I shook my head. "You can't be serious, Lori."

"Unfortunately, I am. Plus, it does look a little bad with us girls hanging out with you. Our husbands all work with Cole at the department, and well, he's heartbroken over this, Yara. Cole has always been such a stand-up guy. No one understands why you broke his heart like this."

Then why don't you marry the man, Lori Peterson?

I huffed, feeling tears burning at the back of my eyes. "He broke mine first."

"How?" she asked. "He told me you blindsided him with the divorce. He told us he was in therapy and trying, and you didn't care. You walked away as if he hadn't given you an amazing life. How do you think that made him feel? You know... I wasn't going to bring this up, but he mentioned that he feared you might've been seeing someone else. Is that true?"

Seeing someone else?

Me?

I laughed. I laughed so hard because I didn't want to cry. I was stunned by the words she was saying. The lies Cole was spreading. He was making himself out as a good guy, and I turned out to be the story's villain.

"Is that right? Is that what he said?" I asked.

"Oh, sweetheart," Lori said, shaking her head with a grimaced expression. "He said a lot more than that." She leaned in and whispered. "Like how you only did missionary. That breaks my heart for him. A man can't live on missionary alone. They have needs. You could've asked me for advice in the bedroom. My Eric and I are quite adventurous."

My mouth couldn't even form words to speak. Over the past year, I never uttered a bad word about Cole. I didn't want to have the ladies form opinions on him based on my situation. I knew they all got along with him. Why wouldn't they have loved him? He was great in the sunlight. It was in the shadows where he hurt me the most.

I didn't want to be the ex who tainted someone's name because they hurt me. I remained humble when they didn't know my struggles behind closed doors. They didn't know how cruel Cole could get. How he'd cuss me out before events just because he needed a punching bag. How he'd sometimes find it funny to judge my body during intimate moments. How he'd laugh when I'd cry. I was so good at hiding it from the rest of the world while he crashed his rage and humiliation against me. I was so good at protecting his image as he quietly destroyed mine.

Yet this whole time, he was out on a smear campaign. He

THE PROBLEM WITH DATING

spread vile lies about me to make himself the hero of some fictional story.

And why was he speaking to Lori about our intimate sex life? That crossed a million lines and made me feel more vulnerable than ever. I might as well have been standing there naked in front of Lori because of how much embarrassment I was dripping in.

And yes, Cole and I did only have missionary-style sex, but that was because he would make me feel insecure about any folds my stomach found during those moments. Imagine trying to make love to only have a man tell you that you were looking extra pudgy as of late. Imagine kissing his lips as he whispered that you should consider a new diet. I'd never felt ashamed of my body until he told me where my shame should've lived.

Lori stood taller. "Now, I have to get going, sweetheart, but I thought you deserved to hear face-to-face why you can't be a part of Sip & Dish anymore. You know how it is. When a couple breaks up, one can't straddle the line. We had to pick a side, and since Cole is the chief over our guys, it only makes sense to stick with family. I'll see you around town, though! I'll be sure to say hi."

"By all means, Lori," I said through gritted teeth, "don't."

She gasped as if stunned by my words. "Cole was right. You are coming off as a bit of a bitch lately."

After she left, I proceeded to drink all the piña coladas on my own before I collapsed into my bed and cried into my pillow, hoping to find better dreams than my current reality.

As I was nestled comfortably in my queen-sized bed, my alarm clock went off unexpectedly at three in the morning. I stirred a little until the realization settled in that it wasn't, in fact, my alarm. It was a fire alarm blasting throughout my apartment, sending me into a tailspin of high red-alert panic.

Without thought, I shot up from my bed and began to hustle. Unfortunately for me, I slept in a tank top and my underwear, so I scrambled around to find pants to toss on. I grabbed my brown sweatpants lying across my chair stacked high with unfolded clothes and hurried to put my legs into them. My hands shook from panic at the thought of the building being on fire. I didn't take the time to grab my glasses, so I flew with impaired vision through my apartment space, searching for my keys.

Once I located the keys between the cushions of my orange sofa, I tossed on my slippers, grabbed my wallet, and shot out the front door hastily.

"Is this a real thing?" my neighbor, Pam, asked as I entered the hallway. She was taking her sweet time debating whether it was a real fire. "Do we have to leave?"

"That's the rule, Pam!" I spat out as I darted past her.

"Well, let me make my coffee first," she said. "I can't do a dang thing without my coffee."

"No time, Pam!" I shouted. "Come on!"

"Okay, hold the elevator for me, will you?"

"No elevators during fires, Pam! Take the stairs," I yelled over my shoulder.

"Okay, but my Stanley hates the stairs."

I paused.

My eyes widened at the mention of Stanley, Pam's dog.

Oh crap, Cocoa!

I spun on my feet and darted back to my apartment. As I scrambled for my keys, I dropped them twice before unlocking my door and opening it to find sweet Cocoa standing in my doorway giving me the most intense side-eye a dog could give. I could hear her thoughts now.

This is why you should've left me at Dad's, Mom.

"Sorry!" I exclaimed as I scooped my dog and hurried out of the apartment again.

"Wow, you left Cocoa, huh?" Pam asked, shaking her head in disappointment.

"Get out of the building, Pam!" I ordered before darting into the hallway and down the stairs to the front of the building. Once I reached the outside, I found others standing around, waiting to see what was happening. Many had their pets with them, while Cocoa gave me the, "You were going to let me suffer in there, huh?" look of death.

"I said I'm sorry," I muttered as I put her down on a patch of grass for her morning business. She began sniffing the grass as I sat on the curbside of the sidewalk and looked up at the building.

I didn't see any smoke, which was a good sign. Then again, my vision wasn't the best without my glasses or contacts.

But you know what I could see well enough? My crush. Standing on the other side of the building, he looked as if he'd just stepped out of a *GQ* magazine photo shoot at three in the morning. Even without my glasses, I could make out his good looks. Gosh, I bet he smelled good, too. Like blueberry biscuits and vanilla scones. As he turned around to face my direction, true panic hit me.

I was not in the right position to be face-to-face with John-Jake at that very moment. He couldn't see me in my natural state of being! My hair was in a bonnet, half on; if I removed it, I was almost certain it would stick straight up like a troll doll. My breath smelled like a mixture of old eggs and dirty socks, and I wasn't wearing a bra.

My hands flew to my chest as reality settled in. I ran outside of a maybe burning building not wearing a bra! No part of me could get away with not wearing a bra. I wasn't gifted a set of girls that could just be free willying life whenever they wished. No. I was one of those women who needed a cage within a cage that was built with strong steel all around. I needed the lifting genie to grant me its services daily through bras because my Phineas and Ferb dual would've been on a mission to wave at my belly button without them.

"Shit!" someone hollered behind me.

"I know, right?" I replied, holding my hands to my chest and turning my back toward JohnJake.

"No, your shit! I stepped in your dog's shit!" a man grumbled from behind.

I spun around to find the new kid on the block, Alex Ramírez, with his grumpy frown, hopping all over as he tried to rub poop from the bottom of his shoes. The shoes were all white and looked brand spanking new, minus, you know, the dog crap.

"Oh, I'm sorry!" I blurted out, reaching to grab Cocoa as she gladly came trotting back toward me, completely happy and relieved.

"Don't be sorry. You should've cleaned up your dog's shit," Alex snapped, a little too aggressive if you asked me.

"I didn't see that she finished. I always clean it up."

"Always is the wrong word," he huffed, his deep voice dripping with annoyance. *Somebody* wasn't a morning person. Though, it was three a.m. Maybe he was sleepwalking.

Still, I smiled. "I'm sorry. The whole fire alarm threw me off this morning. And it seems Cocoa wandered farther than she normally would've."

He grimaced, unamused. "There're leash laws for a reason."

I laughed. Leash laws and Honey Creek didn't go together that well. We were the land of the dogs and the home of the barks. If anything, you'd be more likely to see humans on leashes than dogs.

"It's not funny," Alex ordered. He woke up on the wrong side of the bed and needed an espresso IV.

"Again, I'm sorry."

"How are your apologies helping me?" he barked a little too loudly. "These are new shoes!" People began glancing around toward us, including JohnJake, which was the last thing I needed.

"*Lower your voice!*" I whisper-shouted as I pressed Cocoa to my chest. "Your bad attitude is drawing attention."

"Pretty sure your dog's shit is the cause of said attitude."

"That's neither here nor there. Just shush, okay?" I said as I stood.

As I looked to my left, I noticed JohnJake staring at me. He smiled the moment he saw me, so what did I do?

I ran.

I stepped fully into my Looney Tunes Road Runner speed and booked it around the corner of the building to hide my unbra'ed chest and bonnet.

I waited around the corner for fifteen minutes until the fire department finished their assessment, only to announce that it was a false alarm and we could return to our building. As I rounded the corner, I peeked to make sure JohnJake was nowhere to be found.

I shot onto the elevator like a fruit fly to a banana peel. The moment I entered, I released the sigh I'd been holding in. Right after I hit the button for the sixteenth floor, a leg entered the elevator, stopping it from shutting.

Alex Ramírez.

I shot him a stern glare. He scowled. I wondered if his face knew how to do anything else.

Cocoa and I stood in the corner as he hit the fifteenth floor.

"Hold the elevator, please!" a voice shouted.

I stood straight, noting the accent.

"*Shut the door!*" I whispered-shouted as I dove toward the button to close the elevator.

"What's wrong with you?" Alex asked as he placed his hand in the way of the door.

"A lot, actually! Now if you would just—*oh heyyy!*" I sang to JohnJake as he stepped into the elevator.

"Hey, neighbor," he said the moment he saw me. He then looked at Alex. "Thanks for holding that."

Alex nodded in response.

"I just moved in not too long ago. I'm Josh," he stated to Alex. Josh! Of course his name was Josh. *That's right. Duh.*

"Alex," he dryly replied with his stupid-looking face, not knowing that he was now my ultimate enemy for the betrayal of allowing my sweet Josh onto our elevator.

Okay, I lied. Alex wasn't stupid-looking. I could see how some people could find him attractive if they were into the whole dark and mysterious "I may or may not have been the monster from *Beauty and The Beast* in a past life" grump appeal. I, myself, found him attractive until I witnessed his monstrous side.

Josh stepped backward and placed his back against the wall of the elevator. He sniffed the air. "It kind of smells like crap in here, no?"

Alex looked toward me, then back at Josh. "Don't look at me," he muttered. He gestured at me. "Rumor has it she stepped in dog shit outside. That or she shat herself."

Ohmygosh. I was riding the elevator with the worst human alive. The tall, dark, and annoyingly handsome Alex Ramírez, folks. The newest pain in my ass.

My cheeks flushed as embarrassment built in the pit of my stomach. Before I could say anything, we were already at Alex's stop, and he exited without another word. I figured that was how the worst human alive would've worked—dropped bombs and walked off with a smug look.

The elevator closed, leaving Josh and I alone. Me, him, Cocoa, and the millions of thoughts rushing through my brain. None of which were worthy of leaving my lips.

When the elevator opened to the sixteenth floor, he stepped to the side to allow me out, like a freaking gentleman.

"Thank you," I said, squeezing poor Cocoa to my chest as much as possible to hide my chest.

"Of course, have a good day," he said.

"You too." I started toward my apartment and paused. "Josh?"

"Yeah?"

"I didn't poop myself."

He laughed and it sounded like magical trumpets of joy. "I figured that much, Yara. I'm almost certain that your poop would smell like roses," he said with a wink. "Oh, and Yara?"

"Yes?"

"You have white stuff around your mouth," he said, pointing at my face before unlocking his door and going inside.

Panic filled my chest as I dashed inside my apartment. I hurried to my bathroom mirror to find the lovely remnants of my drunken piña coladas binge. Yet seeing it on my face made it look like something *very* different from piña coladas.

Oh, wasn't life grand?

CHAPTER 5

Yara

After one of the worst days of my life, I tried my best to shake off my bad mood. That wasn't easy when I kept seeing the Sip & Dish ladies in town, who seemed to be going out of their way to avoid me. That was fine by me. I had nothing to say to any of them. Besides, I still had my sisters. They would never kick me out of a group, minus that time when we were kids. We'd play as if we were Destiny's Child, and they kicked me out because I was convinced I was Beyonce, yet they made me Michelle, so I threw a fit.

Outside of that, I had built-in best friends who would never abandon me.

No steps. No halves. Just full.

That was Daddy's motto when it came to my sisters and me.

My sisters and I looked remarkably similar despite not being blood-related. Technically, Avery was my stepsister, and Willow was my half sister, but we didn't believe in those words. *No steps, no halves, just full.* We were nothing less than sisters. They were my full heartbeats from the moment they entered my life.

THE PROBLEM WITH DATING

Daddy always called us the melting pot of love, and Mama used to say that our heartbeats were the same race. I grew up in a home where love was the centerpiece. Mama and Daddy were the definition of soulmates. I wasn't certain I'd believe in true love if it wasn't for them and their love story.

Avery was Mama's first daughter, and after she was born, Mama thought she couldn't have any more children again due to her health issues. Avery's biological father wasn't in the picture, so she never knew much about him. The two met Daddy and me when I was only two, and Avery was four. We met at the annual picnic event, Snack on Hillstack, where Daddy picked Mama's basket. They fell in love right then and there over a peanut butter and jelly sandwich that Avery and I shared. If I were honest, I didn't remember a time before Mama was in my life. I hated that I had to know a time after her.

Even though I wasn't biologically hers, there was no denying that we were destined to be mother and daughter. When I was younger, people would say we had the same eyes, and for some reason, that made me always tear up with happy tears because Mama's brown eyes were always so full of joy. It was an honor to be compared to such a woman.

Besides our looks, we had the same heartbeats. Family had nothing to do with blood but everything to do with heart. Our hearts beat in sync from day one. Daddy said we were destined to love one another. I always liked that idea, too—that people were destined to cross paths just so they could love one another.

That was how it was at the picnic. One day, we were strangers sharing a PB and J sandwich, and then boom—we were family. The day Mama adopted me and Daddy adopted Avery, they each bent down in front of us and said, "Forever," as they wrapped our pinkies with theirs. The ultimate promise.

Willow was a surprise to us all. When I was eight, I overheard Mama crying because she'd found out she was pregnant. Daddy was so worried about Mama's health, but she swore Willow was a blessing from above. I couldn't argue that fact. My little sister was something special—even if she didn't realize it just yet.

I loved that we all held parts of both of our parents in different ways. Avery was a beautiful brunette with full, straight hair like Mama's and freckles all over her cheeks. Her skin was a warm shade of rich mahogany, and her smile stretched far when she allowed it, though she was more into a resting grimace.

My hair, in its natural state, was nothing like Avery's. Mine held tight coil curls that fell slightly below my shoulders. My deep brown skin matched Daddy's, and my laughter echoed his. I always thought Willow received the best of both worlds regarding her looks. She was the perfect blend of Mama and Daddy. She had golden brown natural curls that touched her lower back, sun-kissed smooth skin, and a nose covered in freckles. She had Mama's eyes and Daddy's nose.

I called her my favorite snapshot because whenever I looked into her eyes, it was like I stared straight into Mama's. It felt like the gift that kept on giving.

"Avery's going to have a panic attack," Willow stated as I held the door open to my apartment building. She walked inside and by "walked" in, I meant she floated on her tiptoes. Willow always had a bit of dance in each step she took. She moved like jazz music, with smooth, unique rhythms all her own. Her long legs only made her movements that much more mystical.

"Did you hear about Nathan being back in town?" she asked.

"Oh, I heard, along with Avery. I doubt she's okay."

"I can almost feel her erratic energy in my own body." She shivered in her handmade dress. Willow was the definition of stylish without even trying. When she walked into the building wearing a long lavender spaghetti-strap dress with little green turtles all over it, one would've thought it was the most bizarre fashion choice ever, but for some reason, it looked insanely expensive and classy on her. She belted it with a thin brown rope and tied it together with the same fabric that wrapped her curly hair.

"I thought she'd be here already. Normally, I'm the late one," Willow said. "You think she's off breathing into a brown paper bag?"

"No, I'm not," Avery remarked as she darted into the building. She seemed a bit flustered and red in the face. "And before we start sisters' night, I am stating that the name Nathan Pierce should not leave either of your tongues or so help me I'll throat-punch you."

"Noted," Willow and I said in unison.

After setting into the apartment, I ordered a few pizzas for the night. When they arrived, I headed downstairs to grab them only to run into my new enemy.

Mr. Tall, Dark, and A Pain in my Behind.

As I went to get the pizzas, I noticed the delivery driver was Jason Evans, one of my customers.

"Oh, Yara. Hey. How are you?"

"I'm good, and you?"

"Good, good." He handed me the pizzas. "Look, I'm behind on payments at the dog daycare, but I will catch up soon. I planned to pay last week, but the Taylor Swift tickets went on sale, and I couldn't just not go, you know? It's Taylor Swift, after all. I spent two thousand for my girlfriend and me, but it will be worth it."

I smiled even though I wanted to tell Jason to pay up or piss off. "Oh, it's fine. Whenever you're able to would be great. Have a good night."

He walked off, and I headed back toward the elevator, hoping that one day I'd get a backbone of some kind one day.

Alex stood at the elevator in a navy-blue suit and a cream-colored tie, looking like he'd stepped outside a luxury Beverly Hills country club or something. Even though I despised him, he looked damn good in a suit. I bet it was custom, too. A suit that fit that well had to be custom tailored.

A chill raced throughout my entire system as I stood beside him.

He didn't say anything at first. When the elevator arrived, he followed me in. I pushed the sixteenth floor. He pushed the fifteenth.

We stood on opposite sides of the elevator.

"Do you always let people take advantage of you, or just the pizza guy?" he questioned.

"I beg your pardon?"

"He said he owes you and your business money."

"Oh." I shook my head. "That's none of your business."

"I know. It's *your* business. People will make you broke if you allow them to abuse you like that."

I held the pizza boxes against my chest and cocked an eyebrow. "And what difference does it make to you?"

"Absolutely none. I'm not letting people leave my establishments without paying for my services. But then again, you seem like the type." He glanced my way, eyed me up and down, then turned back to face forward. "No offense."

Uh, offense taken. Dripping in offense! "What does that even mean? I seem like the type?"

"You know"—he gestured toward me—"a pushover."

"I'm not a pushover," I lied. It was my middle name, after all.

"That grown man just told you he spent two thousand dollars on Taylor Swift tickets instead of paying you, and you didn't even consider standing up for yourself."

"You don't understand," I urged. "It's Taylor Alison Swift. It's kind of understandable."

He rolled his eyes. Dang it, why was his eyeroll attractive, too?

He continued. "You're a pushover. A doormat. A weak—"

THE PROBLEM WITH DATING

"I get it," I snapped, cutting him off. The amount of discomfort I found in his words was aggravating.

I felt dizzy.

Hurt, too.

Mostly hurt because I knew he was right. People pushed me around repeatedly, and I hadn't found the courage to shove them back. Maybe because my name was already being dragged through the mud due to Cole. I didn't need more negative press from the pizza delivery man.

The elevator opened to his floor. And before he got out, he turned my way. "They'll keep robbing you as long as you keep your safe open like an idiot."

"I'm not an idiot."

"I didn't say you were an idiot. I said *like* an idiot."

"Why are you being such a jerk?"

"I'm just telling you like it is."

"But it's not true."

"It is. It's called tough love."

I huffed. "Yet there seems to be no love to be found."

He raised and dropped his shoulders. "Then I guess it's just tough."

Chills raced over me as I stared at the darkest soul I'd witnessed in a long time. His approach and his RDF threw me for a loop. He seemed to be the type to live under a dark, gloomy cloud at all times, never feeling the sun's warmth. A vampire of a human. I wondered if he was always like that or what changed him to become that way. Who was his maker? Who was the person who bit him and changed him forever?

"I'm sorry," I whispered, the words leaving my mouth before I could comprehend why I was saying them.

"For what?"

"I don't know." I shrugged. "For whoever it was that broke you and turned you into a monster."

CHAPTER 6

Alex
Eight Years Old

The shouting filled the cramped apartment once more, rattling the thin walls. I hated their loud arguments, especially when they rumbled into the night. Dad's booming voice was powerful enough to shake the walls of our home.

"I can't stand you! Do you even hear yourself? Do you?" Dad's voice thundered at Mom.

"I hear myself just fine!" Mom shouted back.

Huddling on the living room couch, I pressed my hands against my ears to block out the noise. My knees were drawn tightly to my chest while cartoons played silently on the television screen. I should've been in bed but didn't want to walk past their raging storm to reach my bedroom.

"I hate you!" Mom barked. "You're a failure who can't provide for your own family. You have nothing to be proud of. Everything about you is embarrassing. I wish I never met you!"

My eyes clenched shut as their words stung my chest. How could they be so cruel to each other?

THE PROBLEM WITH DATING

"I don't want any of this anymore. I don't want this life, and I don't want you!" Mom declared. "I wish I never said, 'I do.'"

In a flash, a ring sailed through the air, clattering to a halt as it met the edge of the couch. I glanced down and picked it up with shaky fingers. Mom's wedding ring felt heavy in my hand as my stomach twisted in knots.

Did she mean that? Did she mean that she didn't want to be with Dad anymore?

But we were a family.

Family was supposed to stick together.

"Good riddance," Dad spat back, his voice breaking. He didn't mean that. He couldn't have meant that.

"I'm leaving!" Mom bellowed before storming into the living room. She froze as her eyes found me, clutching the wedding ring in my hand. Her gaze shifted from the ring to my tear-streaked face, and something inside her seemed to break.

"Alex," she whispered, her eyes brimming with tears. "I..." Her voice cracked, and she shook her head, suddenly unable to meet my gaze. "Go to bed. I'll be back later."

With that, she grabbed her keys, jacket, and shoes. I hurried over to her. "Take me, too," I begged. "Please." I didn't want to be left with Dad. He didn't like me the way Mom liked me. He was always grumpy. She was happy sometimes, at least with me.

"No. Stay here. I'll be back," she swore. Then she stormed out the front door, slamming it shut behind her, leaving an echoing silence in her wake.

My jaw trembled as I stared at the front door, waiting for her to return inside.

Dad walked into the living room with heavy footsteps. His stare was on to the front door with a look of anger. He huffed as he glanced around the space, almost as if he searched for Mom to be there so they could partake in another shouting fest. His movements were intense as if the storm continued to brew from deep inside him. His nostrils flared with each breath he sucked in. The room echoed with his rage, bouncing to and from the worn-out couches and chairs.

When he realized she was gone, his facial expression shifted. The rage in his eyes flickered out as he blinked a few times. His shoulders dropped as his grimace faded. The house felt still as Dad stood in place with Mom's disappearance. A sudden burst of finality hit the pit of my stomach as we stood in the space that now felt unfamiliar to me. The absence of Mom's presence was the loudest silence I'd ever experienced in my life.

He turned toward me, and I tossed my hands behind my back, hiding the ring in my hold.

His eyebrows relaxed, his mouth parted, and his brown eyes glassed over like Mom's. He looked sad. It was a kind of sad I'd never seen before. The kind that looked as if it would last forever. Instead of the intense warrior he'd been a few moments before, he was now just...Dad. A regular person who was hurting due to love. I didn't know love could hurt so much.

His nostrils stopped flaring as he took short breaths. The shortened inhalations shifted to longer ones as he tried to calm himself down. His trembling lips pressed together as he continued looking at me.

I stared back with a tight chest, wide-eyed with confusion. Dad almost forced a smile but was too exhausted to complete the act. The left corner of his mouth twitched up before it dropped. He didn't frown, either, though. He stood still as all signs of emotions left his system. As his slightly drooped shoulders rose, he began rebuilding himself to a neutral position. His posture straightened, and his exterior shell hardened once more. I'd never seen Dad cry, but he seemed close to tears for a few moments before growing hard again. I wished he had let it happen, but we didn't have that kind of family. Tears weren't a part of our characteristics—only yelling had been. Whenever I felt like crying, I'd punch my pillow instead. I'd learned that from my parents.

Dad's brows bent, and he shook his head slightly. "Go to bed, Alex."

CHAPTER 7

Alex
Present Day

*I*t didn't take long for Nathan to convince me to partner with his family's farm. I'd taken a few trips to Honey Farms to inspect their ingredients and concluded I'd be an idiot not to use their products in my restaurant. The quality was remarkable, and the family took pride in their farmland.

Plus, now I could say I was using Nathan Pierce's tomatoes, which seemed like an odd but grand flex. What I didn't expect over the next few days was a ton of other small-town individuals to show up at my restaurant, pushing their products on me.

When I showed up after a busy day of doing paperwork, I found my new staff standing around at the bar with an older Asian gentleman pouring them all a few glasses of wine.

"You see the difference, right? The crisp hint of honey tones hits your tastebuds," the guy explained as he set down the bottle of wine.

"What the heck is going on?" I barked, startling my staff. It had only been a few days, but it was clear I'd already placed a solid amount of fear in their spirits, which was a win in my book.

"Good afternoon, Chef," they all said in unison, placing their wineglasses down.

I cocked an eyebrow. "Are you all drinking on the clock?"

"Technically, we're working," Eddie, the sommelier, mentioned. "Sammy was going over the menu with us all, and we were sampling the tapas with the wine when Mr. Yang stopped by with samples of his wine from the local winery."

"You must be the owner! Alex Ramírez. I've heard great things." Mr. Yang looked at me with a bright smile. His gray hair matched his beard as he grabbed a glass and poured a sample. He walked over toward me and extended it my way. "I'm Lee Yang, the owner of Honey Bee Winery, and I am excited to showcase a few of my best wines."

"We already have our wine selection pulled," I coldly said. "I'm not sure why Eddie hasn't notified you of this."

"Oh, he did," Lee mentioned, forcing the wine stem into my grip. "I just have a way of being a bit pushy. Plus, Tatiana is a good friend and a long-time Honey Bee Winery supporter."

Tatiana gave me that same smile she'd delivered during her interview. Though, looking back, it was more so that she interviewed me, not vice versa. "Lee is a gem. You'll love his stuff. Trust me."

I cleared my throat. "We already—"

Before I could finish my thought, Lee tilted the glass to my face, forcing me to take a sip, and then he grabbed one of the appetizers and shoved it into my mouth. After almost choking on the drink and food, I swallowed and was about to cuss him out for his aggression, but...I couldn't get over how good the combination was. I narrowed my eyes and grunted as I took another sip of the wine.

What in the world did he put in this stuff?

I gestured toward the bottle of Merlot on the table. "What does that pair with?" I asked.

"The oxtail empanadas, chef," Eddie replied, pouring me a glass. My head chef, Sammy, placed an empanada on a plate. They handed the items to me, and I grudgingly accepted the samples. As I tasted the pairing, I swore my soul entered a far, far away place filled with fireworks and happiness.

I grimaced and arched an eyebrow toward Lee. "How did you do this?"

"The Lang secrecy of wine. It has the Honey Creek special touch."

My annoyance peaked because there was no way I could go without Lee's wines in my shop. Beyond that, I knew I had to sign a deal with him to have his bottles in my other restaurants, too.

"Leave your business card," I directed. "And everyone else, get back to work. We open in a few days."

Tatiana smiled at Lee and nudged him. "That means he's gonna say yes."

"Tatiana," I scolded.

She placed a hand on her hip and raised a brow. "Yes, young man?"

The strength of every mother in the world powered her hand on the hip. I didn't have enough nerve to tell her to stop sending people to my restaurant for partnership. "A word alone."

I walked over to a table and took a seat. She pulled out the chair across from me, sat, and combed her hair behind her ears. "Yes, chef?" she asked.

"You can't keep doing this."

"Doing what?"

"Telling everyone in this small town I can partner with them."

THE PROBLEM WITH DATING

"I'm not doing that. I'm only telling the ones I know you'll partner with."

I grumbled, "You don't know that for a fact. And you're creating false hope for these people."

"It seems Nathan and Lee didn't deal with false hope." She shrugged her shoulders and seemed detached from my trying to scold her.

"Tatiana."

"Alejandro."

I sighed and pinched the bridge of my nose. I thought she would call me chef or Alex, not my full damn name. "I hired you because—"

"Because I am a true asset to the team with my connections to the small town. Let's be honest, Alex. You aren't small town. You don't give off that energy."

"I'm not trying to be small town."

"Well, you have to try, at least. Otherwise, this restaurant will not make it. And I'm the cross point to make it easier for you. If you get the small-town people to like you, you can make this place successful."

"I don't care if these people like me. People will come from out of town."

"Yes, and then they will return to their homes, leaving you with us. You'll need us just as much as we'll need you. You'll need friends. That's the thing about this small town. It's a community. You might as well join it instead of being an outsider. I noticed the harassment some of these people have been giving you."

"You want me to give in to the bullies?" I groaned at the simple idea.

"No. Of course not." She shook her head and reached out for my hand. She patted it and gave me a sense of comfort I didn't ask for. That was…annoying.

And…kind.

Whatever.

"You don't join the bullies of the town, Alex. You join the community. Then the community will be there for you to shut up the bullies. You can't do this alone and shouldn't want to."

I sighed and pulled my hand from her touch. It bothered me that her words felt true.

I pinched the bridge of my nose. "Tatiana?"

"Yes?"

"No more bringing talented people into my restaurant, all right?"

"Oh, but Carol from the chocolate shop down the way—"

"Tatiana."

She tossed her hands up in defeat. "Okay, okay. No more partnerships for now."

"Or ever."

"Never say never. It closes off the possibility of miracles." She stood from her chair. "I'd love to keep talking, but I must get to work. We're opening soon, you know. I have to make sure things are in order 'round these parts."

She excused herself from the table, and I sat there, a bit thrown off about who was in control of our conversation. For some reason, it felt like Tatiana was my employer, not the other way around.

As everyone returned to work, I glanced out the restaurant's front window to the dog shop. I crossed my arms and watched the owner interact with her customers and their dogs. I wasn't sure who was more excited to deal with her—the humans or their pets. Either way, laughter and smiles were spread from that woman as if her middle name was Giggly.

I grumbled as I studied her. She had her hair down and her curls bounced whenever she laughed. She wore a flowy blue dress, and the widest smile I'd ever seen. It was a beautiful grin, and she gave it to everyone who crossed her path. That felt ridiculous to me. Not every person deserved such a genuine smile, which made me think it was...ingenious. Maybe. I didn't know.

All I knew was that I sometimes struggled to look away from her. Her features pulled me in. Deep dimples and dark eyes that smiled almost more than her lips. Curves that made every article of clothing she wore look as if it was custom-designed for her body. Lips that were full, plump, and—

"Tatiana," I called out.

"Yes, Alex?" she replied, walking over to me.

"Who is that?" I asked, nodding toward the woman across the street who was laughing as a huge mutt jumped on her, licking her face to filth. Disgusting.

"That's Yara Kingsley." She clapped her hands, seemingly giddy that I was asking about the woman. "Oh, you have to meet her. I can introduce you if—"

"I don't want to meet her," I snipped.

"Then why are you asking about her?"

"People in town seem fond of her."

"Well, of course they are. She *is* Yara. What's not to like?"

Plenty, I imagine.

"Ohhhh!" Tatiana wore a goofy grin and nudged me in the arm. "Does someone have a crush on her?"

"Don't be ridiculous. I was curious about who she was, that's all."

"Why weren't you curious about anyone else on the street? Many people are around."

But they aren't her.

Why was I curious about her? Why did she stand out so much more than all those others who seemed so black and white compared to her? It was as if she'd rolled in every color in the rainbow while the rest of the world around her remained dull. Maybe that was why I was curious. I understood dullness. I knew mundane and muted. Yara seemed to be none of that. She felt like light, which bothered me because I was so used to the darkness.

I grumbled and rolled my eyes. "I stepped in her dog's crap the other day. I wondered why so many people like a woman like her."

"Oh, it must've been an odd occurrence for you to step in her dog's poop. Yara is a big activist about cleaning up after people's pets. She volunteers to clean it up at the dog park three days a week. That's Yara for you. She's so sweet. And *single*," she added in, singing the last word.

I arched an eyebrow. "Why did you do that?"

"Do what?"

"Emphasize the word single."

"Oh. Did I do that?"

"You did. You said *single*."

"Well, I figured you might want to know that information."

"Why would I care that she's single?"

I wouldn't.

I don't.

Tatiana smiled as if she believed differently. "All I'm saying is, I wouldn't judge you for having a crush on her."

"Why would I have a crush on her? I didn't even know her name until five seconds ago."

"Because Yara Kingsley is quite crushable. If it weren't for her annoying ex-husband, she'd probably have men lining up outside her door for a date."

"Annoying ex?"

"Cole. He's the chief of police in town. Between you and me, I'm not a fan after how he did Yara so wrong in their marriage, but you know. He's the head of the unspoken boys' club."

"What does that mean?"

"You know those people who never grow out of their frat-boy era? The boys will be boys clan? That's Cole, but he only got worse with age. I can't prove it, but I feel like he got every guy in town to do some kind of weird bro-code thing where they'd refused to date sweet Yara after she filed for divorce."

So she married the chief I'd run into earlier that week. That made sense. If she found a way to like him enough to lead to marriage, her taste in things was way off. I knew I didn't like her for a reason.

Then again, she did divorce him. That had to count for something.

Don't make excuses for her, Alex.

"You know, I'm good friends with the Kingsley family," Tatiana mentioned.

"Sounds like you are good friends with everyone."

"What can I say? I'm a people person. You know what? I could walk right over there and give Yara your number if you'd—"

"Tatiana."

"Yes?"

"Get back to work."

She smiled and shook her head and then poked my cheek. *Yup. That's right.* She *poked* my *cheek.* "You're blushing a little, Alex."

I grimaced. "It's hot. Have the staff turn up the air-conditioning."

"Whatever you say, chef," she sang as she danced away, leaving me with my eyes lingering on Yara.

Yara.

She looked like a Yara, too.

Maddeningly beautiful.

CHAPTER 8

Yara

"Yara! Yara!" someone shouted as I sat in the dog park watching Cocoa run around with the other pups in the park. I prided myself in knowing every single dog's name in town. And if I didn't, I introduced myself as soon as possible.

I glanced up to see Tatiana darting my way with a clipboard and the biggest grin on her face. That wasn't shocking. Tatiana was probably one of the happiest people in town—if not on the planet.

She slid beside me on the bench and nudged my arm repeatedly. "How are you?" she asked.

I laughed at her childlike excitement. "I'm good. Hoping one day to be as good as you are," I joked.

"Oh, I think you will. But first"—Tatiana shoved the clipboard toward me—"The fall festival is approaching. I need you to sign up for the annual Snack on Hillstack Picnic Dates."

I sighed and shook my head. "I'll be skipping this year."

THE PROBLEM WITH DATING

"What? You can't! It's been a tradition since before you were born, and you took part in all of them for over a decade."

"Yes," I agreed, "but that was when I had a partner to purchase my basket. Now that Cole and I broke up, I won't stand there and embarrass myself when no one picks me for a date."

"Are you kidding? People will pick you. Plus, it's for a good cause this year."

"What cause is it?"

"The Pup Around the Corner."

My eyes flashed with emotion as I sat back a little. Each year for Snack on Hillstack, the community voted to raise money for a local business. The event took place on the giant hill because of the remarkable view. In one direction, you could see Chicago's skyline in the background, and the lakefront in the other. It was stunning all around.

"What?" I said, stunned by the realization that they would support my shop with the event. "No way. You can't..."

"The board already decided on it. It's a done deal. So you have to partake in the activity." She pointed a stern finger at me. "Don't you dare cry, Yara. I cry when others cry, and I just got my lashes done. I cannot cry for forty-eight hours. Hold it in!"

I sucked in my trembling bottom lip and tried not to release a floodgate. She had no clue how much the business was struggling. She had no clue how helpful this was going to be for me. Unless she did know, which was possible seeing how Tatiana knew everything about everyone.

She probably knew what color underwear I had on in that very moment.

I narrowed my eyes. "Why do I feel like you had something to do with my shop being picked?"

"The perks of being head of the community board," she sang. "Besides. We wanted it to go to someone deserving. That's you, Yara."

"You have no clue how much I needed this."

"Oh, but I do know. You better stop letting those people get away without paying Yara Kingsley. Your mother would've lost her mind if she knew women like Mrs. Levels were pulling a fast one on you."

She was right.

If anyone knew how my mother would've reacted to things, it was Tatiana. She was her best friend, after all. After Mama passed away, Tatiana stepped in for us girls to look up to. We leaned on her most with issues Daddy could never understand. I'd always valued having her in our lives. I couldn't imagine getting through the loss of Mama and the growing pains of being a woman without Tatiana in our corner.

"I'm working on building my backbone," I told her.

"You don't need a backbone to tell someone to piss off and pay up," she replied. That was exactly what Avery and Willow would've said that, too.

"But go ahead," she said, tapping the sign-up sheet for the event. "Add your name."

"Tatiana." I groaned. "Seriously. What if no one bids for my basket?" I would be humiliated. I couldn't imagine standing on that stage without choosing it.

Tatiana seemed less than worried as she waved me off. "Don't be ridiculous. Someone will pick your basket."

"With the way Cole is scaring these men off from me, I wouldn't be shocked if no one purchased it."

"Cole and his stupid followers aren't the ones we want purchasing your basket, anyway. We want a real man to pick it up. Speaking of…"

Oh no.

Her big, goofy smile returned. "You know how the last time we talked, you mentioned being interested in dating again?"

"Yes…"

"And you mentioned how you felt like no man has a crush on you or they are afraid of Cole?"

"Yes. I recall my sad story," I joked. "What's your point?"

"I found a man for you."

I chuckled in disbelief. "I'm sorry, what?"

"I found a man for you," she repeated. "A handsome one at that."

"Is he British?"

"British? No. But his voice is smooth and deep like a dark roast coffee. He's so good-looking, Yara."

So the guy wasn't Josh.

Hmm.

She piqued my interest. "Who is this guy?"

"Alex Ramírez. My new boss."

I almost choked on my next breath. "The owner of Isla Iberia?"

"Yes! That's him."

"The tall, dark, and unapproachable owner?"

She nodded. "You've noticed him!"

That's saying the least.

"I have. I can confidently say that that is *not* the man for me."

"What? He's sweet." I cocked an eyebrow at her. She readjusted her words. "Okay, he's a little rough around the edges."

I huffed. "A little?"

"*A lot.*" She waved her hand around in a dismissive way. "But that's not his fault. He's been through a lot."

"Haven't we all?"

"Yes, but you don't know how awful this town has been to him. Do you know his building has been vandalized four times since he hired me? And before that, who knows how many other times. People are making his transition to this town almost impossible. I'd be grumpy, too."

That thought landed against my heart as I considered it. I couldn't imagine what it was like being so unwelcome in town.

Having your dream and then having people try to destroy it. Sure, he wasn't the nicest guy to me, but could I blame him? He did step in my dog's poop before the sun came up, and who knew what kind of jerks he'd crossed paths with the days prior.

"Think about Max over there. Remember when Max was in the dog shelter?" Tatiana asked, pointing toward the tiny toy poodle playing tug-a-war with Cocoa. "And how snappy and scared he was to everyone no matter what due to how his previous owners treated him? His trust was on high alert. That's Alex. He's on high alert. We just have to keep showing him kindness so he can put his shield down, like Max."

"Are you saying Alex is a toy poodle?"

"Oh gosh, no. He's a Doberman. Sharp and strong. But do you know what I think?"

"I'm sure you'll tell me."

"Every big dog is a tiny, scared puppy that wants to be loved."

"I guess that makes sense…" I warily agreed. My heart and mind were at war with figuring out if Alex was authentically rude or just shaped that way by our townspeople.

"Yes. It does. Plus"—Tatiana drummed her hands against her thighs—"I have it on good authority that he has a crush on you."

My eyes bugged out of my face as I started laughing my head off, tossing it backward in a snickering fit. "That man does not have a crush on me." If anything, he had the opposite of a crush. He had a solid aversion when it came to me.

"Yes! He does! I know it for a fact."

"Is that so?"

"It is." She nodded. "He was asking me all about you the other day. I told him you were single, and he seemed interested."

That made no sense to me at all. From our interactions with one another before, it was the opposite of that. That man did not like me. He could hardly stand me.

"No offense, Tatiana, but I think you're wrong this time," I

THE PROBLEM WITH DATING

said as I signed my name on the clipboard form and handed it back to her.

She shrugged. "I'm just saying. Keep your eyes peeled for that one. Alex is rough around the edges, but if you just take the time to look a little deeper, I think there's a sweet guy who's just been burned one too many times by others."

Maybe.

"You know what you should do? As a peaceful welcome to town for him?" Tatiana asked. "You should make his water dish."

I grimaced. "No. I don't think I will."

"What?! You have to. It's a tradition your mom started, and it would be a shame if it went away. You've made them for every small business in our town. I think it would be a nice welcome to Honey Creek gift for him, to show that not all of us in town are awful."

Ever since I was little, each store on Main Street had a handmade water dish for the community dogs that wandered the streets of Honey Creek. My mother was the one who made them and after she passed, I took on the task. Each bowl was made to match the shop it would be placed in front of.

I'd already made the one for Isla Iberia, but I'd talked myself out of giving it to Alex after our not-so-nice meetings.

Still, Tatiana was right. It was a tradition. I shouldn't have let Alex's bad attitude change how I moved. I made a dish for everyone. He shouldn't have been the exception.

Before I could reply to Tatiana, I noticed Cole walking toward us. She looked up to see what I was staring at and unknowingly rolled her eyes the moment she noticed him.

"That's my cue to go," she said as she stood from the bench. "But keep in mind what I said about Alex. If anything, you should stop by for dinner one night with your sisters and try his menu. It's all remarkable. I've never tasted anything as amazing as his food, Yara. You would love it. Your dad would, too."

"Sounds good." I smiled. "Thanks again for picking my shop for this year."

She placed a hand on my shoulder and squeezed it. "If I could, I'd pick you for every year, Yara. But I don't want to be called out for playing favorites." She leaned in and whispered, "Even though you're my favorite."

As she stood straight, Cole stood right in front of her. He pushed out a small smile. "Good evening, Tatiana."

"It was until you showed up," she dryly replied, giving him a scolding glare. "Bye, Yara. Talk later."

She waved goodbye to me before hurrying off.

Cole sighed and grumbled beneath his breath as he sat on the bench beside me. A little *too* close. I inched away from him so his arm wasn't brushing against mine.

"That woman hates me," he mentioned about Tatiana.

"Can you blame her? She's like a mother to me, and you didn't treat me the best," I offered, gathering Cocoa's things so I could hand her off to Cole for the next few days. The days when I had to leave my sweet Cocoa with my ex were the ones I dreaded the most. It always felt like I was leaving my heart with a stranger even though Cole had always been in her life.

"So let me guess, everything was my fault, and you and your people never did any wrong, huh?"

I didn't reply.

I wouldn't take the bait and comment on him saying those words. No matter what, I felt Cole was always setting up a trap for me to walk into, and I wasn't interested in those traps anymore. I didn't have to walk on eggshells with him anymore, wondering what would trigger him. That was the whole point of our divorce—me getting freedom away from him.

Even though some of me wanted to rage at him for what Lori had told me. I wanted to tell him to clear my name and speak on my behalf. But that would only make him believe I was still invested in us. Or that he still had power over me.

THE PROBLEM WITH DATING

Cole Parker was used to getting his way. He'd never had to work too hard to accomplish anything in town—a perk of being from the founding family of Honey Creek. When his father retired from law enforcement, there was no real debate about who the next chief of police would be. The job position was handed over to Cole on a silver platter. Throughout Cole's life, his mother Lindsay ensured that he never had to work too hard, either. Cole was a mama's boy through and through. That woman spoonfed him all his wishes and dreams.

So, it must've been killing him to know he could no longer have me. I was the one thing off-limits to him. I was convinced he didn't want me as much as he wanted to control me.

He stood with me, taking the leash from my grip. "You're leaving already?"

"Why wouldn't I be leaving? She's yours for the next few days."

He frowned. He looked pathetically sad, too. I almost asked if he was okay, but then I remembered that wasn't my responsibility.

"I thought we could catch up a little," he offered. "We haven't talked in a while."

"That's because there's nothing to talk about."

"Isn't there? I heard you moved into those new apartments. Did Avery finally kick you out? I doubted she'd let you stay much longer."

There it was. The subtle commentary that felt like little digs.

I took a breath before responding. "I moved out of my own accord. Avery wanted me to stay longer."

"That doesn't seem like her. She's always had a stick up her—"

"Don't you dare speak about my sister, Cole," I barked, as my blood boiled.

He smirked after seeing he got a rise out of me.

There it was—the trap. Cole wanted to ruffle my feathers,

and the tiny smirk he delivered afterward showed that he felt victorious.

"I always thought your relationship with your sisters was why ours failed. They were too involved in your life. Inserting themselves into our business."

"Oh? Is that why we failed? It had nothing to do with you inserting yourself in other women?"

Cole's posture tensed for a moment before he shook it off. "You're right. I was the reason it failed. Not them. Which brings me to my next point..."

"What do you want, Cole?" I asked, sensing his odd behavior.

He brushed his hand against the back of his neck. "I'm in therapy, Yara."

"Good for you." I meant that, too. I'd tried to get him to talk to someone for years, but he refused.

"So I can win you back," he finished.

Not so good.

"Cole," I started.

"I'm serious, Yara. I've learned much over the past year, and I miss you. I miss the comfort of you. I miss us doing things together."

I narrowed my eyes at him. "Are you drunk?"

"I'm serious."

"Well, don't be. You're talking ridiculous, Cole. We ended our relationship for a reason, and I do not see reconciliation being an option."

"Why not?"

"Why are you doing this? Why do we have to discuss this?"

His bottom lip twitched, but he shook it off and took three deep breaths as if trying to tame his anger. "Okay. You're right. I came on too strong. We can revisit this at a later time."

"Or never. I'm okay with never."

He laughed and shook his head. "I miss that spitfire personality the most."

I rolled my eyes. "Stop."

"You miss me, too, don't you?"

Not even a little.

Have you ever dated someone, then looked back on said relationship and thought, "What the fuck was that?" That summed up my marriage. It was as if I'd had a bad fever dream and woke ten years later dazed and confused.

"Cole. No. I don't. We're moving on. I'm going to start dating. You're going to date. We're starting our own lives," I explained.

"You're dating? Who?"

"As if I'd tell you."

He laughed again. It sounded like nails on a chalkboard. I used to love his laughter. That was until it was soaked in disloyalty.

"I have to go, but before I do..." I brushed my hand against the back of my neck.

I couldn't help but think about what Tatiana mentioned and the harassment Alex had been facing. Even though that, too, wasn't my business, I felt a tug at my heart to speak up to Cole.

"I wanted to mention something to you," I stated.

He arched an eyebrow. "Oh? What's going on?"

"I've heard a bit about the new restaurant owner, Alex, being harassed with vandalism. Has your team been looking into it?"

He narrowed his eyes. "What interest do you have in Alex?"

I could almost feel his jealousy simmering beneath his words.

"Nothing. I don't think it's right to have anyone in town harassed. We shouldn't have those people doing things and not being caught."

"It's just kids doing kids' stuff."

"Cole, it still isn't right. Maybe you should figure out who it is and teach them a lesson that those actions aren't allowed in our town."

"Or maybe an uppity restaurant owner should find a new place to put his business. My grandfather would've been pissed about what happened to that theater."

"It was a run-down spot that hasn't been used in years."

"It was a staple of our town's history. I took you on our first date there, you know."

Yes, I knew.

He also spilled his whole Slushie on my lap because he was so nervous. What happened to that sweet boy? It still blew my mind how much a person could change throughout the years.

"Cole, can you just watch out and help Alex? It's literally your job."

"Fine." He groaned like he used to when I'd ask him not to leave his dirty underwear on the kitchen countertops. "I'll help him if you let me see your new place."

"*Cole*," I scolded.

"Or let me take you on a date."

"Cole!"

He smirked. "You feel it, don't you?" He gestured back and forth between us. "The heat we're creating?"

"That's not us. It's ninety-three degrees outside right now."

"Yara, mark my word. I'm not going to give up on us."

Please do, Cole.

I sighed, exhausted by the conversation. "You know what? That's my sign to leave."

"All right. If you'd like, I can drop Cocoa off at your new place in a few days."

"No." He'd never step foot in my building if I had it my way. I hated that he even knew where I lived. "I told you. This is just our drop-off and pick-up location, Cole. I don't want to engage in more than that."

"But—"

"Has your therapist taught you about boundaries yet?" I chimed in.

THE PROBLEM WITH DATING

He tossed his hands up in surrender. "All right, all right, I hear you."

"Good. I'll see you here in a few days to pick her back up. Good night." I walked off without allowing him to take any more of my time. He'd already taken enough from me throughout the years.

As I headed home, I hoped to run into Josh, but I wasn't that lucky. I did, however, end up sharing an elevator ride with Alex. Soon enough, I'd start thinking he was stalking me with the number of times we'd crossed paths. He allowed me to step inside first, and he followed after. He pushed both of our floor numbers, clearly remembering mine from before. Then he stood on the opposite side of the elevator. Silence. He didn't even look my way. How could his nonexistent staring make me feel so…vulnerable?

And he had a crush on me?

Where, Tatiana? I needed a magnifying glass to spot said crush.

After he got off the elevator, his head slightly looked back toward me, and his dark eyes locked with mine for a split second. That was all it took from him—one look with those dark, piercing eyes sent my mind straight into a delusional fantasy world. Where nothing made sense.

He was *so* in love with me! It was almost embarrassing. Okay, maybe not love, but he had major *like*. I couldn't tell before because the poor guy suffered so heavily from RDF that I thought he was constipated. But really, that whole time he was showing me major like signals. He didn't look me up and down and wag his tail, but he *did* look my way. The way his eyes locked with mine couldn't have been anything other than signs of a crush.

Thoughts of Alex kept entering my head without permission as I slipped into my pajamas. I was still trying to wrap my mind around the idea he had the hots for me. He didn't seem the type to like anyone, let alone have a full-blown crush. Yet I couldn't stop thinking that perhaps Tatiana was right. Maybe I had to look closer at Alex before shutting that door of possibilities because he looked back at me when he could've kept looking forward.

Oh gosh.

My bare minimum dating bar? It was skirting *pretty* close to hell's quarters.

The delusional part of my brain could understand him being into me, though. I couldn't blame him, of course. I did look extra nice that evening in my overalls and crop top shirt. The stench of wet dog that covered me from my workday had to be a massive turn-on for him.

I wouldn't have been surprised if he'd had wildly inappropriate dreams about me for the remainder of the week.

CHAPTER 9

Alex

Every time I read Teresa's diaries, Honey Creek added another point to it being at the top of my hatred list. How they treated her and her family when they moved from Madrid to the small town drove me mad.

I visited her house to meet the real estate agent helping me put it on the market. Todd Graceson was supposed to be one of the best real estate agents in all of Chicago. I knew he was good, too, seeing as he was the one who sold me the property years ago when my career took off. When Teresa found out I was moving to Chicago from Madrid, she packed her bag that night. She said, "*A donde vayas, yo voy.*"

Where you go, I go.

That was over twelve years ago. I only moved out of Teresa's home in Chicago when I went to live with Catie for a few years. For the most part, that place raised me. Those hallways had stories. Those closets had history. Teresa loved our home, and I loved that I could buy it for her. Seeing as how she raised me in Madrid in her small, two-bedroom apartment, giving her a home big enough for us both to explore and spread out felt good.

The kitchen was her favorite part. She told me that when I built my forever home, I needed a kitchen three times its size. And the one she had was pretty damn big.

I'd miss her late-night coffees at that kitchen island, and I'd miss our morning whiskeys.

With her gone, I had no reason to hold on to the property now with her gone. The house that had once been a home to me was now being put on the market. The warmth Teresa added to it had evaporated through the walls the day she passed away. Now the space felt hollow.

My phone began ringing as Todd walked through the space. It was Noah again. He'd called me for the past few hours, checking in about tomorrow's funeral.

I'd been ignoring him.

I wasn't in the mood to tell him I wasn't going. I'd deal with him scolding me after the event took place.

"Well, it looks remarkable," Todd told me as he walked back into the kitchen. "And I am very confident that with all the renovations you put into it, we can get more than triple what you bought this place for. If you can just sign some paperwork, we can get it listed, and—"

"Not yet," I cut in, feeling a chill race throughout me. An unease that found me whenever he brought up the idea of listing the property. This was the third time he came out to meet me, and the third time I told him to wait.

His brows knitted. "I'm sorry? I thought—"

"I was wrong," I told him. "At least not today. I thought I could do the paperwork today, but I'm not ready. Not with tomorrow being..." I cleared my throat and combed my hand through my hair. "Can we meet next week?"

Todd's defeated look was warranted. I felt like I was becoming a major pain in his ass and wasting his time. But it would be worth it when I signed the paperwork. When I let it go. He'd get his fair cut to compensate for my twisted mind and flawed follow-through.

I'd get there one day.

Just not today.

Just not yet.

Once Todd left, I stayed in the house, sitting at the kitchen island in complete darkness. As the sun went down, my anxiety went up. I battled between going to the funeral and not. How was I supposed to do that, anyhow? How did one say goodbye to the person who saved them repeatedly?

I stared into the darkness a little longer before tossing on my shoes, grabbing my keys, and heading out the front door. I couldn't sit any longer. I needed to move. I needed to cook. I needed to get down to Isla Iberia and cook a few of Teresa's favorite meals.

A few turned into many, and many turned into a lot.

I cooked all night long.

By the time the sun rose, I'd destroyed the kitchen of Isla Iberia. Every dish I could use was dirty, and every item on the menu was made. I finished the last meal around eleven in the morning. My eyes were tired, and I had fourteen missed calls from Noah.

I shot him a text message.

Alex: I'm okay.

Noah: Show up today, or I'll come find you.

Leave it to your best friend to worry about you when you were completely fine. It was beyond normal to cook for hours through the night, not taking a break to think or feel. I didn't need to feel or think. I needed to bury myself deeper into cooking. But unfortunately, Yara caught my attention across the street. She was pacing back and forth, holding some kind of dish in her hands.

It was as if I couldn't get far enough away from her. She was everywhere and seemed to talk to everyone.

Tatiana mentioned that Yara was like the town's golden retriever. That might've been why she stared at me with massive puppy dog eyes the last time I saw her. She looked at me as if she knew a secret I didn't, all giddy. It drove me bonkers.

Still, I couldn't stop staring at her. I couldn't stop taking her in and her erratic pacing outside my building. I studied her so much that I ended up burning my empanadas.

I. Burnt. My. Empanadas.

I didn't burn items. I prided myself on that fact. I'd never burnt anything, but there they were—burnt to a crisp empanadas—all due to the weird woman from across the way.

CHAPTER 10

Yara

"Just drop it off and go, Yara," I said as I stood in front of my shop with the water dish for Alex's restaurant. "Stop, drop, and roll," I muttered. I started walking to cross the street but paused and shot back to my side of the road. Why was I dealing with such a heavy level of panic over the idea of dropping off a freaking bowl? It was just a dish. Nothing more, nothing less.

"Hey, Yara!" Milly said, rounding the corner from her morning walk. "What's that you got there?" she asked loudly as she wore her huge red headphones over her ears that matched her outfit. I swore Milly had a set of headphones to go with every outfit she had.

"Oh, it's nothing. I was—"

"Oh my gosh, are you putting out a doggy dish for that monster of a new restaurant? Don't tell me you're supporting that place, Yara."

"It's a tradition, Milly. Every store on Main Street gets their own water dish."

Milly shook her head in disappointment. "You can't be serious. That dish is more than just a dish. It's a sign that our town accepts this kind of development. That's the last thing we should be doing!"

The way Milly's voice carried made my skin crawl. I hated how she drew in attention when all I was trying to do was stop, drop, and roll.

"You better get back to your walk, Milly. We don't want your heart rate to drop below the cardio zone," I said.

She glanced at her watch and shook her head. "Well, you're right. But reconsider leaving that dish in front of that restaurant. We have to stand in unity," she scolded before looking toward the building across the street. "Is your sweet father working today? I wonder if he'd like this outfit, too."

I pushed out a smile. "Not today, Milly. They finished up with the project over there."

"Oh? Well, maybe he can come help me with a plumbing issue I've been having with my sink."

"He's not a plumber, but you can probably call Eric to get some help."

She waved me off. "Oh, Eric's company charges too much. I'm sure sweet Matthew would do an assessment for free. Even though he's not a plumber, rumor has it he's great with his hands." I shivered in disgust as Milly hurried away. As she traveled, she shouted, "Ditch that dish, Yara!"

I grumbled to myself before rolling my shoulders back and marching over to Isla Iberia. With haste, I went to set the dish down, and as I was kneeling, a voice boomed over my shoulder.

"What are you doing?"

I turned to find Alex staring at me with a stern look of judgment. His brown eyes pierced me with an intensity that made my skin crawl, yet I wasn't sure if it was in a good way or bad. That man made me feel things I wasn't sure how to decipher.

"Oh. Hi." I stood and smoothed my hands over my pink A-line dress. "I was just placing your water dish in front of the restaurant."

"I'm not buying that."

"You don't have to buy it. It's a gift."

"I didn't ask for a water dish."

"Right, of course not." I smiled. He didn't. *Figures.* "It's just something I do for each business. I don't know if you know this, but Honey Creek is a very dog-friendly town—and Walter-friendly."

"Who's Walter?"

"Walter is the community cat that wanders," I explained, pointing toward the orange cat a few stops down drinking from the ice cream shop's water dish. "So I hand craft each store a unique bowl to help keep the pups hydrated on their daily walks."

He grumbled and crossed his arms over his apron covered in flour. I wondered if that was a Mary Sue flour mess or one of his own. "I'm not paying you for that."

I arched an eyebrow. "I already told you it's free. Just a nice 'welcome to Main Street' gift."

"I don't want your gift. Get rid of it," he shot out, his eyes seeming colder than the previous few unpleasant times we'd crossed paths. His grumpiness meter was at an all-time high that morning.

"It's free," I stated again. "It doesn't hurt anyone."

"It hurts my business, and I don't want it here."

"Why are you being a jerk about it? It's just a water dish!"

"One I didn't request. Now, remove it or I will."

I crossed my arms over my chest and stood tall. Even with me standing as tall as possible, I still appeared so small next to his broad frame. "No. It won't even bother you."

"I can assure you that seeing dogs slobber and slurp up water from outside my restaurant will bother me."

I rolled my eyes. "You're being dramatic."

"And you're being rude. I didn't ask for this, so remove it before I do it myself."

"Rude?!" I blurted out, stunned by his word choice. My hands flew to my chest. "I am the opposite of rude. I get along with everyone. People like me."

"Not everyone," he uttered, his words dripping with annoyance. "I don't like you."

My breath caught in my throat as I looked at him, bewildered by his statement. "You don't even know me!"

"I know you let your dog crap wherever it pleases, and that you try to leave water bowls around even when people don't want them. Don't push your dog obsession onto me, Goldie."

"Goldie."

"Like those annoying golden retriever dogs. That's you, Goldie."

"Did you just mean-nickname me?"

"I did, Goldie."

"Don't call me Goldie!"

"I can and I will."

What was wrong with this creature? "Why are you so mean?"

"Because I can be."

"Just because you can be mean doesn't mean you should. You could be nice, you know. That's an option."

"Nice like you?"

"Yes. Nice like me."

He huffed. "You're not nice."

"What? Yes, I am."

"No, you're not. Nice people don't say they're nice. Self-conscious, trying too hard people say they're nice because they are overly obsessed with people liking them."

"I don't care if people like me!" I remarked, which was indeed a lie. I did care. I cared so deeply that if I misspoke to a person, I'd overthink it for hours after the interaction. But I didn't need grumpy-no-water-dish to call me out on my flaws

THE PROBLEM WITH DATING

and insecurities. I already overthought them enough for us both.

"Well, that's a good thing because I don't like you, and you need to take that stupid dog dish and get away from my restaurant!" he shouted. The veins in his neck popped out as he waved his hands in dismissal. His eyes were on me, but they looked so very far away. They swam with rage, or wait...sadness? When he blinked, his eyes looked so sad. As if he was trying his hardest to keep it together.

"What's wrong with you?" I asked, confused about his harsh tone. Sure, we hadn't had the best interactions, but the severity of his anger seemed very misdirected. No one could be that upset over a water dish.

"*You!*" he yelled. "You're what's wrong with me! This whole stupid town is what's wrong with me! This stupid town and their stupid water bowls for their stupid dogs and stupid Walter the cat! This stupid town and their vandalizing, and gossiping mouths, and dumb traditions! This stupid town and how badly they treated her when she was nothing but good!" he hollered, his eyes glassing over with tears and rage and hurt.

So much hurt.

Oh gosh. What happened to this man?

"Who was nothing but good?" I whispered, confused by his words.

He blinked as the rage simmered. He blinked as those tears fought not to fall from his eyes. He blinked, and I saw it—his true self. His hurt self.

He shook it off quickly, and his stare hardened again.

"Nothing. It's nothing. Just go, will you?" he hissed.

"Alex," a voice said, interrupting our argument. Well, more so his argument with the whole world of Honey Creek. I didn't even think he was shouting at me anymore. His frustration seemed too harsh over a water bowl.

"*What?*" he continued yelling as he turned around to see the stranger standing on the sidewalk. The moment he locked eyes with the guy, his anger dissipated. "What are you doing here?" Alex asked.

"Don't be an idiot," he replied.

Alex rubbed the back of his neck but didn't respond. His shoulders dropped. It was as if seeing that guy deflate his anger balloon.

The guy frowned, walked over to Alex, and hugged him. Alex didn't hug him back. His arms stayed to his sides, but the guy didn't seem to mind. He held on so tight as if he feared letting go. Then he said, "Whiskey?"

Alex shook out of his hold and raked a hand through his messy black hair. "I'll get the glasses set up."

"And clean yourself up a bit, will you?" the stranger ordered. "You're filthy."

Alex grumbled. He turned toward me, and all that was left was the sadness in his eyes. He didn't say anything more, though. He simply walked inside, leaving me standing there with the stranger in front of me and the dog dish in my hand.

"Seems you two were in a heated conversation," he told me.

"I was just trying to welcome him to town with a water bowl for the dogs in the community." He smiled. The opposite of something Alex would do. I tilted my head toward him as I narrowed my eyes. "I know you."

He held a hand out toward me. "Noah Colton. Nice to meet you."

My jaw dropped. "Noah Colton, the celebrity chef on the show *Bite Sized*?"

He smirked and shrugged. "The one and only."

"Oh my gosh, I love your show. I'm such a fan. You're friends with this guy? But you seem so nice and he seems so, so, so—"

"Grumpy?"

"And rude! And nasty! And hotheaded."

Noah laughed. "That's my best friend for you."

"Best friends? I'm shocked he has any friends with his attitude."

Noah glanced toward the restaurant at Alex, who was aggressively removing a bottle of whiskey from the bar's shelf. Noah slid his hands into his pockets. "He can be a bit rough around the edges."

"To say the least."

His smile remained, but it fell slightly. "He's had a hard few months. On top of that, today's the funeral for someone very important to him."

"Oh my goodness." My hands flew to my chest. "I had no idea."

"Of course, you didn't. How could you have known? Alex isn't much of an open book. Honestly, I'm pretty sure he superglued his pages shut." Noah sighed and scratched at his beard. "I know he's kind of a dick. It's part of his charm in the industry, oddly enough. The bigger the dick, the better the chef, but he's also a good guy. Normally, he just keeps to himself, but he's been having a tough go at it this past week. He's just in a chapter of his life where he's a bit lost."

"That explains why he's in Honey Creek. He must've taken a wrong turn."

Noah laughed. "Oddly enough, I think this is exactly where he needs to be. You should leave the water dish. It will grow on him."

Before I could reply, the door to the restaurant flew open. "Are you coming in or will you be a pain in my ass and stand outside all day?" Alex growled toward Noah.

His bad attitude didn't faze Noah in the slightest.

"What was your name again?" Noah asked me.

"Yara."

"It was nice to meet you, Yara," he said.

"He's lying," Alex remarked coldly. "He always lies," he grumbled as he waved Noah toward the restaurant entrance.

"You've seen my show, Yara. You know I cannot tell a lie, even if I wanted to. Have a good day."

"You too, Noah."

My stare found Alex's again, and I felt I should've spoken. As if I should've given him my condolences or as if I should've hugged him. There was no reason I should've felt like that, but I did.

CHAPTER 11

Alex

"Nice girl," Noah said as he walked into the restaurant.

I rolled my eyes as I moved toward the bar and poured two shots of whiskey. "She'd be thrilled to know you said that. Nice is her favorite thing to be."

"I would call you out for being grumpy toward her, but with the circumstances..." He took a seat at the bar and I sat beside him.

"You didn't have to come out here. I'm fine."

Noah glanced toward the destroyed kitchen and arched an eyebrow. "Clearly," he sarcastically remarked.

"What do you want me to do, huh? You want me to be sad? You want me to cry? You want me to be overly emotional about Teresa's funeral today?"

"Well...yeah. That would be warranted."

"Too bad. I'm going to clean up this mess and get on with the restaurant opening next week. I don't have time to sit and simmer. Besides, Teresa lived a good life. I'm not going to cry about it."

"Just because she lived a good life doesn't make her passing easier."

"Yes, actually, it does." I downed my shot and poured another round. "So you either can help me clean this place up or—"

He sniffed the air. "Did you burn something?"

I grumbled, remembering the empanadas. "I don't want to talk about it."

"You never burn anything."

"I was distracted."

Noah frowned and patted me on the shoulder. "By your sadness?"

"What? No. By Yara."

He raised a curious brow. "Oh, you've got a thing for the girl next door, huh? Or, more so across the street. I can't blame you. She's beautiful. Nice, too."

There was that word again—nice. Good ole nice Yara.

Why did that bother me so much? Why did she irritate me to my core? People were my least favorite thing in the world. I'd made it a life mission not to care about them, but Yara kept crossing my mind for some reason. It was almost as if she'd unpacked her bags in my head and pitched a tent to live there.

"I don't have a thing for that woman," I grumbled like an old man. "She's a pain and a stereotypical small-town person with a small-town mind."

"What's wrong with that? I like small-town girls. I'm engaged to one, remember?"

"Chicago is not a small town."

"It is when you compare it to New York City," he explained. "It's all about perspective."

"Can we talk about something else?" I said, wanting to move the conversation from Mandy because it always circled back to Catie, and I was beyond done speaking about her.

THE PROBLEM WITH DATING

The best thing about the past was leaving it there.

"Sure. Maybe we can discuss that the last thing you texted me was that you weren't attending the funeral this afternoon."

"I'm not."

"Yes, you are."

"No. I'm not."

"Alex…"

"I'm too busy opening the restaurant. I can't take time off."

"Buddy…"

I sighed. "I don't have time for this, Noah. She died, and it sucked, and I'm dealing with it the best way I can think to, all right?"

"And how exactly are you dealing with it?"

By not dealing with it at all.

He sighed and pinched the bridge of his nose. "It will be a beautiful service. Teresa will like it."

"No, she wouldn't."

He arched an eyebrow. "What do you mean?"

"Teresa hated funerals. She thought they were ridiculous. Besides, a few years ago, we'd walked past a church holding a funeral service, and she told me exactly what she thought of them."

"What did she say?"

I took a deep breath.

I tried not to choke on my next inhale.

"She said, *'Alejandro, cuando muera, no me busque en las iglesias. Encuéntrame entre las ollas y sartenes.'*"

"Wow." He nodded slowly. "Now, in English for your best friend to understand."

I smirked. "*'Alejandro, When I die, don't look for me within a church. Find me in the pots and pans.'*"

Noah sat back in his chair, shook his head, and snickered lightly. "That sounds like Teresa." He gestured toward the kitchen. "Is that why it's a mess in there? Were you looking for her?"

"Yes."

"Did you find her in there?"

"No," I replied. "I only found burnt empanadas."

He patted my shoulder. "It's okay if you found grief, too, Alex."

"I didn't. I'm fine."

"Henry called me this morning. He asked how you were doing."

"And what did you tell him?"

"To piss off."

That's my best friend.

Loyalty was Noah's middle name.

"Thanks," I muttered, uncertain what to think about Henry searching for me after Teresa's passing. Henry was one of the best chefs in the world. It just so happened that with that position, he also managed to be one of the worst humans I knew. I used to look up to him until he stole my restaurant concepts and started sleeping with Catie. Rumor had it that they were living happily ever after together. I always wondered about how cheaters could cheat with one another and then run off into the sunset, leaving others with the trauma of healing from the betrayal. It hurt to be cheated on. It hurt even more to know both parties involved in the scandal.

To say Henry's and my relationship was broken beyond repair would've been an understatement.

"Not a problem," he said and meant it.

"Can we talk about anything other than this?" I asked.

"Like the beautiful girl across the street?"

I rolled my eyes. Turned out, I didn't want to talk at all. Not about Catie. Not about Henry.

And most definitely not about Yara Kingsley. Though, realistically, she was better than the first two options.

"Maybe we can sit in silence," I grumbled.

Noah nodded and clasped his hand around his glass. "I'm fine with that, too."

* * *

NOAH HELPED me clean up the whole kitchen before heading to Chicago later for the service.

After finishing some paperwork, I headed out the front door to lock up shop. After locking the door, I glanced to my left and saw that water bowl.

Son of a...

I snatched the bowl as my chest rose and fell rapidly from annoyance and I darted across the street toward Yara's shop.

"What's the matter with you, huh?" I barked at Yara, who was finishing a transaction with a customer. I would've felt bad if I wasn't such a jerk.

"Who are you talking to like that, young man?" the customer asked, clutching her purse.

"Not you!" I snapped, feeling my whole body heat with anger.

Yara looked at me, then at the woman, and she pushed out a smile. "We'll figure out how to bring your account to date next time, Milly. Have a good evening."

Milly leaned in toward Yara. "I told you about those inner-city drugs."

She then went on her way, pushing herself past me as she exited the shop. Yara released a weighted sigh and then placed her hands on her hips as she turned toward me. Her stupid, beautiful brown eyes locked with mine and she barked, "What the heck is wrong with you?"

"Wrong with me? I told you I didn't want your stupid bowl!"

"Yes, well, Noah said—"

"I don't care what Noah said! I told you in no uncertain

terms that I didn't want this crap," I said, shoving it toward her chest.

"It's not crap," she sternly stated, shoving it back toward me. "And if you weren't in such a mood, you could've probably appreciated it! And I'm sorry, all right? I'm sorry you're in a mood and I understand why you're in a mood."

"You don't understand anything about me. You don't know me."

"You're right. I don't. But Noah told me about—"

"You don't know me!" I blurted out, feeling a wave of emotions rush through me at the mention of Teresa. I wanted to feel those emotions. I wanted to mourn. I wanted to fall apart. I wanted to break into a million pieces. I wanted to be where Teresa had been. I wanted out of this world because a world without her felt like emptiness.

I felt empty.

Void of anything that mattered.

But instead of facing those emotions and processing my loss, I shouted at Yara as if she were the cause of every hurt I'd ever hurt.

"This isn't about my life. This is about you and your pushiness and your stupid bowl. All I said is I don't want your stupid bowl!" I explained.

"Why are you being such a jerk?"

"Why are you being so annoying?"

"I'm not annoying, you freaking prick!" she hammered out, her voice cracking. She then covered her mouth with her hand and shook her head. "Sorry. I'm sorry. I didn't mean that."

"Yes, you did. For once, stand on your words."

"Now, who's acting like they know someone?" she said with flaring nostrils. She seemed conflicted about whether she should've been nicer or let her annoyance with me fly.

Fight me, Goldie.

I needed that. I needed something to be mad at, someone to target this whirlwind of emotions toward.

For some reason, I felt I was the first person she'd ever yelled at based on how flush her face appeared. She looked stunning even when she was upset. That bothered me even more.

She shoved the bowl back toward me. "Just take it!"

"No," I barked back, shoving it toward her.

"Yes," she argued.

"No."

There we were, both beyond irritated with one another, shoving the stupid bowl back and forth, back and forth, back and forth until I simply gave up and stepped backward completely, pulling my hold away from the bowl.

As she shoved it back toward me, she let go, and it slipped from her grip, falling to the floor and shattering into a million pieces.

Within mere seconds, her eyes flooded with tears. She swallowed hard, and her hands flew to cover the sob that choked out of her. All because of a freaking bowl. She darted over to the bowl in a complete fit as tears fell down her cheeks. She began picking up the pieces of the broken bowl with shaky hands, and a pound of guilt hit my chest.

Crap.

Sure, I didn't want the bowl, but I didn't think she'd break into a hissy fit of emotions from the thing breaking.

I grumbled and bent down to help her pick up the pieces. "I'm sorry, I—"

"Just go!" she barked, wiping her tears. "I should've never given you a chance because of a stupid crush that never existed!"

"What are you talking about?"

"It doesn't matter, okay? We don't vibe clearly, so let's stay out of each other's hair. You don't come into my shop, and I'll stay out of yours," she aggressively spat out, her eyes piercing into me.

That was the point when I should've apologized. That was when I should've tucked my tail between my legs and told her I was sorry for being a monster each time we crossed paths. She'd somehow managed to cross my path at the worst moments. It wasn't her fault. But for some reason, I didn't know how to be soft.

How to admit fault.

How to be human.

So I puffed out my chest and hollered, "Trust me, I'll never step foot inside this place again, and I wouldn't have if I didn't have to give you that thing back!"

She stood to her feet, puffed her chest out, and shouted back. "Trust me, I'll never step foot inside your stupid restaurant! You and your stupid fusion crappy food!"

"My food isn't crappy!"

"It's the crappiest crap!" she argued. "And anyone who eats there is a buffoon!"

"That's a lie!"

"No, it's not. Anyone who walks into that stupid place is a clown! You might as well have the hostess put a red nose on each person who shows up."

"You're beyond ridiculous."

"You're even worse than that!"

"Do you have to get the last word in?"

"Do you?!" she rebutted.

"No, I don't!"

"Good then, leave!"

"I am!"

"Go faster!"

"*I am!*" I shouted back, tossing my hands up in frustration.

"*Like now!*"

"*Like I said—I am!*"

THE PROBLEM WITH DATING

But I wasn't. I hadn't moved. I hadn't taken one step toward the front door and didn't know why. I couldn't stop staring at her. I couldn't stop looking at the tears rolling down her cheeks. I couldn't do anything.

So she moved. She stomped toward the front door, swung it open, and then flung her arm to gesture out the door. "And don't come back!" she ordered.

As I left her shop, I stomped my feet like she had, and she slammed the door behind me, locking it instantly.

The moment the fresh air hit my face, I returned to reality, wondering what happened.

I looked through the door window toward Yara, whose back was still to me, and watched as she wiped away the tears from her eyes. Every ounce of aggression I'd felt faded away, leaving me with nothing more than guilt.

Well, guilt and grief.

The worst combination.

Teresa would've scolded me for being such a monster. She would've told me to knock on that door and apologize for being so cold and mean. She would've reminded me of how to be a gentleman. Yet she wasn't around anymore to be the compass that pointed me toward being a better person.

Therefore, all Yara would get was the grumpy man I'd turned into over the past year or so. Cold and heartless. Miserable and alone.

CHAPTER 12

Alex
Ten Years Old

"Please don't leave me here," I begged Dad as we stood before a stranger's house. We'd flown across the world for the longest time because Dad said he couldn't watch after me over the summer. He said he had too much work, and I'd have to spend the summer with my aunt Teresa.

I didn't know who Teresa was, and the last thing I wanted to do was spend time with her in an unfamiliar country. When Dad talked about her, he talked about how weird she was when he was a kid. How she'd eat plain garlic like a vampire and try to feed it to him with honey whenever he came to visit.

I didn't want to eat honey garlic.

I wanted to go home.

"Stop your whining," Dad scolded with his hand tightly wrapped around the suitcase handle. "Most kids would kill to come to Madrid for a summer. You're being ungrateful."

My stomach hurt as I fought the tears that wanted to fall.

THE PROBLEM WITH DATING

"What if Mom comes back while I'm over here? What if I miss her?"

Dad huffed and rolled his eyes. "Your mother left two years ago. I doubt she's going to come looking for you now. Grow up and get over it. It's time for you to be a man."

I didn't know being a man meant I couldn't have a mom. For the past two years, I waited for the living room door to open in my apartment and for Mom to come back inside because she said she'd be back later the last time I saw her. I'd been waiting two years for later, but it never came.

Still.

What if it came when I was in Madrid? What if Mom was looking for me and I was nowhere to be found?

Dad pounded on the apartment door, and soon enough, an older woman opened it, wearing bright, mismatched clothes, a ton of weird necklaces with crosses, big gold earrings, and goofy-looking round glasses. A cigarette sat between her fingers as she looked at Dad.

She smacked his cheek slightly before kissing each one. "You're late."

"Our flight was delayed," Dad explained as he took the cigarette from her fingers and inhaled a drag of it. I hated the smell of smoke. It made my stomach hurt even more.

Teresa snatched the cigarette back and smacked the back of Dad's head. "What are you doing? Don't smoke. It's bad for you." She then turned to me and arched an eyebrow. "Do you smoke?"

I stepped slightly behind Dad's body to hide myself. "I'm a kid."

She narrowed her eyes and studied me with a stern look. Then she burst into laughter. She laughed like a wicked witch, tossing her head backward in a giggling fit. "When I was your age, I smoked a pack daily. But don't you ever start, okay? That's why I sound like an old trucker. My lungs hate me, Alejandro."

She said my whole name. That made me feel weird.

"My name's Alex," I whispered.

She tilted her head. "What was that? Who told you to whisper? We don't whisper in this house. We use our loud voices. Speak up or be unheard. And come out from behind your father. There's no need to hide."

I slowly stepped out so I stood in front of her.

"Good," she mentioned, nodding my way. "Now, speak your words again."

"My name's Alex," I said, a hair louder.

She raised both brows. "You call him Alex?" she asked Dad.

"Yeah."

She turned toward me and lowered herself to my eye level. That didn't take much, seeing as how she was such a tiny person with a big personality. "Do you know where you got your name, Alejandro?"

"From my parents," I said.

"Ah, yes, but do you know who you were named after?"

I shook my head.

She glanced at Dad with daggers before turning back toward me. "You were named after my brother, your grandfather, Alejandro Ramírez. Do you know what a name like that means?"

I shook my head. "No."

She pinched my cheek and patted it lightly. "It means defender of the people. And Ramírez means wise and famous. You see, you were given that name because of the power behind it. Names matter. You are a strong defender, Alejandro. And it is an honor for me to call you that."

I smiled a little.

I never felt strong before, but I liked my name more.

"I'm your great-aunt Teresa, your late grandfather's younger sister, but you can call me Aunt Teresa. The 'great' makes me feel old, even though I am pretty great," she said with a wink. She smelled like cotton candy and cigarettes and had a thick accent but smiled nicely. She smiled like she wanted me to feel good and welcome.

"You have your room set up for you, Alejandro," Teresa said, pointing down the hallway. "You should take your bag there."

"I should get back to the airport," Dad mentioned.

My eyes widened. "You're leaving already?"

"I told you. I was just coming to drop you off. I have meetings in California that I can't miss. I'll be back at the end of the summer to pick you up." He tousled my hair before hugging Aunt Teresa. "Thanks again for watching him this summer."

"I needed some youth in my house. Now go. Let me learn who Alejandro is," she said, waving Dad away.

He didn't hug me goodbye or say he loved me. He just hurried out the door.

The first month, Teresa made me help her around town. We'd go to the farmer's markets, and she'd cook me a meal each night. She was weird but a good cook. The second month, she asked me to chop up some vegetables. I cut my finger badly, and she taught me better skills. The third month, I made fresh tapas while she taught me Spanish.

The fourth month came, and Dad didn't come back.

He called and said business was good.

He called and said he needed more time.

He called less, and less, and less.

I waited for him. I waited for Mom, too. I'd sit in Teresa's living room, waiting for them to return. Waiting for a call saying they were on their way to get me.

CHAPTER 13

Yara
Present Day

I hated the grump next door.

I wasn't one to use the word hate often, but it was there, and it was strong. Unfortunately, I couldn't seem to avoid being in his presence.

The number of times I left my apartment building to avoid him was unreasonable. Yet, still, I always bumped into him in the lobby of the apartment building, the mailroom, or the elevator.

Late one afternoon, after coming home from dinner with my sisters, he stepped into the elevator at the same time as me, and a large group of people followed, shoving Alex and me into the elevator corner, beside one another. Alex called out his floor number for the group to hit, and I did the same. His arm brushed slightly against mine, and I grumbled under my breath at the feeling of his touch. He grumbled back because I was almost certain that was the only sound his stupid mouth could make.

Grumble, grumble, grumpy annoyingly attractive man, grumble, grumble.

I hated that he smelled so good all the time, too. Mean people should smell like a sewer and dirty diapers, but his scents resembled cocoa butter, honey, and oak trees. I loved cocoa butter. I loved honey. I loved, loved, loved oak trees. *These are a few of my favorite things.* If I were a wild woman—which I wasn't—I'd want to snuggle closer to him in the elevator to breathe him in. I'd want to press my nose to his neck and take a ridiculous inhalation, moan against his moisturized skin, and ask him what kind of soap he showered with. I'd want to wrap myself within the fabrics of his clothing, ask about his fabric softener choices, and mark him the same way Cocoa marked all my clothes as her territory.

That was if I were wild.

Which I wasn't.

I was simply Sane Jane. Nothing was weird about me at all. *Totally* normal. Sometimes I had bizarre thoughts, was all.

The sane part of me didn't want to smell him at all. Whenever I saw his permanent scowl, I'd want to punch him in his gut.

His rock-hard gut.

I noticed his abs the other day when he ran shirtless around the neighborhood. No evil person should've looked that fit. It was a pain in my behind how good-looking that man had been. I bet his abs smelled like cocoa butter, too. I bet he lapped handfuls of lotion across every crease of his body in the morning and night. His skin looked too glimmery for him not to have a solid routine.

Stupid Alex and his stupid body.

As he pressed up against me in the elevator, his biceps brushed against my skin, sending tingles down to places in my body that shouldn't tingle from his touch.

"Stop touching me, Goldie," he hissed through gritted teeth.

"I'm not touching you," I replied. Alex glanced down at my arm, resting against his, then back at me. I rolled my eyes.

"*You're touching me!*" I whisper-shouted.

"You're making out with my forearm," he argued.

I ripped my touch away from his and turned slightly to tuck deeper into the elevator corner. "I would never make out with a forearm like your stupid forearm!" I replied, disgusted by the idea of it. "You have awful forearms."

"My forearms are fine."

"Your forearms are hairy! And ugly. And stupid."

"Forearms can't be stupid."

"I thought the same until I saw yours."

He arched an eyebrow. "You're very immature."

"Only to people I hate. And I hate you, Alex Ramírez."

"That's not very nice of you," he sarcastically muttered.

Oh, this man made my skin boil. "Yeah, my niceness leaves the building when my water dish shatters into a million pieces."

"It was just a water di—"

"*It was not just a water dish!*" I shouted, making everyone turn to look my way. I cleared my throat as my nerves hit the pit of my stomach. I smoothed my hands over the fabric of my shirt as the elevator opened to the fourth floor. Everyone hurried out except for Alex and me.

He moved to the left side of the elevator. I stayed on the right.

The elevator opened to the sixteenth floor.

My floor.

I cocked an eyebrow. "Aren't you on the fifteenth floor? Get off my floor!"

He muttered a cuss word under his breath. "Those people didn't hit the fifteenth floor. It skipped mine." He got off the elevator and started following me down the hallway. "And it's not your floor. You just live on it."

"Yeah, well. It's mine now. Get off my floor!"

THE PROBLEM WITH DATING

"I am. I'm taking the stairs down," Alex stated, gesturing toward the staircase exit across from my apartment.

"Take them faster," I urged.

He then proceeded to walk in slow motion.

Now who's immature, Mr. Cocoa Butter?

"Ugh. You're a pain in my—"

"Careful, Goldie," he stated. He glanced down the hallway before moving in closer to whisper. So close that his hot breath melted against my cheek. So close that my heartbeats intensified from his proximity. "You wouldn't want the townsfolk to hear you mutter a bad word. It would destroy your good-girl reputation."

"I hate you," I spat out, feeling so tiny next to his broad frame.

"So you've stated."

"Some things are worth repeating."

"And that was one of them?"

"That was one of them," I agreed.

He brushed his hand across his mouth before dropping it to his side. I stared at his mouth as if in a trance. I hated him. I knew I did. I had to hate him. He was mean, grumpy, and—gosh. What was that with his eyes? Now and again, his eyes would flash with a moment of softness I wanted to unpack. Why did I want to know the story behind his pages? Why did I care about the ink that scribbled against his soul?

"Are you okay?" I blurted out without thought. My chest hurt from seeing that flash in his eyes. I felt like the wind had been knocked out of me from the pained expression he hadn't even known he'd showcased.

Why did I feel the need to hug him? Why did I feel like I wanted to cry?

"What?" he asked.

"Nothing," I replied, shaking off the odd urge that washed over me. "Go away, will you?"

"I'm going."

"Can't wait not to see you again." I sarcastically smiled.

He didn't smile back.

Figured.

He flicked his thumb across his nose. "For the record, I don't hate you, Goldie."

"Why not?" I questioned as my heart did cartwheels and karate chops within my chest. "If you'd like, I'll try harder to annoy you to get you to match my hatred."

"No point in doing that. Hating people takes energy, and I don't want to waste my energy on this."

"You're saying I'm not worth your energy?" I stood taller and placed my hands against my hips. "You're saying I'm that worthless?"

"No," he quickly replied. "I'm saying no person is worth that energy. People are constantly letting others down. They can't disappoint you if you don't expect anything from them. I reserve my energy for other things."

"Like?"

"None of your business," he replied. There it was again—his eyes. He said one thing, but his facial expression showed something else. It was as if he spent all his energy on others his whole life, and they drained him. He didn't hate people because he didn't want to drain his energy. No. He didn't hate people because his battery was already drained. He was a broken-down car left on empty.

I felt it again. The hugging urge.

I stepped toward him. "Alex—"

He shook his head. "No," he whispered, as if he could hear my thoughts and feel them, too. Something about him made me want to fight with him, but it also made me want to hold him. I wanted to shout at him, and I wanted to fall against his chest and tell him that everything would be okay.

Did he feel that, too? Did he feel...me?

"*Don't,*" he pleaded, his voice low and packed with angst.

"Don't what?"

"I don't know." He lowered his head and stared at the floor as his hands flexed in and out of a fist. "Just don't, Goldie," he whispered. He picked up his speed and hurried down the staircase to his rightful floor before I could unpack the odd sensation he'd left me with.

I stood still for a moment, staring at the staircase, hoping he'd come back, but he didn't. I didn't know if what I felt from his departure was me missing him, but when he left, something within me floated away with his soul. Remnants of my spirit were somehow now entangled within his.

I unlocked my apartment door, a bit thrown off by Alex's quick exit. Sometimes, it felt like we were playing tennis with one another in our interactions. A fun yet intense battle of back and forth, seeing who would score a point on the scoreboard first. It always ended with such an intense feeling in my gut that I realized there was more to our interactions. I wasn't sure what was there, but I felt it deep within my spirit.

He was the first person I'd ever been able to stand up to and go toe-to-toe with during our arguments. Why was that? Why didn't my brain freeze up when it came to me hurling comments back his way like it had with everyone else? Why did he make it so easy for me to stand up for myself when others made it almost impossible?

The feeling I'd felt was so foreign to me. It was nothing like butterflies in my stomach. It was like dragons. Fierce, intense, and powerful. I'd never felt that before with another person. I'd never felt connected to something so strongly. I'd wondered if he felt it, too. He'd left with a part of me still twisted within his soul.

A few minutes later, there was a knock on my door. I hurried over to open it, and when I met the person's stare, I swallowed hard and pushed out a smile. "Josh, hey. How are you? What's up?"

My crush! Knocking on my door. Lovely. That would shift my thoughts away from Alex and our odd interactions. Josh crafted butterflies within me. Not dragons, just flutters of beautiful, beautiful butterflies.

His grin stretched far. "Hey, sorry to just stop by like this."

"Don't worry about it." I brushed my hands against my sides, not knowing what to do with them. "What's going on?"

He held up the container in his hand. "I've been a bit busy with work lately, and when I'm overwhelmed, I bake. So I had extra cookies. I wanted to see if you'd like any."

"Oh. Wow. Thanks. Of course I'd love them."

"I'm good at a few things in life, and baking is one. It helps calm me. If I do say so myself, you'll be quite impressed with those cookies."

Oh okay. We can get married any day now, Josh. Do you like Paris in the fall?

I smiled. "That's very sweet, and I volunteer as tribute for any sweets you wish to discard."

"It makes sense for a sweet to like sweets," he said. Was that corny? Yes. Did it somewhat make me swoon? A double yes.

"I also wanted to ask you something else," he mentioned.

"Oh?"

"Yeah. I wanted to ask you out. On a date."

My heart skipped a few beats.

I felt like the Steve Carell GIF with him running around shouting, "It's happening! It's happening!"

"A date?" I questioned.

"Yeah."

"With…me?"

He laughed and rubbed the back of his neck. "That was the hope."

"I'd love that."

He sighed and pressed his hands to his chest. "Oh, great. I was nervous. Are you free Friday night? I know it's last minute, but if you say yes, I already booked a dinner reservation."

Taking the initiative to make reservations. That was a win in my book.

"I'd love that."

"Great! I'm excited. I was lucky to get a reservation at this place. They are booked out for months, it seems. My coworker had a timeslot but had to go to New York for a meeting, so she offered it to me."

"Oh? What's the place?"

"Isla Iberia. It's right across from your shop on Main Street. It's supposed to be one of the best. Did you know Alex is a Michelin star chef? I ran into him the other day, and he told me all about it. Nice guy."

Choking.

I was choking on my tongue.

Alex? A nice guy?!

My poor British future husband was so naive. If only he knew the truth about Alex, he would've thought differently. I almost thought of telling him about how Alex Ramírez went around shattering water dishes, but I refrained from it. I couldn't break his sweet, British heart.

"The reservation is there?" I asked.

"Yeah, is that okay?"

"Oh, yes. *Totally* fine. Not an issue at all. Cool. Cool. Very cool. Neat. Okay. Well, I better get inside and rest. I have a long day tomorrow."

He smiled. "Perfect. I'll meet you at Isla Iberia on Friday night at seven. Have a great evening, Yara."

"You too."

He hurried away, and I closed the door behind me, almost sinking to the floor as the realization settled that I'd have to step inside Alex's restaurant. As I tried to shake off that realization, I opened the container of cookies, picked one up, and took a bite.

That bite instantly flew out of my mouth and back into the container.

"What in the dog food is this?!" I shouted, stunned, appalled, offended.

Did Josh hate me? Why in the world would he feed me something so atrocious?! There was no way he thought those cookies were good. Or, sadly, he lacked taste buds. Josh might've had a lot going for him in life. A great job, a dazzling smile, and a remarkably attractive accent.

But baking?

One out of five stars.

Would not recommend it.

If I could give it zero stars, I would.

CHAPTER 14

Alex

"Shame on you, Alejandro Luis Ramírez!" Tatiana scolded me after she came into work the day after my odd encounter with Yara on the sixteenth floor.

Tatiana must've heard about the less-than-nice exchanges I'd shared with Yara. I'd never seen Tatiana upset, but I was almost certain steam would've been shooting out of her ears if possible.

The restaurant wasn't even open for a few hours. There was no reason she should've been barging into the front door.

I cleared my throat as I stood behind the bar. "Tatiana, can we not—"

"No, we will!" she shouted, shooting over to me. She smacked my arm with her purse. For a sweet lady, she sure had one heck of a strong swing.

"Ow!" I yipped. "You know, you can't get away with hitting your boss. That's completely unprofessional."

"I don't give a rat's behind about being professional. Why in the world did you do that to Yara?"

"I don't know what you're talking about," I lied.

She pointed a stern finger my way and then gestured toward a booth table. "Sit. Now."

"Tatiana. This is ridiculous. I'm not a child, and you can't—"

"Now!" she ordered with a shout. One that sent chills of fear down my spine. Like a little wimp, I hurried over to the booth and sat.

She walked over with her hands on her hips and narrowed her stare on me. "Out with it. Why were you rude to her?"

I grimaced. "Are you going to sit, or will you talk down to me the whole time?"

"I'm going to talk down to you the whole time because your behavior toward Yara warrants that type of reaction until I am proven differently. So speak up. You broke her water dish."

"I had a bad day."

"Nope. Wrong answer. Yara was being nice to you, Alex. Bringing you that water dish. Do you know how much time she spent on making that?"

"I didn't ask for it."

"*That's not the point!*" she shouted, tossing her hands around. "The point is she was doing something nice for you. Something she didn't have to do. You had no right to be so rude toward her."

"I know," I confessed in a low whisper. I hadn't slept in over thirty hours. I hadn't been able to do anything but think about Teresa. And when I wasn't thinking about Teresa, I was thinking about Yara. My brain ping-ponged back and forth between the two. I didn't even know why I felt so haunted by Yara in my thoughts. I didn't know how to get her off my mind. I didn't even know why she was there to begin with.

Tatiana arched an eyebrow. "You know?"

"Yeah. I know. I was triggered. The timing of it all was bad. I should've apologized."

"You still need to apologize." Her voice wasn't dripping with anger as she looked my way. Her eyes softened, too. She frowned slightly as she slid into the boothside across from me. The scolding simmer began to settle as she looked my way. "I get it. This town has been ugly toward you, Alex. They've harassed you, judged you, and made you feel unwelcome as if you were an alien to this place."

"You don't know the half of it..." I muttered.

"You're right, I don't. I'm not the one being attacked. You are. But you can't let these people change who you are. You cannot allow them to make you cold."

"What if I already was cold?" I asked. "What if this is just who I am? A monster?"

Tatiana smiled, stretched her arm across the table, and patted my hand. Just. Like. Teresa.

My monstrous heart cracked a little.

"You're not a monster, Alex. A monster would never question that. You know what I see when I look at you?"

"What's that?"

"A sad, scared little boy who has been hurt too much by this world."

How did she do that? How did she see the parts of me that I worked so hard to keep hidden from the rest of the world? I felt it yesterday, too, with Yara. She saw it. It slipped out. I knew why she asked me if I was okay—my hard shell cracked, and my true hurt spilled out. For a split second, she saw my mess, and instead of twisting the knife, she offered compassion.

Why, though? Why was she so...nice?

"A friendly tip?" Tatiana offered.

"Go for it."

"Don't push away the ones who were never cruel. That's where true loneliness comes from. Discarding the good ones because of the bad ones before them. Yara is a good one. She's one of the few trying to make you feel at home in this silly town."

I grimaced but knew she was right. I hated that she was right because it meant that my heart was still able to feel and not completely frozen over. I didn't want that to happen because feelings made me distrust the rest of the world. If I didn't feel, then I couldn't get hurt. If I couldn't get hurt, then I couldn't be shattered.

A person could only take so many third-degree burns before being destroyed.

Tatiana sat back against the booth and crossed her arms. "What happened this week, Alex?"

"I don't want to talk about it."

"Yes, you do."

Yes, I did.

I grumbled. "I don't want to waste your time."

"My time isn't being wasted. Speak. Now."

Even with her demands, they felt so gentle. Soaked in care. Why did this woman seem to genuinely care about me when she had no clue who I'd been? Why was she so kind? She reminded me of…

Teresa.

Of…

Yara.

Crap.

I was a jerk.

Yara deserved an apology.

I deserved a kick in my ass.

"My great-aunt passed away. The other day when I snapped was her funeral. She was the only family I had left that I still spoke to. I'm just trying to process it all."

Tatiana's eyes widened as if trying to absorb the weight of the information I'd delivered. Her brows furrowed as her mouth slightly parted, and her bottom lip quivered.

There was momentary stillness as she processed the news. Tears flooded her eyes with a profound sadness mixed with disbelief. She was heartbroken over a woman she hadn't even known.

Wait, no.

She was heartbroken for me.

Her sadness made me sadder.

"She's gone?" she asked me, her voice shaky. "I didn't know… I thought…I, uh, I'm so sorry, Alex," she cried.

"It's okay," I told her, feeling odd that she grew so emotional over a stranger.

She shook her head and wiped away the tears falling from her face. "No. It's not. I'm so sorry, Alex. I know what it's like to go through that kind of loss."

I narrowed my eyes. "You don't have family?"

She smiled, yet it was a broken kind of smile. The kind that looked more like a frown. She shook her head. "Family is what you make of it. This town is my family. I've lost a lot, though. I'm the last remaining member of my family line. I had a…" Her words faltered and she shook her head. "Let's just say, I know that struggle. Maybe that's why I felt drawn to you. Because I see the younger version of me in your eyes."

"She was like you, you know," I told her. "My great-aunt."

She sat straighter, wiping her tears. "Insanely charismatic and beautiful?"

I chuckled. "Loud, weird, and bossy. Nosy, too, and ridiculously invested in other people's lives." I took a breath. "And insanely charismatic and beautiful."

"See?" she whispered, leaning in toward me. "A monster could never say anything so sweet."

The comfort she was giving felt too heavy for me to take in. I wasn't certain how to handle it, so I stood. "I should get back to work."

"Yes, okay. And I'll stop yelling at you until later," she joked as she stood.

Then she hugged me, and I allowed it. I almost forgot what hugs felt like until she and Noah reminded me.

When she pulled away, she patted my cheek. "Sweet boy."

It was as if she constantly told me I was good for her words to imprint on my self-consciousness. Teresa used to do the same things. My parents weren't the best. My mother dipped out early on when we lived in Chicago, and my father dropped me off at Teresa's doorstep in Madrid when I was ten so he could pursue his career. No one that young should've been used to people leaving so often. Teresa made sure to be a person who stayed.

I rubbed the back of my neck. "What should I do about Yara?"

"Apologize. She'll accept it."

"And if she doesn't?"

"She will."

"How can you be so sure?"

"Because she's Yara. Holding grudges isn't something she tends to do. Now, I have to get going. I have work to do before I come in for more work."

"Tatiana?"

"Yes?"

"How did you learn my full name?" I questioned.

"I told you. I'm this town's mother. And mothers always find out everything they need to know."

"Right. Of course."

"Do you know what Yara likes, Alex?"

"What's that?"

"Cookies. Chocolate chip cookies."

* * *

Right after Tatiana left, I got to work on my apology. I'd spent the next few days working out how to apologize to Yara

THE PROBLEM WITH DATING

for my cruelty over the past weeks. I was in way over my head with my emotions and took it out on one of the only people in town who were kind to me.

What bothered me the most was that my mind and body didn't know how to act when I was around her. I went through a whirlwind of contradictory emotions when she was near me. I was stuck between loathing and wanting to kiss her until the sun faded. I hated the feeling of conflicting thoughts. It made my head hurt. I couldn't have my head hurting when my heart was already jumbled.

Still.

Not her fault.

Friday evening was busy at Isla Iberia, and I was already figuring out how to go to Yara's apartment to apologize after I locked up for the night. Or, well, I'd wait until morning to apologize, seeing as how I didn't know her apartment number. Though I could've knocked on every door until I found it and—

"Chef? What's this? Should it be tossed?" Sammy said, holding up a tray with desserts on it. "Is this on the menu?"

"What? No. Don't toss it. Put it on a plate and in my office."

Sammy smirked and looked down at the tray. "They look delicious." He went to pinch a piece off.

"*Don't!*" I ordered in a slight growl. "Get back to work!"

He shot his hand away from the tray and hurried away.

After he left, I decided to say screw it and try to catch Yara before she left her shop for the evening. Sure, I swore I'd never step foot in her store again, but that was when I was a mourning, rude jerk. I could pull myself together enough to admit defeat.

Yet before I could step foot out of the restaurant, it shocked me to walk into the dining area and see her sitting at the table closest to the display window.

Yara was in my restaurant.

She sat at one of my tables.

She wore a tight black dress with black high heels.

Her hair was pulled back into a slick, high ponytail.

Her lips were painted crimson.

She looked remarkable. The type of beautiful I hadn't even known existed.

But what was she doing in my restaurant? Sitting at my table? Looking as nervous as ever.

My curiosity was strong enough for me to walk over to her table. This worked out well for me because it gave me a chance to apologize to her for the past few weeks of utter douchebag vibes I'd given her.

I knew I was grouchy, but I wasn't that massive of a jerk.

As I moved toward her, my nerves were rocked upside down. Why did I feel like a little boy as I approached her table? Why did my palms feel sweaty and my chest feel tight? What in the world was this woman doing to me?

When I reached her, she studied her phone with such intensity that I almost felt bad for interrupting. I tried to think of some clever way to get her attention. I tried to figure out the best way to interject myself into her realm. Yet I only thought to say, "I guess you're Bozo."

CHAPTER 15

Yara

I rapidly placed my phone down as I heard Alex's voice from behind me.

"Bozo?" I asked, looking up at him, biting back the tears in my eyes.

He gave me a tiny smile and shrugged. "The clown. You said only clowns would—"

"*I know what I said,*" I snapped, feeling shame over me. I rubbed my moistened hands against the fabric of my dress and tried to shake off my discomfort. "Listen, I'm not in the mood tonight for our opposite of fun banter."

His eyes flashed with a softness I hadn't seen from him before. He cleared his throat. "Sorry. I was just trying to make a joke about—"

"Since when do we have a joking relationship, Alex?" I cut in.

Maybe if he had joked with me prior to that moment. Maybe if he had shown any signs of lightness in the past, I wouldn't have been so shut off. But at that very moment, I felt he were almost mocking me. As if he knew what happened to me, and he walked over to my table to dig the knife in a little deeper.

With how gossip spread in Honey Creek, I wouldn't be shocked if he knew what happened before I'd even found out.

First, Josh told me to meet him at Isla Iberia. Then he told me to go inside, and he'd be there soon enough. Then he texted me that he ran into Cole. That he didn't know I was still entangled with my ex. That he was uncomfortable with taking me out on a date. That he was standing me up.

I'd been stood up.

Stood up in the one space where I claimed I would never step foot inside, with the man who I loved to argue with hovering over me.

I was humiliated.

Alex took a step closer to my table and lowered his voice. "Are you all right?"

I sarcastically laughed and brushed away the stupid tears that decided to slip from my eyes. "Don't act like you care." I sniffled and shrugged. "You win, okay? I'm the silly clown in your restaurant. I'm the silly clown in this town with a stupid ex-husband who scares off any guy who looks at me. I'm the silly clown who was just stood up by a guy I thought liked me."

"British guy?"

"Josh," I corrected. "His name is Josh."

Alex grumbled under his breath and rubbed the back of his neck. "He's a douche."

"Yeah, well, it takes one to know one," I blurted out, then instantly felt remorse for my words. "Ugh. I'm sorry. I didn't mean that. Or maybe I did. I don't know. I'm just...not myself right now. And I can't leave this place because if I leave, people will see that I left, and people will know I was stood up and, well, honestly, the last thing I want to do right now is talk to the guy who hates me about a guy who stood me up, okay?"

He stood there like a statue, staring at me so intensely. I got

THE PROBLEM WITH DATING

lost in his dark brown eyes, uncertain what to say, so I said the only thing that came to mind. "Why are you staring at me like that?"

"Like what?"

"Like you have something to say, but you're not saying it? Listen. I'm hungry and tired. You win. I'm the clown. I'd be quite happy if the clown could get some complimentary bread like the other tables."

His mouth parted, and he nodded. "Sure, of course."

He hurried away, and not long after, he came with fresh-baked bread, still steaming, a fancy kind of butter, a wine glass, and a bottle of merlot.

"I didn't order that," I said, pointing toward the wine.

He set the bread down, the butter, and the glass. He then reached into his back pocket and pulled out a wine opener. As he uncorked the bottle, he remained quiet and poured me a *very* full glass.

"I'm not paying for that," I told him. "I mean, I'm going to drink it, but I'm not paying for it."

"It's on the house. The whole meal."

I arched an eyebrow. "The whole meal?"

"Yup."

"Like I can order anything?"

"Whatever you want."

"You do know your prices aren't cheap, right? To be honest, it seems you're a bit big for your britches, if you ask me."

"I'm glad I didn't ask."

I leaned in toward him and whispered, tapping the menu. "I mean, really. Twenty dollars for two croquetas balls?"

"That's very cheap, considering."

"For two balls? No balls are that good."

"You haven't tasted my balls yet."

I grew slightly flustered from his words. "Touché, Chef."

"My croquetas balls, I mean," he corrected, growing a bit off-kilter. His cheeks reddened slightly. Good. It was about time I wasn't the only one making a fool of myself.

"All I'm saying is, twenty bucks for two croquetas is highway robbery. I just wanted you to know about your pricing."

"I'm well aware of my price points."

I narrowed my eyes. "Back to the main issue at hand…I'm going to order everything on the menu."

He shrugged. "You can't go wrong with the menu. That's what I'd do."

"Are you going to spit in my food?"

He smiled a little.

My heart fluttered a little.

"No, I will not spit in your food," he said.

I wasn't quite sure if I should've believed him or not. Needless to say, after being stood up, I had some trust issues.

I held out my pinky. "Pinky promise?"

"I'm not going to pinky promise you."

"Pinky promise?" I urged.

"Listen, I'm already giving more than I'd give to anyone else. Take it or leave it. Without your pinky."

Fair.

"Why are you being nice to me?" I asked.

"I'm nice to all my customers."

"You were screaming at me like a madman the other day."

He grimaced. "Yes. I know. I wasn't myself that day. My…" He took a deep breath and cleared his throat. "I won't make excuses. I just wanted to apologize for my actions."

My conflicted heart softened as I looked at him. He seemed so sincere. So humbled. "Did Tatiana force you to apologize to me?"

"No," he quickly replied. "She might have mentioned that I was an idiot, though. Which, she wasn't wrong."

Admitting fault.

Not bad, Alex.

THE PROBLEM WITH DATING

"You didn't deserve any of my harshness. I apologize, Yara. You've been nothing but kind to me and I am sorry for breaking your dish." He went on to say, "Order anything on the menu. That wine is the best in-house, from Honey Bee Winery, too. It pairs perfectly with the bread."

I smiled.

He didn't.

I missed the tiny grin he'd given me a few moments ago.

"Thank you," I expressed, not knowing what else to say to him.

"Not a problem." As he turned to walk away, he paused with his back toward me. Then he looked back my way. "Yara?"

"Yes?"

"I don't hate you."

"I know. The whole energy thing blah, blah, blah. But sometimes it feels like you do."

"Yes, well..." He crossed his broad arms across his chest. "Sometimes my hatred for myself spills out and accidentally hits others. I'm sorry for my spills. I'm working on cleaning them up. Also, you should try the house sangria, too. It pairs great with my balls," he teased as he winked my way.

He teased and winked at me!

Oh my goodness. He was flirting with me!

Well, I think he's flirting. Maybe. I don't know.

I was the dog whisperer, after all. Not the man whisperer.

But he *did* wink. Winking felt like a flirty thing to do.

Or was he just blinking? Did a fruit fly shoot into his eyeball? Ugh. This was all too much to unpack. But I did know that the man just before me was *not* the man I saw nights prior.

Maybe the real Alex was kidnapped, and I was dealing with his clone version. If that was the case, I'd hoped the clone would stick around while the other version was off somewhere stepping in mounds of dog poop.

The fluttering of butterflies in my stomach was confusing,

leaving me on high alert. How did a man who made my blood pressure rise so high a few days ago now have my cheeks become a canvas of rosy hues?

With that, he disappeared back to the kitchen. When my server returned, I shook off the odd interaction with Alex. I couldn't help but wonder which version of the man I'd crossed paths with was the real one. Was he the gentle giant or the stinging wasp?

"Hi, are you ready to order?" the server asked. "Or do you want me to go over the menu? The tapas are quite popular here."

I leaned in toward her, crossing my arms against the table. "I'll have one of every tapa."

"Of *every* one?" she questioned, a bit of shock to her tone. A tone I didn't very much like, but whatever, it was free dollars and free cents that evening. *When in Rome.* Or Madrid, that was.

"Every single one. Oh! And I want to order the oxtail paella. It says to place that order in early because it takes a while to cook."

"Okay..." The server looked at me as if I had three heads. "Are you like...an undercover food critic?"

She must've been one of those Chicago staff members that Alex brought into town. Everyone else knew me as the dog whisperer.

But when you can't beat them, join them.

"Yup, that's me," I lied. "If you can ensure everything is cooked perfectly without any spit, I'll leave a very positive review." She nodded in understanding and started off. "Oh! And sangria, please! I'll take the sangria."

"I'll take a sangria, too," a voice said from behind me, making a wave of rage rush through my system because I knew that voice a little too well.

Cole slid into the chair across from me with a smirk. Oh, how I wanted to knock that smirk from his face!

"What are you doing here?" I whisper-shouted as my anger built to category five within seconds of his arrival.

"I heard a rumor that you might've been stood up and—"

"You have got to be kidding me. Cole, you have a lot of nerve showing up here after ruining my date tonight."

"Was that a date?" he asked, ripping off a piece of bread. My bread. My free bread! The hatred I felt for him stealing bread from me was now high on my list of reasons I loathed my ex-husband. "He didn't seem like your type."

I snatched the bread from his hand and shoved it into my mouth. "You know nothing about my type," I muttered with a stuffed mouth.

Cole arched an eyebrow. "I think I know you better than you know yourself, Yara."

"Maybe that used to be true, but it's not anymore."

"Yara."

"What, Cole?" I snapped, annoyed by his stupid face.

"Come home."

I crackled out a chuckle. "What?"

"I think you've made your point, okay? Billy told me you went to the courthouse to change your last name from Parker today."

"I did. I'm a Kingsley."

His hand formed a fist at that statement, but I didn't care enough to shield his feelings. He ambushed my date. He'd scared off Josh and then he had the nerve to try to eat my bread. All because he was upset that I was moving on with my life.

Changing my name felt like another step toward my independence. And shame on Billy at the courthouse for blabbering his big mouth off to Cole about the paperwork I'd submitted.

"What do you want, Cole?" I asked.

"Is everything all right over here?" someone spoke over me. When I looked up, Alex stood there holding two dishes. He arched an eyebrow at me.

I shook my head. "I was hoping to have a solo dinner tonight, that's all."

Alex turned toward Cole. "You heard the lady. She'd like to be left alone."

Cole placed his hand against his chief's belt, on his gun, and raised his brow. "Listen, new guy in town. This is a private conversation between my girl and me."

"She's not your girl," Alex said sternly. The way those words fell from his mouth made chills of pleasure run up and down my spine. His deep, smoky voice had so much authority that I almost applauded him for telling Cole off.

"Also, she stated that she wishes to dine alone. Besides," Alex stated, "we have a dress code here."

"Oh?" Cole sat straighter. "And what code is that? No uniforms?"

"No dicks," he deadpanned.

Oh snap! Take that, Cole Parker. You piece of crap!

My jaw dropped as I mentally cheered on Alex for not being bothered by Cole's apparent threat with his hand on his holster.

"Excuse me?" Cole spat out, standing to his feet and getting in Alex's face. Alex didn't falter, though. He didn't back down. He stood tall and stepped even closer to Cole.

"Leave," he replied.

"You got a lot of dang nerve—" Cole started, but I hopped up and slid between the two men. Alex's body pressed against my back as I faced Cole. His heat brushing against me sent electricity throughout my system as I looked up at Cole.

"It's time for you to leave tonight," I demanded.

Cole looked down at me. His eyes were filled with rage. A rage I knew too well. A rage I tried hard to ignore for years within our marriage. A rage that used to keep me quiet. But he could no longer shut me up because I was free from him and no longer had his name.

It did help my confidence slightly that an over six-foot

Doberman type of man was standing behind me, ready to attack if need be. Alex's existence alone at that moment gave me a boost I'd been lacking when it came to Cole. He gave me courage.

"Now," I ordered. Not a stutter from my tongue. I felt big. I felt powerful. I felt safe. I felt Alex. I felt *all* of him, pressed up against me. *My, my, my.* Talk about being stuck between a dick and a hard place.

At that moment, I'd be forever grateful for Alex Ramírez's protection.

Cole muttered something under his breath and took a step backward. "I didn't want to eat this shit food, anyway," he said before he stormed out of the restaurant.

I released a breath I didn't even know I was holding. As I turned to face Alex, I ran straight into his hard, stone chest. I wondered if it would be inappropriate to stroke each ab *just* a little bit as a thank you. A little stroke, stroke, pat, pat action.

I took a step backward and shook my head. "Sorry about that. He's just..." I couldn't even find words for what Cole had been. Cruel. Controlling. Unhinged.

"Are you okay?" Alex asked. His voice was low and tender. I didn't know that man knew what tenderness was, let alone that he could showcase its sound.

"Yeah. I'm fine," I lied.

He grimaced and placed the dishes on the table. "Are you okay?" he asked again. His voice dripped with sincerity. "No lies this time, Goldie."

"No," I whispered. "I'm not."

"How can I help?"

I slipped back into my chair and shook off the anxiety dripping all over my body. "Keep the sangria coming."

"You got it."

He turned to walk away and I called out to him. "Alex?"

"Yes?"

"Do you always serve each table your guests sit at?"

"No. Just yours."

Just mine.

I didn't know why, but that idea twisted my thoughts into flurries.

As he walked off, I dove into my tapas, not wanting to allow Cole to completely ruin my life the way he seemed so determined to do. If anything, I would not be okay with a good meal in front of me.

It turned out Alex's balls had the perfect amount of saltiness. Just how I liked them.

CHAPTER 16

Alex

Yara was the last one standing in my restaurant that night and the drunkest of them all. After the second to last table left, I found Yara at her table, full of tapas and sangria, singing three blind mice. Why that song? Who knew. She was plastered. Drunk people did a lot of weird things that didn't make sense.

"Poor angel," Tatiana said as she straightened up the hostess stand. "I should figure out a way to get her home."

"I can walk her home," I told Tatiana. "We live in the same building. Can you make sure everyone finishes off their tasks for the night and can you lock up?"

"Of course, Alex, and thank you," she said, touching my arm. "For making sure she makes it home safely."

"Sure."

Tatiana kept her hand on my arm and looked toward Yara. "Even though she's a little tipsy, she's radiant, isn't she?"

"She is," I said without thought. The words rolled off my tongue as if they were automatically produced from the idea that Yara was stunning. It was true, though. She didn't have a bad angle, and for some reason, I'd taken in every single one of hers. Yara Kingsley made it hard to look away. Even when I was trying my hardest to dislike her.

When I stopped looking at Yara, I turned to find Tatiana smiling up toward me with the biggest goofy grin.

"Stop it," I ordered, dropping my mouth into a grimace. I knew exactly what that look she was giving me meant.

"*You like her!*" Tatiana whispered, smacking my arm.

"You're being annoying, Tatiana."

"Annoyingly right," she countered.

"Good night."

She kept her silly smile plastered to her face before she patted my hand in hers. Just. Like. Teresa. Tatiana did that a lot—little mannerisms that reminded me of my great-aunt. She didn't even have a clue she was doing the actions, but the comfort that raced through my body every time was remarkable. Each time she did it, I silently thanked her for the greatest memories being brought to the forefront of my mind.

Who knew a hand tap could mean so much?

"You're a great boy, mi amor," Teresa would say every night when she came into my room to tuck me in for bed. I felt a bit weird being tucked in by my great-aunt into my late teen years. Once, I told her I was too old to be tucked in, to which she replied, "But not too old to be loved. Love shows up in many ways. Being tucked in each night is just one form of love." She'd then pat my hand within hers, as she did every evening, kiss my forehead, and say good night.

My chest tightened a little at the memory of Teresa. It was funny how a memory could give both comfort and cause ache all at once. The complexities of human experience.

After Tatiana wandered off, I headed to my office to get my keys. Once I gathered my items, I headed over to Yara's table and gave her a halfway smile. "Your ride home is here."

She looked up, glassy eyes and all, and asked, "Are you Uber?"

"Yes."

"I didn't call for an Uber."

"It's your lucky day. But we're walking home." I held a hand out toward her and she frowned.

"Walking? I'm so going to leave you four stars." She took my hand into hers and allowed me to pull her to her feet. "Whoa," she mumbled, almost falling over instantly in her heels. My chest stopped her from crashing and she steadied herself. "Alex?"

"Yes?"

"You have abs." Her hands ran up and down my chest. "I like your abs."

I chuckled a little. "You're drunk."

"And sad. A drunken sad girl. But that sangria?" She moaned from pleasure. "That was the good stuff."

"A little too good, I supposed."

"No, just right." She began to try to walk, but she almost broke her ankles in those high heels. It would've been a longer walk if the woman ended up snapping her ankles, so I had to shift the situation.

"Here," I offered, stepping out of my dress shoes. "Switch."

She arched an eyebrow. "You like high heels, Mr. Ramírez?"

"No, I like the idea of you not breaking your ankles."

"For someone who doesn't care about people, you sure seem to care about people."

"Only when they're drunk."

She tossed her hands up in the air. "Well, I shall forever be drunk around you from this day forth."

"Shoes off, Goldie."

She stepped out of them and then slipped my dress shoes on. "You know, I might've been the clown tonight, but you have the clown feet, Bozo."

I snickered. She was a sassy drunk. "Fair assessment." I lifted her heels off the sidewalk, and she linked her arm through mine to keep steady. "But you know what they say about men with big feet."

"They have long toes," she replied, matter-of-fact.

"You're ridiculous."

"You like it."

Yes.

I couldn't tell her that, though.

I'd hardly even told myself.

"You should be careful letting me lean on you too much," Yara expressed. "Cole is probably flying a drone overhead to watch my whereabouts. If he found out you walked me home, shoes and all, he might put you in jail."

"I'm not scared of that man."

"I am. Sometimes."

"Why?"

"Because I fear he'll never let me go."

"Aren't you divorced? You already got away."

"Tell that to the psycho who crashed my date tonight."

Touché.

"It's annoying because if he'd shown me this much attention during our marriage, I would've never left. But the problem was he showed this much attention to people who weren't me."

I arched an eyebrow. "He cheated on you?"

"And cheated and cheated and…cheated."

I grimaced. "I know what that's like."

Her eyes softened as she looked at me. "You too?"

"Yup."

"Is that why you're so hard?"

"You think I'm hard, Goldie?"

"Like a diamond."

I shrugged. "It's one of the reasons."

"How many reasons do you have?"

"More than I could count."

She frowned and somehow seeing her sad made it hard for me to take my next breath. "I'm sorry that life has hardened you, Alex."

"It's okay."

"No," she disagreed. "It's not."

She was right. It wasn't. Still, it was my reality.

She paused her steps and tilted her head to study me. "What was her name?"

"Her name?"

"The one who cheated."

I hesitated for a moment as I moved forward with my steps. She floated with me as her arm was still looped with mine. "You're too tipsy for this conversation."

"I'll sober up for it," she replied.

"Why do you care?"

"Because Tatiana is convinced you and me are supposed to be friends."

"Friends?"

"Yup. During my third glass of sangria, she came over and told me that you want to be my friend."

I arched an eyebrow. "Is that so?"

"Yes." She nodded. "It is so."

"But do you want to be friends with me?"

"Of course I want to be friends with you."

I shook my head. "No, you don't."

"Why do you say that?"

"I've been mean to you."

She shrugged. "You apologized, and since you've apologized, you've been quite nice since then."

I leaned toward her and whispered, "That's the sangria."

She leaned in closer. "No. That's just your true self slipping out. If Tatiana says you're nice, then you're nice."

"You trust her that much?"

"I do. She was my mama's best friend. I'd trust Tatiana with anything. Though one thing did throw me off that she told me about you."

"And what's that?"

She swayed from side to side as she took her steps, with me still holding her. "That you have a crush on me."

"What?" I coughed out, shaken by the realization.

"I know." She nodded. "I thought it was far-fetched, too." She gazed at me. "But it's not outlandish. I'd have a crush on me, too, if I were you."

"Oh?"

"I'm a good thing, Alex."

Why did I feel as if that wasn't a lie? For the next ten minutes, Yara talked and talked and talked. She yapped on and on about any and everything. She talked about dogs, flowers, penguin waddles, Cole's cruelty, global warming, and Ritz crackers with cream cheese.

"I'm just saying, you should add that to your tapas list. It would pair great with your balls," she said.

"I'll consider it," I said when we approached the apartment building. As we walked inside, I held the door open for her and walked her to the elevator. We went straight to her floor, even though she told me she could make it to her apartment. There was no way I was not going to not make sure she entered said apartment safely, though. I told Tatiana I'd get her home in one piece, and that meant watching her close the door in my face and hearing her turn the bolt lock.

Unfortunately, the moment we reached Yara's door, she paused. She patted her sides. She patted her chest. She patted her ass. She then turned to me and pouted. "Keys."

I arched an eyebrow. "You don't have your keys?"

She patted her body all over once more, then shook her head. "I don't have my keys."

"Where's your purse?"

She shrugged. "Don't know." A long, exhausted yawn fell from her lips. "I left it at your restaurant maybe. I'll go get it."

She turned in my clown shoes and started for the elevator. I reached out and grabbed her arm. "No. We'll get it in the morning. You can stay at my place tonight."

Yara's face grew flush and she dramatically placed her hands on her hips. "Are you trying to get lucky tonight, Alex? Because I'm not an easy girl."

"Don't worry. That's the last thing on my mind."

She pouted once more. "The *last* thing?"

I smiled a little. "Maybe not the last thing, Goldie."

Her high cheeks rose higher as she grew bashful. I liked that about her. I appreciated it when she got shy. It was one of the cutest things she did. And she did a lot of cute crap.

Fuck me. Why was I noticing her cute stuff?

"Besides"—I stepped closer to her and smirked as I leaned in toward her ear—"I don't like easy women. I like the complex ones."

"Oh my goodness," she whispered through her slightly parted, plump lips. She playfully shoved my chest. "You totally have a crush on me!"

I stood straight and smoothed my hands over my chest. "I don't know what you're talking about."

She kept swatting my chest. "You do! You have the hots for me." She struck a pose. "Is it because of my witty charm? My wicked sense of humor? My undeniable beauty?"

Yes.

And yes.

And absolutely yes.

"Let's get you to bed," I said, linking my arm with hers once more. "You're drunk and tired."

"You totally like me." She giggled like a schoolgirl, pleased she came to the realization on her own. As we walked, she slightly danced from side to side, humming to herself before saying, "And to think I thought you hated me only twenty-four hours ago."

I pushed the button to the elevator, and it opened instantly. As it did, British guy appeared, his eyes wide from seeing both Yara and me.

"Yara. Hi," he pushed out those two words as if they pained him to say.

Yara and I tilted our heads toward him and arched an eyebrow. In unison, she and I said, "Fuck off," before pushing past him and entering the elevator as he exited it. Hearing the word 'fuck' roll off Yara's tongue did something to my whole system. Especially in my lower region.

As the door closed, Yara leaned back against the railing as I hit the fifteenth floor. I leaned beside her.

"Can you believe him?" she asked as if she was disgusted, but I saw the hurt in her eyes. "I'm so happy I dodged that bullet. I bet his accent isn't even real. I'm so happy." Her words said one thing while her eyes read another. She pretended to be okay. My sweet, complex woman.

My?

WTF?

Shut up, Alex.

I almost debated whether I had any sangria in my system with how my thoughts had been over the past few minutes.

As we entered the apartment, Yara stepped out of my shoes and moved around freely, directly to my bar set up in my kitchen. She grabbed the bottle of whiskey and waved it around in the air.

"I would like to make an observation, if I may," she said.

"By all means."

"It turns out I know what the issue is with dating. Do you know what it is?" she asked.

"What's that?"

"*Men,*" she blurted out. "That's it. Penises are the problem!"

I chuckled a little and shook my head. "Women don't make it easy for us, either."

She pouted as she stared my way. I wondered how many heads I had floating around in her mind, based on how much alcohol she'd consumed. She then plopped down on the sofa beside the fireplace and stared at me. "Oh yeah. Women can cheat and ghost, too."

"Unfortunately, yes." I sat beside her.

"You said someone cheated on you?"

My gut tightened up. How did we get back to that topic? "They did."

"Did you love her?"

"I did."

"How long did it take you to get over it?"

I snickered and shrugged my left shoulder. "Pretty quick. She cheated with someone who I knew. It's easy to get over a person when they do something like that."

Yara's eyes glassed over and she looked to be seconds from crying.

"Don't do that, Goldie."

"Don't do what?"

"Cry because you feel bad for me."

"But…that's really sad."

"Sad things happen. That's life."

"People suck," she blurted out before hiccupping and taking a swig from the bottle. She held the bottle out toward me. "Bottoms up."

I shook my head. "Perhaps one of us should be sober tonight."

She frowned. "But…if you're sober, that means I'm just drunk and sad alone. I don't want to be drunk and sad alone."

"You can be drunk and sad, but you won't be alone tonight."

Tears fell down her cheeks, and I wanted to hug her. I

wanted to hold her. I wanted to wake with her in my arms and —*what?!*

Shut up, Alex!

She wiped her few tears away. "Promise, Alex?"

"Promise, Goldie."

She smiled a little and even her drunk, sad smiles were picturesque. "I like that, you know. I like that you call me Goldie. At first, I thought it was mean, but it has a nice ring to it."

I grinned. "Good. It's a fitting name." Before she could reply, I leaned toward her and lifted an eyelash from her cheek. I held it in front of her lips. "My aunt used to say if someone picks an eyelash from one's face, the person has to make a wish and blow it away. Make a wish, Goldie."

"Glimmer," she whispered as her smile deepened, revealing her dimples. My gosh, she was beautiful. Every kind of beautiful. The loud kind and quiet. The soft kind and hard. The silly kind and serious. Every type of beautiful lived within that girl, and I almost missed noticing it because I walked within my own cloud of darkness.

"What's a glimmer?" I asked.

She sat back and clapped her hands together. "A glimmer is like the opposite of a trigger. It's the micro moments in life that are just so unexpectedly beautiful and quiet. They fill a person with chills of wonder throughout their body instead of anxiety and fear."

"You just had a glimmer from me asking you to make a wish on your eyelash?"

She nodded. "One hundred percent. And from you smiling. Your smiles are few and far between, but wow, do I like them."

Who was this woman, and why was she turning my world upside down with every syllable that fell from her tongue?

She pursed her lips together, closed her eyes, and blew the eyelash away, making a wish.

When her brown eyes reappeared, they smiled more than her lips. My whole body found warmth merely from staring into her eyes.

"Are you going to tell me what you wished for?" I asked.

"That would cancel it out. You're not supposed to share your wishes with others."

I leaned in toward her and whispered, "Don't worry. I'm hardly a person."

She leaned in closer toward me. "You seem very person-like to me."

"That's just the effects of sangria. Really, I'm a monster."

Yara bit her bottom lip, and all I wanted to do was nuzzle it, too. I needed to stop staring at her mouth. The more I stared, the more my thoughts became clouded. What was she doing to me?

"If I tell you my wish," she softly spoke, narrowing her eyes as she locked them with mine, "you have to promise not to tell another soul."

"That's easy enough. I don't talk to people."

"You talk to Tatiana."

"That doesn't count. Tatiana is like…"

"A fairy godmother." Yara giggled. "She's weird and perfect and always right."

As far as I knew, I couldn't disagree with that fact.

Yara took another sip, humming to herself.

For a moment, I sat there and took her in. She was heartbroken and drunk and beautiful and drunk and sad and drunk and perfectly imperfect. I hated that bad things could happen to good people because they didn't seem to deserve it at all. And Yara Kingsley was a good person. She was the kind of person who made me almost consider being good, too.

"I don't have one for you," she randomly said.

"What do you mean?"

"A nickname. You call me Goldie, and I call you Alex." She tilted her head to the side to look at me. "You need a nickname."

"To be fair, Alex is my nickname."

"Short for Alexander?"

I shook my head. "Alejandro. I was named after my great-grandfather."

"That's a beautiful name."

"Goldie?"

"Yes?"

"Why are you crying?"

She laughed as tears rolled down her cheeks. "I don't know. I just really like that name. Can I un-nickname you and call you Alejandro?"

I laughed. "You're drunk. You probably won't even remember this tomorrow."

"I swear I will if you say I can call you it. Does anyone call you that?"

I shook my head. "My great-aunt Teresa was the only one who called me it."

"Oh." She paused and sat up more. "So it was her thing. I don't want to take her thing."

I smiled. "You can take that thing. But only you can call me it. No one else."

"Is it because you think I'm nice?" she said, pursing her lips together, hopeful.

"I think you're awful."

She swung her legs back over the sofa arm and inched closer to me. "I think you're lying."

"I think I'm lying, too."

She smiled and I wanted to do everything in my power to keep that smile on her face. How idiotic past Alex was to think that Yara was a liar due to her niceness to everyone. It just turned out that she was, in fact…nice. She was beyond nice. She was the kind of good that poets wrote love sonnets about. The

THE PROBLEM WITH DATING

kind of good that people prayed to cross paths with. The kind of good that people hurt the most.

"Kitty Kat?" she asked, arching a brow.

"What?"

"Can I call you Kitty Kat?"

I stared at her as if she'd grown five heads. "Excuse me?"

"It's another nickname option. I'm a golden retriever, and you're a black cat. I figured I could call you Kitty Kat."

"In no way, shape, or form should you ever call me Kitty Kat."

She pouted and crossed her arms with a heavy huff. "You're no fun."

"Whoever told you I was fun?"

"My imagination." She fussed for a second before pointing toward me. "Oh! I got it. I'll call you Mr. Black."

"Mr. Black?"

"You know...black cat. Plus, it's mysterious. Like you."

I smiled. "It's better than Kitty Kat."

"I still like Kitty Kat, Mr. Black."

"I'm sure you do, Goldie."

"Hey."

"Yeah?"

"Remember when my psycho ex told my crush not to go out with me?"

"Yeah, Goldie. I remember that."

"And then my psycho ex showed up to dinner?"

"Yup."

"That kind of sucked."

"He kind of sucks."

"Yeah," she agreed. She blew out a big puff of air. "I still don't know what to do about him. Before, it was just hearsay that he was stopping people from dating me, but now I have literal proof from Jake."

"Josh."

"Whatever." She waved me off. "I knew Cole was controlling during our relationship, but I didn't think he'd be that way after the divorce. That was the whole reason I got away from him."

"Look at it this way. You're weeding out the weak. Any real man wouldn't be scared off by your ex."

"It's just hard because I know Cole loved me the best way he could. Sure, he cheated, but I think he truly meant it when he said he loved me."

That bothered me deeply. "I'm sorry, Goldie."

"For what?"

"You thinking that's love."

"What is love then?"

"I don't know what it is," I confessed, "but I know what it's not."

She yawned again.

She was exhausted.

I took the bottle from her hands and stood. "Bedtime."

She kept yawning. "Okay, Mr. Black." She held a hand toward me and I grabbed it, pulling her to her feet. I walked her to my bedroom.

"Do you want pajamas?" I asked.

She nodded. "Please."

I grabbed a pair of my sweatpants and an oversized T-shirt that she'd swim in. She headed into my bathroom and changed as I turned down the comforter on my bed for her to climb into. When she emerged from the bathroom, I almost audibly gasped at the sight of her in my clothing. I even thought about what it would be like to take said clothing off her.

Those thoughts didn't belong anywhere near me.

She walked over to the bed and climbed into it. "Thank you, Alex."

"Welcome," I said as I pulled the comforter over her body.

I tucked her in.

I. Tucked. Her. In.

What was I doing?

She smiled as she snuggled against the pillow, wrapping her arms around it and hugging it. "My wish was that you'd be nice to me tomorrow like you were to me today," she whispered.

"Your wish is my command."

Her eyes sparkled as a few tears fell from her eyes once more. This time, the tears seemed happier. That girl felt everything. Things I hadn't felt in years. She felt deep emotions when I felt empty. It was remarkable to witness—someone who could cry both happy tears and sad and be completely complex and real. I hadn't seen such realness in a person in a long time.

"Good night, Goldie."

"Good night, Mr. Black."

CHAPTER 17

Yara

I stirred a little in my bed with my eyes shut tightly, due to the pounding taking place in my head. Gosh. I felt awful. As memories of the previous night came flooding back to me, that unpleasant feeling didn't fade. That was until I reached the memories of Alex.

I pushed myself to a sitting position on the mattress.

Alex!

My eyes opened and I realized I was in his bedroom, beneath his sheets, sitting in his life. Oh gosh. I'd probably made a blabbering fool of myself the night prior. I bet he couldn't wait for me to get out of his hair.

I dragged myself from his bed and pulled myself to the bathroom attached to said bedroom. The moment I glanced in the mirror, I almost audibly gasped at the level of hot mess staring back at me. Raccoon eyes, smeared lipstick, and my curls all tangled with one another.

I cupped my hand over my mouth, blew in it, and almost gagged from the stench of my own breath.

THE PROBLEM WITH DATING

"Oh my gosh," I muttered, turning on his sink faucet. I washed my hands, then added Alex's toothpaste to my finger and began aggressively brushing my teeth with the finger toothbrush. I gurgled his mouthwash, spat it out, and then washed my face, removing all evidence of my tarnished makeup from the night before.

Though I feared Alex probably saw me at my worst over the past few hours.

As I walked out of the bathroom, I glanced up to see Alex standing in his doorframe with a bottle of water and a bottle of ibuprofen. He arched an eyebrow. "Hey, good morning. Or, well, afternoon."

"It's afternoon?" I breathed out.

"Twelve thirty, yes."

How had I slept so long?

I walked over to him and took the medicine and water bottle from his grip. "Thanks." I tossed the pills into my mouth, took a swig of water, and swallowed. "For...everything."

He smiled.

He smiled! Like on purpose. At me.

"Not a problem," he replied. "I headed to the restaurant earlier and got your purse for you. I also cooked you up a few things if you're hungry. It's staying warm in the oven."

I raised an eyebrow. "You cooked for me?"

"I cooked for you."

"Why?"

He grew slightly timid and shrugged his left shoulder as he leaned against the doorframe. His voice dropped a few octaves, and his lips turned up once again. "Your wish is my command."

My eyelash wish. He was being nice to me because of my drunken wish I'd made.

Glimmer.

He led me to the dining room and served me a plate with

food. All the food. Hash browns, homemade cinnamon rolls, bacon, and scrambled eggs. Scones! He'd made me scones.

"Would you like orange juice?" he asked.

"Uh, yes. I always want orange juice. And water, please," I requested as I sat comfortably at the head of his table.

After grabbing the drinks for me, he made himself a plate and sat across from me. We ate in silence for a while. I didn't know if it was his nerves or my own that were making the gathering of words almost impossible. The butterflies fluttered in my stomach as his words kept echoing in my mind.

Your wish is my command.

If I had known that was true, I would've wished for a few more things from Alex. Like his smiles. And his laughter. His friendship. Sure, we had a rocky start, to say the least, but I bet Alex was a remarkable friend. Noah was living proof of that.

"I'm sorry if I made a fool of myself last night," I said as I bit into a piece of bacon.

"You didn't, and if you had made a fool of yourself, it would've been fine, too."

I smiled, leaned toward him, and whispered, "I made a fool of myself, didn't I?"

He leaned forward and whispered back, "A total ass of yourself."

I snickered. "I am what I am, and that's all that I am."

"I wouldn't want that to change."

"Gosh, you're really taking this being nice thing to a whole new level. I should've wished for it to be an always thing, not just one more day."

"That's why you should think out eyelash wishes. Now, I have to be a jerk to you again tomorrow."

"What a shame," I said, plopping back against my chair. "And to think we were almost friends."

He wore a grin that touched the corners of his eyes. His

smiles made my own lips turn up because they sent sparks of energy throughout my whole system.

"I should get going," I said after the late breakfast. "I need a shower. I look a mess."

"You look great."

I laughed and gestured toward my makeup-less tired face. "You think this is beautiful?"

"Like a diamond," he replied.

My heart beat faster and slower all at once. I felt both dizzy and steady somehow. How did he manage to make me feel such conflicting things?

My cheeks heated as I stood. "I was supposed to pick up my dog Cocoa a while ago from Cole, and I'm sure he's having a fit over it."

"I hate him," he blurted out.

"You do?"

"Yes."

"Why?"

"Because of..."—his words faltered—"you."

My heart. It skipped. It danced. It soared. It got confused, too. Alex seemed to be confusing me a lot lately. "Because of me?"

He took a bite of his bacon. "Yes."

"I thought hating took too much energy from you."

"I tapped into my storage unit of energy."

I bit my bottom lip and shimmied a little. "You know what that means, right?"

"What's that?"

"You *like* me."

He rolled his eyes and leaned back in his chair. "Don't go making up stories in your head, Goldie."

"I'm reading the book you're presenting to me, Mr. Black."

"A fictional novel."

"No," I disagreed, "An autobiography. The story of how the grumpy black cat befriended the golden retriever."

"A tale as old as time."

"An instant New York Times bestseller."

"Wallstreet Journal called it a triumphant tale of opposites attract."

"US Weekly said it's the highlight of the year. Rumor has it that the ending of the book—"

"No." He interjected. "Don't tell me you're a person who enjoys spoiling the ending of books. I'd like to see how each chapter plays out day by day." He stood from the table and walked over to me, pulled out my chair and offered me his hand.

I stood to my feet, my mind swirling with thoughts I wasn't certain how to unpack just yet solely from the touch of his hand. Perhaps it didn't need to be unpacked right then and there. Maybe the current chapter of us could simmer and heat up a little longer within my thoughts.

"Thank you for everything," I said to him as I walked to the front door. "Clothing and all," I said, gesturing to the outfit he'd given me.

"Anytime."

"Don't say that unless you mean it," I joked. "Because I will steal all your sweats."

"Well." He gave me a slow once-over, his gaze traveling from my feet up to my eyes. He opened his front door and quirked his lip. "They look better on you, anyway."

Alex, Alex, Alex, don't make me blush.

I sighed. "Can we pretend I have another eyelash so I can make another wish?"

He swiped at my cheek, held his finger in front of my mouth, and showed an invisible lash. "Go for it."

I shut my eyes and murmured in a low voice, "I wish Mr. Black and I could become friends someday."

I blew against his finger.

I lifted my lids to find his brown eyes locking with mine. He inched forward, his thumb grazing his lower lip. He was so close that our faces met in a soft collision as his breath caressed the curve of my ear. His intimate whisper sent shivers skipping down my spine. "Your wish is my command."

* * *

As I walked toward the elevator from Alex's apartment, I turned around once and caught him looking at me. He hurried into his apartment, almost appearing bashful about being caught. I liked that. I liked how he looked at me when he thought I wouldn't notice. There was a gentleness in his stare that I hadn't witnessed before. A softness to him that he was slowly unraveling for me to see.

I felt as if I was walking on cloud nine the whole trip to my apartment—until I found Cole and Cocoa sitting outside my door.

My stomach knotted.

"Cole. What are you doing here?" I asked.

He stood, scooping Cocoa into his arms. He narrowed his eyes. "Looking for you. You weren't at the park for the trade this morning."

"I know. I overslept and—wait. How long have you been here? And how do you know where I live?"

"I was worried, so I did some digging and found out."

"Cole!"

"*What?!*" he barked. "I'm sorry. I didn't know it was unacceptable to be worried about your well-being. But based on your attire, you were just fine and being irresponsible with picking up Cocoa."

I glanced down at Alex's sweatpants and sighed. "I'm sorry I was late."

"You should be. Messing with Cocoa's schedule isn't good."

I rolled my eyes. "I'm pretty sure Cocoa will be just fine. Right, girl?" I said as I took her into my arms. Arms that she freely leaped into as she wagged her tail. "Goodbye, Cole."

"Who is he?" he questioned.

"What?"

"Don't play stupid, Yara. You show up looking like shit wearing some dude's oversized clothes. Who is he?"

I laughed to keep from saying something rude. "We aren't doing this, Cole."

"Was it that British guy? What, he stands you up, so you end up screwing him instead? Real classy, Yar."

"How dare you?" I blurted out. "Two things. One—it's none of your business how I spend my time or how I use my body. And two—it's none of your business how I spend my time or how I use my body," I repeated.

"So you think it's cute running around being easy with any guy who looks your way?"

"Cole. That line? You're crossing it."

"That's just because I care. At least someone has to care about you. Everyone else in town just gossips about you behind your back."

"No, they don't." My body tensed up as he started to chip at those insecurities.

"Yeah, they do. They talk about how desperate you're coming off, trying to date. They think you're the reason we fell apart."

"And let me guess, you're not quick to tell them the truth."

"That is the truth. You left me."

"Because you cheated on me repeatedly! *You* did that. Not me. You left me before I even considered a divorce. Who knows who or how many women it actually was that you left me for."

"Is that what this is about? You're still stuck on wanting to know who I hooked up with?"

THE PROBLEM WITH DATING

I sighed. "No, Cole. I don't, because it doesn't matter. Maybe back then I cared. I stupidly thought it might bring me comfort knowing, but it means nothing to me anymore. You mean nothing to me."

Cole paused for a moment, examining what I said. Hopefully my words were sticking a landing in that peanut-sized brain of his.

He pointed a finger at me and shook his head. "Nope. You still care. I can feel it."

Landing officially *not* stuck.

His hand brushed against his bushy eyebrows and he shrugged. "You know what? Go ahead. Do whatever you have to do to get back at me for hurting you, Yara. Sleep with however many men you wish. I don't care because I know how this will end. You'll come back to me, and we'll get back to our lives."

"That will *never* happen."

"Yeah, well, I'll believe that when you have another man on your arm. But until then, I'll be waiting." He walked over to me and snuggled Cocoa's head. His proximity made chills of disgust race up and down my spine. The opposite of how Alex had made me feel.

At that point, I realized something very important.

I needed a new boyfriend.

Stat.

I walked into my apartment, trying to shake off my irritation with Cole, when there was a knock at my door. I grumbled to myself and swung it open, thinking Cole was returning to steal more of my joy. "*What do you want?!*" I yipped.

Alex stood there with widened eyes holding a gift bag in his hands. "Is that how you always answer the door?"

I sighed. "Sorry. Thought you were someone else. What's up?"

"Didn't mean to bother you again, but I forgot I made you dishes and bones."

I raised my eyebrows. "What?"

He held the gift bag toward me. "I made you dishes and bones. Chocolate chip bone-shaped cookies, I mean. I also made these two water dishes down at the pottery shop to make up for the one I broke."

I took the dishes out of the bag to find them filled with cookies. That boiling blood of anguish that Cole filled me with? Alex quickly brought it down to a calm, rolling simmer.

Upon closer inspection of the dishes, I noticed inscriptions circling their base. The first one said "I'm sorry for" and the second read "Being a dick". I let out a soft chuckle. The self-awareness of the whole situation was rather endearing.

"One dish for water, the other for food," he explained. "I figured they were better as a pair."

"You really made these?"

"Well, I tried. Pottery is hard and messy. Pat did most of the work, but that *is* my handwriting."

"Why did you do this?"

He absentmindedly rubbed the back of his neck. "I'm not like you," he confessed. "Like you said, I'm the black cat, and you're the golden retriever. You see people as innocent until proven guilty. I see them as guilty until proven innocent. You see the light. I see the dark. We're different."

"Yes," I agreed, leaning against the doorframe. "We are."

"But that doesn't mean my ways are right. You were never guilty, and I treated you as if you were. I've been a bit darker than normal lately, and I owed you a real apology."

"Thank you, Alex," my voice barely audible, as those former dragons in my stomach fell into a slumber. "That's actually very sweet."

He gave a slight nod.

"I'm sorry, too," I said, "For my rude remarks I spat back to you before last night."

"Don't apologize for that. I like the fact that you stood chest to chest with me. It reminded me that even golden retrievers still know how to bite. I just hope you bite back to some of the other pricks in town, too."

With that, he disappeared down the hallway, taking the staircase to his apartment. I stood there for a while, staring in the direction he'd wandered before walking into my apartment and taking a bite of his chocolate chip cookie.

"*Ohmygosh!*" I moaned, taken away into pure bliss from the taste of his cookies. What in the world was that burst of flavor that erupted within my mouth?

Five out of five stars.

Highly recommend.

If I could give a million stars, I would.

CHAPTER 18

Alex

TODD

Where are we at on that property, Alex?

* * *

*E*ach day before work, I found myself reading more and more of Teresa's diary entries.

I walked the streets of Honey Creek with her diary in my grip, reading about the places she spoke of. Seeing the places she spoke of. Sitting on the benches where she sat. Eating the foods she picked up years ago.

It was as if I were walking through her time capsule. I envisioned her walking beside me on the sidewalks, telling me in detail the stories of her youth. She danced down these streets with Peter. She cried in those alleyways with him, too. They'd spend hours in the library, reading to one another in whispers, in different languages.

They had their second kiss beneath the clock tower. They'd

first held hands outside of the ice cream parlor. He told her he loved her in the middle of the high school football field. Her father told her they were going back to Madrid in those same football bleachers.

She cried for two weeks straight from that news.

She nannied a ten-year-old girl named Ana, who had a firecracker personality. Those were the main two people Teresa talked about—Ana and Peter. I could tell they were the sparks of light in her life at that time. The two people who kept her going.

She hated Peter's parents because they didn't approve of her for their son.

Assholes.

"It must be a good read," a person mentioned as I traveled through the farmer's market with my nose in the diary.

I looked up to find Yara standing there with a tote of vegetables. Her smile left me feeling as if I'd missed a step, throwing me completely off balance. Her smiles often left me disoriented.

"A good read?" I questioned, my brain still fumbling over how to exist around her since the shift of our interactions.

She gestured toward the diary in my hand. "You seemed as if you were in your own world, that's all."

She straightened her hair that day.

I liked it.

I liked her curls, too.

"Oh." I shut the diary and tucked it under my arm. "Yes."

She looked to my other hand and saw the bundle of flowers I'd bought. Teresa wrote that Peter would buy her favorite flowers from Ruth's Floral Shop every Sunday morning. Since I'd read that, I'd been going out each Sunday and picking up a bundle of tulips.

"For a special someone?" she questioned, looking at the flowers.

"What? No. I, uh," I shook my head. "They're for me."

"Oh, nice. I, too, treat myself to flowers every Sunday. I'm more of a dahlia and peonies girl myself, but tulips are always a good choice."

We stood there for a moment in silence. I grimaced, unsure what to say. "I'm not the best at this."

"At what?"

"New friendships."

"Oh. That's okay." She moved in closer and whispered, "I have a PhD in the arena of friendship making. Though, it comes with toxic people pleasing tendencies, so I don't know if I'm any help."

I chuckled. "Yeah, I noticed you around town talking to any and everyone."

"Wait." She raised an eyebrow. "Was that a laugh?"

I cleared my throat. "No. I choked on air."

She waved a finger. "No, no. That was a chuckle. I know a chuckle when I hear one."

"Allergies," I lied.

She smiled so big.

That full blown grin of hers? Fuck yeah. I liked that.

"How often do you notice me around town?" she asked as she traced her shoe in circles on the concrete.

I huffed and brushed the bridge of my nose with my thumb. "Not often. Hardly ever."

A lot. Always. *All the fucking time, Yara.*

"Oh, yeah, okay," she said sarcastically, nodding with a wink. "Don't worry, Mr. Black. I notice you quite often, too."

She left me slightly confused about the whole exchange. She didn't seem to hold any resentment toward me after I apologized. It was as if she gave me a full second chance. Tatiana was right—Yara was the kind of person to forgive others.

I quietly swore I wouldn't give her another reason to have to forgive me again.

* * *

TODD

Did you see my other text, Alex?

ALEX

Not ready yet. Soon though.

Soon.

* * *

Time was an odd concept. Some days felt as if they lasted forever, and others felt as if they'd flown by. The restaurant was officially a success, and the staff was officially terrified of me. That was all I needed—good reviews and a terrified staff. Teresa would've been thrilled.

As I hurried around the kitchen for yet another busy night, the line cooks worked as hard as they possibly could to keep up with the orders. I knew I could be grumpy toward them all, but I was secretly impressed with their abilities to work in such intense situations.

"Sorry, Alex, can I have a second?" Tatiana asked, stepping into the kitchen, holding her hands against her chest, moving as if to avoid being in the way. "Can I speak to you real fast? Just for one second."

I glanced over my shoulder toward Tatiana before turning back to the jerk chicken paella dish sitting on the stove in front of me, which Sammy was cooking. "Tatiana, if you're not at the hostess stand, then you aren't working," I scolded. "Which means you're not doing your job."

The bustle of the kitchen was my favorite sound of every evening. The banging of pots and pans, people shouting orders up, me yelling at mistakes being made. Luckily for me, after opening my fifth restaurant and holding two Michelin stars, not many mistakes that took place in my kitchens. I made sure of that by hiring the best of the best.

That night at Isla Iberia, each table was full and the kitchen buzzed with intensity. Cooks danced past one another grabbing ingredients, plating meals, and adding the perfect balance of seasonings to each dish. I moved around double and triple-checking each entrée before it left for a table.

The restaurant had been open for only a few weeks now, and every reservation was booked for a year out. Needless to say, Isla Iberia was a success.

Tatiana cleared her throat, following me to and from each station as I approved dishes. "Yes, Alex, I understand. I just, I need a minute to speak to you and—"

"First it was a second, and now it's a minute. Which one, Tatiana?" I spat out, turning to face her.

"Uh, um, a moment's time?" she said, yet it came out as a question. She seemed nervous, which was the opposite of her personality. Normally, she'd quickly check me for speaking back to her in such a way.

"What is it?" I asked. "Are you all right?"

"Yes. I'm fine."

"Then why do you look like you're about to cry? What is it?" I grabbed her arm gently and pulled her to the side of the kitchen for privacy. "Are you hurt?"

She shook her head. "No, no. I'm all right. It's just… There's a situation at the front."

I arched an eyebrow. "Are you going to expand on that?"

"Well, it seems, there seems to be, um…" Before she could finish her sentence, a sound burst out from the front of the restaurant. A sound that remarkably resembled a dog barking. Why would a dog be barking in my restaurant?

"What was that?" I snapped, standing taller as I hovered over Tatiana's small frame.

"That's the situation."

THE PROBLEM WITH DATING

The whole kitchen staff paused, turning their heads to the front of the restaurant. I shot them all a stern look. "What do you think you're all doing? Get back to work!"

"Yes, Chef!" they responded in unison and went back to work.

I sighed. "Tatiana."

"Yes?"

I crossed my arms and moved in closer to her as a deep, rough whisper escaped my lips. "Is there a dog in my restaurant?"

Her skin paled over like a ghost, and her lips trembled as her eyes flooded with tears. "Yes."

"Tatiana."

"Yes, Alex…?"

"*Get the dog out of my restaurant!*" I shouted, tossing my hands up in frustration.

"Yes, okay!" she cried out, her whole body shaking from panic. If I had a second to grasp what was happening, I would've felt bad for the way my voice vibrated through the space. Yet my mind struggled to figure out why she thought it was acceptable to allow an animal into my space.

"It's just that…" She started, her words tripping off her tongue. "The dog is yours."

I narrowed my eyes and placed my hands against my waist. "Excuse me?"

"The dog in the restaurant. It's yours."

"I heard you the first time, but your words don't mean anything, seeing as how they are ridiculous. I would know if I had a dog. So if you're done talking in riddles—"

"Your great-aunt Teresa sent him."

I huffed and brushed my hand against my forehead as my brows knitted. "That's a lie. My aunt Teresa is…" I paused. "Teresa sent him?"

Tatiana nodded. "Yes."

"Tatiana."

"Yes?"

"Stop crying."

She blabbered like it was her own aunt who passed away.

"I can't, but I'll try." She wiped her tears. "Your great-aunt Teresa left you a dog in her will. He's here now. For you. The transport person is waiting for you in the lobby."

Every inch of my body was filled with annoyance, confusion, and nerves.

No way did Teresa leave me a dog. Why in the world would she do that?

Being done with trying to get information from Tatiana, who was having an emotional fit, I marched through the restaurant toward the front lobby where a man stood with a tiny dog that had a muzzle on his face. That little thing was making all that fuss?

"Outside," I ordered the man with a stern look. His eyes widened from the intensity of my demand, and he yanked the dog forcefully to the outside of the restaurant. I followed them as the dog aggressively growled at me and barked nonstop.

"You can't bring that thing into my restaurant again. Take it back to wherever it came from," I told the man.

"Mr. Ramírez—"

I waved my hand in front of him in a dismissive way. "Don't give me your speech. If I don't hear your speech, then I can pretend this never happened."

"But it is happening, and your great-aunt Teresa entrusted you with this Pomeranian. His name is Feliz." He held the leash out toward me.

As he said that word, I rolled my eyes. Of course my aunt would name the most aggressive-sounding dog Feliz—the Spanish word for happy. From the look of the fangs as it barked nonstop, muzzled and all, it was far from a happy dog.

I pushed the leash back toward him. "I don't want it."

THE PROBLEM WITH DATING

"I don't think you have a say in that."

"It's a free country. I don't have to take on a dog if I don't want it."

"You do. And if you don't want it, it's up to you to surrender it to a shelter. Though, most of the shelters are sadly full as we move into the fall season, and Feliz might end up in a kill shelter."

"Don't play the pity card with me. You'd be surprised at my ability not to care," I muttered.

"Look, dude. I'm just trying to do my job, all right?" The guy reached into his back pocket and pulled out an envelope. "This is from Teresa. I'm supposed to deliver you this and Feliz. That's it. So if you can take both and let me get on with my night, that would be great. I have to be in Kansas tomorrow to deliver another pet."

I snatched the envelope from his grip and ripped it open.

My sweet, stubborn nephew who didn't show up to my funeral,

Leave it to Teresa to be straight-forward and all-knowing.

Out of all humans, it's no secret that you are my favorite, so I got you a friend. This is Feliz. He is to be to you what you were to me—your everything. Feliz might appear to be very much like you—stubborn. Hardheaded. Grumpy. Rough around the edges. But I'm sure he's also like you, too, when a person gets to know him. Soft. Gentle. Kind. Caring. A best friend.

I couldn't think of a better pairing. May you each soften one another.

Treat him well, and he'll treat you well.

I love you, my favorite nephew.

Siempre,

Teresa.

After I finished reading the letter, I folded it up and grumbled under my breath. "Listen, I get that my sweet, great-aunt was a bit clueless about who I actually was but—" When I glanced up, I realized the guy who dropped off Feliz had darted for his car after he set down a bucket of Feliz's supplies on top of his leash to hold the dog in place. "Hey!" I shouted, tossing my hand up in frustration. "Are you kidding me?!"

"Good luck!" the guy hollered from his rolled-down window as he drove past me. "And sorry for your loss, dude!"

As if my day couldn't get any worse. I crumpled the paper, shoved it into my back pocket, then stared down at the dog. I moved closer. The dog growled and lunged at me as if it were going to take my hand off.

"Whoa!" I spat out, seeing the aggression in the dog's eyes. "Tatiana!" I yelled. Seconds later, she came out onto the sidewalk.

"Yes, Alex?"

"Tell Sammy to take over the kitchen for the night. I have some things to handle."

"Of course." She smiled at me and then toward Feliz. "He's cute, isn't he?"

"Like a hairy rat," I muttered.

I couldn't help but wonder if Teresa meant I was her least favorite human alive as opposed to her favorite. That ugly, fluffy creature gave me more hate vibes than love. As I tried to approach the dog to figure out how to place it in my car, I circled it repeatedly as it growled at me. A beautiful dance we partook in. One I wished would end.

CHAPTER 19

Yara

Thirty minutes ago, I received an S.O.S. text message from Avery in our sister group chat.

AVERY

Emergency meeting. Peter's NOW!

WILLOW

I was about to put on a mud mask.

AVERY

I don't care. Hurry up. It's important.

YARA

Important enough to have to put my bra back on?

AVERY

Yes. That important.

WILLOW

Did you finally run into Nathan? I'd put on a bra to hear that story in person.

> **YARA**
> You never wear a bra.

WILLOW
> Free the nip!

AVERY
> Ladies. Peter's Café. NOW!

It took me about fifteen minutes to pull myself together and head to the café. It was no surprise I beat Willow. That girl was probably late for her own birth and would be fashionably late to her funeral.

Avery refused to tell me the news without Willow there, so we sat at our table near the front of the café taking in the commotion happening across the street at Alex's restaurant.

"Someone's having a weirder day than me," Avery muttered. "It must be his karma for being rude to you."

"Oh." I shook my head. "I forgot to mention. We're friends now. I think. Kind of. Maybe."

Avery cocked an eyebrow. "I'm sorry, what?"

"It's a long story and happened about a week ago."

"*A week ago?!*" She gasped, eyes wide. "How haven't you told me this?"

"We don't tell each other everything, Avery. It slipped my mind."

She huffed. "Bull crap. Nothing slips your mind. You told me about that British guy saying your poop smelled like roses fifty times over."

"That was different."

"How?"

I didn't exactly know how. My sister was right. I did tell her and Willow everything, but I hadn't mentioned the night I'd spent at Alex's apartment. I felt that if I spoke about it, it would somehow tarnish the special connection we'd had. I wanted to

THE PROBLEM WITH DATING

keep that safe in my heart. Our little secret for a little bit of time.

"Yara—"

"One second," I said, holding up a hand.

My heart raced as I watched Alex interact with the dog in front of him. He wasn't having the easiest time, and the poor dog looked highly stressed.

My chest felt tight as I stared at the commotion.

"I'm going to do it," I said, placing my paper napkin on the table.

Avery gave me a stern look and pointed a finger my way. "Yara, don't you dare. It's none of your business."

"It's literally my business," I urged as I looked out the huge window of the café. Alex was having a very aggressive conversation with a small Pomeranian pup. I wasn't sure who was more stressed out, the man or the dog. Either way, divine intervention was needed, and it just so happened I was feeling quite divine that evening. I feared the little dog would have a panic attack if I didn't step in. Same with Alex.

"It will only be a minute," I told Avery. She gave me her "yeah right" look of disbelief. "Five minutes, tops."

She leaned toward me, placed a hand against mine, and sighed. "Yara, not every dog is your responsibility. You're off the clock."

"A professional dog whisperer is never off the clock. With great power comes something, something, or whatever Spider-Man said." I patted my sister's hand and grinned. "Be right back." I pushed myself away from the table and started toward the front door.

"Five minutes!" Avery shouted.

"Yes! Five minutes! Ten minutes tops."

I could almost feel her eye roll as I hurried outside and crossed the street. As I got closer, Alex, dressed in all black, was

167

trying to approach the dog from the side, which only led to the poor pup getting more aggressive.

"That's a bad idea," I warned him.

The deepened wrinkles on his forehead and the pronounced grimace against his lips were enough to make me almost retreat. Maybe we weren't friends.

"I don't recall asking for your input," he snapped, but then he turned toward me. As he did, his intensity softened. His stern brown eyes eased from the aggression, and he stood. "Yara. Sorry. I...didn't know it was you."

I laughed a little, unsure how to feel about the shift in his demeanor. Did I do that to him? Did I calm the commotion in his eyes?

"Do you snap at everyone but me in this town?" I joked.

"Yes," he quickly said. "But that's only because they treat me like crap."

Fair enough.

"Yes, well, I'm here to help."

"It's okay. I have this handled."

"Okay, it's just..." My eyes fell on the poor dog. "He's scared."

"He's scared? I'm not the one trying to bite him. If anyone should be scared, it's me."

"Imagine a six-foot-one man coming toward you when you're the size of a sofa pillow. That's scary. He's just on high alert."

He muttered, "Six-foot-four."

I arched an eyebrow. "Are you serious right now? That's your concern?"

"All I'm saying is I'm not six-foot-one."

My hands went up in surrender. "Okay. My mistake. I didn't mean to sting your precious masculinity."

"I'm just saying. Three inches can make quite a difference."

"That's exactly what I tell all men, but they refuse to believe me."

THE PROBLEM WITH DATING

He smiled.

Oh! Friends. We were totally friends.

Play it cool, Yara.

I crossed my arms. "What's the story with the dog?"

He paused for a moment before sighing and raking his hand through his messy midnight-colored hair. "He was sent by my great-aunt. She passed away a few weeks ago, and for some reason, she thought I needed a dog to keep me company so I wouldn't get lonely."

"Did she pass away on the day you broke my dish?"

"No. She passed the day before I stepped in your dog crap. Then her funeral was the day of the dish."

And just like that, his grumpiness from the weeks prior made a little more sense.

My hands flew to my chest, and I shook my head. "I'm so sorry for your loss."

"Why are you doing that?" he asked.

"Doing what?"

"Getting emotional."

"Well, you just told me you lost your great-aunt. It's called sympathy. I feel bad for you."

"I didn't ask you to feel bad for me."

"Sympathy doesn't only work on requests."

"I didn't even state if I liked my aunt. I could've despised her for all you know."

"You're right. It's not my place to assume. Regardless, I've been called the dog whisperer before. All you need to do is get the sweet boy into his crate here, I'm guessing, yes? And then into your car?"

"Yes. My car is in the back. I have to pull it around."

I nodded. "You go do that, and by the time you get back, I'll have the dog in the crate for you and will help you load him into your vehicle."

He was wary at first but then agreed. "I'll just be a minute."

"Take your time. I'll be here getting to know…"

"Feliz."

"Feliz." I smiled. "*Happy.*"

"He's the complete opposite of that," he warned.

"So maybe you two do have something in common," I joked.

"Hardy har har," he muttered. "You're so funny, Yara."

I smirked a little, pleased with how I seemed to get under his skin a bit in a playful way. "Go get your car. We'll be ready when you get back."

It was very quiet, but I could've sworn he muttered a thank you before he headed off to grab his vehicle. To my surprise, Feliz and I had quite a quick turnaround. Once the dog realized I wasn't going to hurt him, he allowed me to place him in his crate, and I gathered up his box of goods once Alex came back around the corner.

He parked his car and stepped out with a somewhat shocked expression. "How the heck did you do that?"

"I told you. Dog whisperer."

He opened the backseat of his car. When he went to grab the crate from me, when Feliz began barking aggressively. He tossed his hands up in surrender and grumbled, "Stupid dog."

"He's scared of you. The same way you're scared of him. Give it time. You'll both grow to like one another. Here. Take the box of his goodies, and I'll put him in the car."

Alex did as I said and walked over to the other side of the vehicle. He opened the door and placed Feliz's goods inside, then shut the door.

I put Feliz's crate into the car and smiled down at the dog that was smiling my way. "Take it easy on Alex. It's his first day being a parent."

Feliz licked my hand one final time as a goodbye, and I gave him a scratch behind his ear through the crate doors, then stood and closed the car door. I turned to Alex. "Give Feliz time to

THE PROBLEM WITH DATING

warm up. He's in a new place and scared. If I were you, I'd sign up for training sessions with him."

"Why did he like you so much so soon?"

"I told you, everyone likes me."

He brushed a thumb against his bottom lip. "Little Miss Goldie."

I smiled. "Big Mr. Black."

He smiled back, and I wanted my mind to get a mental photograph of the way his lips turned up.

"Thank you, Goldie," he said, this time louder. More sincere. "And I apologize for my snapping when you walked up. It's been a..." He released a weighted sigh. "Thank you."

I nodded. "Of course. Good luck. Let me know if you need anything else. I'm sorry again for your loss."

He opened the driver's door to his car and hesitated as he held his hand against the door. "I didn't despise her," he softly stated. "She was the salt."

I raised my eyebrows. "The salt?"

"Teresa was the salt of the world—she added flavor to everything. She was eclectic, weird, and unique in the most bizarre ways. She drank wine in the mornings and coffee at night. She didn't believe in organized religion, but she had the strongest amount of faith in God, which I still struggle with. She cursed like a sailor and prayed like a saint. If you ever saw her not wearing a cross necklace, it was because she gave it away to someone on the street who she thought needed it more.

"She was messy. Her house was always stocked high with books because she was packed with knowledge. She never finished high school but was the smartest woman ever. She grew up with nothing and somehow made everything. She marched to the beat of her own drum and lived her life against conformity. She was the opposite of me, but that was a good thing. Because to all my darkness, she added light. She was the only person I've ever known who saw me for who I was and still loved every part. She taught me everything I knew about being in a kitchen, and I owe my life to her." His voice cracked as he took a pause. I felt it, too—his shattering heartbeats. "She was my best friend when I had no one else, and a part of me left this world when she went away without me. The world's a little darker without her here, and all food seems to be missing a little bit of salt."

There he was. The real, gentle Alex he'd kept hidden from the rest of the world.

He didn't give me a chance to reply before he climbed into his car and drove away.

Still, his words lingered in my head as I crossed the street and wiped the tears that found a way to fall down my cheeks for my grumpy business neighbor who loved his aunt so much and missed her so deeply.

As I entered the restaurant, I shook off my emotions and returned to Avery, who held up the clock on her phone to show I was gone for a solid fifteen minutes. "I ate your appetizer because it was getting cold," she told me as she stuffed the last dumpling into her mouth.

I laughed. "Fair enough. We'll order more."

"Sorry, sorry!" Willow shouted, darting into the restaurant. Her curly hair was bundled up into a bun on top of her head with a headband of flowers—flowers she'd probably picked earlier that day while she was hiking. She wore one of her long, flowy dresses with giraffes all over it. One thing about my little sister was she'd always have flowers in her hair and a smile on her face.

She slid into her chair beside Avery and melted into the seat like a deflated balloon. "Am I late?" she asked.

"As always," Avery replied with a disappointed look.

Willow's grin only grew deeper as she placed her hands on Avery's cheeks and leaned in and kissed each one. "Time is only real if you allow it to be."

THE PROBLEM WITH DATING

Avery gave Willow a blank stare and then shook her head. "You're so weird."

"It's why you love me," Willow countered. "So what was the SOS? Why did you want to do dinner?"

Avery took a deep breath and reached for her purse. As she dug through said purse, she pulled out three ring boxes and set them on the table in a line. She then opened each box, revealing three beautiful diamond rings—one pear-shaped, one princess cut, and one emerald.

"Oh my goodness," I breathed out, covering my mouth.

"Did you rob a jewelry store?" Willow asked, picking up one of the rings and studying it up close. "Are you on the run?"

"Wesley proposed," Avery explained. "Well, kind of."

"How does one kind of propose?" I asked.

"He sat me down, put these three boxes in front of me, and said, 'pick one.' I, of course, panicked, shoved the rings into my purse, and then put out the SOS to you both."

"Wait. Wesley proposed and you took the rings without answering him?"

She nodded. "Yup. He's waiting back at home for an answer."

"Avery!" Willow and I scolded at the same time.

"What? This is a big deal. I cannot make a big-deal decision without my sisters." She bit her bottom lip, and her eyes flashed with emotions. "And I mean, what if I'm not a wife?"

"What does that mean?" Willow questioned.

"What if I'm not made for marriage? I honestly never thought I'd get married. And then, over the past weeks, I've been so thrown off by Nathan's return to town that I've been distant with Wesley. Which makes me feel even worse, seeing as how he proposed with three rings. Who proposes with three rings? I feel as if I've been an awful girlfriend. I'd be an awful wife!"

"Probably an awful fiancée, too," Willow joked.

"Don't tease," Avery whimpered. "Seriously. I'm not good enough for him. Wesley deserves better."

"You're overthinking it. Sure, you were knocked off-kilter with Nathan's return, but that's not your fault. It was a trigger. Triggers happen to us all and knock the wind out of us. But you love Wesley, and he loves you," Willow explained.

"Obviously," I agreed, gesturing toward the rings. "Plus, he still wants to marry you after you hijacked said rings and ran off to have a power meeting with your sisters before saying yes."

Avery nervously laughed as she wiped the few tears falling from her eyes. Avery was so tough that it took a lot for her to actually shed tears. Her emotions must've been at an all-time high.

"Oh my gosh, I stole the rings!" she choked out. "And you know what he did after I ran off like a wild woman? He texted me and said, 'I love you and I'll see you when you get back from your sisters. We can get ice cream later.' Can you believe that? He's dating a psycho and still wants to marry me!"

"So marry him!" I urged. "You love him, right?"

She nodded slowly. "I do."

"And he loves you. Now, just take that next step," Willow agreed.

Avery turned toward me. "What if we end up like you and Cole did?" she questioned. "I mean, you two were happy for a while and then it all went downhill."

I didn't know her words would sting me so much. I thought I healed from that heartbreak, but like Willow said—triggers. They snuck up on a person out of nowhere. I didn't blame Avery for thinking Cole and I were happy longer than we'd actually were. I felt as if I had to protect his image from everyone—especially my sisters. If they had known how cruel he'd truly been, he would've been buried six-feet-under by now. If my father had known, it would've been twelve feet.

I tried to push those feelings down, but unfortunately, I wasn't a woman who could hide the hurt that she'd felt. It bled out of my eyes.

"I'm sorry, Yara. I didn't mean it like that. I just mean… what's the guarantee in marriage?" Avery asked. "What're the statistics? Why should we do it? Most marriages end in divorce, so what's the point?"

"I still believe in marriage," I told her and truly meant it. "I believe in love and the commitment of marriage even though mine failed."

"How?" she questioned.

"Because of Mama and Daddy. They both left marriages and found each other. Isn't the idea of what they had something worth fighting for? Even with all that went down—and is still going down—with Cole and me, I still believe in happily ever afters in all ways and for always."

Avery wiped at her tears and sat back. "In all ways and for always. Okay. Okay. I guess I'm a fiancée."

"After he officially asks and you officially accept," I added.

"Which I will. After dinner. I already ordered for us and got Wesley a meal to go," Avery explained.

"For what it's worth, I loved being married, too," Willow said.

I rolled my eyes. "You were married to that fisherman guy for like two days before you ended it. I went through becoming an ordained minister for that ceremony, by the way."

"You know what's weird about that? I don't even remember his name," Willow remarked.

"You never remember their names," Avery tossed out.

"You're not wrong, my bride-to-be." Willow's grin only grew deeper as she placed her hands on Avery's cheeks and leaned in and kissed each one. "Hello, bride-to-be." Avery grew a little bashful from the comment. "Which ring are you picking?"

"This one." Avery pointed at the pear cut—the perfect choice for my sister.

Willow swooned. "Wow! Look at that thing! I bet it could feed a whole village somewhere."

Avery snickered and pulled the rings away from Willow's reach. "Don't start. We all know how you feel about diamonds."

Willow grinned and sat back in her chair. "As long as we're all aware."

"We are," I told her. "And still, I want a princess-cut one, please and thank you."

Avery laughed as Willow grabbed the bottle of wine that was left at the table and poured herself a glass, then topped off the rest of our glasses, too.

Willow held her wineglass and straightened up. "A toast to the eldest. A woman who deserves the very best treatment in the world. I cannot think of anyone more deserving to find a happily ever after, let alone with a rocket scientist who might stop global warming," she semi-joked. If anyone was going to do so, it was Wesley.

I held my glass in the air. "Here's to forever with Wesley. May you two never stop falling in love."

"Cheers!" Avery added. We tapped our glasses together, then took a sip.

Willow smiled. "If I wasn't such a free spirit and anti-commitment, I'd want someone to look at me the way Wesley looks at you, Avery."

"Someday, little sister, you might find someone who makes you want to settle down those feet of yours," I said.

"But running is so fun. Speaking of… I'm off to Chile tomorrow for a race. I met a guy who asked me to join him, and I booked my ticket yesterday."

Avery arched an eyebrow. "You're running off to Chile with a random guy you just met?"

She smiled. "You say that like it's a wild concept."

"Or her first time doing such a thing." I snickered. If our little sister was going to do one thing, it would be moving wherever the wind blew her. Avery and I were forever stressed out by Willow's adventures, but she always seemed to come back

THE PROBLEM WITH DATING

home safely, which was good enough for me. Besides, if we were to tell Willow to do anything, it was almost certain she'd do the opposite. She wasn't one to be told what to do.

"Does Daddy know?" Avery asked with an arched eyebrow.

"No, and he won't know until I tell him I landed safely." She pointed a stern finger and waved it back and forth between Avery and me. "Don't you dare tell him, either."

"Scout's honor," I said, holding up my hand.

I nudged Avery under the table, and she grumbled. "Yeah, yeah, okay. But only if you send me your location and your itinerary for the trip."

"You know I'm not one for itineraries," Willow said, sipping her wine.

"Yeah, well, make an exception this time around. And I need this guy's name and information before you board the plane."

"He goes by Snake."

Avery's high-alert button was pushed as her eyes all but popped out of their sockets. "You're going out with a man who goes by the name of Snake?!"

Willow grew bashful and wiggled in her chair. "It's because he has a way of slithering into one's heart. Don't worry. He's a trained yogi."

"Why does that make me worry even more?" Avery muttered.

"Avery, take your mothering hat off and put on your sister cap, okay? I'll be fine. I always am," Willow warned. Avery did have a way of being a mother figure to both Willow and me, but I didn't blame her. If anything, I was thankful for our older sister. Mama passed away during childbirth with Willow. Avery was only around twelve years old when it happened, but she made sure Willow and I were always taken care of. Of course, Daddy was our haven. We couldn't have asked for a better father, but when it came to the girl things he didn't know much about, Avery stepped up to the plate. From doing our hair to telling us about pads and tampons, she was always in our corner.

Sometimes she and Willow would bump heads about Avery's mothering habits, but I knew it all came from a good place. Besides, for me at least, whenever Avery acted out in that way, I could see Mama in her eyes. It felt like a gift that kept on giving.

Before my two sisters could continue their back-and-forth, I cleared my throat. "Hey, remember when Avery almost got engaged?" I exclaimed.

The two instantly stopped yapping at one another and swooned together as they said in unison. "Yeah, we do."

Avery nudged me. "Solid conversation shift. Speaking of shifts of topic…Willow, did you know that Yara and Alex are now friendly with one another?"

Willow arched an eyebrow. "The poopy shoes guy?"

"The one and only." Avery nodded. "I'm still waiting for the story of how that came to be. So, Yara, the floor is all yours."

"Well. It all started with his clown shoes."

CHAPTER 20

Alex

I woke up to the most horrendous smell hitting my nostrils. The urge to vomit raced over me as I climbed out of my bed. As I approached my guest room, where the stench only grew more intense, I covered my mouth to keep from gagging.

When I glanced within the crate, there lay Feliz, on his back, snoring, covered in his own poop. It was smeared all over the crate, and he looked to be resting as peacefully as a clam after giving me a night of hell.

"For the love of..." I muttered as I moved in closer. The second I took a step, he awakened and flipped over to his feet. As soon as he saw me, he started his nonstop barking and growling routine. That was the sound I'd fallen asleep to the night prior, and let's just say it wasn't the best thing for my ears to be pierced with—especially without espresso in my system.

Feliz looked at me as if he would rip my throat out. Nothing but rage in his eyes.

"You know, you have a lot of nerve being so aggressive as you sit there covered in your own crap," I told him.

"*Woof, woof, woof, you're a dick,*" he replied. Or at least that was what I assumed he would've said if he could speak. Instead, it was just nonstop barking, which sounded like nails on a chalkboard.

I stared at the deranged mutt for a few seconds before turning around and walking toward my kitchen. My patience was being tested, and I couldn't for the life of me figure out why Teresa would think giving me that thing was a wise idea. Nothing about my lifestyle or me screamed that I was a dog person. A part of me was highly annoyed with my great-aunt for leaving such a bad gift at my doorstep. Then a bigger part of me became annoyed with myself for being annoyed with her. She was dead. The last thing I could've done was let her rest in peace.

Still, I was annoyed.

And grumpy.

And not caffeinated.

As I dragged my feet toward the kitchen, I started my espresso machine and grumbled to myself before I grabbed my cell phone and began reading through my text messages with the updates on the restaurant from the night prior. Then I went to my emails and grumbled some more.

Nothing good came from checking your emails and messages before coffee was in your system. I knew that fact, and still, I failed to keep from checking said messages.

Once my espresso made it into my system, I headed to the bathroom, washed my face, brushed my teeth, and debated how to deal with the dog covered in poop in my guest room. Then it clicked that I had someone who could help a floor above me.

Yara.

Maybe she'd end up being the answer to my jaded prayers.

THE PROBLEM WITH DATING

First, I had to suck up my pride and put my tail between my legs to whimper for her help.

I tossed on my tennis shoes and headed upstairs to the sixteenth floor. After knocking—well, *pounding*—on her door, I felt relief when she opened it.

She opened the door with confusion in her eyes. "Alex. What's going on?"

"Hi. I need your help."

"Is everything okay?" She placed a hand on my arm. "Is Feliz okay?" The warmth from her touch threw me off slightly. Why did my body feel the need to lean in to be touched by her again?

"He's fine. Well, I suppose." I cleared my throat and grumbled, "I need your help."

"With?"

"The dog."

A sly smile fell against her face. She crossed her arms and leaned against her doorframe. "You need my help."

"That's what I said."

"No." She poked me against my chest with a big, goofy grin that almost made me smile back. Why, though? Why did that woman make me want to smile when I'd spent most of my days living with frowns? "You." *Poke.* "Need." *Poke.* "My." *Poke poke.* "Help!"

I groaned as I raked my hand through my messy hair. "You're going to be annoying about this, aren't you?"

"So annoying, yes." She rocked on her heels, narrowing her eyes at me. "Give me a good reason I should help you."

"Because I..." I grumbled, knowing the next words would make her so happy. "I need you."

Her smile stretched further.

I hated that I loved how it looked.

"You *need* me," she sang.

"Stop it."

"I can't because you *need* me."

I grimaced and turned to walk away. "You know what? Forget I asked for your help."

"No, no, wait." She reached out and grabbed my arm, pulling me in toward her. That odd sensation rose again from her touch.

Stop touching me, Goldie.

"What? I asked for your help, and you're mocking me. I'm not going to waste my time here."

"I'm just teasing you a little, Alex. Do you have to be so serious?"

"It's my M.O."

"Trust me, I know." She smiled again, and I couldn't pull my eyes away from her lips. She wore some kind of gloss, and I couldn't help but wonder what it tasted like.

"I'm enjoying this," she expressed. "You needing me."

"I don't need anyone," I snipped.

"That's not what I'm witnessing now," she replied. "Would it be too much for me to ask you to beg a little, too?"

"What do you want from me, Goldie? You want me to get down on my knees and whimper?"

"With a leash around your neck, maybe, yes. Then maybe I could dog walk you around for a bit," she teased. "It wouldn't hurt if you barked, too."

I softly chuckled at her ridiculousness.

Her eyes twinkled. "Those dang allergies are getting to you again, huh?"

"It's the dog dander," I joked.

"Whatever you say, Alex. Whatever you say. So how can I help you?"

"There's a situation in my apartment with the dog."

"A situation?"

I groaned and pinched the bridge of my nose. "The dog shat all over himself in his crate last night, and now it's a mess, and I don't know how to get him cleaned up because if I get half a step too close to him, he'll bark and try to bite me."

She laughed.

Yes.

She laughed at me!

"It's not funny!" I barked, feeling my chest tightening. There I was. Barking. Wonderful. She threw her head back in a giggling fit. I hated that I loved how she laughed.

"It's a little funny because…" She kept shaking her head in laughter. "It's like dog poop is following you around. First my Cocoa and now Feliz."

"I'm glad you're getting a chuckle out of this."

"What can I say? I'm easily amused."

"Are you going to help or not?"

"Of course. I'll help clean him up."

"I need you to stay with him all day."

She scrunched up her face. "What? Alex, I have a job."

"Yes. I need you to take today off. I can't stay with him all day, and I feel bad leaving him alone."

"You can bring him to my daycare if you need to."

"No. It took me forever to get him out of my car last night, and I refuse to go through that again today. I need you to stay with him and dog-sit at my place."

"I can get him to my shop after I clean him up."

"Grand. And if you could watch him afterward here, that would help me."

She bit her bottom lip. "And what do I get out of this exchange?"

"I'll pay whatever you would've made for the day times four."

"I don't want your money. I actually have a better idea. I can help you with Feliz every day for as long as you need me to."

I arched an eyebrow. "You can?"

"Yeah. There's only one small request I have for you."

"And that is?" I started for the staircase, and thankfully, Yara was quick to slide on her slippers and follow me to my apartment.

As I opened the door, the smell hit us straight in the face.

"Oh my gosh, that's bad," Yara remarked, covering her nose.

"Tell me about it." I allowed her to step inside the apartment. "What was your request?"

"Oh, right. You see, you're going to need more help with Feliz. I can get him to not only put up with you but also love you within a few weeks. It's what I do. I can give you the VIP dog whisperer package. Before you know it, this dog will be your best friend, guaranteed."

"I don't think you can guarantee something like that."

"Guaranteed," she insisted. "But in order for me to help you, you have to do one small thing for me."

"Which is?"

"Be my fake boyfriend."

I choked out a laugh. "What?"

"I need you to be my fake boyfriend for the autumn season. At least for the next two-ish months. September to November, tops. We could end things right before Thanksgiving to avoid all the holiday mumbo jumbo. But fall is the best season. We can do so many activities to show off our fake relationship. The Fall into Fall Harvest Festival. Snack on Hillstack picnics on the hilltop. Apple picking at Amy's Apple Farm! Oh, oh, and pumpkin bowling! Do you know this time of year is called cuffing season, which means—"

"I know what cuffing season is, Yara."

"Oh good. Let's be cuffed. Together. You and me. The fake cuffing of Alex and Yara. The tag team of all tag teams. It will be great."

"Why the heck do you need a fake boyfriend?"

"To get Cole off my back. He said he's not going to believe I moved on until I have a man claiming me in this very town.

THE PROBLEM WITH DATING

That man will be you. For two months, at least. Then you're free to go."

I narrowed my eyes. "You want me to fake date you to ward off your ex, and you'll train my dog in exchange?"

"Yup. I'll even pick him up and take him to work. But I'll need you to do morning and afternoon walks with me and trips to the dog park just so you and Feliz can bond."

"No."

She pouted. "No?"

"I can't. Cole already has it out for me. Especially after I kicked him out of my restaurant. I just got an email that the place was covered with silly string and toilet paper late last night. I doubt Cole will give a damn. I don't need to be even more on his bad side if people keep vandalizing my property."

Her pout deepened. "That makes sense. I hate that that makes sense."

"I can pay you, though," I offered. "And take part in the walks and training sessions."

Yara's brows knitted for a moment. "I could actually use the extra money since work is struggling a bit."

I narrowed my eyes. "How? Your business is always packed with people and dogs. It looks like you're thriving."

"If only those people kept up with payments," she muttered. Before I could reply, she held a hand out toward me. "I, Yara Kingsley, the dog whisperer, agree to train Feliz for a price point we can agree on later. I am officially reporting for duty." She snickered to herself.

I arched an eyebrow. "What's so funny?"

"I'm reporting for duty…like doody…like the poop situation you're dealing with. It's just funny."

"Nothing about this situation is funny."

"There is. You're just not spotting the humor."

Before I could say anything else, Feliz began barking and whimpering from my guest room. Yara's eyes moved in the direction of his noise, and her shoulders dropped. She sighed as her eyes softened to the realm of compassion. "Poor baby. Let me handle Feliz. I'll use your guest bathroom to get him cleaned up."

"Down the hall to the left. It's right across from the guest room, where he is situated."

She nodded in understanding and started in that direction.

I followed her footsteps, and she turned quickly and held a hand up toward me. "Oh, no, no, no. You can't be involved with this now. Feliz is already stressed out, and he doesn't need"—she waved her hands around at me with a look of disgust—"this."

"What do you mean by"—I narrowed my eyes and dramatically waved my hands toward myself—"this?"

"You. Your energy. I don't know if you know this, but sometimes you have some of the worst energy about you. You can head out for the day and run errands if you'd like."

My brows knitted toward one another. The idea of being able to go down to the restaurant and check on things was somewhat tempting. Along with getting out of the smelly house.

"I have to work later tonight than normal, too. I have to catch up on some things with my other restaurants and stop in Chicago. Is that okay?"

"I charge by the hour," she semi-joked. "Besides, poor Feliz could probably use a good spa day with me after his travels. Get going. I'll take him in to work with me for the day, then bring him back here if you leave me a key. We'll be here when you make it back home."

"Sounds good. I'm going to shower fast and get going. Anything in the house is free for you to use. The television, anything in the kitchen... by all means, have at it."

Then she smiled, and it was beautiful. Everything about her was sort of beautiful, even her sassy attitude. I found myself taking her in a lot more each time I crossed paths with her.

That morning, she wore a crop top with oversized black

sweatpants that hugged her hips. I struggled a little to pull my stare away from those hips. Unfortunately, when I did manage to look away, my eyes found her lips.

They were full and plump, and whenever they curved up into a smile, I almost felt the urge to kiss her.

If I had agreed to a fake relationship, would there have been fake kissing?

It didn't matter.

We weren't doing it.

Still.

I wondered.

I got out of her way and let her handle getting Feliz into the bathroom to wash him up. I didn't know how she'd manage to get him to trust her enough to give him a bath, but I supposed that was between her and Feliz. She was the dog whisperer, after all, not me.

I headed to the bathroom in my bedroom and shut the door. Hopefully, a shower would wake me up and make me less of a grouch for the rest of the day.

CHAPTER 21

Yara

I was the official dog whisperer for Alex Ramírez. You know, the person I claimed to hate a few days ago.

It was funny how life turned around so drastically in such a short period.

Alex did have a few good things going for him that I found hard to overlook. One, he was an amazing chef. The bone-shaped cookies he'd made were remarkable, too. Josh could *never* make cookies that tasty. As far as apologies went, that was top-tier.

Two, he was easy on the eyes. I didn't completely hate looking at him even though I tried to convince myself otherwise. Alex's attractiveness ran rampant, especially when he wasn't being rude.

And last, three, he had a dog. It was a scientific fact that men with dogs were better than those without. It added bonus points to their whole existence. Did Alex want a dog? No. Probably

THE PROBLEM WITH DATING

not. But he kept Feliz when he did have the option of surrendering him to a shelter. Instead, he came to me for help.

Deep down, there had to be a part that didn't hate the idea of Feliz being around. I felt lonely when Cocoa was with Cole. I couldn't imagine the loneliness Alex felt with always being on his own.

Besides, Feliz was a good boy. He'd simply had a rough few days.

I'd be pooping my pants, too, and barking up a storm nonstop if I was sent to live with a stranger. Oftentimes, humans forgot that we weren't the only creatures who experienced fear and sadness.

At least we, humans, were able to communicate our feelings with words. All Feliz could do was whimper and cry, which he'd began to do once his aggression subsided and I placed him in the bathtub.

Ten minutes later, he was brand spanking new and ready for a solid blow-drying.

"That wasn't so bad now, was it?" I asked the small dog as I finished rinsing him off in the tub. It took a bit of work and my bite-free gloves to get Feliz into the bathtub, but once he realized I was there to help him and not hurt him, he somewhat surrendered to the idea of me bathing him.

That, or he was terrified into a state of calmness. I'd been there before—so scared that I allowed people to have free will over me and my heart.

Every time Feliz whimpered out of fear, my heart shattered a bit more for him. He was such a sweet boy who was misunderstood.

As I grabbed a towel to dry Feliz, there was a knock on the bathroom door.

"Yes?" I called out.

Alex cleared his throat. "Everything okay in there?"

The moment Feliz heard his voice, he began to growl. I wrapped him up in a towel and started drying him.

"Peachy," I replied. "But if you can refrain from speaking, that would be great. It appears your voice irritates him."

I heard Alex grumble some.

Feliz growled at that, too, and grumbled along with Alex.

I laughed.

It turned out those two had something in common—they were two grumpy old men.

"We'll see you soon," I told Alex. "Leave your phone number and key on the kitchen counter, and I'll use it if anything goes wrong, but it shouldn't. I'll see you later tonight."

"O—"

"Don't talk!" I shouted.

More grumbles from outside the door followed by foot stomping and the front door slamming.

I smiled down at Feliz, who still looked at me with those perfect eyes. "Don't worry, buddy. Scrooge is gone. It's just you and me now for the rest of the day. Though, he's not that bad once you give him a chance."

Feliz began wagging his tail as if he understood me, and I started blow-drying his coat, using the pet brush from my backpack to make sure none of his fur ended up matted. After I cleaned up his mess in his crate to make a comfortable place for him and leave Alex's home smelling less like crap, I set Feliz's food up, which he scarfed down within minutes.

Walking him over to The Pup Around the Corner was easy, too. Clearly, Feliz could tell I wasn't out to hurt him. Though every now and again, someone would cross our paths, and he'd try to take out their ankles. But then again, I, too, wanted to take out people's ankles sometimes.

"Oh, who is this cutie?" Keri asked as I walked into the shop. She smiled at Feliz, and he lunged toward her with the most

THE PROBLEM WITH DATING

intense barking I'd seen the guy showcase. "Whoa!" Keri gasped, jumping backward. "Feisty, huh?"

I tried to calm Feliz, but he kept trying to shoot toward her, completely zoned in as if he wasn't only going for her ankles, but he wanted to rip her throat out. He was acting even worse than he had when Alex first met him.

"Feliz, it's okay. It's just Keri," I explained, pulling him closer to me and lifting him into my arms.

"Dogs like me!" Keri chimed in with her bright smile. "It's okay, buddy." She stepped toward us, and Feliz almost shot straight out of my arms to attack Keri. "Maybe he needs time to warm up. I'll go get Lucy in the back. She's better with the smaller dogs."

I agreed with her. The moment Keri left the room, Feliz calmed down. Lucy came out and had no issues taking him in the back for extra tender love and care. While they worked in the back, I headed to my office to do paperwork.

Oh, paperwork and how much I hate you.

The books were behind, clients weren't catching up on their tabs, and I couldn't help but think that Mr. Parker was rolling over in his grave at how bad I was at the business side of things. I felt strongly that I was letting him down, but I had no clue how to reverse it at all. I couldn't give them pay cuts, either, because I knew my employees already worked harder than they should've. If anything, they deserved raises.

I'd already shaved my cut as much as I could, too. If I decreased my salary any more, I couldn't be able to afford my apartment.

I wished I could've ignored the hard parts of life. Shoved it deeply in the back of a dresser drawer and never thought of it again. But the problem with shoving your issues into a dresser drawer was that they built up more and more each time until they overflowed, forcing you to deal with the mess you made.

I was almost at the dealing part of the issues.

Almost.

I was also quietly praying that the Fall into Fall Festival would help raise enough money for The Pup Around the Corner. It was my last hope. Even if we could raise five thousand dollars, I'd be grateful.

"If you keep furrowing like that, you'll get forehead wrinkles," a voice said. I looked up to see my father standing in the doorway of my office. He tapped his forehead. "Trust me, I know."

I shoved the paperwork into the drawer. "Don't worry, I use wrinkle cream," I joked, pushing out a smile to try to combat my anxiety. "What's going on, Daddy?"

He grimaced and lowered his brows. "You tell me. What's on your mind?"

"Nothing. Just work stuff. I'm good."

"Liar."

Liar.

I smiled more. "It's fine. It will all work out."

"Sometimes it doesn't hurt to ask for help, baby girl. Sometimes, by asking for help, that's the way it all works out. So if you need your papa to write a check—"

"Daddy," I cut in. "I'm good. I promise."

What a lying promise that had been. He knew it, too, but he didn't push. I knew how hard my father worked for every cent he made. A hardworking construction man, he built his business from the ground up. My sisters and I tried to convince him to stop working so hard, but he'd always say, "What if my girls need something? I want to make sure I have it to give."

You couldn't talk a good man out of providing for his family, no matter what.

"What brings you in today?" I asked, gesturing to the basket he held in his hands.

"Ah, yes. A lunch date. Before the annual picnic auctions. I had my date with Avery yesterday, and today is yours. I need at least thirty minutes of your time so you can eat with the first man who loved you."

My chest filled with love at how adorable my father was. Every year, he'd have picnics with each of us girls. It was a reminder of exactly what he'd said—one of the best loves we'd ever known.

I knew I was blessed to have a father who cared for me the way he did. Some people dreamed of such a thing—I lived it.

"Well, isn't that exciting," I replied. I made space on my desk, and he began pulling out the same items he packed in the basket each year. The same things Mama had made when Daddy brought her the basket on Hillstack many moons ago—peanut butter and jelly sandwiches, barbecue chips, apple juice, and orange slices.

"I would have this meal with Willow, but did you know my baby girl was running around Chile with a strange man who went by the name Snake?" Dad asked as he sat down across from me.

I bit my bottom lip. "I plead the Fifth?"

He grumbled and shoved a handful of chips into his mouth. "It's like you girls are trying to give your father a heart attack. You see this?" he said, pointing at his hair. "Every gray hair is from each of you girls. You have me looking like Black Santa out here."

I laughed. "The gray looks good on you."

"Well, you're not wrong." He opened the container of sandwiches, cut into stars like they were when we were kids, and handed me one. "What's this I hear about you leaving Isla Iberia with that Alex Ramírez the other night?"

"News travels fast, huh?"

"It's Honey Creek. Would you expect anything else?" He nodded my way. "Are you two involved?"

My stomach turned from the question. "We're friends, I

think." Sort of. Kind of. Maybe. "It's hard to explain. Kind of getting to know one another. He helped me out that night."

"You like him, though," he said, pointing a finger at me. "You know how I can tell? Your eyes sparkle when you talk about him."

I huffed and waved him off. "No, that's just the lighting fixture in here. I don't like Alex. I mean, I don't *not* like Alex. I mean—" Wait. Did I like Alex? What? No. Absolutely not. There was no way I liked him when I hated him forty-eight hours ago. If anything, we were acquaintances at best. Business neighbors. Nothing more, nothing less, except for the friendship we were trying to cultivate and—ohmygosh, why did my stomach feel like a swarm of butterflies filled it as I wondered if I liked Alex? What happened to the dragons?

Go away, butterflies! You do not belong here.

"It's a complicated thing," I choked out.

"A complicated *thing?*" he echoed. "You younger generations and your overthinking of stuff. You know, in my day, dating was much easier. You weren't going person to person, dating fifty people at once, like you were a juggler. No. You set your eyes on one individual, stated proudly that you were seeing them, and you let the man court you. Do men not do that anymore? Court women?"

I snickered. "There's a lot that men and women don't do anymore when it comes to the world of dating."

He grumbled and shook his head. "That's unfortunate. Listen, I know change is good, and we should grow as a world. I'm not one of those old farts going on and on about how things used to be, but dating used to feel good. Now, it sounds like you all run high on anxiety, swiping right and left on your phones, not giving people a long enough shot because someone else always lurks around the corner. When dating, men and women bicker about what the other should and shouldn't do. Then, there're like fifty things before actual

THE PROBLEM WITH DATING

dating. What's that thing called? I heard it on the radio the other day." He snapped his fingers, trying to remember the word.

"A situationship."

"Yes! That! What is that? Someone called in for advice and said they were in a situationship for two years. Two years, Yara! Can you believe that? She said the guy told her he wasn't ready to commit to just dating. I thought we committed to marriage. I didn't know we had to commit to just calling someone yours."

"I think people made all of these different words and levels to dating because they're trying to protect themselves from getting hurt."

Daddy huffed and waved it off. "They made a mistake. People build up brick walls, going in wary and expecting the worst, instead of placing gates that are still safe but open up to at least give others a chance to come inside. That's the problem with your generation. Too many walls, not enough fences."

"That's a good point."

"And don't get me wrong—some people are dangerous. Some people, like a certain ex-husband I won't mention, don't care how they hurt others. That's where discernment comes in. That's when you close your gate and bolt lock it. But I like to believe that most people are just looking for love and to be loved in a world that's forgotten what true love is."

Matthew Kingsley, always with the words of wisdom. It's probably where Willow got that trait from.

"It is scary, though," I countered. "To put your heart on the line."

"Yes, it is. Especially after you've been burned," he agreed. "But you know what's even scarier?"

"What's that?"

"Missing out on the soothing balm that new love can bring. If I stopped believing in love after your biological mother walked out, I would've never met your mama. We wouldn't have

Avery or Willow. Could you imagine a world without their hearts?"

"Not for a second."

"Exactly. So that's why, even after the burns, we try again. Because love brings miracles we'd never dreamed of."

My father. The hopeless romantic. Even after all the hardships he's faced.

"You know, he who we don't speak of showed up to my house not that long ago," he mentioned.

"Oh? Why?"

"He wanted me to talk to you and try to convince you to give him another chance. He knows how close we are and figured you'd give him a shot if he asked me for my approval. Which is funny because the dummy didn't even ask my permission for marriage."

I laughed. Daddy never got over Cole not coming to him about the proposal.

"What did you tell him?" I questioned.

"I told him I'd talk to you. And since I'm a man of my word, this is me doing exactly that. This is me talking to you. Now, you listen to me, Yara, and you listen closely." He leaned in and said, "Don't you ever go back to the things that cut you so deeply. They still have the knives in their cabinets that they used before to hurt you. Even if they smile and pretend they don't. And sometimes, they even sharpened them more."

I smiled. "No back steps."

"We move forward." He shifted in his chair and grabbed a few orange slices. "But this complicated *thing* of yours with Alex."

My cheeks heated from the conversation shifting to Alex.

He continued. "I like him for you."

I laughed. "What? Don't be ridiculous. You don't like any men for us."

"That's true, but I like Alex. He has a good foundation."

"What do you mean?"

"I worked with him on the restaurant for months and months. I watched people harass him, bully him, and try to run him out of town. Still, he kept building. He kept persevering. If that doesn't speak of a person's character, then I don't know what does. You need a person like that. A person who won't quit when things get hard. A person who won't have a wandering eye when you're on a down slope. A person who builds stronger things when the world expects him to crumple."

"Daddy—"

"Every relationship has ebbs and flows, Yara. Ups and downs. You aren't always at the peak, in la-la land of the honeymoon stage. Sometimes, you're in the trenches. That's why you need someone with a strong foundation. Someone who loves you enough to get to tomorrow without hurting you even if they don't like you today."

I wanted that feeling.

I wanted that level of trust in another person, but sometimes I wondered if true love even existed. Because with Cole, I loved him through every storm. It just took me a while to realize it had to be a mutual love. I also realized that the one creating said storms was the one I was trying to shield from the rain.

"Let me be clear, I like him, Yara. I do. But don't get me wrong. If he's not the one for you, then he's not the one. All I'm saying is don't be afraid to try something new. You never know where something new can lead you."

"I love you," I told him.

"I love you," he replied.

After we finished our meal, he packed up his things and headed out. Somehow, though, he managed to slip a few hundred dollars onto my desk, which I didn't notice until he left. He folded it into a few napkins, which read the words, "For my girl."

I loved that man more than words could ever express.

The rest of the day went really well. Feliz and I headed back to Alex's apartment after the workday. I ordered a pizza, and Feliz ordered dog treats. He then found a comfy spot on Alex's living room couch, circled four times, and plopped down for a nap. The sweet baby deserved the rest, but I looked forward to taking him on a walk later that afternoon. Truthfully, Feliz was a very laid-back dog. He was just misunderstood from first, second, and third impressions.

Kind of like a certain man I'd recently met.

CHAPTER 22

Alex

After a long workday and a few more diary entries, I opened the front door to my apartment and walked inside to a silent home that smelled...good. It smelled like peaches, a great change from the smells occupying the space when I left earlier that day.

There wasn't even a yapping dog trying to claw my throat out.

I removed my shoes before rolling up the sleeves of my white button-down shirt. As I tiptoed into the living room toward the sound of two snoring creatures, I found Yara laid out on the couch with Feliz resting on top of her. Yara's arms were wrapped loosely around Feliz, who looked as if he was smiling from his dreams. I didn't even know dogs smiled.

At that moment, he didn't look too much like Cujo. If anything, he looked...sweet.

What the heck did you do to that dog today, Yara Kingsley?

I cleared my throat, and Feliz shook himself awake. The moment his stare met mine, his teeth clenched together, and he returned to his deep growling and began barking rapidly toward me. Oh yes. There he was. The vicious guy I was beginning to know very well.

"Ah! What happened?!" Yara freaked out, shaking herself awake from the sound of Feliz's barking. She rubbed the exhaustion from her eyes, and without a second of hesitation, she reached forward to grab Feliz before he could attack me.

"I guess I don't need to be worried about intruders," I said, taking a handful of steps backward.

"Give me a second," Yara replied. She stood and hurried away toward my spare bedroom, where she opened the door and placed Feliz inside before shutting the door once more. She walked back out toward me and yawned. "You're late."

"I didn't give a time."

"Still, you're late. No one should work past midnight."

"The life of a restaurant owner. It seems like you had a good day."

"Feliz is a sweetheart. I didn't mind spending the day with him."

"Since you guys get along so well, maybe he'd be better off with you," I semi-joked.

She laughed, and it sounded like light. Bright and full even though she'd just awakened. "My Cocoa isn't quite ready for a new roommate."

"Figures." I brushed my thumb against my nose.

"You should get some sleep, or at least as much as Feliz allows you," Yara said. "I'll be by in the morning to take him to work."

"Okay. And, Yara?"

"Yeah?"

"Thank you."

"You're welcome."

"Yara?" I repeated.

"Yes?"

"Thank you," I said once more.

She arched an eyebrow. "What is that thank-you for?"

"Just for you being you."

* * *

MY BODY and mind wanted to sleep, but Feliz had different plans for me.

"Please stop barking." I sighed as I sat outside the spare bedroom. I had little to no sleep the night prior, seeing as how Feliz decided to howl all night long. Earlier, I tried to peek into the room to make sure he had enough food, and that was when he lunged for the door. I shut it quickly before he could attack me.

How did Yara manage to tame him?

Seeing as how I was in charge of keeping him alive, that dog had a lot of nerve to treat me like crap.

"What were you thinking, Teresa?" I muttered to myself, resting my head against the hallway wall. Right that second, there was a knock on my front door. I stood and answered it to find Yara. She was wide-eyed and looked well-rested.

"Good morning!" she chimed.

"What's so good about it?" I muttered.

"He kept you up all night, huh?" she asked, entering my apartment.

"All. Night."

"Well, how about this. How about you go sleep for a few hours, and I'll take Feliz into work. While I'm gone, I'll text you a list of things to get for your place. You should get a gate for the guest bedroom. Then Feliz can see you and get used to you instead of keeping this door shut."

"So he can bark at me nonstop?" I grumbled.

"I know it seems nonstop, but this will be a far-off memory at some point. You two will be best friends."

"Don't hold your breath," I replied as I yawned. "But I will take you up on a nap." I felt as if I hadn't had a good night's sleep in a long time. I began to drag my feet toward my bedroom, and Yara called out to me.

"Wait!"

I turned to face her, and Feliz was snuggled up in her arms, trying so hard to lick her face. What kind of magic spell did she put on that dog? Then again, I couldn't blame Feliz. I had a few moments over the past few days when I, too, thought of licking Yara Kingsley.

"Yeah?" I asked.

"Come pet his head."

"What? No."

She nodded as she walked over toward me. The closer they drew, the more tense Feliz became as he released a low growl. Yara was still convinced, though. "Pet. His. Head, Alex."

"He's going to bite me."

"He's not going to bite you."

"How do you know?"

"Because you're going to reach into the back pocket of my jeans and pull out the treat I stored for you to give to him."

I arched an eyebrow. "He might still bite me."

"No," she disagreed, "he won't."

Feliz's fangs told a different story. "But—"

"Alejandro," she sang, and it felt good hearing my full name roll off her tongue. "Reach into my back pocket and get the treat out."

I grumbled for a second yet did as she said. As my hand reached into the back pocket of her tight jeans, I had to remind myself not to linger too long to try to get a feel of her ass, which I'd found myself watching as she exited rooms lately.

I picked up the treat, then turned back to her. Feliz was already barking like mad, looking as if he wanted to drain every drop of blood from my system.

"Good boy," she said. I wasn't sure if she was talking to me or the dog, but oddly enough, it turned me on.

"Now what?" I asked.

"Hold the treat in front of his nose."

I cocked an eyebrow. "You mean in front of his teeth he's baring at me?"

"Yup"—she nodded—"right there. Let him smell it."

"But—"

"Do you trust me?" she asked.

Oddly enough, for no reason whatsoever, I did.

I waved the treat in front of Feliz's nose. He paused for a moment and went back to barking. Then he stopped once more, smelled the treat, and lunged at me. Okay, he didn't lunge at me, but he took the treat and ate it.

"There! Now, pet his head," Yara instructed.

With haste, I pat the dog's head three times.

One, two, three.

Feliz was too into his treat to realize what had just happened.

So food was the way to his heart, huh?

That was worth noting.

"Yesterday, I realized he had a way for treats. He'd pretty much let us do anything to him at the shop if treats were involved."

"Maybe he and I have more in common than I thought," I muttered. Right then, he finished his treat and tried to lunge back toward me. I leaped backward. "Geez!"

Yara giggled.

"That's funny to you?" I questioned after almost losing my life from Cujo.

"A little. You're so big, he's so little, and you're so...scared."

"I'm not scared," I argued.

Yara narrowed her eyes. "Swear?"

"Swear."

She held Feliz out toward me, and I lurched backward, almost running straight into a wall.

Okay, maybe I was a little scared.

"I'm going to sleep," I told her, muttering under my breath. Oddly enough, Yara appeared in my dreams, too.

* * *

THE FOLLOWING DAYS WERE WASH, rinse, and repeat with Feliz. The only difference was I put up a gate at the guest bedroom, so the little rat was forced to look at me instead of closing his bedroom door. He might not have liked looking at me, but he would have to get used to me being around.

I also found myself online looking up recipes for dog treats I could make. The ingredients in the treats I'd found in the stores seemed to be filled with crap. I would never feed that to a human, so why would I feed it to my dog? My dog. I had a dog, and I was making the spoiled brat homemade treats. Along with homemade dog food, too.

"Here," I said as I sat in front of the gate with him barking and hopping around like a Ping-Pong ball. "Shut up and just try it, will you?" I held the treat out toward him. A sweet potato soaked in gravy and wrapped with homemade jerky.

Feliz yipped but inched closer and closer until he ripped the jerky from my hand and hurried off to the opposite corner of his bedroom to eat in solitude.

"You're welcome," I replied.

He barked once my way before he went back to eating. The slight wag of his tail showed me he liked it. Then the grumpy jerk came back, barking at me but requesting more. The little shit.

I slid another sweet potato through the gate. He yanked it from my grip and hurried away.

"A thank-you wouldn't hurt."

He yapped and growled.

But he loved the treat. That felt like a win.

Yara showed up each morning to walk him before taking him to town to her dog shop. When I opened the door for her, she wore the same smile she'd always had. The same smile that made me feel things for her that I wasn't certain I should be feeling.

"Morning. I brought you a coffee," she offered, holding it out toward me. "I figured you'd like it black like your spirit."

I chuckled. "I would argue that, but it is how I like my coffee. Let me guess, you're a chai tea extra foam upside down, spin around caramel drizzle with five pumps of poison white chocolate latte type of girl?"

She placed a hand on her hip and gasped. "How did you know?"

"I'm a quick study."

"That's good to know," she mentioned. "Because today's the day."

"For...?"

"Our first trip to the dog park with Feliz."

"That's today?"

"That's right now. Chop, chop, Mr. Black," she said. "Let's go."

* * *

YARA WASN'T KIDDING when she said she was the dog whisperer. If I didn't know better, I'd think Feliz was swapped out for another dog whenever she was around us.

When we arrived at the dog park, Feliz instantly took off running with Yara. She was convinced that if she tired him out, he'd sleep through the night. He was still waking after midnight for a few trips outside. Trips that were messing with my sleep.

I watched the two of them dart around with the other dogs

and people at the park as I stood with my coffee. Everything seemed all good until someone spoke from behind me.

"Alex?"

The voice made every hair on my body stand. For a moment, I thought about dashing, but then I remembered that Feliz was around the corner with the golden retriever of a woman.

With a deep sigh, I turned to greet the person who said my name. The second I saw her, an old yet familiar rage began to boil throughout my system.

Catie.

I raised an eyebrow and took her in. She looked good. I hated that she looked so good. Her lips were painted a deep crimson, and her jewelry was all silver. She dressed in all black, just like her soul, and she had enough nerve to smile my way.

"Catie," I dryly replied. "What are you doing here?"

"I'm here to see you and heard you might be here. The real question is, what are you doing at a dog park? You hate dogs."

"I never said I hated dogs."

"Well, you never said you liked them. We never even talked about pets when we were together."

"Probably because our relationship was based on lies." I shifted. "Why are you here to see me?"

"I'm here because Mandy and Noah's wedding is coming up. I figured I should see how we're doing after everything that went down last year. Plus, I heard about Teresa passing. I'm sorry to hear that."

The way she brought up Teresa bothered me more than it should've. Maybe because my great-aunt hated Catie. She always thought she wasn't the right one for me. Clearly, Teresa was right.

"You wasted a trip. There's nothing to talk about. I'll be fine at the wedding with you there. I'm not a child."

"I'm bringing Henry," she said. That felt like a knife to my chest.

THE PROBLEM WITH DATING

"Noah said you weren't bringing him."

She shook her head. "I wasn't going to. But we've been together for a while now, and when I look back on my sister's wedding, I'd like him in the photographs. I wanted to give you a heads-up, so it wasn't a surprise."

"You hid your affair with him for a good while, so no need to be upfront with me now," I bitterly replied.

"I get that you're hurt because of what went down between Henry and me, but—"

"You cheated on me with him. That's what went down. That was the end of it, so we need to leave it there."

"It's clear you're not over it."

Annoyance and anger built within me, but I knew I couldn't showcase said annoyance and anger. The last thing Catie needed to know was that she still got under my skin.

"Listen, Alex. I understand you're still hurt by what we did, and you still have feelings for me as you are trying to work through your emotions over the situation, but—"

"I don't have feelings for you," I told her. I meant that, too. "It's been over a year. I've moved on."

The condescending frown she shot my way made my nerves crawl. "I know that's not true."

"Why would it be possible for you to move on and not for me? Sure, you got a head start on your current relationship by screwing him during ours, but I have moved on."

"Come on, Alex. My sister told me you haven't dated since. I know that's not—"

Before she could finish, Feliz and Yara came darting our way. Feliz collapsed at my feet, completely exhausted. So exhausted that he didn't even realize it was my shoe that he was resting against, which meant he wasn't trying to destroy it.

Yara smiled and laughed loudly because that was what Yara always did. If I could've recorded that sound for my morning alarm clock, I probably would've woken up in a better mood. That was if Feliz allowed me to actually sleep.

Yara paused beside me, out of breath. "I swear, if that dog doesn't sleep through the night after that workout, then I don't know what will work."

Catie cocked an eyebrow and crossed her arms over her chest. "I'm sorry, and you are?" she asked.

"This is Yara," I cut in. I wrapped my arm around Yara's waist and pulled her to my side. "My girlfriend." Yara stared at me as if I'd grown three heads. I then cleared my throat. "Yara, this is my ex, Catie."

Lucky for me, it didn't take much more for Yara to catch up with what was going on. To my surprise, she leaned closer to my side, pressing her body to mine as if we were always meant to be molded with one another. It was almost ridiculous how well she fit against me.

"Nice to meet you, Catie. I'm Yara. Alex's girlfriend," she echoed, holding a hand toward Catie.

"Girlfriend," Catie echoed before she reluctantly shook her hand. "Nice to meet you." She didn't mean that. Her grimace proved Yara's existence bothered her.

Good.

"So you're bringing a plus-one to the wedding, too?" Catie asked, warily.

"I am. We're both looking forward to it," I said as I dug a deeper and deeper hole for myself.

"I'm really looking forward to it," Yara chimed in, going along with my madness. "It's going to be amazing."

"We have to get going," I said as I looked over at Yara, and for a moment, I couldn't even understand why I was lucky enough to have her by my side. Sure, perhaps the situation at that moment was fake, but her touch, her warmth, her commitment to my lie… That felt real to me.

As we walked away, Yara on one side of me and Feliz on the

other, I felt no pull of my heartstrings toward Catie. Oddly enough, that felt like closure. I was stepping into something new.

"It wasn't a good breakup, was it?" Yara asked.

"No. She's the one who cheated with an acquaintance of mine."

"I hate her," she replied, matter-of-factly.

I snickered. "You don't know how to hate people, Goldie."

"I can learn for you. Besides, even golden retrievers know how to bite," she said, echoing my words.

"Touché." I rubbed the back of my neck. "You do know what this means, though, right?"

"What's that?"

"If you're posing as my fake girlfriend, it's only right that I pose as your fake boyfriend in town. Fair is fair."

Her eyes lit up as if I'd just given her the winning lottery numbers. "You'll do it?"

"I owe you that much."

She snuggled into my side a little more. "I guess that makes me yours," she said with a smile that had been slowly defrosting the same heart Catie froze over a year ago.

"Yeah," I agreed. "You are mine."

CHAPTER 23

Alex
One Year Ago

A small, hinged box sat atop my nightstand. It was made of lush black leather that was soft to my touch. It was the first day it sat on top of the nightstand instead of within one of the drawers. The edges were curved, and the box textured. Within the box was an emerald-cut diamond that I never thought I could afford fifteen years ago. Within a few moments, that ring would be released from the box that held it for the past six months and placed on the finger of the woman who held my heart.

I wasn't an emotional man. The only person to ever witness me cry was probably my mother on the day I was born. That wasn't to say I didn't have emotions. I was just much more of an analytic person than a feelings guy. Some called me rough around the edges. Others called me a closed-off recluse. A select few called me a jerk—rightfully so. To be fair, I didn't call those individuals the nicest of names, either. But still, regardless of my downfalls, another was able to get ahold of my grumpy heart and claim it as hers.

I didn't know much about life, but I knew I loved her.

That seemed to be enough for me to take our relationship to the next stage. I'd been with Catie for the past five years, and she'd been through every up and down of my life in that time.

We met at one of my restaurants. She was at dinner with her four girlfriends, celebrating graduation from their master's program, and I was in the back overseeing their meals. I'd never forget when Catie had the server bring me to their table because she wanted to speak with the restaurant owner.

As I approached her, the first thing I noticed was her smile. It stretched so far and wide. Full lips and a genuine softness to her. When her green eyes locked with mine, I knew right then that woman was going to change me. I remembered everything about that night. She ordered the Hawaiian glazed salmon, a Caesar salad, and a side of French fries. She drank a Cosmopolitan as she wore her tight, white bandage dress with a slim gold belt and chunky gold earrings. Her nails were painted dusty blue, and she tapped them repeatedly against the tablecloth.

"You're the chef?" Catie asked.

"I am."

She leaned in toward me and shook her head. "I have a complaint to make to you."

I arched an eyebrow and crossed my arms over my chest. "That will be a first."

"Yes, well, I worry everyone else is too nice to speak up about issues, but I'm not, so here goes." She sat back in her chair and tossed her hands up in defeat. "You've just cooked me the most perfect salmon in the world, and I fear there's no coming back from that. Which is a problem."

"How is that a problem?"

"Because now, whenever I try salmon anywhere else, I'll be forced to compare it to yours."

A small smile slipped from me. I didn't give those away easily. "I'm glad you enjoyed it, but I don't feel bad for ruining all salmon for you. I suppose you'll have to keep coming back in order to have your favorite."

"I guess I'll see you next Friday."

And she did.

Every Friday after, she showed up. Sometimes alone at the bar, other times with friends, and it became a tradition between us. Each week, I'd ask her if she'd found better salmon. Each week, she'd tell me she'd failed the quest.

Then she left me her number. Then I called her. I'd been calling her ever since.

The timer on the oven went off, pulling me from my flashbacks as I stared at the box on the nightstand. I snatched it up and slid it into the inside pocket of my blazer. Hurrying into the kitchen, I grabbed oven mitts and pulled out the salmon dish.

It was perfect, of course. I held a record for never burning a meal.

I quickly fried up some fries, mixed up the salad, and set the dining room table with candles and flowers. I poured two glasses of white wine and checked my watch before I dimmed the lighting.

The table was set with the same meal from the night I met her, and the whirl of anxiety I felt as I waited for her to enter the house was unnerving. I kept checking my phone for the time and to see if she responded to my messages, which had been left on read. Before I could shoot off another one, the front door key began to jingle, and right as Catie walked in, she was in my viewpoint.

I got down on one knee and held open the box.

She gasped. "What's going on, Alex?"

THE PROBLEM WITH DATING

I smiled a bit as I held the ring out toward her. "Asking you for forever."

Tears poured out of her eyes as her body began to tremble. At first, I thought it was from excitement, but then her sobs became more intense and painful, even.

"Get up, Alex," she whispered, shaking her head.

I laughed slightly. "I think you're supposed to answer first."

She hurried over to me and grabbed my arm. "No, get up. Get up. You can't do this."

"Am I missing something? What's going—"

"I'm in love with Henry," she blurted out, covering her mouth with her hands. The tears raced down her face as if she was the one with a broken heart. As if her heart was being shattered.

"Henry who?" I choked out.

She choked on her tears and shook her head. "Henry. Your Henry."

"My Henry?" I echoed again, confused by her words because there was no way... There was no way she was in love with the man who stabbed me in the fucking back years ago. She was in love with the man who tried to ruin my career?

"I was coming tonight to tell you that I was moving out, Alex... I'm leaving."

My heart didn't shatter, no. It froze.

She kept talking, her words feeling empty as they trickled through my ears. Then she packed up her things as I remained in the apartment foyer, completely still. She moved past me and left me alone to remove any ounce of light that was still left within me.

CHAPTER 24

Yara
Present Day

"Henry trained me when I came back to the United States with my aunt. I was a stupid kid, straight out of culinary school, and somehow, I landed a job at his restaurant. I studied under him for years. For a long time, I looked up to him as a father figure after mine walked out on me," Alex explained as we walked home from running into Catie. "Sure, Henry was arrogant and a know-it-all, but he was damn good at his craft. He had enough accolades to warrant his cocky persona. It was no secret that he was a womanizer, and lived a wild life, but I never thought he'd turn on me. He always treated me well, until he didn't."

"What made him change?"

"Once my career took off, Henry became very intrigued with my goals. Me, being a stupid kid, told him about my dreams. I shared secret recipes with him. I told him about my restaurant. I pretty much poured my soul out to him, and he stole my work. He opened a restaurant using my menu without telling me."

My hand flew to my mouth, stifling an involuntary gasp. "He stole your menu?"

"Worse. He even stole the restaurant name."

"You're kidding."

His smile was a quiet reflection of his past regrets. "I wish I was. That place ranked as one of the top five restaurants across the nation that year, and the menu was voted as a top three treasure."

"But it was yours! Did he get in trouble?"

"Nope. There was no way I could prove he stole anything from me. After that, we stopped talking. Yet, we'd unfortunately run into one another at events. That was how Catie met him. When I surpassed him for awards, his resentment toward me grew. Even though it should've been the other way around. It was as if he couldn't deal with the fact that I was winning. He couldn't deal with the fact that I didn't need him either."

"So he slept with your girlfriend."

"Yeah. You know what's funny? When I called him out on it, he told me that she basically threw herself at him. That he had no option to say no to her. Imagine that. This fifty-year-old cocky fucker couldn't help but sleep with the woman I was with."

"What a monster."

"You have no idea."

"Did knowing who Catie slept with make it easier for you to get over her? Do you think it would've been harder if you didn't know?"

"No. If anything, it just cut deeper. Especially since it was with someone I hated."

I stared down at the sidewalk as Feliz walked beside me. "For a while I wished I knew, because then I could get closure, but now that I think about it that wouldn't be closure. It would just be more...hurt."

"Exactly. Sometimes closure is just not giving a damn

anymore." He bit his bottom lip for a second. "Looking back, it's probably the best thing that happened to me. Catie wasn't the one for me. I convinced myself that she had been because she stuck around for a while. After my parents walked out on me, I sadly became a little obsessed with anyone who would stay. What about you?" he questioned, nudging me. "How the heck did you end up with someone like Cole?"

I blew out a cloud of hot smoke. "Truthfully? I think I missed my mom."

"What does that have to do with Cole?"

"Cole lived across the street from us growing up. After my mom passed away, I'd watch him from my window when he'd play with his mom, Lindsay, in their front yard. She was a very hands-on mom throughout all the seasons. From building snowmen in the winter to setting off fireworks during the Fourth of July. I just started wandering over there to join in the activities, and one day, Cole and I were a thing. I don't think I was looking for him, though. I was looking for a mom who made me feel included in the ways my mom used to during each season."

"That oddly makes sense."

"Yeah. By the time Cole and I were in high school, I knew he wasn't the one. Deep in my gut, I saw him shift from his sweet preteen self into someone different. He started becoming popular, and he found the same kind of cockiness that his father had. He started undercutting everything I loved just to get laughter out of others, too."

"Why did you stay?"

I gave a wistful chuckle. "Because if I lost him, I would've lost Lindsay, too. It sounds stupid, but it took me years of abuse to realize that I had to let her go, too. Whenever there was a fight between Cole and I, whenever I was almost ready to let go, she'd pull me back in and convinced me that he loved me. At the end of the day, she'd always be in his corner because she was his mother, not mine. She would always back her son. After the breakup, I tried to remain in contact with her, but it was too hard. She was really pushing for me and Cole to work things out. I haven't spoken to her in a while."

"Does that make you sad?"

A smile touched my lips for a bit before fading as the chill wind brushed against my face. "Yeah, it does."

"It was hard for me to let go of Catie's family. Her parents were amazing. I'm sure they still are, and well, Mandy is fantastic. Letting go of Catie's parents felt cruel because they were always so welcoming to me. I missed them more than I'd ever missed her."

"Exactly."

"Goldie, do you know what you just made me realize?"

"What's that?"

"Sometimes it's just as hard to leave someone as it is to be left behind."

As we walked, we moved beneath a maple tree as a burst of wind fluttered past, shaking a handful of leaves over us. I smiled toward the sky as a few leaves fell against my skin.

"Gosh, I love fall." I blissfully sighed. "When I was a kid, my mom used to gather as many leaves as possible and build a huge pile in the front yard while I was at school. When the school bus pulled up to our house, I'd run from the bus and dive straight into the gigantic pile. She'd join me and make it a big deal every single day until there were no more leaves to dive into."

"She sounds like she was wonderful."

"You have no clue. I'd only had her around for a few years, but I'd give my whole life to have her for a little bit more."

"Can I ask what happened to her?"

My mouth grew slightly dry as I rubbed a hand against my neck. "When she was pregnant with my younger sister Willow, there were complications at birth. She didn't make it."

Alex's eyes showed deep sorrow. "I'm sorry to hear that."

"Yeah. Me too. She was a remarkable woman. If I could be half the mother she was, then I'd be happy."

"You want kids some day?"

"Yes." I nodded. "A litter of them," I semi-joked.

He let out a small smile. "You'd be a good mom."

"You think so?"

"I do. You have patience like no other. Not only did you put up with Feliz, but you put up with my dumbass, too."

"You're right. I'm a saint," I teased. "Do you want kids?"

His brows knitted as he fell into thought. "I do. I just sometimes wonder if that's in my cards. Just because a person wants something doesn't mean it will always happen."

"Yes." I nudged him in the arm. "But we should always expect the unexpected. Good things can happen, too. You just have to believe that after some dark days, there is some kind of light waiting around the corner."

He laughed. "You sound like my great-aunt Teresa. Always so positive."

"If I've learned anything from life it's that it doesn't hurt to hope for better tomorrows. It gives me a little comfort knowing that maybe I have yet to live my best days. The idea that the best is yet to come keeps me on my toes."

"Yara?"

"Yeah?"

"I hope someday I can see it like you."

"See what like me?"

"The world."

CHAPTER 25

Alex

Once Yara and I decided to fake date, she went straight into prep work to spread the news around Honey Creek that she and I were an item. She stood at my kitchen island with a glass of water and said, "The hard launch of our relationship will be at the Fall into Fall Festival."

"Should that mean something to me?"

"Yes, it should. In about a week or so is the festival to launch off autumn in our town. It's also the day of the annual picnic auction to raise money for a small business. This year, it's for my shop, The Pup Around the Corner. The picnic event is called Snack on Hillstack. Essentially, people make picnic baskets, and others bid for a date with the person and their basket on the hilltop. It's a fun event. I need you to show up and bid on my basket."

"This feels very *Gilmore Girls* of this town. Though, I shouldn't be surprised. This whole town is full of small-town crap."

She brushed a curl behind her ear, and somehow I found

that small movement fucking beautiful. "That's the whole point of a small town. Why live in one if it doesn't have hints of cheesiness?" She bent her brows. "Wait, you watched *Gilmore Girls?*"

"I've seen an episode or two," I muttered, not wanting to dive any deeper into my slight obsession. For the record, Team Jess. "How much do I bid on your basket?" I asked, shifting the conversation.

"Uh, however much it takes to outbid Cole. I know he'll show up and be a pain. So if you outbid him, we'll go on our date, and then the town can see us together. It will be our first public outing. But don't worry, Cole is a cheapskate. He never spent over fifty bucks on my basket in the past years. And that was because I'd given him fifty dollars to spend."

"You paid for your own basket?"

"When you say it like that, it sounds depressing."

"That's because it is depressing."

Her smile faltered, and a flash of despair hit her eyes. I'd hit a trigger point.

I cleared my throat. "I didn't mean that in—"

"No," she cut in. "You're right. It is depressing. I did a lot of depressing things when I was with him. All birthday gifts, holiday presents, vacations. I bought and planned them all for myself. All Cole had to do was show up, and when he did, he'd be so mean about it all."

"I've overheard people in town talk about you two and how it seems cruel that you won't give him another chance."

"That's because the people in town don't really know who he is. To them, he's this good guy whose wife left him."

"Why don't you tell them what really happened?"

Her brows furrowed and she fell into thought before shrugging. "I guess a part of me thought he might've stood up for me when people were saying those things. That he'd speak the truth and tell them he was the one who left me long before I brought up the divorce. Maybe not physically, but Cole checked out years before we canceled our I dos."

"I'm sorry you went through that, Goldie."

She smiled shyly, and I realized it wasn't a real smile. It was one she used to cover up her pain. I wanted to question her on it, but she shifted the conversation too quickly. "We can soft launch our fake dating on our walk today," she explained. "If people see us together, they will start to talk. Especially Milly and Mary West."

I grumbled, "The evil twins."

"Yeah. Milly should be getting ready to hit her daily walk within a few minutes. We'll cross paths with her, and by noon, the whole town will know about our budding relationship."

"Your own town's *Gossip Girl*."

Yara's hand flew to her chest. "You know the show *Gossip Girl*?"

I snickered. "I'm not proud of that fact. Teresa was obsessed, and I started watching with her. She got me into *Gilmore Girls*, too."

"The more you talk about Teresa, the more I like her."

"You would've loved her. She would've loved you, too."

Yara smile started in her eyes before spreading down to her lips. "You think so?"

"I know so. Let's get going. But don't mind me if I walk slightly behind you. I have a feeling Feliz might go for my ankles."

"Okay, but the key to making this work is getting the West sisters on our side. So they can spread good news about us being seen together," Yara explained.

"How do I do that?"

"It's easy with those two. You just compliment them, and they will melt into putty for you."

"How can we be certain that will work? Those women have been giving me a hard time for months now."

"Trust me," Yara urged. "It will work. Those women are like moths to a flame when it comes to sugary compliments. They will be easily controlled if you make them swoon."

The walk started with me keeping a strong distance between Feliz and Yara. The closer we drew to Main Street, the more exhausted Feliz grew, which gave me a bit more confidence to walk closer to Yara. And, like clockwork, right outside of The Pup Around the Corner, Milly came powerwalking down the sidewalk.

Her footsteps halted the moment she locked eyes with Yara and me.

She slid off her headphones and arched an eyebrow. "Well, hello there," she said with a bewildered stare.

"Hi, Milly. Good morning." Yara grinned brightly. "Great weather we have today, isn't it? I can smell autumn in the le—"

"What is this?" she asked, gesturing toward Yara and me. "What's going on here?"

"Oh." Yara placed a hand on my chest and smiled at Milly. She was really laying on the charm with the chest touch. That seemed bolder than bold. It also seemed to make a twitch happen within my pants. "Have you met Alex yet? He owns the new restaurant. Alex, this is Milly West."

I nodded and held a hand out toward Milly. "Nice to meet you."

She eyed me up and down, then my hand, and held hers close to her side, not shaking mine. She turned back toward Yara. "You're helping him with his dog?" she asked.

"Yes, and, well…" Yara giggled like a schoolgirl and somehow managed to make herself seem shy as she shrugged. "Alex and I are becoming really good friends."

"Maybe even more than that if I play my cards right," I added with a wink.

Milly gasped. "You?" she questioned, pointing at me. "And you?" she asked, eyes popping out of her head. "A thing?"

THE PROBLEM WITH DATING

Yara grinned and shrugged once more. "Maybe. Like he said, he has to play his cards right." She leaned toward Milly and whispered, "But he has a really good hand if you know what I mean."

"No, I do not know what you mean, Yara Kingsley!" Milly huffed, stunned. "I am a lady and would never understand what you mean."

I began to sniff the air around me and then narrowed my eyes at Milly. "Is that you?"

"Is what me?"

"The thing that smells exceptional." I moved in closer to her and waved my hand from her toward my nose. "My gosh. You smell remarkable. Is it a perfume?"

Milly's whole posture shifted. She grew a bit flustered and her cheeks reddened. "Oh, no. That's just my natural scent."

"It's the best thing I've ever smelled in my life. It pairs well with that breathtaking smile of yours."

She blinked rapidly, taken aback by the unexpected compliment. Her fingers fidgeted at the neckline of her shirt as her knees almost buckled in.

Really? Was she that easy?

"Oh, Alex." She blushed, waving me off. "Stop it." She then looked over toward Yara, completely flustered. "You know, I've heard good things about his restaurant."

"Yes, it's amazing. I actually ate there a few days ago," Yara mentioned.

"Oh, honey, I know. When you were stood up by a gentleman. How embarrassing that must've been for you," Milly said.

My chest tightened as I felt as if I were about to fall deep into a protective mode. "Now listen here, you b—" I started, my voice deep and growling. Yara quickly shoved me in the side. I met her stare and sighed. I could almost read her mind. *Be nice, Alex.* "You beautiful woman…I'd love for you to come into Isla

Iberia for a free meal some time. I'll give you the best table in the house."

"Yes, well. I would appreciate that. I'd love to bring my sister, Mary, too. Did you know there're two of us?"

"I did. Double trouble," I remarked, wanting to stab my eyes out for being nice to the evil twins. "I'll make sure she has a seat, too."

"Well, aren't you sweet? He's sweet, Yara," Milly sang.

"Like a fresh cinnamon roll on a Sunday morning," Yara agreed.

Milly narrowed her eyes as she glanced between us, determining what to make of the situation. She then waved us off. "I must get back to my workout. I can't let my heart rate drop too low. I can't lose this figure."

"And what a figure it is," I said, whistling low.

She giggled like a child as her face turned the color of a tomato. "Oh, Alex. You and your charm. You kids have a good day. And thanks again, Alex, for the praise. Your mother must've raised you right."

If only she knew how wrong she was.

As she continued on her walk, we witnessed her pull out her cell phone and make a call. "Hey, Mary, it's Milly. You won't believe who I've just run into. Yara Kingsley was seen with Alex Ramírez. You know that man you called a shit? Yes, him! And they're an item! I couldn't believe it either. Anyway, we have reservations at his restaurant soon. He's actually a pretty nice guy. You should apologize for what you did to him. Shame on you, Mary. He's quite handsome, too."

"And that is how we get Gossip Girl going through this town," Yara cheered with victory.

"Spotted outside of The Pup Around the Corner. Could it be that opposites truly did attract? You know what they say: every black cat needs a golden retriever. Will these two blossom into something more, or will their leaves rot and drift away? Only time will tell. XoXo."

Yara's jaw dropped. "Did you just Gossip Girl our fake relationship?"

"I might've Gossip Girl'd our fake relationship."

"Oh my gosh!" She shoved my arm. "All this time, I thought you were dark, cool, and mysterious, but you were secretly corny."

"I'm not corny," I grumbled, pushing out a grimace. "I'm mean and hard and tough."

"You're corn-on-a-cob corny."

"Whatever. I'm going to work. I'll see you later for the walk home."

"Okay, my corny black cat."

She said "my" as if I were hers.

I didn't hate that idea. Why didn't I hate that idea?

"Shut up, Yara," I told her with a huff and puff.

"Never." She kept smiling, and I kept falling. She had to stop that at some point. Being so…perfect. "What were you going to call Milly? When she mentioned me being stood up? A butthead?"

"I was actually thinking of a stronger B word."

CHAPTER 26

Yara

The rumors of Alex spread just as quickly as I'd hoped. Unfortunately, individuals from my past also heard said rumors, which meant I had to face a few shadows from my previous life.

The hardest part about being a people pleaser was that you oftentimes forgot to please yourself. You placed every person in front of you. If someone had a cart filled with groceries, you let them skip you in line, even though you only had bananas to purchase. You scrunched yourself into a ball to take up as little space as possible because you didn't want others to feel your presence too much.

You spread yourself so thin, trying to make space for everyone around you, trying to feed their spirits, that you forget to nourish your own. Then, if you did do something for yourself, you'd drop the ball with someone else and that was when good ole guilt would taunt you.

Guilt was an odd sensation. It appeared when you least expected it, too. On my afternoon shopping trip at the grocery

THE PROBLEM WITH DATING

store, I heard my name called out, and I turned to find Lindsay Parker standing there with a bag full of goodies.

I pushed out a smile and walked over to hug her. "Hi, Lindsay. How are you?"

Her eyes glassed over as she wrapped her arms around me. "Oh, sweetheart. I haven't seen you in so long."

There it was—the punch to my heart. Guilt.

I shifted around in my shoes. "I know. Things have been busy with the shop. I meant to call but—"

She frowned as she pulled away, wiping away the falling tears. "But since you've divorced my son, the need isn't there. I get it."

"That's not it, Lindsay," I urged.

"You know, it broke my heart when I found out you and Cole were divorcing. I was sad for my son, but I also worried this would happen. That I'd lose my daughter, too. You've been in my life for decades, Yara, and now you can't even call?"

"Lindsay, I—"

"I don't want your excuses," she warned. "I just want you to know that hurt me deeply. I always looked at you as family and thought you'd the same. But it's clear that you didn't feel the same for me as I did you. The same goes for how you felt about Cole. It was all fake."

My chest felt as if it would explode from how hard my heart pounded. "That's not fair, Lindsay."

"Maybe it's not, but is it really fair that you won't give him another try?"

"I gave that man more tries than I should've ever given him."

She nodded in agreement. "Yes, you did. I know this well. I know my son, Yara. I know how hard he can be. He's like his father. Hard and complicated. But I know he'd never physically hurt you. Doesn't that count for something?"

My eyes narrowed. "That shouldn't be the reason I stayed, Lindsay, because he didn't hurt me physically. He hurt me in every other possible way." Lindsay stared at me as if I were insane. I knew exactly why, too. Because she was right about her husband—he was just like Cole. Cold. Distant. Mean. Yet unlike me, Lindsay stayed.

I'd heard her cry to me over the years about how hard things were at home. I'd watched her suffer at the hands of a man who didn't love her right. I'd witnessed her light begin to diminish after he crushed her spirit time and time again. She became a shell of the vibrant woman she'd once been.

She didn't know it, but she was one of the true reasons why I found the courage to walk away. When I saw Cole growing more and more like his father, I took that as a warning sign. I saw the warning that was right before me. I didn't want to become like Lindsay Parker. I didn't want my next thirty years to become like hers. I didn't want to fall so deeply into the belief that a man was good for you as long as he didn't strike you.

No.

I wanted love.

I wanted warmth.

I wanted not to walk on eggshells when I came home because I didn't know which version of my husband would come through the front door that night.

I wanted to be free from the chains that had somehow slipped around my ankles without me knowing it. I wanted to breathe again.

Still, to this day, Cole tried to suffocate me. Even speaking to Lindsay felt like a pillow over my mouth, ordering me to return to the places that once shattered me.

"He's in therapy," she told me. "He's working on himself, Yara."

"That's good, Lindsay. I'm glad."

"Do you think there's ever a chance—"

"No." I shook my head. "There's not. I closed that chapter of my life."

Her small, fatigued body trembled slightly. "Yes, I understand. You closed not only his door, but mine, too. And here I am taking care of Cocoa for you every few days because that's what family does. We help each other."

I arched an eyebrow. "What do you mean you're taking care of Cocoa? Cole is responsible for her, not you."

"You know he'd forget to feed her and walk her with his schedule. So he drops her to me every time. I don't mind. It's my job to take care of him and that involves Cocoa."

"No," I stated, shaking my head. "That's not your job. And I'd rather Cocoa stay with me all the time than with you. The whole point of the dog swap was because I thought Cole missed her."

"Don't try to take this from me, too, Yara," Lindsay warned. "That dog is the closest thing I have to a grandbaby since you seemed too busy to give me one of those."

More guilt. Piles and piles of heaviness that weren't mine to carry.

I bit my tongue so I wouldn't say something cruel even though many words shot through my brain.

Lindsay shifted her bags in her arms and stood taller. "I hope you can live with the choices you made, Yara. I hope you can face the fact that you didn't only break my son's heart but you shattered mine, too."

That guilt punch landed straight against my heart and bruised my soul. I wondered how many people carried bruises to their soul that were never theirs to withstand?

It felt unfair that I was supposed to feel guilty for the sins of another's actions. It wasn't right that I was left gasping for air when Cole was the one who almost completely choked the life from my lungs.

* * *

"You and Alex Ramírez?" Cole asked as we stood in the dog park to exchange Cocoa the evening after Alex and I soft-launched our relationship. After Cole's mother left me feeling like complete crap. "Are you kidding me, Yara?"

"We shouldn't talk about this, Cole," I replied, secretly happy that he'd found out. I wanted him to realize that I was moving on, so he'd finally back off. I needed him to know that we would not get back together. After my exchange with Lindsay, I knew it was extremely important for it to be clear that the chapter of my life with the Parkers was over. A part of me even wanted to fight with him about Cocoa, but I knew his outburst was more than I wanted to deal with after a somewhat heavy afternoon.

"Was he the one whose sweats you were wearing?" he questioned.

"Cole—"

"I'm not intimidated by him, Yar. If you're just doing it to get back at me—"

"I'm not," I told him, taking Cocoa's leash from his grip. "And anything going on between Alex and me is our private business. You don't get an invite to our life."

"'Our life?' So what? The two of you are an *our* now? Since when?"

"Long enough for it to matter."

"How so? The other day, you were going on a date with Josh. How is this real with Alex?"

I knew there wasn't a good way to explain it, so I did the only thing I could think to do. I lied, lied, lied. "Things with Alex and me started off as friends with benefits, and then we transitioned into something more, okay, Cole? Is that what you wanted to hear? Feelings developed, and neither of us realized it until after the Josh situation happened." I smiled sweetly at him. "I guess I can thank you for that. If you hadn't tell Josh not to date me, then I would've never realized my feelings for Alex."

Cole's face was deep red as the anger built within him. His

nostrils flared as his hands formed fists. "Out of all people, you'd pick someone like him? He's a cocky ass who thinks he can get away with whatever he wants."

"You have no clue who he is. And I've only dated one jerk in my life. I left that chapter behind me. Now, if you'll excuse me, I have a date tonight."

"A date? You're just going to leave Cocoa alone at your place? Some mother you are."

His voice felt like pins and needles against my skin. "Says the man who drops her off at his mother's house every single time we exchange."

The shock in his eyes showed his guilt. "Listen—"

"I don't care. I don't want to hear your lies and excuses. Goodbye, Cole."

I walked off before he could reply, but I could feel his aggression with every step I took. As I walked home, I felt as if a slight weight had been lifted from my shoulders.

CHAPTER 27

Yara

From my point of view, Alex's and my fake relationship was off to a great start. During my walks with him and Feliz, we'd be stopped time and time again by townspeople. They'd engage in conversations with the two of us, and I gladly chatted away. It was often just small talk. Nothing massive. Just simple mindless chatter.

I slowly started noticing the shift in Alex, though, every time a conversation took place. His scowls deepened whenever someone would ask him how he'd been, or mention the weather, or bring up sports. The wrinkles in his forehead intensified as his eyes narrowed in irritation.

When Tim from the local bank asked Alex if he was going to open an account soon and offered some deals, Alex stared him straight in his eyes and said, "I can't do this shit." He proceeded to walk away, stomping his feet the whole time as he turned the corner, leaving Tim and I dazed and confused.

"He's kind of cranky, huh?" Tim asked, stunned by my fake boyfriend's abrupt exit.

THE PROBLEM WITH DATING

I pushed out a smile. "Sorry, Tim. We'll catch up later, okay?"

I hurried around the corner with Feliz to find an ill-tempered Alex, raking his hands through his hair.

"What the heck was that?" I asked.

He turned toward me with a look of defeat. "I can't do this."

"Can't do what?"

"This whole fake dating thing. I'm not built for this, Yara."

I lowered my brows, bewildered. "I'm sorry...did I miss something? Is there a problem?"

"Yes!" he exclaimed, throwing his hands up in frustration. "There's a huge fucking problem."

"With?"

"*You!*" he blurted out.

My chest tightened. I stood straighter. "There's a problem with me?"

"No." he shook his head and sighed. He gestured toward me. "There's nothing wrong with you."

"Oh. Okay. Cool." I let out a sigh, somewhat relieved. That was until he continued speaking.

"There's a problem with *dating* you," he said.

"Uh, I don't know if I should be offended by this or—"

"No, don't be. I'm explaining it wrong." He grumbled a little and pinched the bridge of his nose as he tried to gather his thoughts. "The problem with dating is *you*."

"Okay. Definitely offended now."

"No." He stepped closer and crossed his arms. "The problem with dating *you* is that you're dating *me*."

"If you're trying to confuse me, Alex, it's working."

"You don't get it. You're a good person, Yara."

That soothed my wounds a little. "Okay?" I questioned, still utterly confused.

"You're so good that you can do this thing with people that I can't fucking do."

"And what's that?"

233

"Small talk," he groaned. "I hate small talk, and people in this town love to small talk with you. Now that we are together in this fake relationship, people expect me to small talk back to them like you would! Even when I'm not with you!"

I chuckled a little as my anxiety eased. It turned out my black cat was simply being a black cat. "You hate small talk," I said, understanding a bit more.

"I despise it. Loathed it. And now people are looking at me on the street and smiling. They are telling me about their lives. I don't care about their lives, Yara! Did you know Harrison from the bakery just pulled his grandson's tooth out with pliers? Well, I do! Because he caught me on the street the other day and told me all about little Ryan and his fucking tooth! *Fuck little Ryan and his fucking tooth!*"

I couldn't contain my laughing fit as Alex proceeded to flip out.

"Stop laughing," he muttered, kicking his feet in a huff. "It's not funny."

"It's a little funny."

"Yara," he urged. "I can't be your fake boyfriend if it means I have to be like you."

"Okay," I agreed. "Then don't."

He arched an eyebrow. "What?"

"Don't be like me. Be exactly who you are. Don't do the small talk. Walk away whenever someone bothers you. Don't engage. Growl at people for all I care."

"But people might talk about you dating an asshole."

I shrugged. "They were already talking about me, anyway, since the divorce. Let's give them something juicy to talk about. Besides, the whole point of the fake dating was to get Cole off my back. You don't have to make friends because of me."

He grumbled a little more. "I don't?"

"No, silly. Just be your cute, grumpy self. It works for you.

Besides, maybe with your grumpiness, people will stop telling me so much about their lives, too."

He narrowed his eyes and whispered. "Do you secretly hate small talk, too?"

"Oh, yes. I despise it," I whispered back, stepping closer. "So be exactly who you are, Alex. I like you that way."

He huffed and puffed and grimaced with comfort. "Good. As long as we're on the same page. Now, let's get back to the apartments before anyone else sees us coming."

* * *

THE NIGHT before the Fall into Fall Festival, I made a plan to introduce Cocoa and Feliz. It would be the first night the two dogs would be meeting one another. I was nervous about introducing the two, but unlike mine and Alex's and my not-so-meet-cute, Feliz and Cocoa darted around my apartment as if they'd been friends from day one.

I almost cried seeing their interactions because Feliz was turning into a completely different dog right before my eyes. On the first day I had him at the day care, the first day he wouldn't go near other dogs. Slowly, though, he began to open up little by little. Piece by piece.

I felt as if his owner was doing the same thing with me. Giving me a little more each day. Piece by piece.

By midnight, the two cuddled together, sleeping as if they were brother and sister.

Around one in the morning, there was a knock on my door. I stood to answer to find an exhausted-looking Alex with containers in his hands. "Hey, Goldie."

"Hey, you." I stepped to the side to let him in.

He came inside and glanced at the two sleeping dogs. "Did my Cujo make a new friend?"

"To say the least. She's the peanut butter to his jelly, it appears."

"Sorry I'm late. I ended up cooking after the restaurant shut down for the night." He moved to the dining room table and set down the containers. "I made you dinner. Based on your love for Ritz crackers with cream cheese, I figured you'd only have some box mac and cheese or ramen noodles."

"You made me dinner?"

"Yeah. And don't say you're not hungry because if you stay awake past midnight, you've earned a second dinner."

"I told Cole you'd make me dinner. I mean, I was lying just to get him off my back, but I didn't think you'd…" My heartbeats raced faster and faster. My Cujo made me dinner. "That's really nice, Alex."

"Don't cry, Goldie. Just get two plates, will you?"

He was learning me so well that he knew when I was on the brink of tears. I did as I was told and grabbed a few plates. "Wine?" I asked. "I have some cheap bottles in my cabinet."

"I brought a bottle, too, from work. Sit. I'll serve you."

I'll serve you.

I didn't think he meant for those words to turn me on slightly, but alas. Turned on, I was.

I took my seat, and my stomach instantly rumbled as he took the lids off the food. Second dinner was *definitely* a thing when it came to Alex's food. I wished this could be a tradition from here on out.

He made my plate and set it in front of me. "Honey glazed chicken and a kale brussels sprout salad. For dessert, a birthday cake," he explained.

I giggled a little. "A birthday cake? That seems random."

"It's not that random, seeing as how it's my birthday. Well, was, up until an hour ago."

I slammed my hands against the table. "Wait, what?! It's your birthday?!"

THE PROBLEM WITH DATING

"Was," he corrected. "An hour ago."

"Alex! Why didn't you tell me! I would've made you a cake. I would've gotten balloons. I would've—"

"Done too much, yes. That's why I didn't tell you. You seem like the type of person who loves birthdays."

"Uh, yeah. That's because they're birthdays. Birthdays are a big deal."

"They're just days."

"They're important days."

He shrugged. "Not to me. My great-aunt always made them a big deal, too. She always went over-the-top."

"How old are you?"

"Thirty-five."

"*Thirty-five?*" I blurted out, almost shouting as I tossed my hands in the air in shock. The dogs stirred from my shout but went back to sleep quickly. Their cuddle fest must've been a good one. "Your thirty-fifth birthday is today, Alex, and you didn't tell me?!"

"Yesterday, if you want to be technical."

"I don't want to be technical. Oh my goodness, it's your birthday. It's your birthday, and you cooked me dinner. Everything about this situation is wrong. I should be making you mac and cheese and ramen."

He smiled, made his plate, and sat beside me. "I wouldn't eat your ramen, Yara."

"I bet you would. You see, the trick is draining the water slightly and adding a slice of American cheese and—oh my gosh you're thirty-five! Thirty-five is a big birthday, Alex."

He laughed. "To who?"

"To me! Every birthday is a big birthday. Even half birthdays are big birthdays to me."

"Eat," he urged. I didn't. He picked up my fork, sliced my chicken, and shoved it into my mouth. "Eat," he ordered.

I chewed. I moaned. I swallowed.

"That is…" I moaned some more as I shoved more food into my mouth. "I want to make love to this food," I said with a stuffed mouth. How did he do that? How did he cook like this?

Alex sat back in his chair, pleased. "And that is the best birthday present you could've given me."

I pouted. "It makes me sad that I don't have a gift for you."

"It makes me sad that that would make you sad. It's not a big deal."

We spent the next few hours discussing our fake dating, drinking wine, and eating cake. The best cake I'd ever had in my life, mind you.

"My basket at the festival will seem very underrated compared to this meal," I said as I stood to clean up the mess. Alex placed his hand against mine and stopped me.

"I'll clean it up. You relax." I went to argue, but he stopped me. "It's my birthday wish."

I laughed. "To clean up after me?"

"To take care of you."

His hand was still against mine and the flutters in my stomach intensified within me. "Alex?"

"Yes?"

"I think you're a better fake boyfriend than most real boyfriends."

"I aim to please," he joked, picking up my plate. He leaned in closer, brushing his face slightly against mine as he whispered in my ear, "And just so you know. I can't wait to eat everything in your picnic basket tomorrow."

And just like that, I realized it to be true.

I had a crush on Alex Ramírez.

Crap.

CHAPTER 28

Yara

The following afternoon, Main Street was in a frenzy with the excitement of the festival. I could smell corn roasting as tents were set up for all the different vendors in town.

Keri helped close the shop early, so we could all celebrate the start of autumn in our town. Fall was in the air, and I couldn't help but feel as if I was stepping into the next season of my life.

"So are the rumors true about you and Alex?" Keri asked as I stepped outside with my picnic basket in my hands. She had her own smaller basket, which she was putting up for auction, too.

"It seems we are…something," I stated. I didn't even think that was a lie. No matter what, I felt some odd pull toward Alex. Something about him as of late only made me want to discover more. What was his favorite holiday? Did he like road trips? If he could travel anywhere in the world, where would he go? Did he feel the feelings I'd been feeling, too?

That last question was the one I was most interested in getting to know.

"I think this is great, Yara! I know your past relationship was hard on you, and you deserve a happy ending. Things with Cole didn't seem the best."

"They weren't," I agreed. "I'm just happy to be in a better place."

"Yeah. It seems he's looking to move on, too, right?" she asked.

I huffed out laughter. "Cole? Yeah, right. He's still oddly convinced we're getting back together."

"Really? I heard he was seeing someone..." Her words faded off and she shook her head. "But those were just rumors. You know how this town is. Gossip and hearsay."

"Yeah, I do. But if he is seeing someone else, I pray for her. Because just a few hours ago, he was trying to get back with me. It was clear he was pretty jealous of the Alex situation, too."

"Men," Keri said, rolling her eyes. "You can't live with them, but you *can* live without them."

"I like to think that not all of them are as bad as Cole. Some actually seem..." I glanced across the street toward Alex, who was walking out of his restaurant at the same time. "Sweet."

Keri nudged my arm. "Oh my gosh, you're smitten with him, aren't you?"

"What? No. I'm just...he's just..." I smiled at Keri and sighed. "Have fun with the auction today, okay?"

She held up her basket. "My first ever Snack on Hillstack. Hopefully, I can help raise some good money for the shop with some store-bought pasta salad and ham sandwiches," she joked.

"Are you kidding me? Men will be pushing one another over to get that basket of yours." I knew that for a fact, too. Keri was a young, beautiful girl. She'd just turned twenty-three not that long ago, and it was no secret that the men were into her. Guys stopped into our store without a dog in tow just to speak with her. It didn't hurt that she was also one of the sweetest women

THE PROBLEM WITH DATING

in town. If there was ever an issue, Keri was willing to step up and help out, no matter what.

"Fingers crossed," she said. "Now, I'll stop bothering you and let you go get your man."

She waved goodbye as she walked off to join the others preparing for the picnic auction. Before I could make my way over to Alex, another arm looped around mine and tugged me in the opposite direction.

"What in the hallelujah is going on?!" Avery barked my way, almost yanking my arm from its socket. "Why am I hearing around the streets that you and Alex Ramírez are a thing?!"

Oh yeah.

I forgot to tell my sisters.

If Willow wasn't off with Snake Bite or whatever his name was, I was certain she'd have some choice words for me, too.

"I forgot to—" I started, but she cut me off.

"Yara Zuri Kingsley, do not tell me you forgot to mention that you have been seeing that man! I will disown you as my sister if you tell me that."

"Fine, fine. I won't. But it all happened very quickly, and I didn't get a chance to tell you that Alex and I are dating."

"Bull crap. You're not dating him."

"I am. We are *totally* a thing."

She narrowed her eyes and pointed a stern finger at me. "You're lying!"

"What?" I snickered and shook my head. "I am not."

"You are. When you lie, your nose scrunches up."

"No, it doesn't," I said, working hard to hold my nose still.

"There! You did it again! Out with it. The real truth."

I groaned, knowing I wouldn't be able to pull a fast one on Avery. The rest of the town? Sure. My big sister? Not so much. "Cole was giving me a hard time, and I convinced Alex to be my fake boyfriend to ward off Cole in exchange for my services."

"Oh my goodness," Avery cried out, her jaw dropping open. "My sister's a hooker."

"What?! No, I'm not!"

"You said you're giving him your services! If that's not a come to mama, spread one's legs kind of thing, then I don't know what is."

"My dog services, you weirdo."

Avery arched an eyebrow. "Is that some kind of kink thing? You mean doggy style?"

"No! I mean, I'm helping him train Feliz—"

"Is that the name for his penis?"

"Avery!"

"Okay, okay, you're not a hooker. Continue."

"I'm training his recently adopted dog, Feliz, and in exchange, he's pretending to be my boyfriend."

Avery's brows lowered. "So it's not real?"

I shook my head. "As fake as a relationship could ever be." *I think. Maybe.*

A sigh rumbled through her lips. "Good. Because if you were in a real relationship, and I heard it through the grapevine of Mary West, we would've had some real hard-core issues between us, sister. I'm still a bit annoyed that I didn't hear about the fake relationship from you, though."

"Don't worry. The next time I get a pretend boyfriend, you'll be the first to know." I gestured toward her basket. "You're taking part in the auction this year? You never do it."

"Uh, yeah, because it's dehumanizing to have women stand on a stage and be auctioned off to men."

"Careful, you're sounding a bit like Willow," I teased.

"Sometimes that girl is right. Bizarre, but right. Anyway, for some reason, Wesley wanted me to do it this year. So whatever. Plus, it kind of reminds me of Mama, and I've been missing her lately with the whole engagement thing. Sitting at Hillstack with Wesley seems sort of cute, seeing as how that's where Mama and Daddy met."

"That is cute."

She rolled her eyes. "Whatever. It's stupid."

"It's not stupid. I think it's sweet. And it's a beautiful ring. Mama would've loved it."

"Listen, I don't like crying, so I'm going to walk away. Besides, your fake boyfriend is on his way over, and from the way he's looking at you, you might want to remind him that this is a fake relationship."

I glanced over my shoulder to see Alex approaching. He wore a plain white T-shirt and blue jeans, looking as good as he always had. The closer he drew, the more those honey, cocoa butter, and oak tree scents were revealed. Gosh, I loved how he smelled.

"Introduce me," Avery whispered the closer he drew.

"What?" I asked, a bit awestruck with Alex coming my way.

Avery grumbled, stepped in front of me, and shot Alex her a cold look. "I'm Avery, Yara's older sister."

Alex smiled slightly and held a hand toward her. "I'm Alex, her—"

"Fake boyfriend, yeah, I know." She shook his hand and held on a little too tight. "But I think you still need to hear me and hear me clearly. If you break my sister's heart, real or fake, I will shatter your kneecaps."

Alex started to laugh until he saw the serious look in her eyes. He then looked toward me. "She's kidding, right?"

I shrugged. "She's really good with baseball bats and has impeccable swings."

Alex swallowed hard and then turned back to Avery. "I promise I'll take care of her."

Avery dropped her hold of his hand and huffed. "I almost believe you." She glanced at his biceps and wrapped her hand around them. "Impressive build. What are you squatting?"

"Avery," I scolded.

"What? I just want to know if I'm stronger than him," she replied. I gave her a look that told her to behave, and she dropped her hold on Alex's arm. "Fine, fine. I'm leaving. But remember, I have my eye on you," she told him.

"I wouldn't expect anything less," he said.

She began walking away and gestured toward the two of us. "I have to admit. For something made up, y'all kind of look cute together."

"It's all her," Alex mentioned. "And it seems those good looks run in the family."

"Flattery only works on the West twins, Ramírez," Avery said. "If you want to impress me, tell me how much you bench."

"Goodbye, Ave!" I shouted, snickering to myself, because I knew she was telling the truth. One of Avery's favorite pastimes was outlifting men.

The second she was out of sight, Alex shook off his whole body. "She sure knows how to make a man nervous."

"She'd be happy to know that fact."

"Is your other sister as intimidating as her?" he asked.

"Oh no, but she might try to get you to eat bugs or something weird. Or join a cult. It's a tossup with her."

"Why do I get the feeling that the Kingsley sisters are a handful?"

"We are complex characters, to say the least." I held my picnic basket in the air. "Are you ready to pick me?"

"I was made for this moment. Shall we?" he asked, holding his hand out toward me. "I figured if we walked into the festival holding hands, it might add some drama."

My mind went into a frenzy as I held his hand. His touch had a way of warming my whole body as the cool air of September rippled across my skin. I missed that. I missed holding someone's hand. I couldn't even remember the last time I held someone's hand. Cole never liked to hold hands or display any kind of PDA at all. I was fine with it, mainly because I was fine with anything he did. It was his way or the highway, and I lost so many things about me that I actually enjoyed.

Like holding hands.

I liked that feeling.

No.

I *loved* that feeling.

I loved the feeling of being connected to someone, as if I didn't know where my touch began and where his ended. As if we were one connection, moving in sync.

Before we started to walk, Alex released his hold so he could move to the other side of me, took the basket out of my grip, and then he took my hand once more. He was making sure I walked on the inside of the sidewalk.

And at that moment, before the noise of the festival filled my ears, I quietly, gently, unapologetically began to fall for the man who was only supposed to be pretend.

Pretend.

Wait.

What if he was just pretending? What if his actions weren't his own, but just a script he'd developed in his head to make this arrangement of ours seem real to everyone else around us?

Stop falling, heart, I ordered to myself. *This isn't real.*

The Prince Charming I made Alex out to be was exactly that—a fairy tale. A made-up story filled with fables. Still, a part of me that wondered what it would be like if it were real. Would his touch still heat me the way it had? Would he still want to hold my hand? Would he bid on my basket, even if I didn't request him to do so?

Yes, he would, my heart told me.

Stupid heart and how it felt.

Beautiful heart and how it felt.

"Goldie," Alex whispered, burying himself closer to me the more we approached to the crowd. So close that if I moved an inch closer, our chests would be brushing. His proximity to me felt wrong in the most righteous of ways.

"Yes?" I breathed out, almost forgetting that we were in public.

His mouth brushed against my cheek, and he kissed it gently, allowing his lips to linger against my skin. The feel of his lips sent my whole world into a tailspin of emotions. His kiss was so soft, so intimate, that I almost turned my head slightly to place my mouth against his.

"This will be easy," he softly spoke, his voice deep and authoritative as his mouth moved to the edge of my ear. "If he regrets losing you already, I swear to you, he'll regret losing you forever after the way he sees me worship you," Alex whispered, his mouth now sitting at the edge of my earlobe, which he gently kissed and sucked before pulling away.

I froze in place, my mind flipping upside down as my body tried to decipher the words that fell from Alex's lips. I mentally tried to unpack the sucking of the earlobe.

We were fake. There was no getting around that, but that moment? The tenderness he'd delivered to me? That felt real. It had to be real. It had to be—

Someone cleared their throat.

I looked up to see Cole standing in front of us.

My heart sank slightly as I crashed back down to reality.

Fake. The kisses, the intimacy, the closeness. It was fake. A show for Cole, who Alex must've witnessed approaching. It was fine because that was exactly what I wanted Alex to do—perform. I just didn't expect him to be such a fantastic leading actor. *Somebody give that fucker an Oscar.*

Stupid heart and how it felt.

Sensitive heart and how it felt.

Cole looked right past Alex and straight at me as he puffed out his chest. He stepped forward and grabbed my arm. "We need to talk, Yara," he demanded.

THE PROBLEM WITH DATING

I ripped my arm away from his. "No, we don't. And I'm late. I have to get to the auction." I went to grab the basket from Alex. I forced out a smile, even though my mind was still dizzy. "Thanks for walking me. I'll see you in the audience."

Alex nodded and stared at me with such intense eyes, it was as if he were asking if I was okay.

I nodded back.

I'm fine, Alex. Just a little dizzy from you and your lips.

"I said we need to talk, now," Cole urged, taking hold of me once more, this time tighter.

"Ouch!" I yipped.

That sound was enough to have Alex step between Cole and me. He shoved him backward, and Cole almost lost his footing.

"Watch it," Alex growled, the bass in his voice rumbling through his gritted teeth.

"Who do you think you are?" Cole fought back, not backing down, even though he sat quite a few inches below Alex. And as stated before, three inches could make quite a difference.

"I'm the guy telling you to back off," Alex sternly stated. "Touch my girl again, and I'll break your jaw."

My girl.

Oh, I was screwed.

"You're really threatening an officer?" Cole scolded, his nostrils flaring as he stepped closer to Alex. They looked like two gorillas who were seconds away from pounding their freaking chests.

"No threats, just promises," Alex replied.

"Okay, I think that's enough testosterone for one conversation. Alex, it's okay. Thank you, but it's okay." I grabbed his arm to pull him back. He didn't budge, though. He kept his strong stance as he stared at Cole with hatred in his eyes. Was that fake, too? I tugged on his arm again. "You can go," I told him. Still, no forward movement. Cole didn't falter, either.

"Alex," I begged, standing on my tiptoes. I brushed my lips

against his ear and whispered, "Please." His eyes shut as my touch met his skin. I felt his whole body relax against me, and when his eyes opened, they were softened. The aggression he held for Cole dissipated when he turned to look at me.

I placed a hand on his cheek and smiled. "There he is," I whispered.

He seemed disoriented but brushed his hand against his chin. "I'll see you at the auction."

"Sounds good," he agreed.

Right as he was about to step away from me, Cole called out, "Yeah, be a good puppy and scurry away."

Alex didn't turn to face Cole. Instead, he wrapped his arm around my waist and pulled me in closer to him. His chest pressed against mine, and he tilted my chin up with his free hand. His eyes locked with mine, a stare packed with anticipation and want and need and—he kissed me.

My eyes closed as his lips found mine. I pressed my body into the palm of his hand holding me up, knowing that if he pulled away, I'd melt into a pile of nothingness. He kissed me with all he had. Every inch of his existence finding its home against my lips. I became drunk on him, on his kiss, on his touches, on every piece of him. He might've been the town's poison, but he was my remedy. My favorite black cat.

I kissed him back, slowly parting his mouth with my tongue. He kissed me deeper, not leaving space for us to take in more breaths, but somehow his mouth had become my lifeline. My body was in heat as his hand massaged my lower back. I wanted him. I wanted his taste for the remainder of the day, well into nightfall, too. I felt dizzy and whole at the same time. Alex gently nibbled on my bottom lip for a moment before pulling away from me. He planted a soft peck against my mouth one last time.

Whoa.

Was that what kissing was?

Oh my goodness.

It was pretty humbling to realize at the ripe age of thirty that you'd never actually been kissed before. That exchange wasn't just Alex's mouth touching mine. No. That was fireworks erupting all throughout my body. I felt that kiss vibrate all the way to the tips of my toes.

"I'll see you soon," he said before smacking my behind and walking past Cole. If that wasn't the greatest mic drop, then I didn't know what was.

CHAPTER 29

Alex

Yara Kingsley and her lips.

I'd be lying if I said I hadn't been dreaming about what that woman tasted like for a while. Cole just gave me the perfect opportunity to find out. My mind stayed trapped at that moment as I stood in the crowd forming around the clock tower on Main Street where the auction was taking place.

I was ready to spend as much as I needed to in order to get that basket from Yara. I watched the whole process unfold with a few of the women who went before Yara. Tatiana, of course, was the hostess with the mostest as she spoke to the crowd and auctioned off each basket.

The women posed on stage with their creations, and the crowd started the bidding off low. A few fifty dollars here, a few one hundred dollars there. After about fifteen baskets were sold, Avery was up for auction. I had to admit, a picnic date with her would've scared me because there was a solid chance it would come with a black eye. Nothing about Avery Kingsley read soft,

THE PROBLEM WITH DATING

like Yara. She was hard, stern, and moody. Kind of like me, I supposed. She must've been the Kingsleys' black cat.

Avery sat on the barstool in the middle of the stage, holding her basket in her lap. As Tatiana introduced her, Avery reached for the mic and said, "Just so you know, I think this whole thing is predated and a bit dehumanizing, but happy autumn. Support your local dog spa and start making good on the late payments you owe my sister, you dic—"

"Okayyy, thank you, Avery." Tatiana smiled as she yanked the microphone back and gestured toward Avery. "Let's hear it for Avery! She has this cute basket with a yellow ribbon, waiting for the perfect companion to share it with on the hill tonight while watching the fireworks display. Let's start the bidding process at fifty dollars."

"Five hundred," a gentleman called out, getting a bit of applause from the crowd. He winked at Avery, and she grew a bit bashful, which seemed not to be her norm. He must've been the guy who'd put that massive ring on her finger.

He walked up confidently to claim his basket, when all of a sudden, another voice echoed in the crowd. "One thousand."

I turned to see Nathan Pierce standing with his arms crossed over his broad chest. He wore a backward baseball cap and a smirk that made Avery's eyes widen in surprise.

The first bidder cleared his throat and stood up taller. "One thousand five hundred."

"One thousand seven hundred," Nathan countered.

Sweat started to form at the brim of the guy's forehead as he wiped his hand against the back of his neck. He then held his hand up. "Two thousand."

Before Nathan could reply, which he was ready to do, Avery snatched the microphone from Tatiana and shouted, "Sold to Wesley for two thousand dollars!" She then hurried off stage and ran straight into her fiancé's arms.

The look on Nathan's face felt heavy. He and Avery clearly

had some kind of connection, though I wasn't sure what it had been. I couldn't help but want to question Yara on the topic later on—after I won her picnic basket.

Yara walked on stage, being the last basket of the afternoon to be auctioned off. Tatiana introduced her and spoke about The Pup Around the Corner, giving a speech about the shop's history and how Yara stepped up when the previous owner passed away. Yara must not have liked all eyes on her because I noticed how she fidgeted with her nails and such as Tatiana praised her name.

Out of the corner of my eye, I noticed Cole walking up beside me, determined to outbid me. He shot me a cold look, but I ignored it. I kept my eyes on the prize. I kept my eyes on her.

When she darted her gaze through the crowd, her brown stare found mine. I smiled a little. She made me do that a lot lately—smile.

"I think for such a special lady, for such a special basket, we should start the bidding around two hundred dollars, shall we?" Tatiana said.

Cole's hand started to fly up to bid, but I spoke loudly and boldly before he could. "Twenty thousand."

Everyone gasped from shock, and I was almost certain I'd heard Yara mutter her first bad word.

She grabbed the microphone from Tatiana. "He didn't mean that, everyone, don't worry."

"I meant that," I corrected. Cole's hand dropped swiftly, a clear sign he wasn't going to debate me at all. "Twenty thousand dollars."

Before Yara could speak again, Tatiana grabbed the microphone and said, "Sold, to the handsome gentleman with the best empanadas in town."

"Oh my goodness, what's wrong with you?" Yara shouted as her eyes bugged out of her head. Her shock was more than

THE PROBLEM WITH DATING

enough to make every dollar worth it. Little did she know, I was ready to spend fifty thousand. Each year, I made it a mission to donate to a good cause, and I couldn't think of a better one than Yara. Plus, the defeated look on Cole's face was enough to make it worthwhile.

"You just wasted your money," Cole grumpily stated as he walked past me. "I've had her basket for years. Not worth it."

"I suppose she's just out of your budget range nowadays," I replied.

His face was the shade of a tomato as he stomped off.

"Thank you, everyone, for donating! And please, keep the celebration going! All venues for the festival are donating ten percent of their sales to The Pup Around the Corner, so go spend your money for a good cause," Tatiana said. "And all you picnic basket cuties, go on and pick out your spot for the night firework display for your dates under the stars. Hillstack is now open for the picnic spreads to be unleashed."

Yara walked off the stage and headed toward me at a quick pace. The moment she reached me, she shoved my shoulder. "Are you mad?"

"Quite happy, actually, thank you for asking."

"I'm serious, Alex. That's too much money."

"You deserve it. It's fine."

"No, it's not. I can't let you do that."

I slid my hands into the pockets of my pants and shrugged. "Too bad, Goldie. It's already done."

Her eyes flashed with emotions, and she bit her bottom lip. "You don't know how much that will help me right now. I don't have enough words...but..."

"Don't cry," I whispered, stepping closer to her. "I hate it when you cry."

"Tough, buddy. I cry over everything. The other day, I saw a commercial about a bird dying and sobbed through it. Then I saw the Lewis Capaldi video for 'Wish You the Best', and I sobbed so hard I thought I'd lose a lung from a maddening breathing pattern. Then I rewatched the video so I could feel again. I. Am. A. Crybaby," she breathed out, with tears slipping from her eyes.

"Fine. But if you cry," I said, moving my thumb to her cheek, "you'll have to deal with me wiping the tears away."

"Fair enough."

I wanted to kiss her again. I hadn't stopped wanting to kiss her. I wanted her mouth to find mine, and her tongue to find mine, too. I wanted to taste her and hold her and—

"Okay, well, I need to go set up our picnic spot," she mentioned, breaking me from my thoughts that I shouldn't have been thinking. "You should meet me at Hillstack at seven."

"How will I know where you are?"

"Trust me." She grinned. Swinging her hips from side to side, she was downright giddy. "You won't miss me. I'll see you soon." She began to walk away, and my eyes moved directly to her bottom half. "Oh, and, Alex?" She flipped around quickly and caught me staring. Busted.

I cleared my throat and redirected my eyes to hers. "Yeah?"

"That kiss." Her dimples deepened, and she mouthed, "*Oh my gosh,*" toward me as her hands fell to her chest before she continued walking away. "And stop looking at my butt," she said.

I wouldn't.

I couldn't.

But she wasn't wrong about one thing.

That kiss.

* * *

WHEN YARA SAID I wouldn't have any trouble spotting her, she wasn't kidding. As I walked up the hill to find her, I saw a display of balloons that read, Happy 35th Birthday. In front of said balloons were two wrapped gifts, and a smiley Yara wearing a light-pink dress was on the picnic blanket.

"Happy birthday!" she cheered, tossing her hands up into the air as she hopped up from her sitting position. She hurried over to me and hugged me. "One day late, that is."

Her hug felt familiar like I'd been hugging her my entire life. When she started to pull away, I tugged her closer. I just needed a few more seconds of holding her in my arms. She smelled like roses. Her hair, her neck. I wanted to breathe her in as long as possible.

"You didn't have to do this," I whispered as my chin rested on top of her head. "But thank you."

"Birthdays are important. It's important to celebrate each one. Now, come on, sit. I've made you quite the twenty-thousand-dollar spread, if I do say so myself."

I rolled up the sleeves of my shirt and took a seat on the blanket.

She sat beside me and clapped her hands together. "Actually, let's do gifts first."

"You didn't have to get me gifts."

"Birthdays mean gifts, Alex." She picked up the first box and held it out toward me. "Happy birthday," she repeated.

I smirked. "You're ridiculous."

"I think you like it a little."

A little.

Maybe.

I began to unwrap the gift and smiled when I saw what was inside. "Air Force Ones, huh?"

"I figured I should replace the ones from our first meeting. I found out your size when I was dog-sitting for you."

"Sneaky, Goldie."

"I'm a great gift giver, which brings me to my next gift." She held out a smaller box to me.

I took it. I found a gold chain necklace with a tiny capsule holding something within it as I opened it.

I arched an eyebrow. "What is this?"

"Salt," she replied. "To remind you of your great-aunt Teresa. You said she was the salt in your life, so I figured you should have a reminder of said salt around your neck."

I remained quiet. My mind went into shutdown mode as I stared at the capsule in my hands.

Yara placed a hand on my forearm. "Oh, I'm sorry. I didn't mean to upset you. If you hate it, you don't have to—"

"Thank you," I choked out, biting back the tears that wanted to flood my stare. "This is the most amazing gift I've ever received."

"I thought it might be nice."

"It's more than nice. It's everything. Thank you, Yara."

"Always."

I wanted to kiss her again.

And again.

And again.

Our moment was interrupted as a photographer walked over and held up his camera. "Hey, sorry! I was hoping I could get a photo of the happy couple for the newspaper article on the festival."

"Of course," Yara said.

Without thought, I pulled her toward me, into my lap, and wrapped my arms around her. She seemed a bit surprised by my actions, but I whispered in her ear, "For the fake relationship."

"Oh." She nodded slowly, getting comfortable within my lap.

I forgot to tell her the truthful part, though. The part where I secretly just wanted to hold her in my arms. That I craved her touch. That I wanted her to stay against me until the sun set and rose again.

We took the photograph, and I kissed her cheek as the camera flashed.

THE PROBLEM WITH DATING

The cameraman smiled. "It's good to see such a happy couple. You two look great together. Thanks!"

He hurried away, and Yara slightly twisted her body to face me. "Did you hear that? We look great together."

I brushed my nose against hers and whispered, "It's all you."

She scrunched up her nose and smiled, her lips so close to mine. "It's all you," she replied.

Us.

Even if it were merely make-believe, it was all us.

Her mouth brushed against mine for a moment, but she suddenly shook her head and crawled out of my lap. "Sorry. Make-believe." She giggled nervously. "I almost forgot."

Oh, how I wished she had.

She went to her picnic basket and unpacked the goodies she'd made. "It's a charcuterie board, Yara style."

I laughed as I looked down at the spread. Ritz crackers and cream cheese. That was it. That was all.

Well worth twenty thousand dollars.

It also came with her goofy smile packed with joy.

For that, I would've paid double.

We spent the remainder of the evening under the stars. She told me stories about her life, and I shared a few of my own.

"My mom started the tradition of the water dishes for the small businesses," she explained as she lay on her back with her hands behind her head, looking at the stars. "She made them down at Pat's Pottery. She passed away when I was eight, but I kept making them when new businesses came into town."

I sat up. "The one I broke was based on a tradition your mother started?"

She nodded. "Yeah. That's why I said it's not just a water dish."

I shifted and turned my body toward her. "Yara, I—"

"Don't apologize," she urged. "You already did."

"That was before I knew the history of it. That was important, and I ruined it. I truly am sorry."

"Alex, I'm going to say this one last time, just so you truly believe me deep in your gut. I forgive you. For all the mishaps we've had. We're good." She stood to her feet. "I almost forgot about dessert. Stay here. I saw Hadley's peach pies were out at the festival, and I think you need to taste that to experience the best pie of your life. I'll be right back."

She hurried away, and I watched as she disappeared into the festival lights.

CHAPTER 30

Yara

After paying for the peach pie, I grabbed two plastic forks and happily started my journey back to Alex. I didn't think my heart stopped beating so fast since we sat on that blanket with one another. Everything I learned about him felt like the most special treat. The man who was once so hard was slowly opening up to me. Piece by piece, he showed me his soul, and I loved what he revealed.

"Yara." I turned to find Cole.

Just like that, my floating feeling was snatched away. In came Cole—the joy sucker.

"I don't have time to talk, Cole," I said, stepping forward.

He hurried over to me and shook his head. "No, wait. Just...I need to talk to you."

I sighed and turned toward him. "Aren't you tired of this, Cole? This chase. I don't want to be with you anymore. I don't feel anything for you and—"

"The first time it was a random stranger. She was passing through town late one night and I pulled her over. She didn't want a ticket, and well, long story short, we had sex in the back of her car."

I narrowed my eyes. "What are you doing?"

"The second time it was with Lori, but it was a mistake. We were drunk and stupid. It only happened once."

"Cole. Shut up," I urged, feeling sick to my stomach from the facts he revealed. "I don't want to hear—"

"But the main one was Keri," he blurted out, making me pause my words.

I tilted my head toward him, confused. "Keri?"

He nodded. "She was the woman I was having an affair with. For years, actually. For the longest time, I thought that telling you would hurt you, but then it clicked that back then, you asked me repeatedly who the other woman was, and I lied. I didn't want to hurt you. But, seeing you do all of this with Alex to get my attention, just to bother me, showed that you still cared. So I figured I should be upfront with it all and tell you. It was Keri."

"No," I choked out, my eyes burning with tears forming. "It wasn't."

"Yes." He nodded. "It was. I mean, she still wants us to be a thing, but I told her that I wasn't interested. I only want you. And—"

I started walking off in a daze. Confused. Hurt. Angry. Betrayed. I felt dirty. As if Cole had just rubbed all his sins in my face, trying to get a little more ache out of my heart. Trying to stab me with the same knives he'd been sharpening for months now. I hated how it hurt, too. I hated how he'd cut me. I hated how my mind spiraled, thinking about how Keri had been in my face for the past few years, pretending to be a friend. Pretending to care. Pretending that she wasn't a cruel woman I'd employed.

"Yar," Cole said, grabbing for my shoulder.

"Don't," I barked through gritted teeth, yanking myself away from his touch. I pointed a stern finger toward him. "Don't ever

THE PROBLEM WITH DATING

touch me again, Cole. I mean it. Don't ever speak to me again," I warned.

Tears scaled down my face, and I hated that he witnessed it. I felt as if it gave him some sort of pleasure, indulging in my pain. He probably got off on knowing that he was still able to hurt me even though I'd left. That he was able to stab me so deeply and twist the knife.

But it wasn't because of him that I was hurting.

It was because of her.

I walked back up to the hill, tears streaming down my cheeks. Before reaching Alex, I paused in front of Keri and her date's picnic. She was laughing, carefree, tossing her head back and looking as beautiful as ever.

When she looked up, she had a smile on her face. That was until her stare met mine. Her face shifted as she rose from her seat. "Yara, I-I can explain," she started.

"You're fired," I blurted out through the tears. My heart felt as if it had been ripped from my chest and hammered in as I looked into eyes that I believed were once so friendly. "From my shop and from my life," I told her.

She began to cry, and I wanted to drown her in her tears because how selfish could she have been? How diabolical could a person be to sit in another's face for so long and pretend as if they weren't doing the worst thing imaginable?

"I'm so sorry." She sobbed. "I'm so, so sorry."

But I knew the apology was empty because it was only offered once she was caught.

I moved over to Alex's and my blanket. My body shut down as everything began to blur. My knees felt weak as I stood before him. The second he saw me, he stood.

"Yara, what is it?" he asked, alert.

I felt light-headed. I felt sick. I felt like, at any moment, I'd pass out.

Everyone's eyes were on me. I felt them. Everyone stared my

way and judged me. I couldn't escape. My mind was too far gone from being able to move.

"I, I, I think, I, I'm, I'm, I'm having—" I tried to push out my words as the pie dropped from my shaky hands. My voice was choppy and broken, like my heartbeats.

"A panic attack," Alex said, taking my hands into his. "You're having a panic attack."

Yes, I thought. *That.*

As my legs were about to collapse, Alex caught me. He went into authoritative mode and led me down the hillside. He moved me through the festival as people stared at me. As they judged me. As they whispered about what had been happening.

He led me to his restaurant and moved me through the kitchen. When we entered the space, he swung open the large refrigerator and had us move inside.

"I-I can't breathe," I whispered, still shaking. Still crumpling. Still breaking.

"You can, and you will. Just slow down, Goldie. I've got you," he said, wrapping his arms around me. "Slow down."

I fell against his chest as he held me close to him.

The chilled fridge relaxed my overheated body as I lay against Alex. He held me so close that even if I wanted to hit the ground, it wasn't a possibility. I felt embarrassed and ashamed that he found me in such a state of panic.

I kept my breakdowns to myself.

I put on a happy face for the whole world to see. I had panic attacks in the privacy of my own home and office when the doors were closed. Never in front of others. Always by myself. I'd been so alone for so long in my states of panic that I didn't even know there could be a safe place outside of me, myself, and I to fall apart. I didn't know that breaks could happen in the arms of another. I didn't know other people could catch me when I fell.

I wanted to apologize to Alex. I wanted to tell him that this wasn't me, that I wasn't the broken woman who fell apart, but instead, when he gave me his shoulder, I cried against it.

"I-I'm sorry," I choked out.

"Shh, you're fine. Just slow down," he repeated. "It's okay. You can break here. I'll catch your pieces."

That did me in.

When he told me to let go, I unleashed it all.

He held me through it.

Every tear, every howl, and every break, he held on tight.

* * *

AFTER MINUTES OF FALLING APART, we sat on the refrigerator floor. I fiddled with my hands, still a little embarrassed as I told him what happened with Cole and Keri.

"I detest the majority of humans," Alex said. "But they are now at the top of my list."

"Yeah," I agreed. "Me too. Don't get me wrong, I already despised Cole. But Keri…she smiled at me every day during the affair and every day after. I cried into her arms about it. She comforted me. That felt so cruel." For the longest time, I'd convinced myself it was Lori. I had it made out in my brain that she was the one who Cole had betrayed me with. It made sense to me. Keri did not.

"I'll never understand those types of people."

"Me neither." I wiped my eyes and laughed quietly. "I never cried in front of another person like that. I normally hide my hurts."

"I have to admit, for a while, I thought you weren't capable of being heartbroken like that. You put on such a brave face."

"Yeah, well. People pleasers learn how not to show their bad days. You get a fear that you might push people away. Like now, I worry that you saw too much, and you might pull away."

He reached out and took my hand. "I'm right here, Goldie. You didn't scare me off."

I tried to push out a smile, but he told me not to force it. I didn't have to put on a mask with him that evening. I could be all of me—the good, the bad, and the broken.

I glanced around the refrigerator. "I have to admit, this place comes in handy for panic attacks. It chilled my overheated body instantly."

"Yeah, it does that."

I raised my eyebrows. "How many panic attacks have you had in here before?"

Alex's brow knitted, and he shrugged. "Enough to know the cold air helps."

My poor black cat.

I rubbed my hands together. "Look at us. Just two damaged people sitting in a fridge, working through their trauma."

He snickered. "Who would've thought we'd get here? I will say it's nice to see this side of you."

I chuckled and rolled my eyes. "What? Me being broken?"

"No," he clarified. "You being real."

CHAPTER 31

Alex

Yara's and my photograph made front page news for the Honey Creek newspaper, and we became inseparable after the Snack on Hillstack. Seeing her open up to me, trust me enough to see her fall apart, made me want to do the same with her. I wanted to share my bad days and my good. I wanted to tell her things that I kept to myself. I wanted to show more of me the way she showed herself.

Being around her was making me better. Being near her was making me whole again.

Between the training with Feliz, dog park trips, and fake dating activities, we seen each other more often than not. I wasn't complaining about it at all. Being around her made the long days feel less hard.

But dog training wasn't the only kind of training that was taking place. One early morning while we were apple picking, I had to sit her down on a hayride and call her out.

"I ran into Avery the other day, and she told me you're letting people get away with robbing you," I mentioned.

"Since when are you and Avery on speaking terms?"

"Since she told me to call you out on the fact that people are taking advantage of you at your shop, and you won't listen to them and beat them with bats."

She laughed, and I wanted to kiss each of her dimples. "It's really fine. The festival helped me a lot."

"And what about after that?" I asked her. "After that money is gone? Yara, you can't continue this. So I am going to train you now." I placed my hands on her shoulders and stared straight into her eyes. "We are going to practice you telling these people to piss off. I'll be the customer, and you'll be you but like a me version of you."

She raised an eyebrow. "You want me to be a black cat?"

"Exactly!"

She rolled her shoulders back and shimmied a little. "Okay, got it. I can do that. Let's do it."

I rubbed my hands together and lowered my brows. "Hi, Yara. I know I owe you almost a thousand dollars. But you see, my grandmother's best friend's secret lover Lloyd needs a hip replacement and—"

"Oh my goodness, is Lloyd going to be okay?!" she cut in.

I pointed a stern finger her way. "Yara, no."

She pouted. "Oh, right." She cleared her throat and puffed out her chest. "I'm sorry to hear about Lloyd, and I'm sending you my thoughts."

I patted her knee. "Well, sweetheart, thoughts and prayers aren't going to pay for Lloyd's hip. You know, it's his fifteenth surgery in the last five weeks, this poor guy. And this is the final one that will heal him from his toes to his forehead."

Her eyes flashed with emotions over a fictional character. "Poor Lloyd!"

"Goldie!"

"What! Sorry, that's a lot of surgeries and—"

"Goldie."

THE PROBLEM WITH DATING

She sighed. "I'm sorry you're going through that, but if I wish to keep this dog day care open, we have to charge people for the services."

I leaned in and whispered, "And I, Yara, know that my services are worth what I'm charging."

She nodded and repeated my words. "And I, Yara, know that my services are worth what I'm charging."

I whispered again, "Now pay up, you cheapskate, before I call my sister to beat you up."

She laughed. "I'm not saying that."

"You should say that."

"I'll consider it."

I leaned back. "Seriously, Yara. Stop letting these people walk all over you. Be stern. Be direct. Be bold. And when they try to make you waver, stand strong. Don't bend."

"Don't bend." She nodded. She grasped my hands with hers. "Now that that's handled. Can I ask you something very important and very serious, Mr. Black?"

"Anything."

She inched closer to me and locked her eyes with mine. "Can we get a few pumpkins after this, then go home and carve them? And can you make some super yummy apple dessert with these? And then we can roast pumpkin seeds?"

I chuckled. "That's your serious question?"

"Yes. Extremely serious. And I know that our fake relationship is supposed to be for outside activities and such, but…I figured even if we are just friends, maybe we can do friends dates inside."

Friends.

Why did that word feel so deeply painful to me? When did my heart's position shift on the idea of her, too? There was a day when I thought the mere idea of her was ridiculous. Now, I couldn't imagine a morning without her knocking on my door for morning walks. I couldn't imagine not seeing her smile, hearing her laughter, and holding her hand—fake or not.

I liked her.

I liked her so much that it made me want to vomit because I knew whatever we were was simply to get Cole off her back. But at some point, the pretending began to feel a little too real.

Then again, I wasn't certain I'd ever started to pretend in the first place.

I liked Yara Kingsley, and there she was, calling me her friend.

Stab me through the heart, why don't you?

She might as well have called me her sworn enemy the way that made me feel. I'd been friend-zoned when I only wanted to take her into my apartment, wrap her up in my sheets, and stay there until morning.

Later that night, we pulled out the pumpkin's guts and slammed it onto the newspaper covering Yara's coffee table. The oven was already cooking the apple crisp I'd made for us as we began our carving adventures. My pumpkin was supposed to be a golden retriever, and hers was a black cat.

Clearly, she got the easier tracing cutout. My dog would end up looking ridiculous.

"So Noah's wedding is this coming weekend," Yara mentioned as she carved the pumpkin.

"Yup."

"I'm nervous," she confessed.

"Nervous?"

"Yes. The more you tell me about it, the fancier it feels."

"I won't lie. Mandy and Noah are really fancy people. There're going be about four hundred people, too, which is wild to me. My wedding would have like...two people. But that's my social butterfly best friend for you. He's my friend golden retriever."

She smiled. "You black cats are always secretly searching for us."

"No. You just run wildly with your tongues out and crash into us."

"That's... Accurate."

"You shouldn't be nervous, though. It's going to be an epic party."

"I have no doubt about that. A fancy wedding in a fancy Chicago mansion for a fancy chef? I'm pretty sure I dream of experiences like this. I can already imagine how remarkable the food will be."

I snickered. "It's going to be a foodie's heaven, that's for sure. Friday night is the rehearsal dinner, and Saturday is the wedding. Since I have to be there the day before, I will set up a car to come pick you up."

"Oh no, it's fine. I'll drive myself. I can get there early, too, then do any extra tasks if you guys need help."

"Are you sure?"

"Of course. There's always some last-minute thing needed. It's nice to have a runner. A weekend of extravagance." She swooned. "I just hope I look worthy enough in my dress to be on your arm. I've been worried about what to wear and how to behave around such people."

"Be exactly who you are. There's no way people wouldn't like you. And anything you wear will be perfect," I informed her. "I'm lucky to have you on my arm."

A nervous titter escaped her lips as her stare fell to the carpet. "Is that fake boyfriend Alex or real friend Alex speaking to me?"

I smiled. "Both."

Her gaze settled on me with newfound solemnity. "It's kind of sad, isn't it?" she asked, picking pumpkin guts out from beneath her nails.

"What's that?"

"I told you that we'd fake date for two months, and October is almost over. The wedding is the last event we have together, and that's around the corner. Therefore, our fake dating is coming to an end. The wedding is like our last hurrah of this ridiculous situation." She tried to laugh it off, but the sound was coated with a tinge of sadness.

Was she sad that the fake relationship was coming to an end? Because I was.

I was dreading the day I could no longer call her mine—even if it was fake. Even if she was never really mine to begin with. The idea of not being able to hold her whenever I wanted to and kiss her when others were looking was starting to get to me. I needed just a little bit more.

More moments with her. More moments with us. More of Yara Kingsley.

I didn't only want her when we were in the public eye, either. No. I wanted to kiss her in the dark when no one else was around. I wanted to whisper against her ear when others weren't looking. I wanted to go to her on my bad days because she always made them good. I wanted to have her not only in the public, but I craved her in my private life, too.

Yet if we changed things, if we shifted from something fake to something real, there was a whole new realm we'd have to figure out.

If we were real, then hearts could break someday.

If we were real, then she could leave. I was so damn tired of people leaving.

That fear alone was enough to leave me stagnant.

CHAPTER 32

Yara

*E*ven if I wanted to, I wasn't certain I had the strength to stop myself from falling more and more for Alex based on how many feelings he'd built within me.

So many feelings.

Feelings and Alejandro Ramírez.

"I'm just saying, Hamburger Helper isn't exactly cooking, Yara," Alex explained as we took on our Sunday farmers' market trip. He held Feliz's leash as I held Cocoa's. I told Cole we were taking a break from exchanging Cocoa for a while. I didn't like the idea of sending her off to him—well, more so his mother—especially after what he'd done. He didn't put up much of a fight about it. It was clear he only took Cocoa to get under my skin, not because he cared about her.

"I think it's cooking. I'd even go as far as to say it's luxury cuisine," I expressed as he picked up a container of eggs to inspect.

"I was thinking of making us breakfast for dinner. Maybe a Spanish tortilla with bacon and scrambled eggs," he offered.

You can scramble my eggs up if you want, Alex Ramírez.

I cleared my throat, trying to keep my mind from floating away. "Sure. If you're that against my Hamburger Helper."

"I am."

I shrugged. "I think Hamburger Helper tastes just like anything at Isla Iberia."

He narrowed his eyes and shot me a stern look. "You take that back right now."

"Never."

He grumbled and muttered under his breath. "Let's split up since people are already shutting down their stands. We need a few more things. I also need to break from you and that disturbing comparison you've made. You go get the potatoes for tonight. I'll get the herbs. Meet me by the tomato display, then we can head out."

"Deal. And if you see candy corn on your way, get me a bag!"

"Candy corn is only liked by people who are insane."

I tossed my hands in the air. "Just call me Annie Wilkes, baby."

He chuckled before wandering off. Every time I made him laugh, I felt as if I'd unlocked his heart a little bit more.

As I collected the final items, I was approached by the three Sip & Dish girls, who looked so disappointed when they saw me. I tried my best not to let my nerves take over.

Rory smiled at me while the other two did the complete opposite. Rory parted her mouth to speak, but Lori cut her off. "How dare you keep Cole's dog from him. That's so childish, Yara."

"Oddly enough, I didn't ask your opinion, Lori," I told her as I picked up the potatoes and started to walk away.

"Cole was right. You are desperate," Lori said, making me pause my steps. "I mean, screwing the restaurant owner because no one else will look your way screams desperate."

"Lori, take it easy," Rory mentioned. "Let's just go."

THE PROBLEM WITH DATING

"No. I'm sick of everyone acting like what's happening is right. The way she's flaunting this man in poor Cole's face is disgusting," Lori kept going on.

"Poor Cole?" I hissed, feeling my anger rising. I was so tired of Lori and her judgmental ways. She seemed so upset for Cole that it was driving me bonkers. "He cheated on me, Lori, and I know you know with who. So excuse me if I don't feel bad for him or give a damn what you think."

Lori rolled her eyes. "He only did that because he was trying to get your attention, but you were too busy trying to be a businesswoman, and now you're too busy trying to be a whore."

"What the fuck did you just say to her?"

We all turned to see Alex standing behind me with the sharpest stare shooting straight at Lori. I was shocked she didn't fall over instantly from the daggers he'd shot her way.

I stepped in front of Alex, my Doberman, and told him it was okay.

"It's not okay. People don't get to speak to you like that," he scolded. "Not with me around."

"Yeah, I know. But I got this," I whispered before turning back to Lori. This was it. This was the moment. I placed my hands on my hips, built up all the bark I had within me, and bit. *"What the fuck did you just say to me?"* I spat out. I took a step toward her. "I'm sick of you and your defending of shitty people. I get it—shit defends shit—but it's becoming really annoying. Cole is a jerk, and I'm lucky to be done with him. If you care so much about his well-being, how about you go screw him again for all I care?"

Rory gasped. "You slept with Cole, Lori?"

Lori's face went as white as a ghost. She must not have known the news Cole shared with me. "I don't know what she's talking about. She's delusional."

"Yeah, okay. Do what you do best—lie. But trust me, Cole is all yours. Have at him. But for the love of all things, *leave me alone, you fucking psychopath!*" I shouted, my chest burning from the rage that'd been building up for longer than I thought.

The three women gasped, stunned by my outburst. They hurried away, leaving me standing there with weighted breaths.

Alex stepped closer to me and looked just as shocked as the women.

"Well damn," he muttered as he pulled me in and kissed my temple. "Good girl."

CHAPTER 33

Alex

TODD

Hey, Alex! Happy mid-October. I had a client come in searching for a certain type of property. I think yours is perfect. What are your thoughts on listing?

* * *

When it was time for Noah and Mandy's big weekend, I was far from mentally prepared.

I felt an odd sense of nerves as I approached the mansion for Noah's wedding rehearsal. I knew I wouldn't only have to face Catie, but I'd have to come up against her whole family, too. A family that I thought one day I'd be a part of.

I didn't have any bad blood or feelings toward any of Catie's family members. If anything, I thought they were all kind people. Most of them were like Mandy—good. They always welcomed me in, and when I'd asked her father, James, for

Catie's hand in marriage, he gave me a very loud yes. We smoked cigars together and sipped whiskey to celebrate.

Clearly, I hadn't seen James since everything went down, and I had enough nerves to want to avoid the interaction completely. But that weekend wasn't about me. It was about Noah and Mandy. So I'd put on my big boy pants and I'd perform the act of best man because that was exactly what Noah deserved—the best.

Thankfully, the only person who gave me a heartbreaking look when I entered their space was Catie's mother, Sarah. Sarah always looked as if she was on the verge of heartbreak, though, so it didn't sting me too badly.

Noah approached me the moment he saw me and wrapped me in a big bear hug. "You made it."

"Wouldn't miss it for the world," I replied, hugging him back.

"First question." He pulled back and patted my shoulders. "Where's the girl?"

"She'll be at the wedding tomorrow."

"Great, wonderful. Next question. Who's the girl?"

I snickered. The only information I'd given him was that I needed a plus-one. He made me promise to spill the beans the moment I saw him.

"Remember Yara? The girl from across Isla Iberia?"

"Ah!" His eyes widened as a wicked smirk hit him. He shoved me. "The nice girl!"

"Yup. The nice girl."

"I told you that you liked her," he claimed, smug about the fact, too. "Good for you, man. You deserve something good."

Yara Kingsley was, indeed, a good thing. I still wasn't convinced that I deserved her, though. I wasn't certain any man alive deserved that woman.

Besides…

She wasn't even mine.

Not for real, at least.

THE PROBLEM WITH DATING

"Come on, buddy." I squeezed Noah's shoulder and nodded toward everyone waiting for us. "Let's go get you fake married tonight until we get you real married tomorrow."

When they paired us to walk down the aisle, I begrudged that I had to walk with Catie, but I didn't show my irritation. Sadly enough, the best man had to be paired with the maid of honor.

Catie wrapped her arm with mine, and we practiced walking down the ridiculously long path. Unfortunately, when you had four hundred guests, there had to be a long path to the altar, due to all the rows of seating.

"You look really great, Alex," Catie said as we walked down the aisle.

I grimaced and kept my steps forward. "Don't talk to me."

"Really? Are you going to be that childish?"

"Trust me, Catie, if I didn't love Noah so much, there would never be a chance of me ever laying a hand on you again."

Out of the corner of my eye, I saw her pained expression as if my words had cut her deep. For a moment, I thought of taking them back. But then I remembered who she was and what she had done. I didn't owe her my kindness. I didn't owe her a thing. As we walked down the aisle, there was only one thought crossed my mind.

I wondered what Yara was doing back in Honey Creek.

I was counting down the hours until she joined me in the morning.

After the rehearsal, we all headed to dinner at one of the best Italian restaurants in town. The spot had a cigar lounge inside, and after the meal, James tapped me on the shoulder and asked if I'd like to join him, Noah, and the other groomsmen for a smoke while the women shared a few glasses of wine and gossiped.

I agreed, taking my glass of whiskey to the other room.

"How have you been?" James asked as an employee brought

out a tray of cigars. We sat beside one another in large, leather chairs that looked like thrones. The lighting was moody, dimly lit, and puffs of smoke could be seen from all viewpoints. "I know it's been a while since we'd last chatted, and well, after the talk we shared I thought I would've been at your wedding to my daughter," he explained.

"Funny how things change."

"Funny, but not funny 'haha' more like funny 'what the hell, Catie?'" We picked out our cigars, and James lit them for us. "That's my daughter for you—unpredictable. Still, that unconditional love has me locked in."

"That's a good thing. I wished my parents had that skill."

James gave me a sad smile before taking a puff of his cigar. He'd known the situation with my parents and how they'd abandoned me. Hell, we'd had a handful of heart-to-heart conversations about how I shouldn't have let that define me, and that I was a person worth sticking around for. I would've really fucking loved to have that guy as a father-in-law. Noah was a lucky bastard when it came to his soon-to-be in-laws.

"Are you doing good, though? Noah was going on and on about how successful your new spot is. I've been meaning to check it out but…" His words faded off. I understood. It would've been crossing a line. "Well, all I really wanted to say is I'm proud of you, Alex. You've got a strong head on your shoulders. I wish I'd had your drive when I was your age."

"I appreciate that, James. I do."

"Now, I know I'm not supposed to say this, but fuck it, I'm old. I can say whatever I want." He leaned in and nudged my knee. "Henry is a piece of shit and I think my daughter lost her mind letting you go."

I chuckled. "That's the whiskey talking."

"No, no. I mean it. Sarah and I talk about it all the time. That scumbag has nothing compared to you."

"Well, he does have about thirteen successful restaurants around the world and a crap ton more money than me."

James waved a dismissive hand. "Who cares about that stuff? That doesn't mean anything. He can't take those things to the grave with him. Besides, he's missing the biggest thing that you have in spades."

"And what's that?"

"Honor. You're an honorable guy. I always respected that about you." I snickered a little, uncertain how to take the compliment. James must've noticed my discomfort, so he stood from the chair. "I won't keep you. I just wanted to let you know that Sarah and I still think about you all the time. She still says your name during her prayers at night, too."

"Thanks, James."

He rubbed the top of his head, messing up his fluffy white hair. "Not a problem. And for the record, Alex, it would've been an honor to call you son."

I gave James a halfgrin and nodded goodbye as he walked away.

After he was gone, all I could think about was how I'd want to share that odd conversation with Yara. Heck, I wanted to share everything with that woman.

I pulled out my phone and shot her a text message.

Alex: How's my Feliz?

Yara: Shouldn't you be off socializing instead of on your phone?

Alex: Momentary break. Is he okay? I miss him a little.

She sent a snapshot of her with Feliz on her chest sleeping.

Yara: We miss you a little, too.

We miss you.

I didn't know it could feel so good to be missed by a dog and a woman named Yara.

CHAPTER 34

Alex

In a perfect world, the wedding would've gone off without a single hiccup. Everything would've been smooth sailing from beginning to end, yet that wasn't how life worked. We lived in an imperfect world where things went wrong.

Luckily, Yara was around to do last-minute errands to stores for safety pins, superglue, and the list of random tasks I'd kept shooting her way via text.

"The officiant isn't here," Noah told me, holding his phone in his hand as he paced back and forth. "The officiant isn't here! I guess he ate at some crappy seafood place last night and has been sick all morning. He just now told us. Fifteen minutes before the wedding!"

Inside, I panicked. Outside, I kept my cool because that was the best man's job. To panic inside while remaining cool, calm, and collected on the outside.

"It's okay," I told him, patting his shoulder. "We'll figure it out."

THE PROBLEM WITH DATING

"How?" he said. "We need an officiant for the wedding. We can't do it without one," Noah exclaimed, his worry growing by the second.

"Uh, sorry to interrupt, but I have the superglue that was requested," Yara said, walking into the men's dressing room. I turned to find her and almost lost my breath.

She looked breathtaking as she stood in front of me. She wore a long, ruffled peach strapless gown that danced across the front of her cream heels. Her hair was pulled back into a high bun, except for a few curls that framed her face. Her makeup was light but perfect. Everything about her was perfect.

"Sorry," she apologized again. She smiled at Noah. "I overheard the officiant issue, and well, if you need one, I'm ordained."

I cocked an eyebrow. "You are?"

"Yeah. My sister Willow randomly thought she fell in love once with this fisherman from Alaska. Long story short, they got married on a fishing boat, and I officiated it. They ended things two days later after Willow became a vegan, but alas. I still have my license."

"No way." Noah gasped, placing his hands on the sides of his head in shock. "You'll do it?"

"Of course. If you get me a program, I can see the order of the ceremony and write a few words to make sure it flows well. Not a big deal," she said.

"It's a big deal," Noah and I said in sync.

Yara smiled. "I'm just here to help."

Noah dove into Yara's arms and hugged her tightly. "Perfect. Thank you. I gotta tell the girls to let Mandy know we are all good to go. But thank you, Yara. Seriously." Noah turned to me and pointed sternly. "Break her heart, and I'll break your back, dude."

I laughed. "Noted."

Noah scattered off to let the others know of the bomb had been defused.

I turned back to Yara and shook my head. She smiled at me.

"You look," we said at the same time.

A small laugh fell from both of our mouths. "You first," I said.

"You look like royalty," she told me. "And you smell delicious, too."

I smirked. "Thank you."

"Now," she said, stepping back and doing a spin. "How do I look?"

My heart skipped as I took her in. "Like every dream come true."

Her eyes fluttered from my words. "Thank you, Alex." She moved in closer and straightened my bow tie. She softly spoke words that fucked with my mind. "I can't believe it, actually."

"Believe what?"

"That anyone has ever let you go."

"Goldie?"

"Yes?"

"Sometimes I think about kissing you even when we're not pretending."

She stepped back, taken aback by my words. I couldn't tell if that was a good or a bad thing.

Before she could reply, Noah came rushing over with a notebook and a program. "Here you go, Yara! So you can get started."

She shook her head, clearing the moment we were about to share and smiled. "I better get to work." With that, she was off to work to save the day.

* * *

THE CEREMONY WAS BEAUTIFUL, and Yara was magnificent. As she read through the script she wrote fifteen minutes before

THE PROBLEM WITH DATING

showtime, I couldn't look away from her. She looked remarkable standing before everyone, and the sunbeams fell against her as if they were crafted solo for her.

While everyone else's eyes were on the bride, mine fell on Yara. On her lips, on her words.

Yara spoke like poetry. Her words weren't just words, but they were something more. Something uniquely crafted and dipped in profound understanding. She spoke about love in a way that made it seem like her heart had never been shattered.

Something was special about someone who could do that—still have such a purity to them when life gave them the opposite.

"Now, I haven't had the privilege to spend much time with this beautiful couple, but sometimes you don't have to spend much time to understand when two people were meant to be. Mandy and Noah, your love moved hundreds of people to show up here today to witness it. Your love inspires others to search out happily ever afters. Your love creates more love within this world. I hope you remember these words as you go on this journey toward forever. Marriage isn't about the ability to keep falling in love with one another, it's about the steady steps that come after the love has been formed. It's about choosing each other day in and day out, even when your foundation is rocked. It's about reaching out to one another and holding on tight so that when one is unstable, the other is able to grab them and bring them back to their steady steps. As you move forward together as husband and wife, remember to keep taking those forward movements after the I do's. Take those steps on the good days and take extra ones on the hard nights. This is the beginning of your walk into your future. Oh, and I hope it's the most beautiful future you'll ever live, and I pray your footsteps leave a trail of hundreds of beautiful memories along the way."

I didn't know how to explain it, but her words...

Her words had heartbeats.

They were an order of operation that made each breath I took a little bit easier. I felt every syllable within every fiber of my being. Her words made me slow down and remember what love could be, how it could move. How it could feel. Her words reminded me that it still existed within me—love. I thought it had vanished from me through the years. But somehow, love was still there—even though I thought I'd never discover it again. It hid in the quiet corners of my soul, broken and bruised, but it was still there. And Yara brought it out of the shadows and into the light.

As I stood there, watching my best friend say "I do," my heart turned back on because Yara Kingsley somehow found the key to unlock it.

Everything about her made me want more.

The way she smiled.

Glimmer.

The way she talked.

Glimmer.

The way she stood.

Glimmer.

The way she laughed.

Glimmer.

After she finished the ceremony, she smiled my way and every piece of me wanted to taste her lips and to feel her smile against mine.

Glimmer, glimmer, glimmer.

Everything about Yara was a glimmer. She was the beautiful micro-moments in every single moment that existed. I wasn't simply falling for her, no.

I was crashing.

* * *

THE PROBLEM WITH DATING

AFTER THE CEREMONY, everyone enjoyed themselves at the most remarkable reception I'd ever attended. Noah and Mandy did not leave a single stone unturned when it came to the details of their black-tie event. Hundreds of string lights and lanterns. Colorful floor lighting all around the venue space. Ice sculptures. Food trucks. Violinists. Probably thousands of flowers. No stone was left unturned for the event, and every penny spent seemed worth it. Everyone was having the times of their lives.

When I could reconnect with Yara after completing my best man duties, I pulled her straight to the dance floor when the first slow dance came on.

"Are you sure it was okay? I felt nervous up there. It was all right?" she asked me for the seven hundredth time about the ceremony. "I felt as if I was fumbling my words."

"It was the best performance I've ever seen. You did amazing. Especially with such short notice."

She sighed. "Okay. I'll stop overthinking."

I laughed. "You won't."

"You're right, I won't. How are you though?" she questioned. "I know having Catie here with Henry has to be—"

"I don't care," I confessed, shaking my head. "I thought it would be hard to deal with, but I don't care. Not even a little. I think it's because my soul moved on to something better." Truth be told, I hadn't even thought of the two of them. They didn't cross my mind for a split second after Yara showed up, looking remarkable as ever.

She smiled. "I think some would call that growth."

"I call it the Yara effect."

As we slow danced, I pulled her closer to me, dreading the moment when the song would end.

"Alex?"

"Yes?"

"I forgot to tell you earlier. I've been thinking about kissing you, too."

I pulled her back slightly as I arched my eyebrow. "Yeah?"

"Yeah."

She laid her head against my shoulder and we returned to our sway. My fingers gently began to massage her lower back as I held her against me.

"Careful when you hold me like this," she whispered.

"Why?"

"Because," she faltered, "I might mess up and start to believe in the lie."

CHAPTER 35

Yara

I'd never seen so much food at a wedding in my life. From the rotating appetizers during cocktail hour and multiple veggie and fruit displays, to the pasta bars, carving stations, and food trucks, Mandy and Noah's wedding was destined to add fifteen pounds to my bottom by night's end.

The problem with me was I understood that I'd probably never find myself in that situation again, so I would partake in every single food item out there, even if my stomach suffered the following morning.

I was almost certain I was going to break into the meat sweats sooner than later. Still, I needed to try the glazed ham that I heard another table going on and on about.

"Tonight has been amazing," a gentleman said as he crossed paths with me at the carving station. It was Mandy's father, James. I'd met him earlier after the ceremony had taken place. He thanked me for stepping up to help out.

He picked up a plate and handed it to me before grabbing his own. "It looks like you two lovebirds are having a great time, too," he said.

"Yeah." I smiled after he spoke about Alex and me. As I turned to see Alex talking to a few others, I couldn't help but feel a slight tug in my heart. He looked amazing in his olive-green tuxedo. I hadn't been able to take my eyes off him since he'd walked down the aisle during the ceremony. "It's been a fantastic time."

"Definitely." James had the carver place a piece of ham on his plate, followed by a slice of prime rib. "Now, I know we don't know each other, and it's probably odd for me to ask anything of you since I'm the father of Alex's ex. But I'm going to go out on a limb. Do you think you can do one thing for me?"

"Sure. What is it?"

"Take care of him;" he requested with a cracked voice. "Don't break that boy's heart. I know he acts tough and puts up a good poker face, but truth be told, I don't think he has many more breaks left within him."

The sincerity in James's voice sent chills racing down my spine. "I'll do my best."

"Do even better than that, please." He looked over at Alex, and a tiny smirk found his lips. "But I think the two of you are safe. You look at him the same way he looks at you, and I've never seen him look like that before. Not even with my daughter."

"Look like what?"

"Happy."

* * *

After too much food, I headed over to one of the many bar stations to try the Candy Mandy signature cocktail that came with a nice size of cotton candy attached to it. Since I was on a food high, I might've well have added a sugar high to the list, too.

As I waited for my drink to be made, I turned to examine the room before me. Alex was at a table, laughing freely with a few of Noah's family members. Seeing him happy did something to me. I wanted to keep him in that utopia as long as possible. I'd realized, too, the whole night whenever he wandered off, I'd find myself searching for him. It felt as if a magnet was constantly trying to pull me closer to him.

"Well aren't you smitten," an older man said as he stumbled to the bar beside me, clearly intoxicated. My body instantly tensed, as I recognized him from how Catie interacted with him the whole night.

Henry.

The scumbag.

He gave me a wicked grin and grabbed a toothpick from the bar counter. He stabbed a few olives in the mason jar and shoved them into his mouth. I was almost certain that was exactly how he stabbed Alex in the back.

"I'm Henry—"

"I know who you are," I cut in, impatiently waiting for my drink. He smelled like bourbon and was bathed in cockiness.

He raised an eyebrow. "Do I have that big of a reputation?"

"To say the least," I muttered, slightly turning my body away from him. He was the last person I wanted to be engaging with.

"Wow. Alex has a feisty one this time. Then again," he leaned on the bar and allowed his arm to slightly brush with mine. "That's kind of what I found attractive about Catie, too. So, what do you say? Are you interested in giving this old man a spin when you're done with Alex?"

What a freaking pervert.

I snatched my arm away from him and grabbed my drink as it came out. "You're a disgusting man, and I hope you burn in hell."

He laughed. A sinister chuckle. "I could use the tan."

"It's not funny," I spat out. "Alex looked up to you. He trusted you. So, if you get a kick out of hurting people, that's on you. If you find it funny that someone suffered from your actions, cool. But believe me when I say this—he's better off without you." I glanced past Henry to see Catie standing there. I wondered how much she'd overheard.

From the way her eyes glassed over, it was enough.

I lifted my drink from the counter, and brushed past Henry, walking straight toward Catie.

"You made the wrong choice," I told her. "You picked the wrong guy."

As I walked past her, tears began to fall down her cheeks. It was clear that she knew I was right. I couldn't for the life of me imagine doing what she'd done to Alex.

How did you go from luxury streets paved with gold to a dirty pot-hole of a man? How did she let Alex go only to run into the arms of a creep who was quick to hit on anything with a vagina between their legs?

When Alex found me on my way back to our table, he reached for my arm gently. "Hey. I saw you talking to Henry. You looked upset walking away. Are you okay? Did he say something—"

My eyes held his before I leaned in and cut into his words. I pressed my mouth to his, kissing him into silence. My kisses melted against his lips as I stood on my tiptoes, falling into him. I kissed him deeply, losing myself and finding him for the few seconds that our mouths interlocked. With each kiss, I wanted him to feel the truths that I wished to plant within his spirit. I wanted him to know that he was worthy of having someone stick around. He was worthy of love and of being loved. He was worth the commitment, worth the promises that love brought with him.

I kissed him for his past hurts, and he kissed me back without even knowing he was kissing my former pains, too. I never knew lips could heal until his fell against mine.

His hands wrapped around my body, and he held me so

THE PROBLEM WITH DATING

close. As the music blasted around us and others danced past in a blur, I felt as if I were floating ten feet high. I felt intoxicated, yet more sober than ever before. As I pulled back, I tenderly nuzzled his bottom lip before kissing him one last time.

"Real or fake?" he whispered against my mouth, his gaze deep and mesmerizing with a timid warmth that drew me closer.

"Real," I replied.

Oh, so real.

After a few more hours of dancing and celebration, the beautiful couple raced through the sparklers, giggling nonstop with one another as they entered their getaway car. Across from me in the sparkler line was Alex. Laughing as he watched his best friend race toward his happily ever after. I'd never seen a person seem so utterly overjoyed for another. The love he had for Noah was so loud through the way his eyes showcased said affection.

Then he looked at me.

His eyes locked with mine across the sparklers and his lips turned into the biggest smile I'd yet to see from him.

My cheeks felt as if they would burst from joy seeing how full of life he'd been. There were a million reasons he should've felt off that night. He was faced with people who hurt him to his core. People who broke his heart and kicked around the shattered pieces. Yet he didn't fall backward into the traps they'd tried to set for him. He rose and was the bigger person.

Daddy was right—Alex had a solid foundation. He didn't lean when the world tried to shove him. He stayed firmly planted in place. He stood tall against adversity. He did not falter.

But me, on the other hand?

I crumpled solely from his smile. I melted from his eyes. And I kept falling, falling, falling for his soul.

As Alex looked at me, he hadn't even known it was happening, that I was falling so deeply for him.

Once the sparklers died down, he crossed over to me, took my sparkler, and tossed it into the bin with the rest of the sticks. He pulled me into a hug and whispered a thank you to me.

"For what?"

"Being the best wedding date I've ever had."

I felt like crying into him as those words left his mouth. At that moment, I wanted us to be real. I wanted the chance to feel the type of love he might've someday given to me if we weren't wrapped in a fake fairy tale. I wanted to see what it meant to be loved by a man such as him. I didn't want to break his heart, but I wanted to witness it heal as he healed my own. I wanted the old parts of our hurts to be drowned by the new discovery of our happiness. I wanted him. All of him. Every piece, every drop. I wanted to drown in his love.

But we weren't real.

"Don't let go yet," I urged, burying myself against his body. Feeling his warmth, his heat radiating against my chilled bones as the autumn breeze pushed through the atmosphere.

"What is it?" he asked as I hugged him tightly. "What's wrong?"

"Nothing," I confessed. "And I think that's the problem."

"The problem is that nothing's wrong?"

"Yes," I agreed. "Because Cole is no longer a concern, and the wedding is over, which is why we began this fake dating thing. So now I have this terrible fear that at the stroke of midnight, we'll go back to whatever it was before we made this arrangement, and I don't know if I want to go back to that just yet. I just…I want to pretend some more with you. I just want a little bit more."

"Okay," he said, pulling away from me. He took off his jacket and draped it over my shoulders. He held his hand out toward me. "Let's go home and pretend just a little bit more."

CHAPTER 36

Alex

*A*fter the wedding weekend, Yara had full control of my thoughts.

When I wasn't with her, I thought about her.

When I was with her, I dreaded the moment she'd leave.

Who was I as of late? When did I allow my heart to defrost once more? And what was I supposed to do with all these new feelings? I couldn't get enough of her. She was becoming my strong morning coffee and my favorite late-night gin.

When I finally hit my breaking point, I reached out for some friendly advice.

I lay on my couch, talking it out to get some help or feedback on my emotions. "You see, I worry that if I tell her how I'm feeling, I'd be opening myself up for heartbreak again. And that sucks, you know what I mean? But then again, if I don't open myself up to her, she might never know, and she might move on to someone else. Which would suck too, you know? Because the idea of her being with someone else makes me want to rage even though we aren't real. We aren't real. But it feels real. What am I supposed to do, man? Any advice would be helpful," I said, sighing.

I turned to my left to look at my partner in crime.

Feliz just stared blankly my way as he lay on his back, wagging his tail, wanting belly rubs. Then he barked.

"Yeah," I grumbled. "My thoughts exactly."

CHAPTER 37

Yara

Whenever a message showed up from Alex, butterflies appeared, too. It was simple conversations, but each one felt important.

ALEX
You won't believe what's happening right now.

I smiled down at my phone seeing his name appear.

YARA
Do tell.

Seconds later, I received a picture of Feliz sitting on the couch with Alex. Sure, he was on the other half of said couch, but…he was there. Sleeping. Not barking his head off.

YARA
This is amazing!

ALEX
Worthy of celebration.

> YARA
>
> One hundred percent.

> ALEX
>
> I don't work tomorrow. Maybe we could celebrate together by trying a different dog park with Feliz and Cocoa in Chicago? If you're not busy, of course.

I smiled at his message. Then right after, another came through.

> ALEX
>
> If you're busy, it's fine. That was a stupid idea. Ignore it.

I bit my bottom lip.

> YARA
>
> Meet me at my apartment at six?

> ALEX
>
> See you then.

* * *

Alex sent me a photograph.

> ALEX
>
> This tapa looks like the massive hat Milly West wore to my restaurant last weekend.

> YARA
>
> I can almost hear her yelling ridiculous things just from seeing that. Also, bring me leftovers. A few extra balls, too.

THE PROBLEM WITH DATING

ALEX

They're already packed.

* * *

YARA

Why did the tomato turn red?

ALEX

Is this going to be a bad joke?

YARA

I don't tell bad jokes.

ALEX

You tell awful jokes.

YARA

I do not!

ALEX

I could make a list of your bad jokes and it would form a full-length novel.

YARA

Whatever, Alex. Why did the tomato turn red?

ALEX

I don't know, Yara. Why?

YARA

Because it saw the salad dressing.

ALEX

Lose my number.

* * *

ALEX

Yara?

YARA
Yes?

ALEX
Don't lose my number.

* * *

YARA
Thanksgiving plans?

ALEX
A turkey leg with Feliz.

YARA
Come to my dad's house to celebrate with my family. Tatiana will be there, too.

ALEX
What dish should I bring?

YARA
Take the day off, Chef. We'll handle the meal. You just show up.

CHAPTER 38

Alex

One afternoon when I had some free time at the restaurant, I cooked a quick lunch for Yara and walked over to The Pup Around the Corner to drop off the food. As I walked into the shop, I saw her speaking with a customer, who gave Yara some sob story.

"You understand, right, Yara? It's just that bills are so high right now, and I know I'm five months behind, but I'll make my accounts up to date sooner than later," the woman explained.

Five months behind?

She couldn't be serious. "Weren't you just spending over three hundred dollars at my restaurant last weekend?" I mentioned, making the woman and Yara look up at me.

The woman's eyes widened. "Well, that was a special situation and—"

"And this is, too. Either pay up now or take your dog home," I told her.

"How dare you speak to me like that," the woman said, holding a hand on her hip. "Do you know who I am?"

"No, and I don't care. You owe money. Pay it."

"I'll only pay if Yara says I have to, and sweet Yara would never—"

"You owe four hundred and fifty dollars, Mrs. Levels," Yara cut in. Her voice trembled, but she was stern. That was good enough for me. She was allowed to be nervous, but she wasn't allowed to be taken advantage of.

"Are you joking?" Mrs. Levels asked her. "Why, the owner before you would never—"

"Unfortunately, he's no longer with us. And if we hope to keep his legacy running with this shop, we'll need to have our clients pay for our services. Now, Mrs. Levels, if that isn't possible for you at this time, we can even work together to set up an automatic payment schedule. Otherwise, I can have an employee go into the back and bring your dog up front to head home with you."

Mrs. Levels huffed. "Well, I never…" she complained with a deep scowl. But she took out her wallet and swiped her card, paying in full. "You're lucky my sweet boy loves it here. Otherwise, I'd switch to another location."

"Thank you for your assistance, Mrs. Levels. Have a puptastic day," Yara sang, handing her the receipt.

Mrs. Levels hurried out of the shop, and the moment she was gone, Yara skipped over to me and struck a pose. "Did you see that? Did you see me tell her off?"

"I did. Bravo." I held out the containers. "I had some leftovers from lunch. I figured you might want something to eat."

"Careful, Alex. If you keep feeding me, I might want you to be my real boyfriend."

That wouldn't be the worst thing in the world. "What are you doing tomorrow night?" I asked.

"No plans."

"Good. I planned a date for us. I need you to pretend with me at seven."

Her eyes sparkled with the same joy her lips found. "I would love to pretend with you."

CHAPTER 39

Yara

He planned a date for us, then texted me to wear something I didn't care about getting messy. When he texted the address, I knew exactly where he was taking me on said date. Pat's Pottery.

When I arrived, he stood outside with a bouquet of dahlia and peonies. My heart beat faster and faster as I approached him.

"Hi, Goldie."

"Hi, Mr. Black."

He took a step closer and held the flowers out to me. "For you."

"You didn't have to do that, Alex. Thank you. They are beautiful."

"What kind of fake boyfriend would I be if I didn't get you flowers?"

I laughed a little. "I never had a real boyfriend, or husband, get me flowers before. Cole's mother would always order flowers for me, though, and say they were from him."

THE PROBLEM WITH DATING

He grimaced a little and brushed his palm against his chin. "No offense, but I don't think you've ever been in a real relationship."

"I don't know if that statement should make me laugh or cry," I joked.

He placed one hand on my back and held the door to Pat's Pottery studio for me to walk inside. The second I entered, I gasped, seeing the room lit with candles and romantic music playing. The space had a table set up with a huge charcuterie spread—much more than Ritz crackers and cream cheese.

"Oh my goodness, Alex. You did all of this?"

"Yeah. I rented out the studio for the night."

"What? How? Pat is very serious about getting as many guests in as possible on the weekends. How did you talk her into doing this?"

"Well, I tried flirting with her, but that technique seems to only work with the West sisters. So I offered to partner with her shop and do catering for her big parties."

"Look at you, making deals and partnerships with the small-town crew."

"Your golden retriever energy is rubbing off on me." He took my flowers and placed them in a vase he'd already had set up on the table. He then rolled up his sleeves as he grabbed aprons for us both. "I will say, though, Pat pretty much made the other water dishes I gave you, so you'll have to guide me through this."

My eyes widened. "We're making water dishes?"

"Of course we are. We have to replace the one that the stupid black cat shattered a few weeks ago. Plus, Feliz needs a nice custom dish from the queen of water dishes."

Glimmer.

"Don't worry, I'm a great teacher," I told him. He walked over to me and placed the apron around my neck, his hand brushing gently against my skin, making every hair on my body stand straight up. He walked behind me to tie the apron around my waist.

His proximity still surprised me, even though I knew we were acting out a relationship. Though a part of me wondered what was the point of the date was if others weren't viewing it? Why were there so many tender moments if we were alone in our solitude, without eyes to witness said moments?

Once he finished knotting me up, I shook off the feelings and moved over to the stations. Pat had already set them up with all the tools and clay we'd need to make our creations. "I hope you're okay getting messy," I warned him.

"I've been waiting for the day I could get messy with you."

My cheeks heated, as I tried to shake off every feeling of falling for him. But I kept finding myself tripping, stumbling whenever he spoke my way.

"Okay, you control the wheel with the pedal and just push it to make it go," I explained. I then showed him how to start molding the clay, pushing it down with my thumbs and working my hands into it to get the desired shape. Alex followed my guidance, but his ended up being a sloppy mess. I couldn't help but laugh at the frustration in his eyes. It was clear that my Mr. Black was a bit of a perfectionist, so his failure at pottery made his grimaces come back.

"You're using too much pressure," I told him.

"I don't know how to do it any lighter."

"Here, let me show you." I stood from my station and walked over to him. I placed my hands over his. "Let up on the wheel a little. Slow it down. If you push it too hard, it won't create the piece you're after. It's a balancing act."

He slowed down the machine.

I placed my hands on top of his, guiding his fingers. "Now, go slow and work your fingers toward the bottom to start with the shape, okay?"

I moved my fingers on top of his, ordering his steps.

He stopped the wheel and wrapped an arm around my waist. He placed me in his lap and grinned. "You can guide my hands better from here."

I could do a lot of things better from here, I thought.

Clearing my throat, I wiggled myself into his lap and placed my hands back on top of his. He slowly pressed his foot to the pedal, and the wheel began spinning again. Slow. Steady. Gentle.

My hands were covered in clay and Alex was covered with me as my hands guided him. He leaned forward slightly, pressing his chest against my back, glancing over my shoulder at the water dish.

"That looks a little better," he mentioned.

"That's why you can't just be forceful. Sometimes you have to go *slow*."

"I'm good at slowing down my speed, too," he said, his hot breaths falling against my neck.

"Alex?" I whispered.

"Yes?"

I slightly turned my head to feel his cheek brush against mine. "Can I be honest with you?"

"Always."

"Sometimes you say things that make my lady parts dance because said locations of my body do not know we're pretending, even though we *are* pretending, so if you could not say such things in order to keep me from going into heat, that would be great."

The wheel stopped spinning.

His thumbs stopped thumbing.

He turned me around to face him as I sat in his lap, my legs falling to the outside of his. Those brown eyes narrowed as he covered my arms in clay from holding me.

"Are you saying I turn you on, Goldie?" he asked, his voice low with a ridiculously smug smirk on his face.

"What? No." I waved him off, shaking my head. "That's not what I'm saying."

"Then what are you saying?"

"I'm just saying that sometimes you turn off the unprofessional parts of my body and ignite the parts that haven't been used in quite some time. That's all I'm getting at."

"That's it, that's all?"

I nodded. "That's it, that's all."

"That's too bad," he mentioned. "Because truthfully, I've been wondering if you've felt what I felt."

"What do you feel?"

He gave a shy smile and shrugged. "Everything. Which is odd and overwhelming for a person like me who'd spent a good period not feeling a thing."

I placed his hands in mine, the clay against our fingers blending together. "Does that scare you?"

"Yes," he confessed. "It terrifies me."

"Why?"

"Because I have a history of caring for people who didn't care for me back. Some might say I have an abandonment issue."

"You're afraid that if you get too close to someone, they will...?"

"Leave."

"That can't be true about everyone in your life, Alex."

"It's been true enough to create some scars. Plus, you build up some strong walls when your parents abandoned you as a kid and your girlfriend leaves you for someone who wronged you."

"My dad said people should put up gates, not walls. It's easier to let people in."

"Which is exactly why I build walls. If it's easy for them to come in, it's easy for them to go, too."

I looked down at his hands laced with mine. My heart pounded in my chest as I studied our closeness. How could he say those words when it felt like this, though? How could he not want to give this a real shot?

"You're scared of this," I whispered, placing his hand against my chest, over my heartbeats.

"Yes."

"Because you think I'll hurt you and leave?"

"Yes." His mouth grazed mine so gently as he spoke so low. "I think fear is my default setting now."

"Sounds to me like you just need a reprogramming with the right person."

"Are you saying you're that person?"

"I want to be. If you allow me."

"I know this is supposed to be a fake relationship, but…" He brushed his mouth against mine and whispered, "This feels real to me."

I kissed him gently, slowly, without hesitation. "This feels real to me."

"Yara." He moved his mouth to the edge of my ear and his hot breaths melted against my skin, sending tingles of desire down my spine. "Can I tell you a secret?"

"Yes?"

"You were never fake for me."

I couldn't hold it in any longer. My mouth found his, and I kissed him harder and deeper than ever before. My hands began roaming all over his chest as he kissed me back. His large hand wrapped around my neck, covering it in clay as my hips began to grind against his hardness.

"I want you," I whimpered against him as his free hand wrapped around the hem of my shirt. "I want you so much, Alex."

His hand moved up my shirt as I undid his apron. I pulled it over his head, along with his shirt, and tossed them on top of the pottery wheel. My hands caressed his abs as my mind tried to make sure I wasn't daydreaming.

This was happening.

He was kissing me.

He was massaging me.

He was undressing me.

This was real. This was no longer make believe.

Alex fumbled with the button on my jeans as I glided my tongue to the curve of his neck and—

"*Hey!*" someone shouted as they walked into the pottery shop. "What the hell, man!"

We both paused and turned to find Pat standing in the doorway, staring at me and a half naked Alex, covered in clay.

"You said you were going to be making water dishes, not babies!" Pat called out, stunned.

My face instantly blushed over as Alex turned the color of a tomato. Pat walked over, picked up Alex's shirt, and flung it toward him.

"You're going to have to pay extra to bleach my chairs," Pat ordered.

I nervously giggled as I buried my face into Alex's neck from embarrassment. Alex snickered quietly and whispered. "Worth it."

CHAPTER 40

Alex

After getting caught with my hand almost down Yara's pants, we'd decided to keep any kissing activities within our apartments. Which was fine with me. I was just damn happy to be able to kiss her in the dark. I'd spent most of the following days replaying the night at Pat's in my head. If there was ever a night filled with glimmers, it was that one.

Unfortunately, when I wasn't daydreaming about Yara and her mouth, I was busy working nonstop at the restaurant.

Saturday evenings at Isla Iberia always buzzed with life. The staff hardly had any breathing room to make a mistake. Luckily for me, the team lived in a good solid fear of messing up, therefore most things ran smoothly. The chefs nailed the preparation of each dish. I knew after the glowing reviews we'd recently received we'd have more customers keeping us on our toes.

As I rushed around the kitchen, my whole body tensed up at the sound of shattering glass in the main dining area, along with shouts of fear.

Darting through the door, I found Tatiana standing at the

hostess stand, which was covered with shattered glass and a brick. My eyes fell on Tatiana who had blood dripping from her forearm.

"Are you all right?" I asked as a grabbed a napkin from under the stand. I wrapped it around her forearm after examining it for more shards of glass. My eyes glanced at the shattered front door before moving back to Tatiana.

She had tears in her eyes, alarmed by the situation. The happy-go-lucky version of her was shook to her core from panic.

"That brick almost hit me," she stuttered. "If I was a little to my left—" tears began falling down her cheeks and she shook her head. "Sorry. I'm just a bit shaken up, that's all."

"Don't apologize. Did you see who it was?"

"Just some kids on their bikes. They were wearing ski masks, though. I didn't get a good view. It happened so fast and I, I…" her words fumbled away as the fear and intensity of the situation overwhelmed her.

I pulled her to my chest and held on as she fell apart.

"Is everything okay?" a man asked, walking over from his table. "I saw the jerks ride by with the brick. Wish I could've seen their faces, the little punks." He and a few other guests went to help clean up the mess. I stopped them as my staff came out with brooms and dust pans. Tatiana was still stunned. I surveyed the room and all the guests seemed uneased from the situation. An employee picked up the brick and studied it before placing it on the hostess stand in front of me.

I looked at it and saw the words scribbled across it in red paint.

Go home, Chicago.

This was officially past boys being boys. This was much more than some apple pies and silly string. Tatiana was injured. She or others could've been seriously hurt. It had all gone too far now, and I knew exactly who I needed to talk to—even though I didn't want to at all.

* * *

"Hey!" I exclaimed as I barged into the police station, straight to Cole's desk. I slammed the brick onto his desk. "Do something about this."

He arched a brow and surveyed the brick. "You've been finger-painting or something?"

"Some kid threw that brick through the front door of my restaurant tonight."

A sinister smirk spread across his face. "It sounds like kids just being—"

"Stop the shit, Cole! Tatiana was injured. It could've been a lot worse, too."

"What do you want me to do about it? I sent some of my guys down there."

"I want you to start actually giving a fuck. These vandalizations have been happening for months now, and for some reason your department can't seem to figure out who these kids in ski masks are. You need to do your job."

He sat back in his chair and folded his hands together. "You want me to do my job?"

"Yeah, I do."

"Fine," he agreed, "as long as you leave Yara alone. You want to know whose doing this to your place? I'll dig deeper once you leave my wife alone."

"*Ex*-wife," I corrected. "And what's that? Blackmail? You think getting me to stop seeing her is going to what, magically make her want you back? Get real."

"Real? You want to talk about real? Fine. Let's chat. I did some digging on you, Alex," he coldly stated. "I saw that you were abandoned by your parents. Shipped off to Madrid. Then your girlfriend left you, too. Are you seeing a trend?"

"Piss off," I murmured, feeling my rage building. I knew what he was doing. He was trying to get under my skin. He was trying to shake me.

"You're a rebound for Yara," he said. "You're not end game. You're the passing fancy. Not the final stop."

"It must kill you, huh? Seeing her with me. Seeing her happy and knowing you'll never have that again."

His mouth twitched as his face reddened. If he was going to get under my skin, I was going to return the favor. "Screw you, Ramírez."

"Look, I didn't come here to talk about her. I came to get some real help down at my restaurant. My employees and my customers don't deserve that harassment. Especially with people getting injured."

He pushed out a hard laugh. "I don't care."

"What?"

"I don't care about your customers or employees. Did you really think I'd give a damn about the harassment, especially now?" Cole questioned. "Between you and me, I hope the thing burns down to the ground."

I should've known I'd be wasting my time talking to him. He was such a maniac that trying to talk sense to him was too farfetched. Without another word, I turned and started to leave.

"She's going to leave you, Ramírez," Cole called out. "And when she does, I hope it hurts like hell."

"Oh." I turned back to him and took him in. I really looked at him and saw the pain in his eyes. "I get it. You think I'm your competition."

"I don't know what you're talking about."

"Yeah, you do. That's why you tried to bring up the stuff from my past to trigger me. But Yara already showed me too many glimmers. My past doesn't hurt the way it used to."

THE PROBLEM WITH DATING

"What the hell is a glimmer?"

"You would know if you knew Yara. That's the issue, though. You don't know her. You have no clue who that woman is, and I'm not sure you ever did know her. You think you and I are in a race for Yara's love. You think if you can get rid of me then you'll win, but you already lost. You lost her before I existed in her mind. You lost her before she muttered my name." I crossed my arms. "Sure. Maybe she will leave me. Maybe she'll walk away and not look back. But I'll be able to sleep peacefully knowing there is no way she'll ever go back to you. She has too much self-respect to do that again."

* * *

I WENT BACK to the restaurant to cover the door with wooden planks, but to my surprise, my staff already handled it. I was damn lucky to have that team. After all was settled there, I ended up at Yara's apartment.

She opened her front door with concern in her eyes. "Hi. Sorry. I fell asleep for a while and woke up to messages about the restaurant. Is everything okay?"

I sighed as I stood in her apartment doorway after the longest day. I felt defeated. Tired. Sad. But seeing her made it a little easier. My blood pressure dropped just from being closer to her.

I leaned against one side of her doorframe and crossed my arms. A small smile found me. "Hey," I whispered.

"Hey," She said, still worried. "Are you okay?"

"No."

"Do you want to talk about it?"

I shook my head. "No."

"Okay." She leaned against the other side of the door frame and crossed her arms, mirroring me. "How can I help?"

I held a hand toward her. She took mine into hers. I pulled her into my chest and held her close. "This works."

She looked at me with questioning eyes. "Just this?"

"Yeah. Just this."

Holding her calmed the loudest noises in my head. Just having her close was enough to make a bad day not hurt as much. She soothed the deepest cuts solely with her touch.

"Goldie?"

"Yes?"

"Don't let go, all right?"

She held on tighter.

CHAPTER 41

Alex

When Thanksgiving came around, Feliz and I pulled up to Matthew's home around noon I knew I was told not to bring a dish, but I couldn't show up empty-handed. Therefore, I spent the morning making Teresa's favorite empanadas and a tortilla de patatas.

"Hey there, stranger." I turned to find Tatiana walking up with a dish in her hands, too. "Happy Thanksgiving."

"You too," I responded. "What do you have there?"

"Coxinha. It's a Brazilian dish. My mother used to make them every Thanksgiving. I still keep that going with the Kingsleys. I just have to fry them inside." She glanced down at my hands, which had two dishes. "Is that all you brought?"

"I was told not to bring anything, but I couldn't show up empty-handed."

She frowned. "So you're letting them do all the cooking?"

"Why do you say it like that?"

She shook her head. "Oh, sweetie, you'll see. The Kingsleys

are known for a lot of things, but cooking isn't their strong suit."

That was…concerning.

Was I about to be stuffed with cream cheese, Ritz crackers, and some cheesy ramen noodles?

We headed up the front steps, and the moment we reached the door, a woman swung the door open and burst into cheers. "Happy Thanksgiving!"

"Willow! I thought you were still running around with some oddity called Snake," Tatiana remarked. Willow. Yara's younger sister.

"Came back late last night." Willow moved her long golden-brown hair to the side and revealed her neck to show a tattoo. "I got a few snake bite tattoos, though."

"Willow Kingsley!" Tatiana remarked. "Are you kidding?!"

Willow laughed, and it sounded just like Yara's. Infectious. "It's a temporary tattoo, but I figured I'd give Daddy a heart attack for fun."

"You are such a fool," Tatiana said, shaking her head. "But I would enjoy seeing Matthew freak out."

"Did you hear the news?" Willow asked her. "He's deep-frying the turkey this year."

Tatiana's eyes flew open, and she darted into the house. "*Matthew Samuel Kingsley, don't you dare!*"

I snickered a little at Tatiana running into the house. It would be an interesting afternoon. I was looking forward to it. If it wasn't for the invite from Yara, I was almost certain I'd be sitting at home in a mood from being alone for the first time on Thanksgiving. It was one of Teresa's favorite holidays. It was nice to get out to celebrate it because it forced me not to overthink everything.

Willow smiled at me and placed her hands on her hips. "So you must be the guy."

"The guy?"

"The one who has my sister acting all giddy and giggly."

I couldn't help but grin at the idea that I made Yara giddy.

Willow pointed at me. "Yup. She has that exact goofy grin. I'm Willow. Nice to meet you," she said, taking a dish from my hand and carrying it in. "And who's the cutie hanging out by your feet?"

"Oh, this is my buddy, Feliz."

"Well, hello, Happy," Willow said, kneeling. "Aren't you just a sweetheart?"

Feliz wagged his tail as if he were meeting his soulmate. I wished I had gotten that warm meeting when we first met.

Willow then stood and released a soft sigh. "Oh," she whispered. "He likes you," she stated, speaking of Feliz. "He feels safe with you."

"The feeling is mutual."

"Now, when do I get to tell you embarrassing stories about Yara?"

"*Never*," a voice said, slicing through the atmosphere. Yara darted from around the corner, and her lips turned up when she met my stare. "Hey, you."

"Hey, you," I replied.

We stood there for a moment, staring at each other with the goofy grins that Willow was probably talking about. I couldn't help it, though. Whenever I saw her, I felt like a damn kid again.

"Okay, weirdos, let me take these from Alex. Drop Feliz's leash, will you? Then you two can be awkward together alone," Willow mentioned. I handed her the other dish and dropped Feliz, who was quick to follow her.

I brushed my hand against my neck. "Happy Thanksgiving, Goldie."

"Happy Thanksgiving, Mr. Black."

She hugged me tightly and then pulled back. "Are you ready for the Kingsley madness of the holiday?"

"Uh, I think?"

"Good. Because we're starting the first game of Scrabble in the living room. Please don't be offended when I beat you time and time again."

I smirked and rolled up my sleeves. "Game on."

* * *

The day was packed with laughter, apple cider cocktails, and a perfectly burnt turkey, which was replaced with frozen pizzas. The last time I was in a house with so much laughter was when Teresa danced in the kitchen of her place with music blasting out of the speakers.

When the table was set, I noticed a few extra settings for the meal. I raised my eyebrow as I took my seat beside Yara, who was the only one in the room so far. All the others ordered me to stop trying to help and to sit down since I was a guest. "Are more people coming?" I asked.

"No. Those are for the ones we wish could be here today," she explained. She pointed at the first plate. "My mother." She gestured to the next. "And Teresa."

"I love you," I said without thought. It was as if my heart had robbed my tongue and spoke of its own accord. I hesitated for a moment as fear tried to slip in, but at that very point, fear had no way to exist due to the amount of love I felt. For the first time in a long time, I felt alive again. I felt whole. I felt…in love. "I love you," I echoed. The words somersaulted from my tongue, landing into the atmosphere. "I'm sorry, I just, I know that's fast and odd and too much probably, seeing as we only met a few months ago, but I…I love you, Yara."

She reached a hand slowly across to me and placed it against my cheek. She pulled me in closer and brushed her lips against mine. "I love you, too."

That was what I was thankful for the most that year—Yara's love. I hadn't even known I was missing so much until I found her and her passion.

The rest of the group joined us, and Matthew said grace over the food before we dove into what was one of the worst-tasting meals of my life, but I didn't care. Too much joy was spread around to care about the inedible dishes in front of us.

Watching Yara's family reminded me of what made a house into a home. It was the people. The laughter. The lives. The love.

I needed that family on that Thanksgiving Day to show me once again that even after loss, life could return once more. And houses could once again begin to feel like home.

* * *

After dinner, I headed outside to the back porch to get a breath of fresh air. I wanted a small moment to breathe in and out and think about everything that had happened over the past year. I'd thought of the saddest days, and I thought of the best ones. The ups and downs. The heartbreak and the heart repairs.

"Are you all right, Alex?" Tatiana asked as she stepped onto the back porch with me.

I sniffled a bit, turning around to face her. "Yeah, I'm good. I just needed a moment of air."

She held a little chest in her hands. "I have something for you."

"What is it?"

"Teresa gave it to me to give to you. She told me to deliver it on a good day, and I think today is a good day."

I arched an eyebrow, perplexed about what Tatiana meant. "What do you mean Teresa told you to give it to me?" My brows knitted. "You knew my aunt?"

"When I was a little girl," she mentioned. "My family called me Ana."

My chest tightened as the realization settled in. "You're the little girl Teresa nannied?"

"That's me." She chuckled as she showed me the locket around her neck. The one I'd read about in Teresa's diary. "The one and only."

What in the world was happening?

"Tatiana... I'm a bit confused," I told her.

She nodded. "Yeah, I know. I figured as much. About a year ago, Teresa showed up to me with these letters. I remembered her the moment she smiled my way. She had that kind of smile. The kind a person could never forget. We caught up for a while, and she told me she was sick and didn't have much time left. Then she asked me if I could do something for her great-nephew."

I stood taller, trying to force my knees not to buckle in. "What did she want you to do?"

"Make sure you got to know a sweet girl named Yara Kingsley. She and Mr. Parker both came together over the past few years through these letters they sent back and forth with one another. They were almost certain that you and Yara were meant to at least meet one another, and perhaps be friends, so they started scheming up a way to get you both to meet. Insert Feliz. Teresa knew you'd keep the dog, and Mr. Parker knew Yara would help you train him. These are the letters, and Teresa told me to give them to you on a good day. Today felt right."

I took the small chest from Tatiana, with my mind still spinning at the reveal of what was happening.

Tatiana was Ana.

Teresa was her nanny.

And I was so confused.

"This is a lot to process," I confessed. "So you were a part of the scheming this whole time?"

"Yeah. Even down to me forcing you to give me a job. I wasn't certain it would work, but Teresa said you'd hire me."

"That was Teresa for you. Always so sure."

Tatiana smiled and moved over to me. She patted my hand in hers, just like Teresa, and then patted my cheek and said, "Sweet boy." Just like Teresa. It was all adding up. The little things that reminded me of my great-aunt lived within Tatiana because she, too, was raised by Teresa's love.

"When your great-aunt moved back to Madrid, my heart broke as a kid. I loved my parents, but Teresa made me feel *extra* loved."

"She had that effect on people."

"Yes." She laughed, nodding. "She did. Then when I met her again last year, I felt that same love and was so upset that I missed so many years of feeling it. I felt robbed of having her in my life. That's why I fell apart when you shared that she passed away. She was a good thing, and I wasn't certain I'd feel that kind of warmth from a person again. Then I met you. Alejandro, you are Teresa's living legacy, and I'm so proud to have witnessed your healing."

I huffed and snickered, shaking my head. "It's like you're trying to make me cry, Tatiana."

"Yeah, well. What's a holiday without a few tears?"

Before I could reply, Yara came darting out of the house with a panicked look. "Alex. We have to go."

I stood taller, alert. "What's wrong?"

"I just got a message about Isla Iberia. It was vandalized again, and I guess this time it's bad. We need to go. *Now.*"

CHAPTER 42

Yara

They'd destroyed it.

Whoever went on a mission to destroy Isla Iberia had succeeded. My gut sat in knots as I stared at everything before me. A crowd had formed outside the restaurant, gossiping voices surrounding the place. Police car lights flashed, painting the darkened night with reds and whites as my family and I stood beside Alex, speechless.

All the windows were shattered.

Graffiti was sprayed all over the outside—and inside.

The sign was only half hung, with the other half dangling over the front door. The front door was kicked in. Alex began to walk toward the building. His hands were in fists, yet his movements were slow and steady. I followed his steps, moving across broken glass as we entered the establishment.

Knives slashed the chairs and booths. Tables were flipped upside down, and chairs were tossed across the space. The kitchen was destroyed. Food was pulled out of the storage rooms, and flour was dumped over everything. The oven

THE PROBLEM WITH DATING

racks were removed and hammered. Everything was destroyed.

I placed a hand on Alex's shoulder from behind him, and his body tensed up.

"Yara, I...I can't..." His words stumbled from his tongue. "I can't have you here right now, all right?"

"What? No. I'm not going to leave you."

He turned to face me, and I saw his eyes were bloodshot from the tears he fought to keep from falling. "No, you don't understand. I'm seconds from losing my shit, and I can't lose my shit in front of you I can't. I, I can't—"

"*Breathe*," I finished for him, seeing it in his eyes. He couldn't breathe. I saw him choking on each inhalation he was trying to discover. I saw him struggling to form his sentences. He was having a panic attack. He was seconds away from falling apart. And everyone in town was watching him about to descend to nothingness right before their eyes. A few even had their cell phones out, recording it like a television show.

"Come on," I said, taking his hand into mine.

"I can't," he whispered.

"You can. Just follow me," I ordered, pulling him out of the eyesight of others. I pulled him toward the refrigerator, and we stepped inside. I shut the door behind us, and Alex bent down to his knees and covered his face as he began to try to grasp any breath he could find. I bent down beside him and wrapped my arms around him.

"Slow down," I instructed him, like he had me when I fell apart. "Just slow down, Alex," I begged. "And then break. It's okay to break."

With that instruction, he allowed himself to fall apart. He began to sob against my shoulder. He lost himself as reality set in on how much damage had been done to something he'd worked so hard to create. I couldn't imagine what he was feeling. I couldn't comprehend the demons at work trying to destroy his thoughts. All I could do was hold him and let him know he wasn't alone. All I could do was stay by his side when he needed me the most.

* * *

"We can't stay in here forever," Alex whispered after he calmed down enough to be able to find his words. "You're freezing."

"I'm okay," I lied.

"You're shivering."

"I'm fine," I lied again.

"Goldie," he said, his voice low. "It's okay. I have to talk to the cops outside. I need to face this."

"I'll help," I said, rising as he stood. "Whatever you need."

"No. It's fine. Really. I need to do this on my own. There's probably a lot of paperwork and calls I have to make. Make sure your family is all right and tell them I'm sorry for ruining their evening."

"Don't you dare apologize for that, Alex." I couldn't even believe that thought crossed his mind. "But I'll ask a few people to see if they saw anything. All hands on deck."

He nodded. "Thank you, Yara."

"Of course. And, Alex?"

"Yeah?"

"Everything will be all right. I don't know how, but it will."

He gave me a smile that felt like heartbreak. His beautiful brown eyes looked defeated before he walked off to speak to a few officers.

As I stepped out of the building, I saw that the most important person on the staff was missing from the investigation—the scumbag chief himself.

* * *

"What are you doing, Cole?!" I barked as I stormed into the police station to find him sitting at his desk, shoving his mouth full of a Thanksgiving dinner plate Lindsay had probably dropped off to him.

He looked up and cocked an eyebrow. "Uh, my job."

"The hell you are. You're the chief in this town. You should be at Alex's restaurant, seeing what's happening and figuring out who damaged that place." I gestured to the other officers in the office. "The whole team should be down there. It's a mess, Cole."

"Yeah, well, sometimes messes happen. I sent out a few boys to check it out. But it's hard to get a good read on who could've done it. It appears they wore masks, so there's not much we can do."

"Not much you can do?" I huffed. "You could at least pretend to care?"

His voice dropped an octave, and he snickered at me. "You expect me to go out of my way for the man you're seeing, Yar? I could think of a million other things I'd rather be doing than helping that dick. Like eating my mama's sweet potato pie," he said. He lifted a forkful of the pie, and I swatted it out of his hand before throwing the whole plate against the wall.

"Whoa!" he snapped, shooting to his feet. "Have you lost your mind?"

"Have you?!" I spat back at him, my chest rising and falling from anger. I'd never felt so disgusted by a person in my life. He was really doing this. He wasn't helping Alex's business because he was jealous of me moving on. "You're acting like a coward. A weak ass who was given a job he never deserved or earned." I turned toward the other officers and pointed at them each. "And shame on all of you for not standing up to him. For covering for him and for not doing your jobs."

Cole snickered. "It seems that I still get under your—"

Slap.

I slapped him. I didn't even realize my hand rose and landed against his face until he stumbled backward. His eyes bugged out, shocked by what happened. I was shocked, too, as my hand stung from the impact with his face.

He shook it off, and a sinister smirk landed on his face. "Assaulting an officer, huh? Nice move, Yar. Real mature," he scolded. "Jeff, come over here and toss Yara into a cell for a while. An hour or two should do her well. She's a bit feisty around the holidays."

Officer Jeff stood, uncertain of what to do. He cleared his throat. "Listen, boss—"

"Now!" Cole ordered, pounding his hand against his desk.

Chills raced down my spine as I saw the monster within him unleash.

Jeff walked over to me and grabbed my arm. "Sorry, Yara."

"Are you joking right now?" I hissed, stunned. "You're going to let him get away with this?"

"I'm just doing my job," he stated, dragging me off to one of the cells. He placed me inside and locked the door. "You know I like you, Yara. It's not personal."

"It sure as hell feels that way."

He grimaced and rubbed his forehead. "I'll let you out in an hour. Don't worry."

As he turned to walk away, I called out to him, holding my hands against the cell door. "If you don't stand up for what is right, you might as well turn in that badge of yours, Jeff, because you are exactly what's wrong with this world. Shame on you for helping that monster."

He didn't say another word.

He left me in that cell, and I worried about Alex the whole time I sat.

When an hour had passed, Jeff released me, and I walked to the front of the station.

Cole still had that ugly smirk and said, "I hope you learned a valuable lesson from your time-out."

I flipped him off and went on my way.

THE PROBLEM WITH DATING

Alex was nowhere to be found when I returned to Isla Iberia after my oh-so-pleasant time-out. I darted around, asking people if they'd seen him, but everyone stated it'd been a while. His car was gone, too. My heart pounded against my ribs, feeling as if it would shoot out of my chest at any moment. I tried calling him, but his phone went straight to voicemail.

I didn't know what to do, so I went across the street, sat on the bench, and waited for him to return. He had to come back at some point. He just had to.

"Yara," Tatiana called out toward me. She jogged over and sat down on the bench. "I think I know where he is."

"Where? How?"

"Teresa told me…" She shook her head. "I think he's at his great-aunt's home. I have the address, and I can drive you over there."

"What? Why would he go there?"

"Because I think that's where he goes when he feels far away from home. Also, this is for you," she mentioned, pulling out a letter. "I was going to give it to you tonight before everything went to crap."

"What is this?"

"It's a letter from Mr. Parker. He left it for you. I've been holding on to it for a while, waiting for the right time to give it to you."

I arched an eyebrow. "What do you mean he left it for me? And what did you mean by Teresa told you something? How did you know her? What's going on, Tatiana?"

"I'll explain everything on the drive. Plus, Teresa told me a phrase once that I loved. I think you should say to him when you see him. But first, you should read that letter."

* * *

Dear Yara,

If you're reading this, everything is going according to plan. Well, hopefully. Hopefully, you aren't still with that bonehead grandson of mine who would ruin everything good about you. He's a vampire, sucking the goodness from those around him.

But if you are reading this and have met a man named Alejandro, I urge you to honestly look into your heart and see what you're feeling. If Teresa was right about that young man, and I was right about you, then you both are a match made in heaven—even if you are just friends. You need good friends in your life, outside of your sisters. And someone who is straightforward like Alex could be great for you.

Now, I know Teresa and I playing friend matchmaker is odd and slightly morbid, seeing how I'm dead, but throughout the letters we'd exchanged over the past few years, I realized she and I both had one thing in common—regret. I loved her, Yara. I'd never loved another the way I loved Teresa Ramírez, and my biggest mistake was not acting on that love when I was younger. I was afraid of hurting my family. I was scared of losing my home. Then, when I realized she was my home, I went to Madrid to win her back, only to find her with another man.

It broke something within me, and I came back home defeated. Later, I learned that it was just a friend I saw her with, but my pride back then was too strong to push through.

If I had known then what I know now, I would've followed Teresa to the moon.

If there is a heaven, I know she'll one day be there, and I plan to spend eternity searching for her smile so I can have one more chance of forever with her.

It's okay if Teresa and I are wrong about Alejandro and you. If you two don't click, then that is okay. Don't settle just to make me happy. I'm dead. It doesn't matter what I think. But if there's a slight chance that you've found a person who's a true friend and makes you feel alive... If you feel more like yourself than ever before, then explore that feeling.

Don't miss out on your forever on Earth, Yara.

Don't let fear keep that from you.

I'll see you later—but not too soon.
-Mr. Parker

P.S. Get out of your head. You're doing great with the dog day care. I left it to you because I believe in you. Now, it's time for you to believe in yourself.

CHAPTER 43

Alex

I couldn't stay at the restaurant. The space buzzed with energy I wasn't certain I could deal with. My mind got too clogged up, so I left and went home.

At least to the only home I'd truly known.

I walked into the house searching for Teresa, needing her love to get me through the hard parts of my current state. What I built for her, for her memory, was destroyed that night. That felt like a heavy weight sitting against my chest.

I sat in the empty house that was once a home to both Teresa and me, reading through the dozens of letters exchanged between her and Mr. Parker. I knew the letters existed because she told me about them before she passed away. What I didn't know was that they spoke about Yara and me. I didn't know that so much of what had happened over the past few months was all divinely planned out before I came into town.

Still, it was odd to see the actual letters.

When I reached the last letter in the bunch, it was addressed to me from Teresa. As I opened it, everything began to finally make sense.

Dear Alejandro,

If you're reading this, that means Ana has delivered the letter to you. Good. It's about time.

Have you read my diaries yet? And my letters from Peter, have you dove into those intimate moments?

Who am I kidding? Of course you have, you nosy bug. That's a good thing, though. I needed you to read them so you could understand why I had to take you to Honey Creek across from that dog shop. I had to get you to understand that sometimes, you needed a guiding hand to find the happily ever afters. From what I've heard about her, Yara Kingsley is a good girl. That's why I got you the dog—so you'll be forced to be around someone good for you. If a friendship blossoms, then by all means, open up to her, Alejandro. You deserve good people in your life, because you are a good person. You deserve the ability to trust others again after so many have done you wrong.

I know life hasn't been easy for you, my Alejandro. I know life has pushed you around one too many times, but within you is a fighter. Never stop fighting. Never surrender. And never give up on love.

And unlike me, don't you dare let it slip away from you.

Hold on tight.

Love loudly.

I'll see you later. (Much, much later.)

-Teresa

I sat there for a while, stunned by the words I'd read in her letter to me and her letters with Peter. This was a setup. All of it. They'd spent years sending letters back and forth between one another, talking about how much Yara and I would be the best of friends.

The whole idea of it was hard to wrap my mind around.

Those sneaky two planned for all of this to go down. I could only imagine Teresa giggling and kicking her feet about playing matchmaker in my life. The way they went into detail over it all felt so sincere, too. Reading their words felt like I was reading into a love story frozen in time. They knew they wouldn't get another chance with one another, but they also believed in love so deeply that they tried to set up a simple friendship for Yara and me.

And…it worked. It worked a little *too* well.

I fell in love with her. I fell in love with every piece of her.

I needed to find her because I now knew home wasn't the walls that I was sitting in. It was Yara. She was home to me, and I needed to be wherever she was.

Before I could even stand to go grab my cell phone, there was knocking on the front door. As I went to answer, I was shocked to see Yara standing there.

"What…" I stuttered.

"Hi, Alejandro," she breathed out.

"Hi, Yara."

Confusion swirled in my head. "What, how are you here? How did you even know where here was?"

"Tatiana brought me." She reached into her pocket and pulled out a letter. "It turns out a few from the other side have been playing matchmaker."

"Is that from Mr. Parker?"

"Yeah, it is." She placed the letter back into her pocket before pulling me into a hug. "Are you okay?"

"No," I confessed. I buried myself against her. "They destroyed the restaurant. I'm still trying to process it. I'm sorry I missed your messages. I just needed some time to clear my head. You didn't have to come all the way out here, though."

She took a breath. "*A donde vayas, yo voy.*"

And just like that, my heart didn't hurt as much as before.

Where you go, I go.

I took her hands and kissed her palms gently before pulling her back into my chest. We stood there for the longest time. We stood there as the sun began to set. We stood there as the moon began to shine. I held on to her, knowing that I'd do it for the rest of my life because, unlike everyone else before her, she did something different. She stayed.

CHAPTER 44

Alex
One Year Ago

"Here?" I muttered as I sat on a bench at nightfall, staring across the street at an old run-down movie theater in the middle of a tucked-away small town called Honey Creek, Illinois. The town was packed with cornfields and paved sidewalks with no stoplights to be seen for miles. The town's centerpiece was the huge clock tower on the red-brick Main Street, where the shops of Honey Creek all resided, including an old, abandoned theater.

The property seemed somewhat out of place beside the preserved Victorian-style shops that surrounded the building. It was hard to believe that Chicago was only a twenty-minute drive from Honey Creek. Being in that town felt as if I'd gone back forty years in time and landed in my personalized torture chamber.

I hated small towns. They came with small-minded people who gossiped more than they worked. I didn't live a life where gossip was the norm. At least not so much in one's face. Chicago had a different way of handling things. For the most part, I worked hard to keep to myself. It was almost impossible to do such a thing like that in a place like Honey Creek.

It smelled so stereotypically small town: wafts of fresh-baked bread and apple pies perfumed the air. It was predictable to the point of being cloying. It seemed that the only culinary redemption this town had was its apple pie.

I hated apple pie.

"Here," my great-aunt, Teresa, retorted with an air of finality as her delicate frame sat on the bench beside me, holding her walking cane in her right hand. Her old, worn handknit sweater hung loosely against her shoulders as she stared at the building in front of us with a tiny smile on her face. The tiny smile matched her brown eyes that twinkled with unyielding certainty. Though barely five feet tall, Teresa's vivacity made her seem larger than life.

"You can't be serious."

"It has charm."

"And a legion of rodents," I grumbled, frustration mounting. I leaned against the bench backing and sighed. "When you mentioned Illinois, I envisioned a high-end Chicago location. Not..." I gestured vaguely toward the decaying theater.

She dismissed my grumbles with a wave of her hand. "You already have a Chicago restaurant. That's boring. But this, this is something new." She gestured toward the theater. "This is a challenge."

"Why fix what isn't broken? My other four restaurants are thriving, and I don't see how this new and challenging placement would benefit anyone."

"This venture will be no different from the others," she said. "Success will come."

I narrowed my eyes. "This town barely has a thousand people. How am I supposed to sustain a high-end restaurant here? People aren't here, and those who live here are eating at" —I waved my hand behind me—"Peter's Café."

"This is the spot," Teresa affirmed, undeterred by my skepticism. "Ever since you promised me a restaurant when you were just a boy, I've envisioned it here."

"That promise can be fulfilled in Chicago."

"You said I can pick the location. I pick this one, Alejandro Luis Ramírez."

She used my full name.

A sign of her finalization.

Exasperated, I leaned back against the bench. "Why here? I was willing to open a restaurant anywhere, even in Madrid. Wouldn't you want it in your homeland?"

"Home isn't a place, Alejandro. Home is a person, and that person was from here."

"Your person was from the middle of nowhere town in Illinois?" I asked, utterly bemused.

"Yes."

"And this person is...?"

"*Was*," she corrected gently. "Peter," she said, a soft whisper of remembrance.

"Who's Peter?"

"Peter Parker."

I cocked an eyebrow and turned to face her straight on. "Spider-Man?"

"What on earth is a Spider-Man?"

I laughed. "The superhero. Peter Parker."

Her eyes widened. "You know my Peter Parker?"

"I have a feeling we aren't talking about the same Peter. Tell me about yours."

With a sigh and a wistful smile, Teresa embarked on her tale. As she spun the threads of her history, I was struck by a realization. Beneath my great-aunt's well-curated image of a perennial playgirl was a woman who had experienced, then lost a profound love.

Teresa in love?

It was an odd concept to wrap my brain around.

Ever since I was a child, she'd have a different guy doting on her every want and need. Even her flat in Madrid was paid in full by a man she'd hardly liked and would only date on Saturdays because he'd always bring her the best wine, and she'd get drunk enough to dance with him until the sun came up. Miguel, I believed his name had been. Or Cristian. Heck if I remembered.

But that was the thing—each man was a passing fancy of hers. While these men worshipped her as if she were royalty, she hardly recalled their last names.

"Peter was my everything," she confessed. "After you, of course."

"Why haven't you mentioned him before?" I asked, startled by her casual revelation.

A somber silence fell over us before she finally spoke, her voice laced with memories and regret. "Sometimes the greatest joys in life are the hardest to speak of." She glanced over her shoulder toward the café behind us, then back toward the abandoned movie theater. "When I was sixteen, my father moved us to America for a few years. To this very town. I met a young man named Peter. He was studying at a café that I was at, too. I was reading out loud as I was trying to learn English, and I kept saying a word wrong. Peter overheard me and came over to help. It turned out he was trying to learn Spanish, too, so each week, we met at the café and would teach one another. Peter's family founded this town. Hence, the café being called Peter's Café. The café even has a sandwich called the Teresa."

"What happened with Peter?" I questioned. "Where did that go?"

"Oh, we spent the next few years falling in love in this dang small town. He gave me my set of firsts."

"Set of firsts?"

"Yes. My first romantic butterflies. First set of tearful laughing. First meaningful kiss." She pointed across toward the movie theater. "And last meaningful kiss right inside that building." Her smile somewhat faltered, and I saw the shift in her personality. "Our story was a tale as old as time." She shared her history with Peter, a love story that began in Honey Creek. Their romance was a whirlwind affair tainted with a family's disapproval and life circumstances tearing them apart.

Despite the years and miles between them, it was clear that whatever connection they held was real, and Teresa still held those memories within her heart.

"I'm sorry to hear how it ended," I told her.

"Thank you." She shook off her emotions. "Over ten years ago, I received a email from Peter. He found me online."

"An email?"

"Yes. He told me about his life back in Honey Creek. How he married, and had children, grandchildren. How he helped run this town and how much it meant to him. I wrote him back, and we became pen pals. At first, I felt guilty over the words I left him on the page. Then I felt safe. It was like talking to a ghost almost. An old friend who remembered the best days of your life. He wrote me in Spanish, too. I replied in English, showing how far we'd come with our studies. We'd send picture updates and tell all the stories we'd missed the opportunity to share over the past decades."

"For the past ten years, you've been emailing this guy?"

"Yup."

"You've been back in the United States for over twelve years. We're right in Chicago. Why didn't you reach out to him? Why didn't you try to meet him?"

"Oh." She waved a dismissive hand. "He had his whole world

here. It wasn't my place to come mix it up. I couldn't even talk to him on the phone because I felt as if it would become...I don't know. Real, maybe. The thought of hearing his voice was too much for me because I felt as if maybe I'd still be in love."

"It sounds like you never stopped being in love."

"Maybe that's what love is—something that never really stops."

"How does someone know when it's real love?"

"*Latidos del corazón*," she said. "It's in one's heartbeats. The heart can't lie, even when the brain tries to deceive it. Every person who's ever been in love—good or bad—feels it deep within their souls forever. That's the thing with real love—it's for better or worse."

"What was this guy Peter to you? Was he for better or for worse?"

She snickered quietly. "He was for best."

That made me sad for her. The best love she'd ever had was in her youth. I couldn't help but wonder if it was even worth experiencing, with it being so short-lived.

"The emails stopped?" I asked.

"Yes. They did. He became sick and told me he didn't have much time left. The last one he wrote me, he signed it see you later. I'm holding on to that promise, too. Peter wasn't one to ever break promises."

"Teresa, I'm sor—"

"Don't apologize, nephew," she warned. "Because I was blessed to know a love like that. Most people don't get those kinds of opportunities. I had it twice. When I was young, and now in my later years, his emails gave me that feeling again." She held the key around her neck and took it off. "In his last he told me he left me something. After he passed away, I was delivered this key."

"To?"

She gestured toward the movie theater. "He said to do with

it as I please, and I think I'd like a restaurant there. So maybe other young souls could have their first kisses there, too, and fall in love and get the happily ever after Peter and I missed."

I chuckled, shaking my head. "Who would've ever thought my aunt Teresa was a hopeless romantic."

"Hopeful," she corrected. "A hopeful romantic. There's a difference. Speaking of…" She tapped my leg with her cane. "What is this I hear about your proposal to Catie?"

"Who told you about that?" I asked, knowing who it had been.

"Noah. He called me for our Sunday chat."

Noah was my best friend and had known Teresa for years. He felt as if she was the grandmother he'd never had growing up. I swore, sometimes they talked to one another more than I spoke to them both, and I lived with the woman. Teresa said I was always too busy swimming in my thoughts to actually communicate with others.

"Of course he told you," I mumbled, not wanting to get too much into the conversation.

She placed a hand on top of mine, which was resting in my lap. "I'm sorry, Alejandro."

"I'm fine. It doesn't matter."

"It does. And it's not fair what they did to you."

They.

As in plural.

"It doesn't matter," I repeated.

"It does," she said once more. "Why didn't you tell me about what happened? Or why didn't you tell Noah? He's your best friend, and he heard about it through Catie's sister. Why didn't you mention it to us?"

"Why didn't I mention that my girlfriend denied my engagement because she was cheating on me?" I huffed; a bit too cold with my words toward Teresa.

"Yes," she said, not taking insult from my harsh attitude. She had a way of knowing when I didn't mean harm with my bad mood.

I began picking at my fingernails and shrugged. "Sometimes the worst things in life are the hardest to speak on," I muttered.

She smiled at me. She then patted my cheek. "Sweet boy."

I smiled back before it dropped away, and I stared across the street. The streetlamp flickered in and out, affecting our pool of light. "What kind of restaurant are you thinking?" I asked her.

"A fusion of sorts. Maybe Caribbean and Spanish. Peter told me he loved Caribbean food."

"You think an uppity fusion restaurant could make it in a small town like this?"

"The way I believe in you, I think you could build a restaurant on Mars tomorrow and have a line that wrapped all the way around Jupiter."

I laughed. My biggest cheerleader. "Well, you know what they say. Whatever Teresa wants…"

Her grin widened as she placed the key into my hand. "Teresa gets. Besides…maybe you, too, will find love within these streets someday."

"I'm not looking for love, Teresa."

"Yes," she agreed. "That's normally when it decides to show its face."

I lowered my head. "What did the doctor tell you today? How long did he say we have?"

She smiled. "We can't worry about the future so much, Alejandro. It spoils today. And today, I'm still here. Besides…" She leaned in and patted my hand. "I'll never leave you, Alejandro, even after death, because we are family. We are connected by something bigger than life alone. You'll feel me everywhere you go because your breath is my breath, your heart is my heart, and your love is my love. Therefore, I am always with you. When you can no longer see me with your eyes, then find me within your soul. *A donde vayas, yo voy.*"

CHAPTER 45

Yara
Present Day

The following morning, I woke in Alex's arms. It was exactly where I was meant to be.

As I sat up slightly, my phone dinged on the drawer. As I reached over to check it, I noticed a collection of text messages from Tatiana and my sisters.

TATIANA

I know you and Alex are probably chatting it up or doing things I don't need to know about. But I need you both to get down to city hall by ten.

AVERY

Dude, where are you? Answer my calls.

WILLOW

Earth to Yara, where are you? Get to city hall by ten this morning. It's going to be a circus. The town is turning on Cole.

I glanced at the time, then nudged Alex.

He stirred a little before waking. "What's going on?" He yawned, sitting up in the bed.

"I think we're supposed to head back into town. I've been receiving calls and messages from my sisters and Tatiana nonstop."

He reached for his phone, and his eyes widened. "Yeah, me too. Let's go."

I shot off a few texts to the ladies.

YARA

We're on our way.

* * *

WHEN WE ARRIVED IN TOWN, the city hall was packed with people. Cole sat on stage, trying to calm the angry crowd, as Tatiana stood on stage opposite Cole. Behind Cole were a few of his police officers, clearly they were there to protect him.

What in the world was happening?

Cole sweated bullets as he stood in front of the crowd. He never was great at public speaking, but he looked awful. "Listen, everyone, I hear your grievances, and I can assure you the chief's department is looking into everything and—"

"And what's to stop this from happening to my shop down the way?!" Pat shouted, cutting Cole off. "What happened to Alex's restaurant is unacceptable, and you're doing a half-assed job figuring out who's been harassing the man for months now! Sure, Alex is kind of a dick with a 'don't ever talk to me' kind of persona. And, sure, he tried to bang Yara in my shop while they were covered in clay—"

"Wait, what?" Daddy hollered, hearing about Alex and I almost hooking up in the pottery shop.

More for me to add to the 'discussions for my future therapist' list.

Pat continued. "But, he's a decent guy! He's even working with me to have a few of my pieces used in his restaurant as artwork. We talked about expanding into catering for my shop. So, having his spot vandalized is damaging my business, too."

"Now, listen, Pat—" Cole started, but he was cut off again.

"Alex has been nothing but helpful to everyone in this town even though he had a million reasons not to be," Mr. Lee said, shooting up from his seat. "Sure, he's a grouchy guy who doesn't know how to smile. And sure, he acts like every interaction with other humans outside of Yara is like getting a root canal. And, sure, he looks as if he might murder a person if they tried to engage in small talk with him—"

"What the hell? Is this fucking roast Alex hour?" Alex murmured. "I can't tell if they are defending me, or trying to make me cry."

I couldn't help but snicker at all the little digs people were making toward my black cat. They weren't wrong, though. Alex had a way of growling at anyone who wasn't me. I kind of liked the fact that he hated most of the world outside of me.

Lee continued. "—But my business is surpassing my goals due to Alex pushing my wine in his restaurant! He even had it shipped to his other locations and told other chefs about it. People are buying my wine from simply trying it at his spot. To think the law enforcement hasn't done a dang thing to help him is outrageous. You should be ashamed of yourself, Cole!"

Before Cole could get another word in, everyone in town leaped up to shout their anger for what was happening to Alex's restaurant. Everyone voiced their opinions. Some with much more spicy word choices than others.

"What's happening?" Alex whispered as he stood beside me, stunned at how the people had shown up to support him.

I took his hand and squeezed it. "You're seeing the real Honey Creek. This is who we are. This is what we really stand for."

THE PROBLEM WITH DATING

I looked up at Tatiana, who was smirking with a big grin. She winked my way and shrugged. It was clear that she was on stage to destroy Cole, but somehow, he managed to do that all on his own.

"My team and I have been working for weeks to catch the boys harassing Mr. Ramírez's establishment," Cole lied.

"That's not true," a shaky voice said from behind him.

The room grew quieter as Officer Jeff rose to his feet. "Now, I understand that we have a rule of looking out for one another, Chief, but this has gone too far. I pushed it to the side as long as I could, but when Yara came down to the station last night, she was right. If we don't stand up for what's right, then we are what's wrong. You told us not to investigate the incidents with Mr. Ramírez. You told us to bury them."

"And why the hell would I do that?" Cole snapped, his eyes blazing with the same anger I used to see when I lived with him. The rage that kept me quiet for so long.

I tightened my hold on Alex's hand, and he pulled me closer to his side.

"Don't know, sir," Officer Jeff stated. "I just know that you did."

Before Cole could respond, the doors of the city hall flung open, and in walked Milly and Mary Sue with four teenage boys being dragged by the both of them. They walked with their heads high toward the front of the city hall and presented the kids before everyone.

"Here," Milly said, gesturing toward Cole. "Seeing as how you seem incapable of doing your job, I figured me and my sister would get to the bottom of what happened at sweet Alex's restaurant. These are the four boys who did the damage to his property."

Cole cleared his throat and nodded. "Good. See, everyone? Everything is handled, and we now know who the bad boys were in this situation. Now, me and my team—"

"Oh, why don't you shut it, Cole Parker, you little shit," Mary Sue remarked, shooting him a stern look. "These boys already told us that you paid them off to do the damage to Alex's property."

"What? Bullshit. That never happened. And it never would. Now, unless you have proof—"

"Steven?" Milly said to one of the boys.

"Yes?" he replied.

"Show him," she ordered.

Steven pulled out his cell phone and played a video of Cole making the deal with the boys under the table. It was clear as day what went on, and the whole room erupted from madness.

"You little punk," Cole said, shooting toward him. Luckily, the other cops grabbed him and held him back. They put handcuffs on him, too, as Cole's rage hit a new high. "Why the hell would you record that?!" he shouted, his veins popping out of his neck.

"We're Gen Z, dude." Steven shrugged his shoulders. "We record everything."

Before I knew it, everyone was approaching Alex and me, apologizing to us both for what happened. The officers dragged Cole away. I wasn't certain exactly what was going to happen to him, but I knew he'd officially be out of my life. And Cocoa would never have to go to his mother's house again.

"I can't believe you were married to that monster," a few people said to me. The same people who once called me a terrible wife for leaving him. "We're so happy you got out of that."

Tatiana tapped the microphone in her hand. "Okay, everyone. Everyone, quiet down. As we discussed earlier, we will take shifts to help clean up Alex's restaurant. Roe—you already said you'll handle replacing the windows," she said, pointing over to Roe Campbell.

"Yup. And my son is a master at cleaning fabrics. Those chairs will be repaired in no time."

"Perfect." Tatiana gestured toward Haley Smith. "And you, Haley. You're covering the lighting fixtures."

"Already ordered replacements for him. I worked with the contractor in Chicago that you used, Alex. He owed me a favor. They'll be here next week."

"And my team will be out to rehang your sign," Daddy chimed in. "Any structure issues, we have covered."

"Also, dude, I know we're the dicks who messed up the place," one of the teens said, "but if you want, we can make some social media videos for you and make you go viral. Jacob over here has like two million followers on his TikTok—that is, if you don't put us in jail or something. My mom would be pissed."

"I'm already pissed, Timothy!" a voice shouted from the crowd.

Alex snickered slightly, shaking his head.

The list of people helping kept growing and growing. Each time someone spoke, Alex's eyes glassed over more. Tatiana called him to the stage for a few words, and he led me up there with him, never letting go of my hand. I followed his steps, of course, because wherever he went, I went.

Alex took the microphone and cleared his throat, pushing back his tears. "Well, uh, I'm not good with a microphone, but, well… I came into this town with a lot of bad thoughts and opinions about the people who lived here." He shut his eyes for a moment, taking a breath, taking it all in, and then when he opened his stare he rubbed his chin and softly spoke. "Thank you, Honey Creek, for proving me wrong. But don't take this as a sign that I want to have small talk with you all. I still hate that shit."

CHAPTER 46

Alex
Five Months Later

It took five months for Isla Iberia to reopen its doors, but when it did, the whole town came together for the grand reopening. They did what they did best, too—threw a damn festival. What was it about small towns and festivals? They seemed to throw them for any and every reason possible.

I wasn't complaining, though. The way the townspeople rallied around me and helped repair the restaurant and make it excel was shocking. Even the jerk teenagers who did the damage were now running all the social media accounts. Some people said I should've pressed charges, but I figured that with the views they were getting me and the promises they made to stop being total dicks, we were even.

As far as Cole, though, he was off doing some time for the hole he dug for himself. It turned out that I wasn't the only case he'd pushed to the side. He'd been doing a few shady things under the table, and time had caught up with him. I couldn't say

THE PROBLEM WITH DATING

I was sad for him. Truthfully, I hoped he rotted for a good amount of time.

Yara probably wouldn't have thought the same because she was a bit better than me in that way. We didn't really talk about him a lot, though. Once that door was shut, we bolt-locked it to keep that guy out forever.

After the ribbon cutting for the restaurant and the festival, I took Yara to Teresa's home one last time. I'd finally gotten back to Todd to tell him it was time. One last visit felt right before moving on to my new chapter.

"So this is goodbye?" Yara asked as we walked into Teresa's house. It was mostly empty. The only things that remained were everything in the kitchen. I figured I should cook one last meal on that stove.

Over the past few months, I had all the furniture removed along with all the artwork on the walls. Everything was bare, yet the room didn't feel as hollow as when Teresa passed away. It felt cleansed.

"Yeah, this is it." I crossed my arms over my chest. "I told my real estate agent to list it last night. I figured it was about time to let it go. She wouldn't want me holding on to this anymore. Besides, my home is in Honey Creek now. I can leave this chapter behind."

Yara walked through the hallways, taking it all in. "I can only imagine the memories you've made here."

"The best ones." I held a hand toward her. "Let me show you something."

She followed me into one of the bedrooms, where a picnic blanket was laid out with a basket sitting on top of it. Candles surrounded said display, and I raised an eyebrow.

"What's this?" she asked, seemingly surprised.

"We never finished our picnic on Hillstack. So I figured I'd make us a basket as a redo."

"My sweet, romantic black cat."

I gestured for her to take a seat, and she did. I sat down beside her and began to open the basket. It wasn't Ritz crackers, but it turned out to be a thing that made Yara's eyes fill with tears.

"Alejandro, what are you doing?" she breathed out as I laid down the spread.

A few peanut butter and jelly sandwiches, barbecue chips, apple juice, and orange slices. The same items that her mother had in the basket many moons ago when she first met Yara and her father. The basket that began her family. The basket that gave her sisters.

Oh yeah, I pulled out a ring box, too.

I opened the ring box and held it toward her. "I could do a long speech, but I figured I'd stumble over my words and sound like an idiot, so I'll keep it short and sweet. Yara Kingsley—my life was dark until you came in. You reminded me how to feel again. You showed me what love looks like when it stays. So marry me and stay a little longer. Stay until we're old and gray. Stay until we meet Teresa and Peter and get to yell at them for playing the role of Cupid. Just…stay and say yes."

Her hands fell on my forearms, and she pulled me closer and brushed her lips against mine. "Yes."

* * *

WE STAYED in the house for hours. After the picnic basket meal wore off, I cooked her a late meal in Teresa's kitchen. I used my great-aunt's pots and pans. Yara helped me chop the vegetables. We moved our picnic blanket to the balcony around three in the morning, spilling wine and laughing nonstop. Yara smiled at me as we sat on the blanket, her fingers wrapped around the stem of her wineglass.

"Okay, next question. What was the best day of your life?" I asked.

She paused and looked at me. Her lips turned up. She didn't say a word but instead looked back out at the darkened sky. She didn't say the words, but I knew her answer because it was the same as mine.

Here. This.

Us. Now.

We sat out there in the house that raised me, wrapped around one another, completely and wholeheartedly full. I might've lost some salt in my lifetime, but Yara was certain to bring me more. She was my forever, and I knew it to be true because *latidos del corazón.*

She was in my heartbeats.

EPILOGUE

Yara
One Month Later

"Stop it, *Alex*! We have to go." I giggled as he trailed kisses down my neck. We stood in the refrigerator at his restaurant, fumbling around like high school kids under the school bleachers. We'd made out as if we just discovered what kissing was. I felt overpowered with want and need as my body fell against his. His hands roamed over me as a low growl slipped through his lips. I loved that. I loved not only when I could feel his desires, but when he vocalized them, too.

"You smell amazing," he whispered as he lifted me on one of the empty shelves in the fridge. He inched my dress up slightly, grazing his hand against my inner thigh. "I bet you taste even better."

A slight whimper escaped me as I almost fell into the trap that was Alex Ramírez. That filthy mouth of his had a way of making me lose all common sense.

"*No!*" I said, shaking my head and falling back to reality. I

THE PROBLEM WITH DATING

lowered myself from the shelf and playfully shoved him away. "Stop it."

"But, I just"—he let out a wicked grin and started back at me —"want a little bit more."

I pointed a stern finger. "No, Alex. Stay," I ordered. "Be a good boy."

"Oh." He bit his bottom lip. "But I know you like it when I misbehave."

Oh, how I do.

I loved when he broke every command. I was good at training dogs, but Alex seemed to be untrainable when it came to him keeping his paws off me. I hardly ever cared, but that afternoon we were on a strict deadline.

I shook my head. "Okay." I took another step back, creating more distance between us. I smoothed my hands over my dress. It wasn't any ole dress, either. It was my wedding gown. *Oh gosh.* I was getting married today. In fifteen minutes, I'd be marrying the one man who loved me more than I'd ever been loved before. That was if I could get him out of the freaking refrigerator.

"How do I look?" I asked Alex, striking a pose.

His brown eyes smiled at me before his lips had. "Like a dream come true."

My sweet black cat.

I giggled and swatted his arm. "Okay, now go. And pretend we haven't seen each other yet, okay? That's bad luck, I think. But act just as wowed by my beauty as you were when you found me earlier and dragged me into this fridge."

"Trust me, Goldie. The wow factor isn't leaving any time soon. You look astonishing."

My cheeks heated. I still felt bashful whenever he'd compliment me, and he did that quite often. I could be covered in dog slobber and he'd say I was the most beautiful woman he'd ever seen.

I shoved him closer to the exit. "Go. Now. Or I might do things to you that I was saving for after our vows."

He arched an excited brow. "I'm always down for a good meal. Then we can have the leftovers later. I love late-night snacks."

"*Alejandro.*" I laughed. "*Go.*"

He pulled me closer to him and went back to kissing my neck. My body arched toward him from the sensations he'd sent through my system. It was always the neck kisses that made me melt. He knew that, too. He was using his mouth placement to make me desire more kisses.

"Just a little bit more," he moaned against my skin, sliding his hand over my behind and pulling me closer to him. My body pressed against him and I giggled a little from the hardness that brushed against my thigh. I had a feeling that saying our vows in front of our loved ones wasn't currently the top thought dancing through his mind.

"Yes, yes, just like that, my Kitty Kat," I murmured with a slight purr.

He instantly paused and stepped away from me. He shot me a stern glare. "I told you to never call me that!"

I laughed. "Desperate times call for desperate measures. I had to get you off me somehow. Now, leave."

He pouted. "Fine. But I'll meet you back in here after I call you my wife."

I'd be that in a few minutes—his wife.

Mrs. Black, or well, Mrs. Ramírez if one wanted to be technical.

I agreed with his request. "Deal." When he opened the door, I called out one last time. "Mr. Black?"

He looked over his shoulder. I fell in love with those eyes all over again every time they found mine. "Yes, Goldie?"

I huffed and rolled my eyes as I held my hand out. He smirked and placed his hand against mine.

I pulled him closer and then rested my hands against his chest. "Okay, fine. You win." I kissed him nice and slowly as I whispered, "Just a little bit more…"

* * *

In need of some more Honey Creek adventures?

Up next at bat is Avery's story, The Problem with Players, coming Spring 2024!

Preorder Today: The Problem with Players

ACKNOWLEDGMENTS

Hi, there!
Thanks for reading The Problem with Dating! I hope you enjoyed it, and I cannot wait to bring you more of the Kingsley sisters! I'd love to take the time to thank a few people who made this possible:

My mom and my sister, Candace. Thank you for talking plot with me at all times of the day. You are two of the most creative individuals I know, and I am lucky to be able to bounce ideas off your genius brains.

A huge shout out to my agents Flavia and Meire at Bookcase Agency for always working extra hard day and night with my novels.

My editing team: Virginia, Jenny, Emily, and Ellie. Thank you for deleting all those extra commas and words I make up when I'm writing on zero sleep.

Staci Hart, thank you for the beautiful illustrated cover design! And another shout out to Silver Grace from BitterSage Designs for the exclusive cover design. You both are beyond talented. Thank you for seeing my vision when I cannot see it myself.

A thank you to Kumiko for beta reading for me and providing great feedback to make the story stronger.

And the biggest thank you to *you*, readers, for allowing me to explore new territories. Thank you for meeting Alejandro and Yara. I hope you loved them as much as I enjoyed creating these beauties in my mind. I can't wait to bring you more of Honey Creek over the next few years. I cannot wait to dive even deeper into this realm.

I'll see you later,
-BCherry

ABOUT THE AUTHOR

Brittainy Cherry has been in love with words since she took her first breath. She graduated from Carroll University with a bachelor's degree in theater arts and a minor in creative writing. She loves to take part in writing screenplays, acting, and dancing—poorly, of course. Coffee, chai tea, and wine are three things that she thinks every person should partake in. Cherry lives in Milwaukee, Wisconsin, with her family. When she's not running a million errands and crafting stories, she's probably playing with her adorable pets.

Printed in Great Britain
by Amazon